**THREE BILLION DRUGGED HUMANS FACE DES-
TRUCTION UNLESS THE HANDFUL OF MEN STILL
AWAKE REPEL THE ALIEN INVADERS**

Everyone on Earth was in a drugged sleep, lulled into a coma
with the exotic fumes of a strange plant brought by the Llralans—
orange-skinned invaders who planned to take over the planet.

Only a few men—"The Unaffected—were immune to this dreadful
weapon. Desperately, they struggled to discover what strange power
they possessed that had saved them from Llralan control. Could
they waken the SLEEPING PLANET?"

"CRISPLY WRITTEN . . ." (Fort Wayne News-Sentinel)
". . . SUPERB SUSPENSE." (Sunday Oklahoman)

SLEEPING PLANET

PLANET

William R. Burkett, Jr.

PAPERBACK LIBRARY, Inc.

New York

Prologue

At 11 A.M., Greenwich time, 2432 A.D., upon what was to be his last day on Mars, Donald Shey was rudely awakened by the shrill ululation of sirens passing beneath his third-floor hotel window. He sat bolt upright in bed, listening tensely. *So soon?* he wondered. *If so, I've overslept or they've jumped the gun.*

His eyes lighted on the bedside clock and his tenseness vanished. No. The time was not yet. It was 1 P.M. in Cairo and twelve o'clock in Rome and there were still ten hours to go. And the sirens had been of the police, not Civil Defense.

Nearby, the sirens died horrible moaning deaths, and anxiety of a new kind gripped him. Had he been sniffed out at last? With so little time left to trickle away, was he to be taken? Were feet already pounding on stairs, shifting impatiently on escalators bearing them to his floor? Were guns in hands, fingers ready on triggers?

With such thoughts galvanizing his actions he leaped out of bed and started throwing on clothes, shoving his feet into the insulated half-boots that were standard Martian footgear. Then he was fumbling with the boots' laces and cursing his slowness. Plague of the Black Stars, would those laces *never* fit properly over their grommets?

A heavy knock came at his door.

He froze, laces forgotten, hand on his gun. "Who is it?"

"Room clerk, sir. Just remindin' you that check-out time is twelve sharp, Green. And th' Earth ferry you booked passage on leaves at two. It's getting on towards time."

5

Immensely relieved, Shey replied, "Uh . . . was just about to come down. Thanks."

"All part o' th' service." Footfalls retreated down the hall, paused. Came a muffled knock, then an indistinguishable exchange between the clerk and some other late-abed customer.

Shey took several minutes to let his twanging nerves recover before he finished dressing. Six months—on any calendar—was just too *long* for this kind of assignment. He was jumpy as a . . . but time later to dwell on the drawbacks of his profession. Right now he had a job to attend to.

Sighing wearily, he put on his coat, picked up his travel bag and left the room. At least he didn't have to leave in the grand old manner known as "shooting his way out." At least he was spared that. That and the rooftop and alleyway chase sure to follow, with flamerfire crackling about like summer lightning.

Downstairs he hurried through the formalities of checking out, knowing his haste would be looked upon as that of one who doesn't relish throwing away the price of another day's lodging. Then he went into the hotel dining room, ordered breakfast and sat long over a cup of coffee waiting for Martian night to fall. In the early dusk he hailed a cab and named the spaceport on the northern edge of town as his destination.

Traffic was heavy by virtue of the fact that several of the Rusted Plains mines were changing shifts. While the cab threaded its way north, Shey kept a close watch for signs of a tail. By the time he reached the spaceport he was fairly sure he wasn't being followed; nevertheless, to be on the safe side, he went inside and mingled with the crowd a bit before departing by a side exit and taking a cab at a stand belonging to a different company. Giving the driver an address on the far side of the city he sat back and forced his nerves to unkink by sheer will power. *It's getting,* he thought morosely, *where I'm afraid to go on the streets.*

But in nine hours it would all be over. He hoped.

The cab dropped him within a block of the garage apartment he had rented under the name of William Howards and the driver said, "Two-ten."

Shey handed him three ones, yawned broadly. "Sure feel sleepy today. Must be the weather. How about you?"

"Nah. I'm used to it."

"Not sleepy at all?"

"Nah. Anybody gets used to it if they're here long enough —but the air and these turned-around days get 'em all at first."

Shey smiled. "Yes, I imagine it does." He waved away his change, watched the cab's taillights out of sight before heading for the apartment. *You may not be sleepy now,* he thought. *But give yourself time.*

Give the entire population of the Solar System time.

About nine hours' worth.

That's all they've got left.

He let himself into the apartment, went upstairs and changed into heavily insulated clothing suitable for wear beyond the city's atmospheric enricheners and radiant heating. Then he went down to the garage.

The three-wheel jetcar within had its tanks full, its engine checked and its tires flattened for sand travel; in its luggage compartment resided a heap of tools commonly used for prospecting Mars's barren plains. Standing beside it, he took out all documents signifying that he was one Donald Shey, Terran businessman, and burned them thoroughly, and scattered the ashes. A battered billfold replaced his pigskin one, complete with papers certifying the fact that he was William Howards, dune rat.

All that remained now was to ascertain that his inhalator was in his mackinaw pocket and in workable order, and to leave his discarded clothing and travel bag in a tool locker by the door. He entered the car, punched the remote stud for the doors and swung carefully out into the street, jets throttled down. A while later he was miles away, roaring over an expressway that led to the Outer Gates. Here the outskirts of Rusted Plains dwindled away and ended a half mile short of the big bomb-screen generators and a mile from where the screen would rise when in use. Beyond lay open, untamed Mars.

He approached the Outer Gates, rolled into the slot with the lighted *attended* sign and cut his motors. A burly individual with the unmistakable gait of a born Martian ambled up as he dropped his window.

7

"Prospector?" he inquired.

Shey nodded.

"See your license, please?"

He handed it across confidently. The forgery would pass muster; of that he was sure. The attendant wasn't here to doubt the validity of licenses; what he was placed here to doubt was the sand-worthiness of vehicles venturing out.

The prospecting permit was handed back. "Your sand pilot's certificate?"

That got the same brief scrutiny. Then Shey got out and stood shivering in the wind coming off the open dunes while the Martian inspected his car, poking here, prying there, revving the motor, kicking a tire and noting each action carefully in a small notebook. Finally he stepped back.

"You're all okay, Mr. Howards. Have a good trip."

"Thanks." Shey got back in. "See you."

"Yeh. Good luck."

He throttled up and rolled through the Gates onto the cold bleak surface of virgin Mars, ghostly in the pale light of the planet's twin moons.

Two hours later the jetcar sat silently on the lip of a millennia-dry watercourse and Shey was crouching miserably in a shallow indentation in the gully's side, hands numb, his breath coming in gasps even the inhalator couldn't altogether calm. From the squat black box before him came a muted humming that gently vibrated the single, slender antenna that extended to a height approximately level with the car above. He watched the telltale grimly, afraid to retreat to the warmth of the jetcar's cabin for fear of missing the response to that silent summons now flashing starward.

Following his thoughts, he looked up at the stark splendor of the Martian night sky. Somewhere out there in the void, unknown and unsuspected, the fleet awaited his signal. And time was growing short. *Why don't they answer . . . ?*

The telltale glowed.

He pounced on the headset, slipped it into place.

". . . acknowledging. Sleeper acknowledging. Sleeper acknowledging . . ."

He triggered a stud, cutting short that chant "This is DS on Mars. Ready to report."

8

He waited patiently for the time lag to bring his answer back: "Go ahead. Ready to receive."

"The word"—Shey paused, took a deep breath, suddenly overwhelmingly aware of the tide of events he was setting into motion—"the word is go."

"The word is go," came back the distant voice, repeating.

"That's right."

"All right . . . " The voice hesitated, and he got the impression that the word was being passed. Then, "You've done a commendable job; the general thanks you."

Shey grinned. "He can thank me personally before too long. Tell him that for me, will you?"

"Will do." The voice sounded dubious. "Over."

"And out," he responded. The telltale faded away. Contact was broken. He looked at his wristwatch. There were a little more than six hours left.

He closed down the transmitter, tucked it back into its hideaway in the gully's wall and clambered back up to the car. Minutes later he was skimming back for Rusted Plains in a swinging arc that would bring him to a gate other than the one he had left by. There was no point in arousing the burly gateman's suspicions as to the reason for the brevity of his trip.

It would never do to spend his last few hours on Mars in a Terran Security prison.

Chapter One

The sky was dark over London when Bradford Donovan took his delivery truck out into the streets and began his nightly run. The tires spun as they hit the level after climbing out of

9

the subterranean garage, and left a little rubber on the pavement, for this was one of the bad nights and Donovan was feeling irritable.

As he rolled, he viewed the darkened streets and buildings with a jaundiced eye. London, the twenty-fifth century. Bigger, higher, deeper—an unkillable man-made growth upon the British Isles, and its distinctive English flavor gone beyond recall, banished by the winds of time and stellar trafficking. London of the twenty-fifth century resembled nothing so much as the New York of the twentieth—big, uncouth and brawling.

Which was why the cool pressure of the gun under his jacket was so reassuring. Kid gangs—yet too young to be drafted and much too combative to confine their exercise to legalized sport —had discovered a new diversion: trap the late-night-delivery vehicle, loot it, burn it and rough up the driver. The insurance companies could stand the gaff and no one was hurt, particularly.

No one except the hapless truck driver.

Donovan growled under his breath. Anyone attempting to slap him around was first going to comb lead out of his eyebrows. Tonight especially, he was trouble looking for a chance to start.

He turned on the radio, got a husky feminine voice singing one of the freshly written and highly popular war ballads, *The Saga of the Scout:*

> ". . . and fast cruisers abaft of his beam.
> 'God,' said the Scout, 'I'll never get out.'
> But nevertheless turned on the steam . . ."

Without waiting to hear if the Scout got out, Donovan changed stations.

Again, the voice was female. Most of the disc jockeys and announcers formerly heard were wearing uniforms and fighting Larrys ninety parsecs out. This time it was news.

". . . *Mad Hatter* will be in Londonport for minor repairs the week of the twenty-ninth. Relatives and friends having men aboard the *Hatter* may contact Base H.Q. for details concerning the possibility of dirtside liberty.

"So much for the comings and goings of our boys in uniform. As for the weather, a continuing warming trend can be expected over much of England for the remainder of the week, but Old Man Winter *is* on the way. For those of you having business on the continents, may we recommend Stop-Wear, the *superior* lubricant for the engines of your aircars. Especially to those who have business in the Americas, Stop-Wear will provide that extra margin of safety for those trips across the wintry North Atlantic . . ."

He tried again.

This time he recognized the voice of Johnny Hatcher, a favorite recording artist before the war, since killed in action on some nameless asteroid somewhere out along the Line.

". . . the stars are shining brightly, hanging in the void—
Their beauty catches at the throat, their cold heat chills the
soul . . .
Space is deep and space is cruel, but a man'd be paranoid
To hate the suns that warm the worlds that are the Black
Sea's shoals . . ."

And again.

". . . the draft call for November is expected to reach an all time high, and the government has announced new emergency measures designed to free more able-bodied men for the war effort. If you are an independent businessman, remember: HIRE THE HANDICAPPED—you'll be freeing a man for the front lines."

Click!

Donovan cursed softly and stared out through the windshield. His left hand strayed from the steering wheel, smacked his thigh soundly. The plastic masked by his pants leg gave back a dull thump.

Plasteel legs and modified robot muscles to give them mobility—mobility superior in some ways to flesh and blood. But according to the Military Board, it made him half a man. And a fifty-year-old half-man is simply not military material.

"Free a man for the front lines."

But not half a man.

Half a man can push a truck normally handled by a brute with more muscles than a gorilla, less brains than a gnat, while the gorilla-gnat points and fires a gun half a galaxy away. Even a robot could handle this run—but robots were too scarce nowadays to sacrifice to the gangs. Not so a cripple such as himself.

Cripple!

He gritted his teeth and his plastic foot nudged the accelerator a little. The truck began to vibrate gently as the extra speed shifted the load. It shot past deserted intersections, under dim or burnt-out street lights—this was one of London's meaner sections.

Cripple!

Had been a time when Bradford Donovan hadn't been a caricature of a man with robot's legs; had been a time . . . twenty years ago . . . when Bradford Donovan had taken a stellar voyage with his bride of six months, a voyage that lasted another half year with the result that their first son was born *in vacuo*.

At the end of that voyage had been Risstair, world of promise and possible wealth; world within, and under the jurisdiction of, the Llralan Empire, but open to Terran trappers. In the years that he was there his lend-lease trapping line had prospered, thanks to his skillful traps and ready rifle. The Donovan brand had become familiar to Terra-side furriers and his signature to bankers dealing in out-world trade. Things were progressing nicely; Jane had given him another son, and a fat bank account awaited their return to Terra. Another two years, he figured, and they could return to Terra wealthy enough to want for nothing the rest of their natural lives.

Then, on a regular run of the traps, there had been the smell of death in the air.

He could never forget it—that distinctive, incredibly delicate odor exuded by all dying Risstairan life. Often he had wondered if any get-rich-quick character would decide to attempt distilling and bottling the essence for sale to Terran females, but no such scheme had developed while he was on Risstair.

The odor of death had been overpowering, drawing him to the woodland glade irresistibly. And in the glade—the mangled bodies of three Risstairan woodcutters clustered about their loaded logging sled and kept company by a pair of marq carcasses, one with an ax-split skull, the other with a crossbow quarrel in its brain.

They had been hit fast, without warning or provocation, and from the rear. His flesh crawled. That meant one thing on Risstair: rogue pack in a kill-sweep.

And the home station was six miles away through the gathering dusk.

Almost, he made it. The sounds of everyday activity around the station were faintly in his ears and the jungle was thinning away to only an occasional thicket growing stubbornly beneath the tall and wide-spaced trees.

That sparsity of cover was the only thing that saved his life.

Out of the corner of his eye he caught sight of a bounding shape that rushed at him with the speed of a greyhound closing on a rabbit. There had been no time to shoot—instead, he leaped straight up. With his still one-gravity-accustomed muscles in the lesser pull of Risstair, it had been a good jump—a fantastic jump. The marq, startled, had lunged after its soaring quarry, but lacked the proper timing. Three-inch fangs had slashed across him at a point halfway up the thigh.

The shock of the hit was such that it deadened the pain. Turning as he fell, Donovan fried the recovering marq with a full-strength squirt from his long-barreled flame rifle and took another slash from a second beast quartering in from the opposite direction. That one died with its head cindered, but there was a third, a fourth, a fifth. . . . He held down the trigger and waved the gun like a wand, laying a path of flaming destruction around him. The squalls of scalded beasts had mingled with the guttering song of his rifle, but they had come right through the flames with the terrible single-minded-ness only a marq in a kill-craze could exhibit. Dying jaws, already headed for the ground, slashed his legs again and again, and the number and seriousness of the wounds had put him on his back and helpless.

But the marqs had finally had enough. With twelve of their number gone and the flame rifle lashing the area all about like blind lightning, even they were at last discouraged and went in search of easier prey.

And the night was still, but someone was screaming and

would not shut up and he realized vaguely that it was himself, and voices were calling his name, but distantly, distantly . . .

And then there was nothing. Nothing until he awoke in a Federation naval hospital back inside Federation territory and was told that his legs were gone—that the choice had been simple for the medic on the ship bringing him in: his legs or his life. And in the months that followed—months in which, he now realized, he had behaved more like a frightened child than the man he thought himself to be—he had come to believe that the medic had made the wrong choice. It had been a long and bitter road down from the lofty status of out-hunter with money in the bank to that of lowly truck driver with a budget that seldom balanced.

This last was the final blow. The Federation could take his sons and train them as fodder for Imperial guns—his young, strong sons with their lives still before them—but it refused an embittered old man the right to give the ending of *his* life some dignity and purpose . . .

Abruptly, without preamble, the raid alarms began to moan from the rooftops.

Donovan came out of his reverie, startled, and looked around.

He had passed into a better section of town, in which aircars moved to and fro over rooftop runways, gleaming groundcars slid through the well-lighted streets and the quality and number of pedestrians had shot upward.

But the aircars were diving for the roofs, the groundcars were pulling in at the curbs and the pedestrians were vanishing from sight with magical speed. As if spewed from sidewalk gratings, characters wearing yellow armbands and helmets topped by amber flashers appeared, gesticulating wildly and mouthing instructions. London's ancient heritage of raids from the sky and experience gained during the past year seemed to have instilled in its populace an instinct for diving promptly, accurately and without question into the nearest hole.

Donovan pulled over, parked and got out. Locking the truck, he glanced at the star-spangled sky and then hurried after a group of citizens looking for their hole. As he joined the tag end a warden joined the van and ushered them through a door that gave onto a foyer and so through to a seemingly endless series of stairs. The group clattered downward in grim silence, and Donovan followed. After long enough to have reached Hell, the warden halted before a steel door, swung it open. Donovan fully expected to see an imp waiting to show them in, but was disappointed. The room in which they found themselves was filled with wooden benches, had a partitioned room in one corner. A long low cabinet took up one wall. A short-wave set resided on the cabinet. Naked, yellow-painted I beams jutted horizontally through the space; dim light bulbs were mounted thereon.

The crowd filled up the benches rapidly. Donovan sat in a pool of shadow and lit a cigarette.

Heavy feet sounded on the stairs, came through the door and became attached to a uniformed policeman. He dogged the door behind him, took two heavy steps into the shelter and gave a quick look round.

His gaze paused briefly on Donovan's cigarette. "Douse the butt," he said, and headed for the short-wave.

Donovan went on smoking.

The cop must have sensed something amiss, for he turned back. For a long moment he seemed at a loss as to how to cope with this bare-faced insubordination. Then he reacted typically for one who has the law in his pocket and glories in abusing the privilege. He took a menacing step forward, hand going to his nightstick.

"Maybe you don't hear so good. I said 'Douse the butt.' "

"I hear fine. Why?"

"Just get rid of it."

"But . . ."

"No buts." The cop unslung his nightstick, used it to point at a plastic-fronted list of shelter conduct rules fastened to the door. "Yuh see that? Them are standard-procedure rules, and I know 'em by heart. They say an officer of the law, whether off duty or on, shall be the authority in any shelter in which he takes refuge."

"So?"

"So douse the butt or grab grief."

In his present mood, Donovan was more inclined to grab grief, but in view of the circumstances he abstained. The cigarette died under his heel. "Satisfied, Bossy?"

"Oh, so you're a wise one, eh?" The cop gave him the cold eye.

"Not at all," contradicted Donovan, undismayed by the glare. "I simply wonder why, when we have purifiers in these holes, you forbid me one of life's few-enough pleasures."

"Purifiers have been known to fail, and we might be locked up in here for quite a spell."

"Oh, come now—that's reaching a bit far, isn't it? Aren't you just throwing your weight around to keep up your own nerve?"

"No," said the cop, unconvincingly. "No, that's not it."

"What then?"

"Just chalk it up to my dislike of smoke getting in my eyes," snapped the arm of the law, growing apoplectic. "Now shaddup!"

With poor grace, Donovan shaddup. Authority when in the hands of chumps—or of anyone else, for that matter—rubbed him the wrong way. Being ordered around was the surest way of unleashing his quick temper. But, again in view of the circumstances, he bowed to stupidity, the same kind of stupidity that kept him earthbound while men with less on the ball than he—but with the proper number of natural limbs—tried to hold back the Larry advance.

The radio crackled, said loudly, "Condition Red Maximum! Condition Red Maximum! Central Control Canada reports three full-strength assault waves inbound past Jupiter. Repeat, Condition Red Maximum. E.T.A. first wave, fifteen minutes; advance scouts, momentarily . . ."

Overhead, sudden deep-throated thunder rolled. It started as a mutter, passed quickly to a bellow, then a deafening howl. At its peak, the shelter trembled ever so slightly and loosened dust shifted in the weak light of the naked bulbs. The occupants of the shelter grew still and tense, waiting.

As suddenly as it had come it was gone, fading to a waspish buzz and then dying away altogether. For a seeming eternity, there was only silence. Then the warden straightened from the instinctive crouch he had dropped into, wiped shiny perspiration from his forehead.

"Wheweee!" he breathed shakily. "That was a close 'un! Bet there ain't a whole pane of glass left in London."

"Glass can be replaced," came a voice from beyond Donovan's eye range. "I'll be happy if there's a *city* left."

"Me too," endorsed another.

The cop scowled darkly. "You shouldn't talk that way—we don't have anything to worry about." Then his authoritative demeanor was spoiled when he gave out with a wide-mouthed yawn.

Donovan turned to his neighbor. "At a time like this, he tells us we shouldn't worry about things like low-flying enemy ships, and then tops it off by gaping like a sick hippopotamus. What do you think . . ."

He never finished the sentence; his thought hung unsaid.

His neighbor, a piglike man nursing a battered briefcase and wearing a wrinkled suit, was slumped untidily against the wall. His mouth was hanging open; from it seeped gentle bubbling noises. Porky was in dreamland.

Incredulously, Donovan looked back at the cop. That worthy was hanging onto an I beam as if it were the proverbial straw and he the drowning man. Even as Donovan watched he slowly and jerkily slid down the beam until he prostrated himself at its base. Now he seemed to be worshiping the sickly 15-watt bulb fixed thereon.

The warden turned from where he had been speaking softly into the short-wave, glanced without much curiosity at the fallen cop. "He seems a ha' fallen down," he observed thickly. Then he yawned.

"And you don't think that's curious?" inquired Donovan.

The warden regarded him owlishly, pushing his helmet further and further back on his head until it fell off and hit the floor with a resounding clang. The amber flasher shattered and went out.

"Wazzat yew say?"

"You don't think his passing out that way is . . ." began Donovan, then hushed as another wash of propulsor noise swept over from the north and dwindled into the southeast. When quiet returned, he noticed a sound not present before in the shelter.

Snores.

He peered hard at the assemblage, and cold prickles began to dance along his spine.

17

Three-quarters of the occupants of the shelter were sprawled or slumped or hunched about with no care for their posture. As he watched, his eyes began to water and he rubbed them violently. The atmosphere of the shelter suddenly seemed unbearably thick. He blinked again. And again. The room seemed to reel just a bit.

Crash!

He swung his head around dopily, wasn't too surprised to see the warden on the floor, one arm draped in brotherly fashion about the cop's broad shoulders, the other pinned beneath the short-wave set where he had dragged it from the cabinet as he fell.

There was movement in the shelter. Donovan glanced up.

The ceiling came rushing down.

He cried out involuntarily, threw up his arms.

There was no impact. He lowered his arms cautiously, stared hard at the ceiling. It was back in place—no, no it wasn't, not quite. Wasn't it creeping downward again, trying to surprise him?

The next moment he was frantically tearing at the door, then bolting up the metal stairs, taking them four at a time with agility remarkable even for robot legs—extremely difficult for a whole man, even in the prime of condition. He made it back to the street in a fraction of the time it had taken him going down, burst through the foyer and into the cold night air. Sagging against a wall, he panted for breath.

Far away, propulsors muttered, and he looked at the sky.

Blue circles were blooming in clumps and pairs everywhere —blooming and drifting down with the gentleness of the first snow of winter. His jaw dropped. Well he knew, having seen news films taken at the front, what those were.

Paratroopers!

Larry space infantry, floating in on anti-grav units. And they were unopposed. Nothing was disturbing their orderly downward drift—no airships, no missiles, no autogun tracers or flamer beams were tearing holes in their descending ranks. Not so much as a stone was being hurled against the invaders.

Again, he began to run.

He tore around two corners and across three streets before he ran into a waiting line of lean, tall figures lounging in an intersection. His sudden precipitation into their midst touched off startled exclamations and momentary confusion. He had time to get his gun out and half empty the clip before they dived for cover, leaving two still forms on the pavement and one that kicked and screamed.

He jumped behind a stalled bus, scooted alongside it and began to gallop frantically away. A pale blue tongue of fire snapped over his head and authoritative shouts rang in the air behind him. Another searbolt passed so close he felt its hot breath. Then he was around another corner and pounding heavily on. His leg stumps were beginning to throb painfully from the unaccustomed exertion when a string of figures again barred his way. He skidded to a halt, stumbled, brought up his gun.

A searbolt smacked into the concrete at his feet. Blued metal gleamed dully as a dozen weapons shifted to cover him.

Picking the tallest of those before him he fired twice, then started working leftward along the line until the hammer dropped on an empty chamber. Only then did he realize that several searbolts had riddled his remarkable legs, and that their controls were dead.

As he stood there swaying uncertainly, another bolt hit his ankle and severed it completely, knocking the foot awry.

Down he went, like a timbered Sequoia.

Chapter Two

Beneath the cloudless blue bowl of the midday sky, the Georgia countryside was a shout of autumnal color, stretching as far as the eye could see in all directions, unbroken by industrial smoke or gleaming skyscraper. In the glades and pastures the golden sunlight ruled, forcing the stubborn chill of November back under the evergreens and into the shade of leaves yet unfallen. Off across the overgrown fields an exact replica of an abandoned farmhouse leaned tiredly against the earth. Bobwhite quail scratched dirt and preened beneath fallen rail fences; rusted and sagging barbed wire hung from decaying wooden posts. Near the house an untended pecan grove laced dead limbs against the sky.

The man sitting flat on his rump with his back propped against a big oak tree puffed contentedly on his pipe and took it all in through the frostbitten branches of a gooseberry bush. The ground was cold beneath his denim-clad legs and the wind blowing in his face made him wish his dungaree jacket's insulation was thicker, but he wouldn't have swapped places with anybody on ten worlds at the moment. James Rierson was in what he considered to be his element, matching wits and gun against the cunning of animals in their native habitat. The ten months of the year in which he lived and matched legal talent and persuasiveness of argument against another attorney before the bar of justice in the air-conditioned and near-hermetically sealed environs of Atlanta were as nothing compared to this.

From the first day of November to the end of the year, Rierson the lawyer underwent a Jekyll-Hyde metamorphosis and became Rierson the country squire, living in a rambling and rustic log dwelling and devoting his exclusive attention to the pursuit of game across the thousand square miles of reclaimed semiwilderness graciously provided by the state of Georgia for just such sentimental reactionaries as himself, men who wistfully recalled the halcyon days of yore, with frost on the pumpkin and a harvest moon and men with shotguns following quartering bird dogs across the back forty.

Not that he was a complete fool; he realized that those days spoken of so longingly by others of his bent had not been entirely without their shadows, without their empires and wars and heartaches. But five centuries is a deadening opiate, and names become empty things, a dusty roll call upon a little-used book-tape. Sherman and Shiloh and the Battle of Atlanta fade into insignificance; and was the Kaiser an automobile or a king? Hiroshima and hypocrisy and the hydrogen bomb; Communism and censorship and cerebral palsy . . .

The names, and the meanings behind the names, fade. But the vague longings somehow manage to perpetuate themselves, handing themselves down from generation to generation, stubbornly refusing to die like the names of old soldiers and old battles and old issues.

Daniel Rierson, his uncle, had had such a longing—a desire for uncluttered skies and fresh air in his nostrils and the feel of a good gun in his hands. And so Daniel Rierson, who scoffed at the reclaimed areas of Earth as phony and artificial, packed his gear and his dreams and boarded a stellar liner heading out beyond the furthermost reaches of the Terran Federation. He had found his dream and had settled in to stay, and had once prevailed upon his brother to allow his nephew to make the long voyage one summer for a visit. The visit had been short, but the fifteen-year-old had managed to kill three tarl—fur-bearing, goatlike forest-dwellers—during his stay, and the flame was ignited. He had returned home a dedicated hunter and determined to rejoin his uncle as soon as his schooling was finished.

That, as it turned out, was not to be. Within the year, worsening relations between Terra and the Llralan Empire had forced the recall of all settlers beyond the boundaries of Terran holdings and Dan Rierson had come home aboard a Federation warship, his dream finished.

James Rierson, twenty-three years later, had modified his own longings to coincide with what lay within the realm of possibility, and thereby managed to attain a balance in life that men with twice his years and forty times his financial status found themselves envying. For ten months of the year he operated as part of the legal machinery that held his society together; for the remaining two, he forsook that society and rolled back the clock five centuries to a less-complicated era—devoid of its own indigenous miseries—took it easy, and enjoyed life.

His pipe had gone out. Rather than relight it, he stuck it in a pocket and lifted the rifle lying across his knees. That was another part of the illusion: outwardly, the weapon was

21

not much different from the sporting arms of five hundred years ago. Its synthetic stock was stained to resemble walnut, its barrel dyed a deep blue-black. The sleek design of the stock, the telescopic sight raised just enough to permit use of the iron sights beneath, the leather carrying sling—all were features straight out of the distant past. The differences in the gun lay beneath the surface—and were still quite in keeping with the tradition. The scope—lighter, more compact—magnified better than its ancient counterparts; the long, tapering cartridges in the gun's magazine reached further and hit harder.

Putting the scope to his eye, he scanned the edge of a meadow eight hundred yards away, where tall, frost-burnt grass ended and a swamp had its beginnings. Just *there*—the cross hairs paused on the spot—was where his quarry should have appeared long since. He started to swing on, but a flicker of movement caught his eye. He held steady, waiting for a repetition.

A deer stepped into his field of view—a bullnecked, heavy-chested buck carrying a massive rack of incredibly symmetrical antlers. Rierson had seen him before—this was the one he had been waiting for—but he had never seen him act quite like he was acting now. He held his fire, watching.

The buck, normally regal in bearing as befitted his advancing age and magnificent physical proportions, was now weaving like a drunk. His head drooped, as if that basketwork of rapier-honed points had suddenly become too much to bear. He braced himself on trembling legs, tried to draw himself up, failed, tried again and partially succeeded, only to lose his footing altogether and go down heavily. He raised his head feebly, a leg thrashed once or twice. Then he fell back and lay still.

Rierson lowered his rifle, and the image of the fallen deer was gone. To the unaided eye, the buck across the fields was simply a brownish splotch blending into the ground. He put the scope back to his eye and the deer was lying exactly as he had fallen, unmoving.

In the time it took him to cross the distance separating his stand from his collapsed quarry the deer didn't stir. When he arrived it was lying exactly as it had been when he last observed through the scope.

There was no wound on the animal; he hadn't thought there would be. The game ranger had said he would have the whole section to himself, and he had heard no shooting to prove the ranger wrong. Most hunters these days were either in the armed forces or sticking close to home, hearthside and the family bombproof in case one of the increasingly frequent Larry nuisance raids managed to penetrate the defenses. The latter group seemed a little ridiculous to Rierson; no Larry bombardier—living or robotic—would waste bombs, if he ever got the chance to use them, on trees. But timid nimrods were not his concern right now. This deer was.

This deer that staggered into the open like a city slicker lubricated with mountain dew and proceeded to collapse in remarkable imitation of same . . .

And lay there breathing far too slowly, breathing in great surging billows so gradual the eye was hard put to catch the movement of its chest . . .

And snored.

Sitting down on a log James Rierson tried to remember all such similar occurrences he had ever heard or read about. After a careful tally, he came up with exactly none. Meaning, something had caused it to act so strangely—meaning, something definitely unusual. And meaning the Wildlife Service should be notified posthaste.

He took his leave of the fallen deer and headed for where he had left his aircar in the early morning hours to take his stand. Before he went out of sight he took one last look back.

The deer was still sleeping peacefully.

He made it back to his aircar in fifteen minutes' steady walking, climbed in and let it drift up just clear of the treetops before scooting for the ranger's cabin. Another ten minutes and he was there. He dropped in for a landing on the graveled expanse before the cabin, went to the check-out station's open door.

The ranger wasn't in, but one of his little robotic assistants was. The five-foot humanoid was busily sticking colored pins in a large map.

"I have a report concerning a sick animal," Rierson told him.

"Where?" The robot continued to impale the map as fast as he could scoop up pins.

"Right there." Rierson pointed out the location on the map.

"Type of animal?"

"Deer."

"Deer," repeated the robot, selecting a green pin and jabbing it into the indicated spot. He pointed to a stack of forms on a counter. "Fill out one of those, please."

Rierson went to the counter, saw that the mimeographed sheets wanted all information known by the individual reporting the sick or hurt animal, and the identity and license number of the reporter. He filled it out quickly, handed it to the robot. "This is a rather unusual case . . ." he began.

The robot stopped his enigmatic exercise with the colored pins and flicked emotionless camera-lens eyes over the form. "What is unusual about it?"

Rierson was taken aback. "You mean it *isn't* unusual?"

"Perhaps in the over-all sense of the word, yes. In relationship to this game management area, no."

"You mean things like this have happened before?"

"Eighty-four times in the past week."

"And before then?"

"Never."

"But . . . but then why haven't I heard about it? Why haven't the newspapers picked it up?"

"That I do not know."

"Would the ranger know?"

"Perhaps."

"Where *is* the ranger?"

"At present, he is investigating a lake where fourteen lesser scaup were drowned."

"*Drowned?* Ducks *drowned?*" Rierson stared at the robot incredulously. "And eighty-four cases similar to the one I just reported in one week alone?"

"Yes."

"I see. Where did you say the ranger was?"

"As I told you, he is—"

"Not that. *Where*. What section? What lake? There's a thousand square miles out there he could be in."

"Hardly, sir," reproved the robot mildly. "His jurisdiction extends over only a tenth of the area, not the whole."

"Then where is he?"

"I don't know. When I last tried to reach him by short-wave he didn't respond. Perhaps he wasn't listening. Did you wish to leave a message for him?"

"No—no, never mind." Rierson started for the door. "Is that all you need me for?"

"Yes, sir. Thank you for your cooperation."

Rierson sent his car up to two hundred feeling vaguely uneasy. Something was in the air—he could sense it, feel it, almost smell it. Something about the very air itself didn't seem quite right. And this matter of the sleeping buck, the eighty-four similar cases—of the drowned ducks. He made a spur-of-the-moment decision to stop by the Chief Ranger's office in Baxter Township to find out what was happening; this management area was his favorite, and if anything untoward was going on he wanted to know about it and what, if anything, he could do to help correct it.

Setting his course for Baxter he leaned back in his seat, letting the autopilot take over. While half of his mind dwelled on the memory of the big whitetail sprawled unconscious, the other half proposed and discarded a hundred fantastic reasons for its being so. He was really reaching when an alien sound intruded itself upon his consciousness, interrupting his train of thought.

His first thought was that it was an irregularity in the beat of his alo engine and he scanned his instruments. Nothing. Then he realized the sound was not coming from his car, but from an outside source. Another ship, then. He made a quick radar sweep, found the ship miles behind and at twelve thousand feet, closing rapidly. He checked his airspeed with thoughts of a Sky Patrol unit, then realized the ship's angle of descent would bring it down far ahead of him.

Within seconds the ship was above him, blunt prow glinting in the sun. It was then that he realized what had been bothering him about the cadence of its engine. Black, oily smoke was pouring out of its motor hatch and pluming away behind, leaving a dirty trail across the clean blue of the sky. As he watched, the ship slewed sideways, corrected, plunged on.

Unpronging his short-wave mike, he switched the selector to general traffic.

"Civilian Craft XD-4538-P calling ship in distress over Robert E. Lee Game Management Area. Do you read?"

There was no response. He tried again.

"Civilian Craft XD-4538-P calling ship in distress. What's your trouble? If your sender's dead, do a mild bank to south-southwest."

The ship bore determinedly onward.

Switching channels he said, "This is CC-XD-4538-P, over REL-GMA. Have sighted ship in distress heading due south, speed . . . do you read me, Savannah Control?"

Savannah Control obviously didn't. There was no answer.

"Savannah Control, this is CC-XD-4538-P, over REL-GMA, reporting ship in distress. Do you read?"

No answer.

He swore. So it was his own radio that was at fault. He could not tell anyone of the other ship's plight. He consulted his map. It said an ancient superhighway—now a truck route—ran through the area from east to west, then bent south into Florida. A truck stop was indicated not far from his present position. Nosing over, he headed for there.

He overran his destination, circled back and put down so hastily he left skid marks on the landing area. No one showed themselves despite his overhead acrobatics and reckless landing; he climbed out and went around to the front. The place was the stereotype of truck stops on any of fifty Federation worlds. The building was surrounded by a sea of concrete broken at intervals by banks of fuel pumps and maintenance racks; the structure itself was large and rectangular, housing a robo-repair unit at one end and a mechanic's office and automat at the other.

A big red groundcar—A Catamount—was pulled up at the pumps nearest the building. Otherwise, the place was deserted. The paunchy individual seated behind the Cat's wheel semed to be the sole occupant. The glass-walled office was empty and no one answered Rierson's hail.

He walked toward the Catamount. "Hey . . . where's the attendant?"

The fat man maintained his hunched, head-down embrace of the steering wheel and offered no answer. He didn't even bother to look up at the big man stalking toward him.

Rierson went around the car to the driver's window. "You deaf or something? I asked you where . . ."

His voice trailed off. The man's eyes were closed, and suddenly his utter laxness was very apparent. He was either dead, very drunk or a sound sleeper.

Rierson reached through the open window, shook him gently by the shoulder.

"Hey . . ."

The fat man's bulk shifted slightly; that was all. His eyelids didn't even flutter.

The lawyer grabbed the door handle, lugged at it. The door swung open—and the driver toppled out. He was caught by surprise but managed to grab a handful of expensive suit fabric to keep the other from dashing his brains out on the pavement. Lowering him gently, he dropped to his knees beside him.

Leaning over, Rierson sniffed his breath suspiciously—there was breathing, at least—but there was no odor of liquor. Just one of strong nicotine. So he wasn't dead and he wasn't drunk. Rierson straightened. What did that leave? Stun shock? Some sort of seizure? Or was the man just a really heavy sleeper?

He let the head down on the pavement carefully, stood up. The shifted position brought forth snores from his unconscious friend. Long-drawn and noisy inhalations followed by a prolonged hesitation and then equally long-drawn and noisy exhalations. There was something about that extreme slowness of breath . . .

Uttering a wordless exclamation, Rierson dropped back to his knees and lifted the other into a sitting position against the side of the car. Then he slapped the flabby face gently—a light blow intended to sting into consciousness.

The fat man didn't even flinch.

He took a deep breath, struck again, harder.

He might as well have been slapping jelly; the consistency and response were about the same.

Rocking back on his heels, he looked around him, feeling cold. There was nothing but the warm golden sunlight, the deserted station and the chill wind rustling pines across the road.

First the deer, now a man. And the robot ranger had said there were eighty-four similar cases among other forms of life. The ducks, he saw with a sudden flash of insight, had drowned because they had become unconscious, even as the deer and Fatso here. And the ranger had not answered his assistant's hail . . .

Rierson left the fat man to his dreams and went in search of the attendant. It wasn't a long search; it ended at the right flank of the Catamount. A dark-haired youth in greasy coveralls was huddled between the fuel pumps and the car, hose still gripped loosely in his right hand. Fuel had leaked from the nozzle to form a reeking pool in which his pants legs were soaking.

He, like the Catamount's driver, was snoring in slow motion.

Getting him under the armpits Rierson dragged him clear, then carried him around the car and deposited him beside the fat man. Then he stepped back and looked them over. To his way of thinking, this had definitely gone beyond the province of the Wildlife Service, had become a matter for the police. He went into the office, found a battered phone with a scarred visiplate and consulted a list of emergency numbers scribbled on a desk calendar. Finding the one he wanted, he dialed it.

The phone rang and rang, without answer.

Finally a voice cut in on the line and the smooth, featureless mug of a worker-class robot appeared on the screen. "What number are you calling, please?"

"Who're you?" countered Rierson.

"South Georgia Switchboard, sir."

"Okay, George—I'm calling EXN-988. Highway Patrol."

"One moment, please."

Rierson waited impatiently, had about given up when George came back with, "The trouble is not with the line, sir. No one is answering."

"All right . . . try Sky Patrol Barracks at Savannah."

"Yes, sir." Again the screen went blank, and Rierson could hear a distant phone jangling. There was no response. George's unlovely face appeared once more. "Sir, there is no answer."

"I heard. Doesn't that strike you as peculiar?"

"Sir?" George sounded puzzled.

"Doesn't the fact that neither of the two forces supposed to protect the public can be reached by the public—that no

28

one is answering the phone in the middle of the afternoon?"

"It *is* a little irregular, sir, but . . ."

"But what?"

"Sir, I wouldn't let it worry you . . . humans are a chronically erratic species." George let go the equivalent of a superior sniff. "There is hardly any logic or order to anything they do."

"Thanks for the compliment," commented Rierson sourly.

"Sir," began George earnestly, "it was not meant as a compliment but as a serious observation upon the follies of—"

He never finished his sentence. The phone went dead and the visiplate did likewise. Completely, utterly dead. Rierson jiggled the receiver, but there was no response. It was as if a curtain had been dropped—a thick, all-absorbent curtain.

He became aware of a muted humming he had not heard before, hunted around until he found a minuscule transistorized radio. It was on, but the station to which it was attuned was very obviously off. He twisted the selector as far as it would go to both sides, turning up the volume.

Not one word did he get. No station seemed to be broadcasting. He looked out at the Catamount, found himself wondering if the radio stations had stopped sending before or after the attendant and fat man had succumbed to . . . to whatever they had succumbed to.

In any event, he couldn't just stand here wondering for the remainder of the day and into the night. Some definite move was called for. Since he had started for Baxter, he might as well continue in that direction—the direction the burning ship had taken.

Thinking of the burning ship brought up another point: whatever was in the wind, it boded no good for airships—not judging from the looks of the only one he'd seen all day. If he were going anywhere, his traveling should be done on the ground.

In keeping with that decision he went out and dragged the two sleepers inside, finished filling the fuel tank of the Catamount, replaced the cap and racked the hose. Then he went to his aircar and got out his rifle and cartridge belt, strapping the latter, with its row of gleaming shells and long-bladed hunting knife, around his middle. He could well imagine the sensation his dirty denim garb, artillery and week's growth of beard was going to cause in Baxter, but that couldn't be helped. The familiar presence of the rifle bolstered his confidence, and at this point—what with dead radios, blanketed phone lines and burning airships, and sleeping deer and sleeping men—his confidence could *use* a little bolstering. As for taking the car, it looked as if Fatso needed medical help worse than he needed the Catamount, and it was necessary for Rierson to requisition the latter in order to provide the former.

Which he hoped would sound plausible to local authorities when he showed up in Baxter armed to the teeth and driving a "borrowed" car. One could never tell how small-town cops would react to anything.

Climbing into the Cat, he pulled out onto the highway and pointed its sleek prow at Baxter.

Chapter Three

Face down, thrashing on the sidewalk like a boated fish, Donovan struggled to reach the spare ammo clip in his jacket pocket. His legs were a dead, unresponsive burden.

He moved in a dream. All sense of reality had fled; he was a performer and this a stage set for some fantasy-melodrama. Things like Larry troopers raining down out of the evening sky simply don't happen in real life.

But it *was* happening. With startling clarity he perceived each little detail of its happening even as he flopped about. Troopers were running forward, jump boots pounding hollowly against the wind whispering through darkened streets. Others were bending over three supine, silent forms on the pavement. Above, thick clusters of blue haloes were still descending, and

—very high up—red stars moved across the sky as the paratroop ships made another run, inundating the city with propulsor noise.

He felt a need for deeper darkness; here he was exposed. He relaxed the muscular tension holding his legs in place, and scrabbled forward on his belly, letting them drag out of his pants legs. When they were gone, the empty legs flapped in the gusting wind like the protesting arms of a ghost.

Hoarse shouts sounded back and forth among the Llralans. They stopped their headlong advance and half of them brought up weapons. Donovan's guts tightened against the expected impact of searing fire.

A blocky specimen near the Terran used his own gun to knock up that of another, uttered a sharp command. His action was almost too late; the soldier's gun discharged upward with a static *fzack!* and a second rifle burned a black rut along the sidewalk that ended just short of Donovan's empty pants.

There was a choked cry from overhead.

The troopers involuntarily craned their necks, seeking the source of that piteous sound. Seeing his chance, Donovan hustled for any alley mouth on knuckles and thigh stumps. Crashed against a wall behind a garbage can. Dug in his pocket and found the clip, discarded the empty and rammed the new one home. Fed the chamber and turned back toward the street.

A blue circle of light was descending not twenty yards away, right over the gawping troopers. It came down very slowly, and one of the Llralans played a hand torch over it.

The gray-clad body suspended from the harness was dangling with a laxity only death can bring. The head lolled on the chest; the arms moved loosely with the pendulumlike motion of the body. In slow motion, the Llralan's jump boots touched the street and he stood grotesquely for a long moment before his legs buckled and he went to his knees slowly settling back on his haunches.

There the gray unit halted its descent. He squatted there on his haunches, head bowed and arms hanging loosely. His position suggested some humble prayer to his alien gods that his soul be wafted home across the stellar wastes. Donovan could now see the ornate, rainbow-colored boards on his shoulders—indication of high rank. Charred remnants of uniform tunic flapped in the wind and the odor of burned flesh came strongly. The officer's upper trunk was a blackened ruin.

While the soldiers stood momentarily awed in the presence of brass-hatted death, Donovan began a careful sneak down the alley.

He had made about thirty feet when something hard and conical rammed deep into his spine. A high-pitched voice said, "Sig vash, frambule!"

He stiffened, half-raised his gun.

"Vash, frambule!" The gun in back jabbed harder. "Vlisor gur stugor."

He hesitated, calculating his chances.

The voice became edged with something akin to hysteria, and the gun jittered nervously on his spine. "Vlisor gur stugor, frambule!"

Obediently, Donovan dropped his gun. He felt bitter as he did it. Whatever was going on, whatever situation on the rest of Terra, he would rather have met it as a man on the loose—even legless—than as a prisoner of war. Especially one that had just made a dent in the opposition. But dead he couldn't accomplish anything, and this Larry behind him seemed just nervous enough to kill him by frying if he resisted too much.

Loud cries sounded in the street and heavy footsteps came on the run. They had noticed his absence and in typical fashion become overwrought. Shouting and running about seemed to be their way of meeting every situation.

His captor called out and guided them. Greenish-beamed torches came alive, converged on him. Behind the glare, boots shifted uneasily and throats were cleared. He could imagine their feelings; the thought of a legless cripple chopping down several of their number and playing hard to get—even for such a brief interim—was disquieting. By simple arithmetic, if a cripple could do so much, then a whole man . . .

He grunted irritably. There was where the logic fell down: no one considered him as an individual. He was classified as *cripple*. Half a man. What half a man can do, a whole man can double or better.

Bull!

The alley was crowded now. An authoritative voice spoke from behind the glare of lights.

"You speak Llralan, Rekk?" The query was in English.

He shrugged. Why try to deny it? "Yio," he gave the Llralan affirmative.

"Good," applauded the other, slipping back into Llralan. "Then let me inform you that you are a prisoner of Empire, upon what is rapidly becoming an Empire-held planet. I tell you this to show the futility of trying to escape. Any such attempt will be dealt with harshly."

"What could I do?" Donovan indicated his legs.

"Plenty!" rasped another voice. "You killed my partner, you stinking . . ."

"Corporal!" reproved the bossy one.

"I am sorry, my captain. I spoke out of turn."

"It is forgotten," returned the officer condescendingly. "When one loses a partner, he is entitled to his grief, his anger." Then, "You, Rekk—what is your name?"

"Donovan."

"And your occupation?"

"Larry-killer."

"H'mm." The captain sounded troubled. "You do not feel the least bit sleepy or unsteady, Donovan?"

"Are you kidding?"

"No, I am not kidding."

"Then you should be. Anyone who'd ask a question like that ought to be kidding."

The captain sighed heavily. "So it's going to be like that, is it?"

"It's going to be like that," Donovan confirmed.

"Ah, well—there are those better qualified than I to ask questions and dig out the answers. Sergeant!"

"Yes, my captain?"

"Take the prisoner in charge, detail a squad and escort him to the nearest checkpoint. Have the flivver pilot there make contact with the mother ship. The commander should be advised of this at once."

"Yes, my captain. My captain . . . ?"

"What is it?"

"The nearest checkpoint is LO-80. That is a good twenty siveb from here—and the prisoner, as you can see . . ."

"Yes. Yes, you have a point. What would you suggest, sergeant?"

"Back along the street, my captain—in a merchant's window —I observed several wheeled tables. The prisoner could be placed upon one of those and pushed. Or Dispensary could be contacted and a wheelchair requisitioned."

"No time," the captain dismissed the second idea. "The wheeled tables sound like a good idea. Carry on, sergeant."

"Yes, my captain."

A gun muzzle found his already tender spine. "Vaga, Rekk!"

Donovan marched. He made his way back to the street surrounded by towering troopers who managed to look exceedingly self-conscious as they paced alongside their stubby captive. Then one of the troopers stepped on a trailing pants leg and sent him sprawling and Donovan cursed him roundly and fluently in Llralan. After that, they watched his dragging clothing and didn't seem quite as embarrassed.

The sergeant sent a pair of troopers off on the run to get the table. They were back in ten minutes, pushing a utility cart of the type used in kitchens and on patios—big rubber tires, a power outlet; large, flat table surface and shelves underneath.

Rough hands got him under the arms, boosted him aboard. "You hang on," said the sergeant grimly, "or off you fall. We'll put you back on, but we won't keep you from falling."

"Oh, no, sergeant, you'll have to do much better than that," Donovan told him. "Much better. According to the captain, I'm a rare specimen. Get me banged up and there'll be a reckoning."

"Reckoning, is it?" inquired the sergeant nastily. He took a menacing step forward, reminding Donovan somewhat of the cop in the bomb shelter. But for the physical difference—four fingers as opposed to five, pointed head as opposed to domed, and orange skin as opposed to pink—they were cut from the same cloth. Toughs—their answer to everything being a fist or club or gun.

Donovan was too numbed from the suddenness of it all, too angry at himself because he had not reacted swiftly enough to

34

avoid capture, to be dismayed by the sergeant's scowl. "Yes, reckoning," he said flatly. "What if I told your commander that I personally saw you shoot that colonel while his attention was on me. Grudge against authority, that sort of thing. Then there'd be a reckoning!"

The sergeant glanced around hastily, lowered his voice to a growl. "It's a long way to LO-80, Rekk—and you just bought yourself a side trip down some dark alley. A one-way trip."

"Then I'll just say my piece here," countered Donovan. He raised his voice. "Captain! Hey, captain!"

"Shh-h-h!" The sergeant made shooing motions. "Shut up, you fool!"

"Why? What do I care if you get the ax? You're the enemy; I've got a weapon. Therefore you're dead. But as to that proposed side trip—you don't dare pull such a stunt."

"Why not?"

"Because no tale you could dream up would save you if I get killed and cannot be questioned. I'm important to the big brass. Incompetent frambules that can't keep a prisoner important to the big brass alive and healthy get shot—you know that. So you're over a barrel, friend—and you might as well admit it."

The sergeant fumed; the troopers fidgeted. But Donovan was right and they knew it.

It was a very, very smooth ride to Checkpoint LO-80, Donovan sitting at ease on the table and managing to convey the impression of a prince surrounded by his vassals.

The flivver pilot at Checkpoint LO-80 got an immediate and vehement response to this message. The commander thought, it ran, that there was supposed to be no opposition to the landings. Therefore what did Checkpoint LO-80 mean by coming up with a Rekk that had killed six men (they were giving him credit for the colonel) and critically wounding another? That just wasn't proper procedure. Not at all. The commander would message the Supreme Commander of the occupational forces at once. Meanwhile, the pilot would hustle the prisoner aboard his craft, abandon LO-80 and head for the grounding site of the mother ship.

The pilot helped the sergeant load Donovan into a too-narrow bucket seat, called his gunner away from a rapt contemplation of fall wearing apparel in a shop window, and saw to it that the sergeant was comfortably ensconced beside the captive with drawn gun. Then he took the flivver up fast, circled out over the Thames. After that, a combination of speed, darkness and violent maneuvering made the Terran lose his bearings. Once the vagrant beams of a new moon sparkled on big water—either the Channel or the Atlantic.

Finally they went down like a falling elevator and Donovan got a confused picture of patchwork fields and hedgerows and neat little cottages before a massive, space-scarred globe loomed up at them, portholes ablaze with light.

They dropped into a cleared space where an honor guard with a motorized warehouse truck awaited. Donovan was lugged out, loaded aboard the truck. The sergeant followed, got on and the driver started up, moving toward the spaceship slowly to allow the guard to keep pace. The flivver from LO-80 dove back into the sky.

There was frenetic and noisy activity around the base and halfway up the flanks of the interstellar leviathan. Burdened warehouse trucks scooted out of the gaping holds and empty ones scooted in; winches rose and fell. Ground armor clanked into the maws of big freight copters and the loaded copters lifted swiftly to make room for others. Higher up, pale lemon tractor beams reached out to enfold the long, slim paratroop ships as they returned from their drops, and warp them home. A steady stream of matériel was being unloaded quickly, but without undue haste. Perspiring Llralans stripped to their undertunics took time from their work to goggle as Donovan's truck moved past, then turned back to their tasks shaking their heads.

From the looks of things, Larry was settling in for a long stay.

The truck climbed a wide ramp and went into a resounding hangar that was rapidly being emptied. It threaded through the confusion, arrived at a wide bank of intraship cars resembling nothing so much as old-fashioned Terran elevators. Donovan was carried unceremoniously into one of the cars and shoved into one corner by the press of guards. The doors closed, the car lurched and began to climb steadily to the accompaniment of a nerve-shattering whine. When it stopped and the doors rattled open, two brawny specimens lifted him bodily and carried him along a metal corridor that stretched into the distance. At an alcove some three hundred feet from the elevator they set him down before a plastic-topped steel counter while a pair of Llralans with blue armbands on their sleeves stared curiously.

"Prisoner for you," said the corporal of the guard.

"What *is* it?" asked the shorter of the two, leaning over the barrier and peering down.

"A vis come straight out of that walsos bottle you've got in your hip pocket," retorted Donovan sharply. "Come to haunt your dreams for all the miserable tricks you've pulled, you misbegotten frambule."

The turnkey recoiled, put a guilty hand to the bulge on his hip. "He speaks our language?"

"And how!" endorsed the sergeant from London, giving Donovan a dirty look.

"Where'd you dig him up?" the other blueband wanted to know.

"In that big burg over on the island," contributed the corporal. "London, they call it."

"Yio? Have any trouble?"

"A little."

"I blasted five of your billy boys," informed Donovan, blowing his own horn. "And I got another one burned, and left still another very sick with lead poisoning."

"Real fresh frambule, ain't you?" inquired the corporal.

"That's right." Donovan sighed. "And since you're about to put me on ice, it looks like I'll stay that way. Real fresh."

His sense of triumph at having maintained a vestige of independence by tongue-lashing his captors was very short-lived. They carried him down the corridor, opened one of many doors and dumped him on a cot within. The door clanged shut behind their departing backs with a sound of utter finality.

Donovan lay on his back and stared at his new home—a small cell about ten by fifteen feet, featureless except for the one blank door, the bunk and a tiny table.

"Damn," he said. Then he repeated it twelve times, with feeling.

It didn't help at all.

He was still in the bowels of an enemy ship sitting somewhere in the countryside of France; he was still legless; he was still under lock and key. He might as well have been nine thousand light-years from London as a short hop across the Channel. His world—and London's—had ended when the raid alarms sounded and the Llralan ships came booming over. As to what came next he had no idea. But it was certain to be unpleasant, probably painful and possibly fatal.

He sighed heavily. If it were fatal, he would at least have the consolation of knowing he had not come cheaply—that he had swapped his life for six and possibly seven out of their ranks. That was something, anyway. He thought of Jane suddenly, and realized that he was *not* nine thousand light-years away—that London and their flat were only a couple of minutes away by air.

And what had that Larry captain said? Something about being a prisoner of Empire on what "is rapidly becoming an Empire-held planet." The Llralans had invaded the ancestral home of humanity, yet the fact of his being awake and kicking had disconcerted them—they were expecting no opposition. Remembering the occupants of the bomb shelter—how they had slumped one by one into unconsciousness—he didn't wonder.

So this, he thought wryly, *is the way the world ends. Not with a bang but with a snore.*

The way the world ends—this is the way the world ends . . .
Not with a bang. No one had time to whimper.
Not with a bang . . . not with a whimper . . .
With a snore.

Chapter Four

The township of Baxter slept peacefully in the slanting rays of the late afternoon sun. Everything was quiet; nothing moved in the stillness save a questing breeze with the nip of winter in its breath.

Rierson stopped the Catamount midway between the city limits and the precisely centered shopping area, rested big hands on the steering wheel and looked around carefully, noticing details.

He was on a two-lane street bordered by well-kept verges and clean sidewalks. Beyond the sidewalks—each in its neat little lot—were pleasant bungalows of various pastel colorings. The lawns were green and close-clipped; the shrubbery showed signs of careful tending. Cars sat here and there along the street, pulled up at the curb or parked before garages. A toy space helmet was lying on the sidewalk not fifteen feet away.

Taken as a whole, it was a tranquil, pastoral scene the likes of which could be found virtually anywhere on Terra now that the brawling, sprawling masses had clustered around the spaceports or gone starward to the colonies.

All it lacked was one essential ingredient:

People.

The wind moved in the short grass, in the exotic plants and manicured hedges; the wind pried leaves from the stately oaks along the street and sent them whirling in helter-skelter confusion.

The wind moved, and only the wind.

The scene bore nightmarish connotations—as if some prankish deity had waited until the wee hour before dawn when the town slumbered deepest, then flipped the whole about on its axis, leaving the unsuspecting sleepers peacefully dreaming on.

Unease prickled in the back of his mind—a tiny voice that shouted something was terribly wrong, that urged him to turn the car around and leave while there yet was time.

He shook off the feeling, touched the accelerator and rolled forward into the business district. These buildings alternated in height between one and three stories; they were square, pastel-colored and possessed of yard upon yard of plate glass. Graveled car parks dotted every other corner or so, and none were over a quarter full. The bulk of the cars were lined along the curbs.

Still no sign of life.

He began to see other things.

The window of a hardware store was smashed; glass fragments sprinkled both the merchandise within and the pavement without. There was a conspicuous gap in a displayed line of sporting rifles, and what had been neatly arranged boxes of cartridges looked like a tornado had whirled through them. A car pulled up at the opposite curb had a badly-dented fender and shattered headlight. Directly across the street from the hardware store, a ladies' apparel shoppe's display window was peppered with symmetrical, bullet-sized holes. Within the window, several manikins were overturned.

The Catamount moved further.

Several other vehicles showed fresh signs of minor collision damage. No other buildings had been disturbed as far as he could tell.

He approached a wide, divided boulevard.

In its center, safety islands bloomed with multi-hued late-season flowers and were festooned with short, healthy palm trees. Tall, graceful light standards arched above. He turned left into the boulevard, continued his slow ride.

Five blocks ahead and on the right, a massive graystone church occupied a full block of real estate. Its architecture—vaguely Spanish—contrasted sharply with the square and modernistic auxiliary building of brick, aluminum and glass enclosing its rear half in a square horseshoe. At the very least, the contrast of structures was eye-catching. The church, facing on a back street running parallel to the boulevard was as devoid of life as the rest of Baxter.

Atop the church's steeple, diluted by the sun, an amber flasher revolved.

So that was it.

Rierson grinned, shaking his head as the tension that had been building in him since he discovered the Catamount's sleeping driver drained away with a rush. While he had been hunting, the Larrys had pulled off another of their incessant nuisance raids, and the staunch local citizenry was cowering in its bomb shelters.

That explained the smoking ship—possibly a crippled Larry drone, perhaps a civilian craft that had not gotten down quickly enough when the shooting started. It would also explain radio silence and the fact that commercial stations were off the air—if not the telephone embargo, which was probably some new measure dreamed up by bureaucrats to make the public more war-conscious. And at this very moment, one of those selfsame bureaucrats was undoubtedly totaling up with vindictive glee the fines to be levied against one James Rierson: operating an aircraft during an alert, breaking radio silence, attempting to use a telephone and various and sundry subsidiary charges. It was going to take a lot of talking to get out of this when confronted by war-hysterical authorities.

If it got too bad, he might even have to hire a lawyer.

With these happy thoughts running through his head, he pulled up opposite the rear of the church and killed the engine. Might as well go on in and surrender to the local raid warden and start facing the indignantly patriotic music.

Fwack!

With his hand on the door handle, he looked down at the puncture in the fabric covering the door. It was the making of that puncture that had caused the sound. He looked up. In the right side of the windshield was a neat round hole with spidery cracks radiating from it.

In seeming slow motion, his brain assimilated the facts and produced a conclusion:

Someone was shooting at him.

Again in seeming slow motion, he reacted. He flung the door wide and fell out onto the street, taking his rifle with him. In his ears racketed the sharp crack of a high-powered rifle. Came a second shot close on the echoes of the first, and fine glass fragments powdered him as he hunched against the Catamount's flank.

He inched down to the front of the car, peered around.

Blowie!

As he ducked back, concrete chips stung his arm. No doubt about it, somebody wanted his scalp and wanted it badly. But at least he knew now where his would-be assassin was: on the roof of the auxiliary church building.

He put his back against the Catamount, checked the loading of his gun. There were five shells in the magazine. He bolted one home, waited.

A fourth shot disturbed the tomblike stillness of Baxter and the slug ricocheted off the roof of the car, screaming away into space. He moved back to the front, scanned the area before him cautiously.

Between himself and the church building was a sidewalk, a lawn and a sign. Nothing else—nothing to afford a scrap of protection. The sign was the only thing resembling cover; he studied it carefully. It was a large affair, approximately five feet by ten, and made of the same fake brick as the auxiliary building. It was surrounded by a petit flower bed lifted above the ground by a brick enclosure; in raised plastic lettering upon both sides of that expanse was spelled BAXTER METHODIST CHURCH.

Rierson eased back to a position of safety and waited some more. The silence of the afternoon returned. The sniper was waiting, too. Waiting for what? Reinforcements? Had he bumped into a gang of hoodlums intent on ransacking the town while the Baxterites hid in their shelters? Sweat trickled down his ribs, made his palms slippery. Was that why he was being shot at? If not, what possible reason could there be?

"You on the roof!" he bellowed. "You hear me?"

Silence answered.

"I said, *can you hear me?*"

No answer.

"God-damnit, why're you shooting at me?" His voice, distorted, flung echoes across the silent boulevard to bounce among the buildings there.

Nothing.

Hot anger coursed through him. This had gone just about as far as it was going to. Shoving himself to his feet, he started around the car, intent on getting satisfaction.

A head and pair of shoulders popped above the edge of the roof, and sunlight glinted on rapidly shifted metal. Rierson dove for the turf. The rifle above cracked, and the bullet plowed a furrow wide of its mark. He came up on his elbows, sighted along the gun barrel beneath the scope tube. The gold bead of his front sight dropped into the notch of the rear and centered on the figure.

The other just wouldn't give up. He made violent motions with his hands—working in another cartridge—and slammed the gun back against his shoulder.

Rierson squeezed his trigger.

The three orange-skinned men were staring morosely at their stove-up scout ship when the first shot sounded. They jerked almost simultaneously, hands going to guns—and then relaxed, exchanging looks of disgust as a second shot followed.

"I wish," said the pilot, "that Agirt would stop shooting off that damned thing."

"Me too," endorsed the gunner. "Didn't he get enough kick out of peppering those store-window dummies?"

"Not Agirt." The lieutenant smiled. "He has an incredible fondness for archaic and alien weapons." He raised the rifle he was holding. "And these are both archaic and alien."

"But hardly a weapon," opined the pilot. "Me, I'll take a crossbow over that thing anytime."

The distant rifle sounded again.

"He's supposed to be standing watch," said the pilot. "Not playing with alien toys."

The lieutenant shrugged tolerantly. "Who's to hear him? The Rekks?"

"Maybe," insisted the pilot doggedly. "Remember that air-car we saw? It could have been—"

Agirt's rifle cracked a fourth time. "It was flying by automatic pilot," said the lieutenant.

"How do you know?"

"Because its living pilot would have succumbed to the Dust

by now. We were informed of the possibility of seeing aircraft still flying—and instructed to let them alone."

"We were also informed there would be no danger from Terran defenses," muttered the gunner. "But where's the landing ship that brought our air squadron down, eh? Where's half our squadron . . . ?"

"That's enough!" The lieutenant's voice assumed the cold weight of authority. "Our landing barge was destroyed by sheer chance—a last-gasp effort of defenders falling asleep at their guns. Now be silent, or you will find yourself on report—"

"Listen!" That was the pilot.

"I heard voices—a voice . . . something . . . from over near Agirt."

"You're imagining things."

"No! I swear it. I . . ."

Agirt fired again.

"Voices or not," said the lieutenant, frowning, "I think Agirt *is* taking this a little too far. I'd better—"

A sixth shot sounded. His voice choked off.

"That," said the pilot unnecessarily, "was not Agirt's rifle."

The lieutenant felt a sudden coldness in his belly. He dropped the Terran rifle, drew his sidearm. "Gunner, you come with me— pilot, you stay with the ship. See if you can lift it—and if the cannon are working." Then he was running toward Agirt's position, with the gunner pounding heavily along behind.

The unknown rifleman flung his arms up and went over backwards, leaving his rifle on the parapet. The abandoned gun teetered precariously for a long heartbeat, then fell end over end to the ground below.

Climbing to his feet, Rierson went across the lawn, around the building and through an arched doorway. Within was a patio formed by the three wings of the Sunday-school building and the rear of the church proper. Shrubbery similar to that adorning the boulevard safety islands lined the walls; the enclosure was bisected by flagstone paths.

A paint-stained plastic ladder leaned against one wing of

the auxiliary building. He went to it, ascending cautiously, using one hand to climb, the other to keep his rifle ready. Reaching the roof, he stepped onto it and found his ambusher.

He was utterly dead.

He was also a Llralan soldier.

Rierson stood there incredulously, seeing the neat hole drilled through the Larry's forehead, seeing the ruin made of the back of his head by the soft-nosed hunting round. The lean body was lying loosely, like a discarded rag doll. It was clad in tight-fitting gray trousers stuffed into space-black knee boots, and a billowy, soft-looking gray blouse. A peaked cap and neatly folded tunic lay beside the parapet, alongside several brightly-colored boxes of Terran hunting ammunition.

For long moments the lawyer stood there, unable to believe what he saw, yet unable to discredit his eyes. A Llralan soldier dead atop the roof of a Sunday-school building in Georgia. There had to be irony in that, but he was in no mood to appreciate it. There was also probably an explanation, but he couldn't think of one offhand.

Right now, only one thought occupied his mind: if there was one, was it not possible that there were more?

As if in answer to his question, there was a furtive movement back in the direction of the business district. He dropped instinctively to the graveled surface of the roof, but no shot was forthcoming. Crawling to the parapet, he peered over.

Sure enough, someone was slinking along, hugging every bit of cover, about three hundred yards away. He leveled his rifle across the parapet, put his eye to the scope.

The slinker was a Llralan.

Uniformed like his dead fellow, but carrying a sear pistol instead of a Terran rifle, he was heading for the church. He was not aware of being observed. His face was taut, eyes narrowed. The shots had probably drawn him from whatever he was about. As Rierson watched, he disappeared behind a building, reappeared fifty yards closer. He felt suddenly cold. Never before had he been stalked by a sentient being, and the idea wasn't particularly appealing.

The Llralan came on. Rierson waited, cross hairs centered on his chest.

His advancing target halted, looked around. A second

sinuous form glided from between two palm trees to join him. Rierson began to sweat in earnest. Two of them now, rangy orange men with sear guns in their hands and murder on their minds.

How many *were* there, anyway? The lawyer began to have visions of a creeping horde, stealthily encircling the church.

However many there were, two less would make the odds that much better for him. Rierson sighted carefully, gently let off the shot.

The right-hand Llralan jackknifed, staggered backwards several yards and went down in a kicking heap. The left-hand one reacted swiftly spinning to his companion's downfall on his heel and sprinting for cover. Rierson worked the bolt smoothly, with ease born of long practice, and swung the gun after the running figure.

The bullet kicked up chips beneath the other's flying heels. Then he was behind a row of cars and running crouched. Rierson snapped a shot at him as he crossed an opening, missed by ten feet. He continued to gallop back the way he had come.

He ran through a yard, vaulted a low fence and steamed at another, higher one, long legs scissoring along with amazing rapidity. As he took to the air like an ungainly water bird, Rierson fired again.

He seemed to trip over some invisible obstacle, went pin-wheeling through the air. He cleared the fence, dropped behind it and was lost to view. Rierson swung back to cover the first one, saw that he was huddled on the sidewalk, head dangling loosely from the curbing. That made one he didn't have to worry about.

Turning, he got to the ladder and down it hastily. Pausing only to reload, he went to a heavy door set in the rear of the church—the one marked with yellow—the bomb shelter entrance. As he had figured, it was locked tight. He debated whether or not to try banging for admittance, decided against it. The place to get was away from here. He headed for the archway, went through it and began to run back toward the Catamount.

To the west, something large and silvery rose above the roof-tops and wavered uncertainly toward the church. The staccato

46

thrum of its engine marked it as no ship of Terran make, though the difference was hard to discern through the coughing irregularity of its beat. Caught in the open, Rierson resorted to the big sign, flattening himself against it as the ship arrived overhead. A round hatch opened in its belly as it hovered, casting a saucer-shaped shadow on the lawn, and a stubby, cone-shaped snout jutted from it. A low buzz became apparent over the throb of the ship's engines; a blue blur formed in the hatch.

Rierson studied that haze thoughtfully. Whatever the frame of mind of the pilot of the craft, it had caused him to forget his cupshields—the force shimmering about that projector was unprotected. Should a material object enter that field at this moment—an object say, the size of a bullet . . .

Suiting action to thoughts, he placed a bullet through the hatch.

The afternoon came apart in a blinding flash of white flame. The sound of the ship-disintegrating blast was rather felt than heard. Rierson lay flat in the flower bed, stunned by the concussion, the bolt of his rifle digging into the pit of his stomach.

It was a long while before he came back to reality and looked around him. His ears still rang; his eyes still smarted. Every window in the Sunday-school building had been blown inward. Likewise the windows across the boulevard. Several trees were uprooted and one light standard leaned drunkenly.

Of the Llralan ship there was no trace. None.

He crawled out of the flower bed, staggered to his feet and picked up his rifle, checking the barrel for obstructions, the mechanism for damage. Satisfied that all was well, he moved unsteadily to the Catamount. The big red car was windowless, and several ragged holes in its body showed where chunks of the airship had disappeared to. Miraculously, the tires were unharmed.

Brushing powdered glass from the seat, he got in. He was still in a state of shock; the possibility of there being more Larrys close to hand never occurred to him. The engine turned over first try, sounding loud in the stillness after the blast.

He began to drive. The wind coming in through the wind-shieldless front window was cold; he fastened his jacket, hunched his neck and drove on, north out of Baxter. The sun was going down with its usual pyrotechnics in the clouds.

When darkness was complete, he abandoned the car and continued on foot. The headlights were smashed and he had no intentions of driving blind. He had no intentions at all, in fact, except to get as far away from Baxter as he could. He was cold, tired, confused. And scared.

Scared as hell.

With dragging footsteps, he kept moving north.

Chapter Five

For Bradford Donovan, time had virtually ceased to exist. In the cell there was no night or day—the lights were never dimmed or darkened. His watch had been taken from him; so had all his other personal belongings—they hadn't even left him cigarettes.

Interrogation, he knew, having been so informed, was coming as soon as the commander got around to him. The commander, it seemed, was presently occupied doing his part in arranging an orderly conquest duty. Until he was called, he would remained jailed, be fed at fairly regular intervals and taken to a multispecies-type head down the hall when he made the wish to do so known.

That was all. His only contact with his captors was when two guards brought him a tray of food—one carrying the tray, the other a wicked-looking truncheon—and returned later to suspiciously count dishes and utensils and then go away until he was compelled to summon an honor guard for a journey to the head. In-between times, he lay on his bunk and gloomed up at the ceiling. He did not know how the battle was progressing—whether the Llralan tactics had succeeded wholly, partially or not at all. He had only the word of his captors and the vast boredom evinced by his guards to judge by—and judging by that, the outlook for Terra was black indeed. He especially believed that the guards could not be so bored if they considered Terran retaliation imminent.

Which would infer that Terra was incapable of retaliation.

Out among the stars, along the Line, Terra had fleets boasting technical superiority but numerical inferiority to those of the enemy. Weaken those fleets to drive Larry off Terra, and the hordes opposing them out there would make a push. Save three worlds, lose fifty—that kind of arithmetic just wouldn't work, even if one of the three was Terra.

Terra, Venus, Mars—the first, second and third planets, respectively, ever to be inhabited by Homo sapiens.

Terra, Venus, Mars—taken in force from the rear, going down to ignominious defeat at the hands of an enemy heretofore considered too stupid to accomplish any such victory.

Terra, Venus, Mars—casualties in a stellar conflict, expended pawns in a game of cosmic chess. Cut off, captured, carried off the board.

Sometime in the far future, when the depths of the Empire of Four Thousand Suns had been plumbed, bombs delivered to its factories and governmental palaces, and blockades thrown across its supply routes—when and if—then the Federation could proclaim victory and declare surrender for the smashed foe. Then, no doubt, the three worlds would be handed back— and any atrocities committed upon the inhabitants thereof repaid in blood and broken necks.

But that was in the future, and this was the present. The grim, grim present. Donovan doubted whether he would have lived to see the end of the war anyway—it threatened to far outlast the remainder of his natural life—but his present situation removed the doubt. He would die in captivity and before the end of the war, whether against a wall, on the rack or in a POW camp. To come to such a futile end had he threaded precariously through fifty years of hazardous life, wandered over parsecs in search of the rainbow's end and struggled to keep certain principles more or less intact. And done so with the deep conviction that he was the main character, held the center stage, and would emerge victorious in the end.

Now from the looks of things, the only victors would be the Larrys. Just how many races, he wondered, must be buried within the sprawling reaches of Empire—races that harbored billions of individuals such as himself, possessed of dreams, loves, hates, and idiosyncrasies; individuals who had died or been subjugated when their races died or fell.

It must be an old, old tale to the lank conquistadors from Llrala.

When an irresistible force meets a movable object, there is only one result; and the Llralan Empire was that irresistible force—a lapping sea of soldiers and guns and ships that eroded and finally inundated any bulwark erected against it, and then moved on.

Homo sapiens, join the honored rolls of the vanished peoples, of the space-island dwellers lost to sight beneath the Llralan wave.

Somewhere, time passed—but for Bradford Donovan, time had ceased to exist. His life became a round of cryptic orange faces and plastic food trays and stumping trips to the head—of fitful periods of sleep in which distorted nightmares left him dripping with sweat when he awoke to the close oppressiveness of the cell.

Returning from one of his journeys down the corridor, a pant leg worked free from where he had tucked it under his belt and began to trail. He stopped, got the dragging leg and began tucking it back in place. His lone escort—a dopey-looking type with which the lower echelons of Larry infantry seemed to be well stocked—stopped obligingly and waited. Donovan noticed that the corner of his mouth twitched convulsively.

"Well," he growled irritably, "what's *your* problem?"

"Problem?" The guard was taken aback. "I have no problem."

"Then why are you staring at me?" Donovan glowered at him. "It seems to me your mother would have taught you it's impolite to stare—if you *had* a mother."

"But I'm not staring!" protested the guard.

50

"Don't hand me that! You're staring, all right—and I know why, too."

"You do?"

"Yio, I do. You're wondering why a cripple should be guarded so closely; you're wondering why the brass thinks I'm so important. Where you come from, legless men are either beggars in the street or—if affluent enough to afford artificial legs—possessors of soft jobs out of deference to their conditions. They are objects of pity—not fear."

The guard stared at him, round-eyed. "How did you know all that?"

"Grandpa's ghost told me," retorted Donovan, occupied with pulling the pant leg up good and tight.

"Gremper?" the guard repeated, butchering the Terran word. "Who is Gremper? You are forbidden to speak to other prisoners"—he indicated the doors lining the corridor—"and there is no guard by that name. My name is Svitta. So who or what is Gremper?"

Donovan looked up at him, thinking he was being kidded. He wasn't; Svitta was dead-serious, his brow corrugated in puzzlement. Somewhere in Donovan's brain, a gear meshed and wheels began to turn . . .

"A *Grandpa*," he explained solemnly, "is the father of your father, or maybe of your mother, but never both."

"Oh," said Svitta relievedly. "That explains it." Then his face clouded. "Doesn't it?"

"Oh, definitely," agreed Donovan, having a hard time keeping a straight face.

"But you said you were *talking* to Gremper!"

"I was. And he was talking to me. We talked together."

"I see . . . I think." Svitta frowned, added perplexedly, "But I remember no visitors being authorized to see you. Of course, he could have come while I was off duty . . . I didn't have a chance to read the log when I came on, but that must be it."

"Yio, that must be," echoed Donovan.

"I shall check the log first thing I report back to the desk," promised Svitta. "If I don't keep up with events, some officer will catch me one day and have me flogged."

51

"It's a hard life," sympathized the Terran.

"Yio, it sure is."

Svitta deposited him in his cell, closed the door with a clang. The stride of his hurriedly departing jump-boots vibrated faintly through the walls.

Donovan lay back on his bunk and waited.

It didn't take long.

Where one pair of boots had departed, two returned and paused before his door while a key scraped in the lock. It opened and Svitta came in, his face a study in bewilderment. He was followed by a heavy, beetle-browed specimen wearing sergeant's insignia. Beetle brow was frowning like a thundercloud.

Donovan pulled himself to a sitting position. "And to what do I owe the pleasure of this unexpected visit?"

"You told me you have a visitor," accused Svitta reproachfully.

"I did."

The sergeant looked from the Terran to his subordinate as if both had taken leave of their senses. Finally he addressed Donovan. "You had a visitor—here in this cell?"

"That is correct."

"There is no record of such a visit," he informed. "If such a breach in procedure had occurred, the day sergeant would have told me. What do you say to that?"

"What should I say? I'm not in charge of your paperwork, nor your jail. I'm but a stranger here; Heaven is my home."

"Huh?"

"I cannot take responsibility for the incompetency of your staff."

"You persist in your claim that you had a visitor here?"

"There's no persistence involved," countered Donovan. "It is a fact—perhaps an unrecorded one, but nevertheless a fact."

"I see."

"There's only one reason I can think of that would excuse your staff from disciplinary measures of the strictest nature," he went on, in a musing voice.

"What?" asked the sergeant, in spite of himself—hooked

by his eagerness to duck painful manifestations of official displeasure.

"Why," said Donovan, in the manner of one pointing out the obvious, "perhaps Grandpa didn't come through official channels at all. That would explain it, wouldn't it?"

"Yio . . ." admitted the sergeant, somewhat hesitantly. "But how could he *get* here without coming through channels?"

"Simple," Donovan told him. "If he didn't come through channels, what's left?"

"What?" prompted the sergeant.

"Why the walls, of course."

"The *walls?* Great Sirri, Rekk—have your brains become addled?"

"Not at all. Grandpa *ought* to be able to come through walls"—he rapped his fist on the bulkhead—"he's had enough practice in the last thirty years."

"What d'you mean?" queried the sergeant suspiciously.

"Well, he's been dead for thirty years, you see, and . . ."

"*Dead?*" yelped the sergeant. "Did you say *dead?*"

Donovan blinked at him in amazement. "But of course—didn't I mention that before? How careless of me . . . but then I'm prone to forget little details like that."

The sergeant simply stared at him in incomprehension. Svitta, however, reacted much more satisfactorily. His face lost color, his eyes widened perceptibly and he swallowed several times.

After a long-drawn moment, the sergeant looked at Svitta. "Let's go."

Svitta obediently led the way out of the cell, eyes shunting around as if to espy any spooks in the process of wall-coming-through. The fact that he saw none seemed to please him immensely. The sergeant stalked out, stuck his head back through the door.

"You will not change your story?"

"What story? I have stated a simple fact—that Grandpa visited me—and you have attached a lot of unnecessary significance to it, that's all. Seems a person can't even visit a relative in bad straits and offer his condolences without a top-level investigation. Why, if I were Grandpa . . ."

Slam went the door.

It was several minutes before Donovan's ears stopped ringing in sympathy. By that time the Llralans had moved beyond the limited earshot afforded by the metal walls.

He leaned back against the wall and contemplated overhead rivets, old and half-forgotten memories of his days among the Llralan stars flooding back. Planets and mountains and seas, cities and villages and people, all parading across his mind's eye in kaleidoscopic array. Local dress, local custom, local superstition . . . foibles, fancies, fantasies.

"May your forebears sleep well and deeply."

It had only been a form of greeting to him then—an expressed hope for one's continued well-being. And on certain festival days, various offerings were made at tiny, faerylike chapels scattered across the countryside to insure that ancestors *did* sleep well. The ceremonies were simple, dignified and touched with a certain hushed awe for those who had gone before—and had been choice fodder for his tourist's camera, while some Imperial Intelligence agent hung around close by, trying to be inconspicuous, and watched to make sure no military installations fell within the range of his lens.

On many of the worlds, the ceremony had become simply part of a way of life, without too much inherent meaning. A labor performed on festival day, that was all, just a meaningless ritual. But on others . . .

Ah, therein lay that which made the wheels go round in his cranium.

"May your forebears sleep well . . ."

In ancient tradition stretching back to the time when Llralans were not haughty rulers of a stellar empire, but simple mud-slogging, planet bound slobs, there was a very good reason for that pious wish: If forebears *didn't* sleep, they hung around their living descendants and bent an ear to hear how oft and kindly they were mentioned. If what they heard didn't please them, they took out their pique on the offenders by methods ruthless and bloody.

"May your forebears sleep . . ."

Well, he had exhumed one of his. Now to see just how old Rumjet Donovan would react to his favorite planet being infested with Larrys, and his favorite grandson incarcerated by same. If Llralans could believe in inimical ancestors, then

54

what was to keep them from swallowing a benevolent one? Benevolent to one Bradford Donovan, that was—and pure hell on Larrys.

Which went to show just how desperate he was for a friend and confidant, he mused sadly. Desperate enough to whistle up a spook. Much more of this, and he'd be seeing things, too.

"Grandpa," he said at length, "Grandpa, bless your rum-soaked old bones, you're finally going to come in useful. I hope."

If Rumjet Donovan had known the use to which his carefully and artfully besmirched name—remembered only by relatives, a modest tombstone and in legend in bars from Singapore to Alpha City—was going to be put, he would have rolled over in his grave, sat up, and called hoarsely for a double Scotch.

Chapter Six

The Llralan gun-truck rolled slowly down the road, twin blast-cannon pointing at the sky in preparation for quick un-limbering in any direction. A lone head, weighed down by a blue-green combat helmet, poked up through a hatch; the Llralan was scanning the underbrush along the road with binoculars. From various vents in the vehicle's armor, per-iscopes did the same. A mounted autogun jutted from the prow, shifting occasionally as the unseen gunner jiggled it.

For what seemed like the thousandth time, James Rierson lay in concealment and sweated.

There could be no doubt now.

Llralans were everywhere. Silent, ghosting patrols in the woods; grinding, gas-reeking vehicles on the roads; whirring flivvers overhead. Roads were closed, and "sleeper" units were infiltrating the area—units that spread out in thin nets, dug in and waited for the unwary to come bumbling into them.

For the past four days he had lived on the brink of discovery, walking shoulder to shoulder with death. Once he had crouched beneath a ground-sweeping cedar tree while a patrol bearing a wounded soldier on a litter went by. Snatches of half-heard conversation informed him that the soldier had been cut down by a jittery watcher.

Three things he knew with utter certainty: Llralans were on Terra in force and virtually unopposed; they had thrown a gigantic trap around Baxter and were slowly squeezing it shut; and he was caught in the center of that trap. Steadily, inexorably—step by step, tree by tree—he was being forced back toward the town he had left so hurriedly five days ago. Whether he slipped up out here, or was pushed back into Baxter—to be systematically cut off and bottled up until no escape was left—it was only a matter of time until he lost the nerve-jangling game.

The irony inherent in the death of an alien soldier atop a Sunday-school building was present here, too. He was a man who had built his life around language and the usage thereof, and yet he was skulking through the woods like a hunted Apache, where even to open one's mouth or clear one's throat was to precipitate a blast of gunfire. A respected attorney at law, he was playing a game as old as history—a game of grim, silent, deadly maneuvering through light and shadow, glade and growth, where the first misstep was also the last.

A lawyer lives by his persuasiveness of argument, and by his wits. His tongue is his foil; he parries and thrusts, he tries to wear down, catch off guard or bewilder his opponent into a position for the fatal blow. A lawyer uses his tongue as a soldier uses his gun—to rattle, scatter, pin down and ultimately destroy. But destructiveness is a relative thing. In a courtroom, destruction is confined to arguments—arguments are destroyed. And even then there is an appeal.

In the tangled flora north of Baxter, a life would be destroyed.

His.

And there would be no appeal.

Cold, constant fear had come to be his companion since he had fled Baxter—a bubbling terror just below the surface that threatened momentarily to well up and choke him. That and the dull, unfamiliar ache of hunger that cramped his stomach and sapped his strength. But apart from the depression brought on by his state of being and the morbid conviction that his fate was sealed, his doom inevitable, a different side of his nature sat up and—albeit in a small voice—raged in indignation that he should be submitted to such treatment. Who did they think they were, these Larrys? By what right did they burst in on a perfectly serene planet and disrupt his life? By what right did they hunt the hunter?

And he knew the answer to that, too: by the right of might. There was no one to say them nay. No Terran rockets, war robots or divisions—no *nothing*.

Just him, a hunting rifle and twenty-three rounds of ammunition.

Those, he felt, were not the best odds in the world.

The truck ground around a curve with a rasp of changing gears, disappeared from view. The engine noise faded gradually, died out altogether. Rierson waited. If the Larrys patrolling this road followed standard procedure, there would be a second truck following at a discreet distance—but close enough to pounce on anyone crossing the road behind the first one. That lesson he had learned painlessly by seeing the method work on a road winding beneath a hill upon which he hid under a tangled windfall while troopers scoured the slopes.

Sure enough, the second truck rolled into view presently, repeated the scanning activities of the first almost perfectly, then moved out of sight.

When it did, Rierson was on his feet and moving swiftly. Out of the trees, across the highway, into the cover beyond. If there were ever a third truck, this maneuver might get him killed—but a third one didn't make sense. No matter how many trucks they had, dozens of them following each other around and around could accomplish nothing more than tire wear and frayed nerves. The patrols were the more serious threat, and even they could be avoided.

Reaching the safety of the other side he slipped through a gap in the solid wall of greenery, crouching along for a bit, then straightened as the tangle thinned and large trees replaced it. He slowed his pace, began to glide from trunk to trunk, pausing often to look and listen, his rifle held ready across his chest. Just such areas were favored by the sleeper patrols, and here was where one should be. Continuing at right angles to the highway just crossed would allow him to skirt Baxter and eventually wind up on the coast.

As it turned out, there was no waiting squad. Whether they had something else in mind—were herding him into some as-yet-unsuspected trap—or had simply missed a bet, he had no way of knowing. He decided to take the setup with several grains of salt and veered toward Baxter. Toward Baxter was probably where they wanted him to go, but this gaping hole in their dragnet reeked of contrivance. So he moved toward Baxter.

He didn't have far to go. He had only been fifty miles away when they slammed the door to the north in his face. Since then he had been pushed back until the city limits couldn't be more than two miles away. Weariness pulled at him; he had not slept more than twenty hours out of the one hundred and twenty since he had last slept peacefully in his hunting cabin. His hunger had only been whetted by scraps of food stolen from isolated farmhouses, but was not yet such that he could put aside his civilized conditioning and eat without cooking some of the various small animals he had come across unconscious. A fire, of course, was out of the question. Tension, fear, lack of food and sleep—all coupled with endless miles of walking—had just about extended him as far as he could go. He wasn't thinking too coherently; only one clear thought remained. One thought, one purpose, that threatened to ride him until he collapsed.

Keep away from the Larrys.

Left foot, right foot; look ahead, look behind; look up, look around . . .

Keep moving.

Stop and you sleep. Sleep and you're caught. Caught and you die.

58

Move. Keep your gun up. Watch. Keep your eyes and ears open. Keep away from the Larrys . . .

Move or you sleep; keep your gun up or you're beaten to the draw; keep your eyes and ears open or you're surprised; keep away from the Larrys or you're dead.

Sleepy. . . . *Don't sleep.* . . . So blasted sleepy . . .

The woods were darkening rapidly with another sunset— the fifth one since he had killed the Larry on the Sunday-school building—when he found the house. It was squarish, two-storied and possessed of a circular landing apron with skidway leading to the garage appended to the main building. The clearing around it was vacant, undisturbed.

He waited until full dark before deciding to chance entry, the promise of food overcoming caution. Once decided he made a bold approach, marched up the front stairs and tried the doorknob. It twisted easily and the door opened. He went in.

He found himself in a parlor straight out of another century, complete with fireplace and overstuffed furniture. The sole glaring inconsistency in the decor consisted of a section of quasi wood paneling swung out at right angles to the wall to reveal a rounded steel door. Going to the steel door, he worked the handle. The door swung back on unoiled hinges, complaining squeakily. Revealed was a flight of stairs leading down into the earth. He went down them. At the lower end of the stairs he found a second door, went through it and into a smallish room equipped with steel let-down bunks and various survival items—a bomb shelter.

Sprawled on one of the bunks was an old codger of ninety or ninety-five; crumpled in the limited floor space was a woman of at least equal age, and a short-legged beagle hound. He checked the trio over, using more or less the same procedure followed at the trucker's stop. They were neither dead, drunk nor normally sleeping. Rierson stepped on the beagle's tail twice, and neither time did the little dog do so much as quiver. He lifted the frail little woman onto the second bunk, moved the beagle out of further harm's way beneath his master's resting place.

The only light in the bomb shelter was provided by a tiny

bulb set into a small radio. It glowed steadily, blood-red. The yellow, orange and white bulbs were not burning.

So the attack alarm had been a Condition Red Maximum—that in itself was a precedent. Never before had a Llralan task force penetrated far enough into Terran space to warrant such an alarm here.

Now they were tramping around outside, thick as quills on a porcupine.

And this old couple and their dog slept peacefully. So too had the men at the truck stop . . . and the whitetail buck, and the various creatures come upon in his four days of wandering.

As for Baxter . . . as for Baxter, he had not seen a soul of its inhabitants during his rather short visit there. But he *had* wondered what the Llralan was doing on the Sunday-school roof—and now the answer was obvious. He had been guarding the bomb shelter. That there had been only that one—only three plus the flivver in the whole town— would infer that they were expecting no trouble.

No trouble? Expecting no trouble from a townful of Terrans? Then they must have a hole card, and a high one. But what? Surely they would expect trouble of some sort, even from civilians, unless . . .

Unless the entire population of Baxter was asleep?

Whatever had put to sleep eighty-four reported heads of game, drowned ducks, keeled over a whitetail buck and overcome four people and a beagle hound was certainly not a freakish twist of nature. It had to be an introduced element. If the Larrys were banking on that element, then they had probably introduced it—and followed up with a full-scale invasion.

Invasion of one town, Baxter, and one state, Georgia, would profit them nothing and get them promptly scattered over the landscape by planetary defense centers. But they had not been splattered.

Which meant the Terrans were powerless to splatter them.

Baxter was asleep. What then would prevent Atlanta from sharing the same fate—or New York, or London? What would prevent the gunners of El Scorpio Southern Planetary Defense Center, in Texas, from succumbing to what had knocked men and women over elsewhere?

Turning, he went upstairs and hunted a kitchen. Finding it, he went to the robotic chef, scanned the list of available items and dialed what he wanted. The unit started humming softly and its metal sides grew warm to the touch; mouth-watering odors began to seep into the room.

While the robochef busied itself with the meal Rierson went to the front of the house and looked out over the silent woods. No shadows moved without; no unnatural outlines bulked suspiciously against the greater darkness. From the looks of things he had found a house as yet unwatched by the hunters. And, now that he was in, he wasn't going to leave until his meal was served up, if it meant fighting the whole Llralan Empire between mouthfuls.

He explored further, found in the garage a trim two-seat aircar with a fast, silent alo-motor. He tried the overhead garage doors, found them unlocked and tested them gingerly. Unlike the rusty shelter door, they moved quietly on their tracks. His next sortie took him upstairs in search of the ignition key. He found it among other pocket junk on a bedside table. In the drawer of that same table resided a lightweight, deadly machine pistol with two clips of ammunition beside it. As to what fear of spooks, burglars or of a violent past catching up to its owner the weapon's presence bespoke, he had no idea; neither did he care. But it might come in handy. He loaded and tucked it in a jacket along with the second clip.

Downstairs, a bell chimed softly. The meal was prepared, the dinner bell being rung.

He wasted no time in heeding its call.

Later, belly full to an almost uncomfortable degree, he was faced with a decision: whether to leave, hoping to find a place in the woods to sleep, or to push his luck and stay here for the night.

When he opened the front door, a chill wind swept in, biting into him after the warmth of the house. He shivered, sleepily imagining himself stumbling around in the dark trying to keep his eyes open and his sense of direction operational. The ultimate result would likely be collapse and unconsciousness for a number of hours. At worst, such an event could bring capture; at least, sleeping in the cold unprotected and with resistance lowered could bring pneumonia. Neither extreme was pleasant to contemplate from the seeming security and undisputed comfort of the house.

He pondered for a while longer, but his mind was made up.

He was staying.

Chapter Seven

The corridor without resounded to the militant tramp of many feet. Donovan, thus alerted, was sitting up facing the door when the van of the small horde entered.

The highest rank visible was lieutenant; then, in descending order, the beetle-browed cell-block sergeant, two specialists and a pair of hard-faced paratroopers.

The sergeant grinned mirthlessly. "May your Gremper help you, Rekk. Your interrogation is at hand."

The lieutenant frowned. "Gremper? Just what, sergeant, is a *gremper?*"

Before the sergeant could answer, Donovan said quickly, "Don't worry, sergeant—he will. And when the time comes, you'll be near the top of his list." There—that sounded sufficiently sinister for an opening gambit. If he was going to instill the fear of the supernatural in these characters, there was no time like the present.

The sergeant was taken aback. "Near the top of his list for what?"

"You'll find out—when the time comes."

The lieutenant looked around wildly. "Will somebody *please* tell me what's going on? What's he talking about?"

"My grandfather's ghost, if it's any of your business—which I don't think it is," responded Donovan snobbishly.

The lieutenant shook his head. "That's for sure! I'm a robot-ocist—not an interrogator doomed to deal with whirly aliens, for which I thank Sirri."

"So you're a nonbeliever, eh? A Sirritei." He made it an indictment.

The lieutenant shrugged, obviously giving him up as hopelessly insane. "I'm here for only one reason—and it isn't to discuss theology."

"Then what *are* you here for?" demanded Donovan, grabbing the initiative while it was his to grab.

The lieutenant looked at the taller specialist, who was burdened with an oblong unwieldy canvas-wrapped bundle "Give them to him."

The specialist, with an assist from his fellow, pulled off the wrappings and came forward bearing two familiar objects.

"My legs!" ejaculated the Terran.

"Precisely," said the lieutenant. "Your legs. Our men are tired of matching their pace to yours, or lugging you around like a warbag, so I was called upon to repair them."

"It is also detrimental to the morale if they are constantly reminded that a handicapped Terran is worth seven of them," observed Donovan shrewdly. "They're liable to do some arithmetic and come up with the conclusion that a whole man can do a heck of a lot more than a cripple. And that is bad for the morale, isn't it, lieutenant?"

"I am not the judge of that," responded the other, refusing to be baited. He nodded to the specialist, who had stopped and silently suffered through this exchange. "Give him his legs."

The specialist complied gladly, retreated to stand with the others.

"Try them on," urged the lieutenant. "Let's see what kind of leg doctor I'd make."

Donovan laid his pants aside, placed the stump of his right thigh into the fitted hollow in the top of the right leg, connected the leads. Tensing his muscles, he experimented. The leg functioned smoothly. Quickly he got the other one in place, noticing the crudely patched burn areas. Other than those blotches, the legs looked entirely real, down to faint tracings of veins under the plastaflesh. He slipped the shoes off his plastic feet, climbed into his pants, replaced the shoes and then paced to and fro across the cell. The lieutenant and his specialists watched the performance professionally, and the former smiled when the legs seemed to work.

The soldiers reacted a little differently.

The troopers and the sergeant bore the unmistakable flat cheekbones of Llralan peasantry; all undoubtedly came from worlds still in the process of colonization and development. The kind of world where ancestor worship still flourished. The kind of world where all but the crudest artificial limbs would be a rarity. To see a man legless one moment and not the next, though having witnessed the metamorphosis from start to finish, seemed to bother them more than slightly. Donovan smiled faintly. Dolts like Svitta and unsophisticates such as these were the base stock of Empire's armed might. It would be to these and others like them—if he could swing it—that Rumjet Donovan would assume inimical life, fleshed in by their own secret fears to dog their waking hours and haunt their nights.

He turned to the lieutenant, "My compliments on your skill as a robotocist."

The lieutenant inclined his head. "It was nothing." He turned to leave, gesturing his men to follow. When they were gone, the sergeant displayed a set of hand manacles.

"Hold out your paws."

He held out his paws, the cuffs were snapped in place, and the two troopers took him away to face his interrogation.

They reached the place appointed for it after a long climbing journey on one of the shrieking intraship elevators and a walk down a corridor that was—by contrast to the bleak cellblock hall—opulent. Heavy tapestries covered the walls; a thick carpet covered the steel decking. Three-dimensional solidographs of Llralan cities and landscapes hung at regular intervals over the tapestry; a faint, not unpleasant odor was wafted through the air by hidden blowers. Officers' country, without a doubt.

The right-hand trooper rapped on the door, received an invitation to enter from a wall grid and they trooped in. The soldiers flanked him to a big desk, stood rigidly to attention as he underwent an appraisal from the officer behind the desk.

On the commander's right hand was an infantry major; on his left, an air force captain.

"This," said the captain, indicating his seated superior, "is Commander Sa-Dzalla Sarak, master of the *Kalistra* and marshal of its air and ground forces."

He was obviously supposed to react in some way, so he bowed mockingly. "Honored . . . I'm almost sure."

The captain and the major stiffened perceptibly; the commander merely raised an eyebrow. He was a thoughtful-looking character with shrewd eyes, and he radiated quiet authority. This one, Donovan decided, was going to be a tough nut.

The tough nut waved at a convenient chair. "Terran, be seated."

Donovan sat, and the troopers retreated to frame the door like book ends. Sarak arranged a sheaf of papers before him, studied the topmost one a long moment, then looked up.

"Now then . . . you are Bradford Donovan?"

"Yes."

"You were captured by soldiers under my command on twelve November, in the city of London and on the island of England?"

"I was captured on the twelfth, and in London. If you say they were your men, I am unable to deny it."

"H'mmm." Sarak looked again to his papers. "Before you were captured, you managed to shoot and kill several Imperial soldiers. Do you remember how many?"

"Perfectly. I killed or wounded five. As to their being stone-dead, I cannot say, as I had no time to examine them. A sixth was still kicking when I last saw him, so I can't claim a kill there; he'll have to be tallied as a cripple."

"You speak of killing men as one would speak of swatting veq," put in the infantry major.

"I speak of killing *invaders*," corrected Donovan. "London is my home; I defended it to the best of my ability. Those dead men have no kick coming—they made themselves liable to death or maiming when they participated in the landing."

"He is right," Sarak chided the major. "You, a soldier, should know that." He turned back to Donovan. "But you have mentioned only six men shot by yourself. What of Colonel Slanel?"

"I know no Colonel Slanel," Donovan told him truthfully.

"He was also killed during your capture—but by searfire, not bullets."

"I had no seargun—only the .40." Donovan shrugged. "Your troopers carry the searguns. You'll have to ask them about Slanel."

"No!" That was the air force captain, driving his fist against the arm of his chair. "You do not wriggle out by trying to make us suspect our own men. They are trained and loyal soldiers—they would neither accidentally nor deliberately shoot a superior—"

Donovan hoisted surprised eyebrows. "Who said anything about accidents or treason? I merely said—"

"I *know* what you said! But you will not get away with it—not here! You will *not* protect your comrades in Georgia—"

"Captain!" Sarak's voiced sliced through his subordinate's anger. "Captain, control yourself. I understand your feelings, but please refrain from such outbursts."

The captain subsided, seething.

"What's eating him?" Donovan wanted to know.

"He has lost a cadet brother, a man who graduated with him from officers' school. They were friends."

"Slanel?"

"No—a flivver commander, killed in Georgia."

"He appears pretty overwrought," Donovan commented. "So did the soldiers in London. Seems pretty funny to me—you come busting in with guns and ships, all set to stomp somebody, and then get all upset if somebody stomps back."

"Our soldiers can die as bravely as any—in battle!" snapped Sarak. "A soldier expects to die. But when his superiors have told him he will have nothing to fear, and it would seem to be so . . . and then, out of nowhere, death, and no one to fight back at . . ."

Donovan had no idea what the commander was talking about, but it did make a likely opening. So he said, "Sounds positively supernatural, doesn't it?" in a knowing tone.

Sarak looked up quickly. "Which brings up another point. This wild tale of an ancestral spirit visiting you in your cell—what possessed you to dream up such a thing?"

"There was no dreaming involved," asserted Donovan. "And

no tale, either— at least no tale told by me. I simply mentioned that I had a visitor, and you treat it like a major crime."

"Look . . . you undoubtedly know that there are certain strata of Llralan peoples who worship ancestral spirits. An old passport in your personal belongings shows that you spent quite some time on Imperial worlds before the war. I think that you decided to use that knowledge to put your guards in awe of you—to perhaps even secure certain privileges—as a favorite descendant of a restless ghost."

"You think I invented Grandpa? Think he's a figment of my imagination?"

"Frankly, yes."

"Then why don't *you* tell *me* what happened in Georgia— and how Slanel came to be shot by his own loyal and well-trained soldiers?"

For the first time, he had the feeling that he had gotten through to the commander. Sarak was a long time in answering. When he did, he went off on a new tack altogether.

"I'm going to tell you a few facts," he said. "Then we'll see what you've got to say about Slanel and Gremper. And Georgia."

"I'm listening."

"First of all—that thickhead Svitta *is* from one of those backward planets where ancestor worship still flourishes. Since you gave him that rigmarole about Gremper, he's spread the word to other believers on this and other ships, and they have spread the word in turn to outside units. They are uneasy—no one likes to tangle with the supernatural. That unease *could* spread to other troops, causing a breakdown in morale and a subsequent disruption of our conquest duty. I intend to stop that before it starts, by making you admit that you fabricated the whole thing . . . and by conclusively proving that the only Donovan in your cell was you."

"Just how do you intend to make me admit anything?"

"By letting you know how we stand in this solar system. You appear to have guessed that we have employed a new and totally indefensible weapon in capturing the three inhabited planets. What you may not have guessed"—he leaned forward, speaking slowly for emphasis—"is that, very likely, you are the last Terran alive or awake on Earth."

The deadly assurance and titanic import of those words chilled Donovan to the marrow of his being. He had guessed as much, hoping against hope that he was wrong, but now there was no guesswork involved. And no hope. *The last Terran alive or awake on Earth.* Abruptly his utter aloneness came welling up in him. Terra was taken, and he was a prisoner aboard an enemy warship. Captured, weaponless and alone.

Sarak and the others were watching him smugly, confident now that they had him where they wanted him. Something he had almost forgotten he possessed—his hair-trigger temper—came to the fore. He mentally gave himself a swift kick in the pants. He, alone, had them worried, or he wouldn't be here—and they wouldn't be trying to scare him speechless.

For that was the only weapon they had left him.

Speech.

And he wasn't alone; he had one potent ally.

The late, unlamented Rumjet Donovan.

Now to use them.

"Well?" prompted Sarak. "What? No smart retort? No clever play of words? Come now . . . don't give up so easily! What do you say about that?"

Assuming an expression of immeasurable woe, Donovan said, "I am sorry. Deeply, truly sorry. Please allow me to extend my condolences to your valiant fleet before it is too late to do so. May you go to your greater reward knowing that your supreme sacrifice here will inspire others to similar bravery when the reckoning comes upon them. The Empire will doubtless award the highest honors, posthumously, to—"

Sarak was left floundering by this sudden reversal of the Terran's attitude. "Condolences? Sacrifice? Posthumously? What words are these?"

"He is just trying to confuse us," opined the captain. "He—"

"Let him speak," Sarak overrode him. "He's trying to make a point. Let him make it." He looked at Donovan. "This better be good."

"It isn't," Donovan told him. "It's bad. Very bad. You have said that I was the only living or sentient native left on Terra. Therefore I felt obligated to offer my condolences."

"Why?"

Looking pious, Donovan replied, "Because I detest wholesale slaughter. Because you are going to need all the condolences you can get."

Not to be put off, Sarak reiterated, "Why? Why will we need them?"

Donovan shrugged helplessly. "Figure it out for yourself. You have on your hands a planet whose occupants have been drugged into some type of prolonged slumber and eventual death . . ."

"Only slumber, not death," Sarak corrected. "But go on."

"Then you have a planet of slumberers. Venus and Mars . . ."

"Have succumbed also," nodded Sarak. "You will get no help from them."

Ignoring that, Donovan continued dramatically, "So you are stuck with a sleeping planet." He considered, added, "In fact, you are stuck with *three* sleeping planets. Three planets populated by the sleeping . . . and the dead."

"The sleeping, anyway," Sarak conceded.

"Oh, the dead we have always with us," pronounced Donovan solemnly. "Since the dawn of our time, men have lived and died on Terra. Even now, with her sons gone starward, the graveyards are not idle, nor funeral parlors nonexistent. Some far-ranging Terrans have even had their bodies or ashes shipped home for interment in parent soil. So the dead we have with us, in numbers uncountable. You know the adage: 'All the world's a grave, and all the men and women mobile corpses.' The great majority of the dead sleep well and deeply, just as your traditional greeting would bid them do—but some do not. And my grandfather is one of those."

"Very moving," complimented Sarak. "Very literate, too— and it might scare a fool or an ancestor worshiper out of his wits."

"Then they'd be smart. It's *enough* to scare somebody—even me. The present, living heirs of Terra are in no shape to assert their rights and push the spirits back into the nether regions where they belong. There is nothing to stop veritable hordes from arising to walk the Earth—and there is nothing in the make-up of an invading army to make them rest the easier.

"And, once freed, they aren't likely to want to be vanquished a second time. They will want what they consider theirs by right of prior claim: the Earth!" He paused, studied his listeners covertly. They appeared to be listening earnestly; he hoped they weren't letting him make a complete fool of himself preparatory to giving him the big ha-ha.

"The forces of the afterlife are gathering," he went on, "and you"—jabbing a finger at Sarak—"and you and you"—two more jabs for the captain and major—"and you and you"—twisting in his seat to include the troopers—"the whole fleet"—a wide, all encompassing wave—"are trespassers upon what they consider to be their private domain, do the shades of the past. They will be irritated—and you can't even claim a common birthright to trade on for leniency. They will take steps to rid themselves of the unwanted guests."

Sarak was beginning to look half-convinced despite himself, and yet could not by rights believe what he heard. The major looked thoughtful; the captain wore an expression of cynicism, but it ill-concealed his underlying uneasiness.

"Steps," said the commander, at length. "What kind of steps?"

"*Unpleasant* ones."

Donovan leaned back in his chair, crossed his artificial legs and endeavored to look sure of himself. He had gone as far as he could go without having an actual specter put in an appearance—and he somehow doubted that Rumjet would be able to make it tonight. Or any other night.

It was solely up to the Llralans, and their imaginations.

If they *had* imaginations.

Chapter Eight

On the sixth day of his fleet's occupation of the Terran home system, Martak Sarno, Supreme Commander of the invasive forces, finally reached a relative lull in his duties and was able to sit back and take stock. Remanding the fleet into the hands of Vice-Commander Blanatta, he retired to his cabin and poured himself a long drink to do just that.

In the midst of reading a report on the over-all state of the invasion, somewhere between an optimistic quote from the admiral in charge of Mars foreseeing no more trouble in the future than he had had to date—in other words, none—and a mention that no new light had been shed upon the mysterious destruction of Scout Flight S-90980 and its crew in Georgia, he leaned back and stared meditatively at the ceiling. Events in this man's galaxy, he decided, moved *fast*. It seemed only yesterday—surely not back in the very first months of the war—that he had been sitting in his office on Risstair and fulfilling his function as military adminstrator to that world by wading through pile after pile of appalling tedious paperwork all concerned in the most explicit detail with every trivial fact of provincial life.

Then, in all that vast sea of boredom, anything vaguely resembling something out of the ordinary was a priceless gem to be pounced on joyfully. And the fact that Terran prisoners of war, clearing military sites in areas rendered so fearsome by venerable native taboo that not even the whips of the Star Gods nor threats of more drastic action could force the local work crews into them, were succumbing to some mysterious

71

malady, was certainly out of the ordinary. The malady took the form of abrupt precipitation into an hours-long coma from which nothing could rouse them. Recovery, it was noted was every bit as swift as the seizure, and ever thereafter the victim was immune to whatever it was that had affected him. One coma to a customer seemed to be the hard-and-fast rule. And always in the taboo areas.

Work stoppage on military sites, no matter how fleeting, was sufficient excuse to lock his office, shed his paperwork burden and go investigating—an opportunity he seldom had. Besides, the facts of the case were intriguing.

So he had played it to the limit. Blanatta, then his chief of police, brought in local witch doctors and questioned them intensively in relation to the taboo. Top medics in the star cluster were requisitioned through the auspices of internal security agencies. His direct superior, the Sector Lord, authorized whatever measures became necessary to discover the cause of the ailment.

With such overwhelming pressure brought to bear it was inevitable that the exotic planet must give up its secret, and Sarno was in at the kill. The culprit, it turned out, was a flower. A very unusual flower of delicate alien beauty and the undelicate constitution of a meat-eater. A carnivore. Since it was not equipped with tooth, claw or mobility, nature had compensated nicely by arming it with a gaseous vapor and the ability to spray it with deadly accuracy when its sensory equipment detected meat on the hoof within range.

The bell-ringer was the fact that, while swift and deadly poison to all Risstairan life, the vapor's effect on Terrans was no more than that of a good sleeping potion. True, it tended to slow all bodily functions down to a level that could almost be classified as hibernation had the Terrans been a hibernating species, but it never lasted. And after one time around, the victim was permanently immune. Subsequent tests revealed that it affected Llralan fauna not at all, and the case was closed forthwith. The medics recommended that Sarno subject all future work gangs to the effects of the flower—"xil'tressk," or blossom of death, in native parlance—and let them have their comas before starting to work on the installations; promised that he would get a footnote in the annals of stellar botany as the discoverer of the effect, packed their bags and left for home.

With the little mystery cleared up and work back to normal, there was nothing for it but to unlock his dusty office and put his nose back to the grindstone. He found himself back at his desk facing even greater mounds of reports, requests and receipts than he had left behind. Stifling an urge to turn a seargun on the lot, he dug in. Hundreds of bills and measures and mandates awaited his personal approval. The Highway Department needed more money (didn't they always?); the Coastal Patrol needed refittings and repairs for its boats; and the smallest incorporated township on the planet needed a new garbage truck. And those were only the top three forms on a stack nearly as tall as himself.

He thought about retirement, then seriously considered suicide. He'd already tried an even dozen times to get out of administration and into the field or onto the bridge of a warship, had received a dozen flat rejections. Top-flight administrators were scarce, ran the wording, and they had to make the best use of each individual in the war effort. So that avenue of escape was closed to him. He was trapped on a backwater planet going slowly insane while visions of budget allowances marched through his aching head.

From that to this in one leap. He took a long pull on his drink and shifted slightly, easing his heavy frame into a more comfortable position. Somewhere between a garbage truck for Altoburv and the tall cool glass of walsos he now held, somewhere between then and now, he had hit upon the magic combination that opened doors and melted obstacles and accelerated events. One moment he was beating his head against a blank wall, the next he had butted through that wall and was being carried into unexplored realms by the impetus of that final thrust.

He could not recall just where the inspiration that the xil'tressk's unusual gas might be utilized as an unorthodox weapon against Terra had come from—all he could seem to remember of those days was his mounting frustration at books that would not balance and a kind of desperation that waxed and waned in exact proportion to the volume of paperwork pouring in from all over the planet. Somehow in his off-

73

hours, which were few and far between, his fevered brain had conjured up the image of sleeping multitudes of Terrans with Llralans standing over them, and himself holding the power of life and death over the sleepers. Perhaps the dream was brought on by what he had seen in the POW camps; or perhaps his military brain, trained long ago and far away to recognize military potential when confronted by it, was struggling in his subconscious to reach the politics-deadened regions of his conscious mind.

And once it had, he had begun musing what a pity it was that the unconscious state lasted only roughly nine Terran hours. Suppose it lasted a day—two days? *Suppose it lasted quite a while longer?*

For the time, it was enough. He now spent his off-hours building a theoretical invasion plan upon the hypothetical Dust of his imagination—the Dust whose effect lasted at least several months. It was a diversion, anyway—a hobby. He began disposing of his paperwork with a will, discovering a vigor within him he would have thought long, lusterless years had drained away long since. His hobby became his obsession, and he began to almost believe that his post on Risstair was only temporary—a cover assignment to be endured until his masterful deathblow to the Federation could be worked out to the fullest. Rusty old talents for logistics and maneuvering for which he had had no use since his days in the Transport Service were brought out and poilshed up. A hundred, a thousand timetables for conquest were drawn up and discarded. Martak Sarno had discovered a new lease on life. His administration of planetary affairs began to reflect his quickened interest in living, and he implemented policies with a flair. Among other things, Altobury got *two* new garbage trucks. His mental rebellion at being relegated to such duties were gone, and he no longer regarded his job as a trap, but as a mere step upward—and the stars were the limit.

In his exhilaration he became excessively bold. He pulled his rank on spaceport personnel shamelessly to gain access to the massive data computers therein. To these he submitted reams of figures and calculations, correcting his mistakes and making new calculations until his figures and those of the computers jibed.

It had been on the last night he intended to use the computers that his world of illusion had been shattered abruptly into a million fragments. All figures at last checked against each other—ships and men, supplies and weapons, timetables and distances. It was all figured to the nth degree, and he was at least as jubilant as if he had really conquered the home system of the Federation and was proceeding with conquest duty plans—all of which he had carefully thought out and made allowances for. He had carefully filled his several briefcases with all the neatly processed data, erased all indications of what he had been doing from the memory banks of the computers and turned to go, with the pale glow of more stars than even the Empire boasted penetrating into the now-darkened spaceport control tower.

And then the lights had flashed on, and the man he had never seen before was stepping forward, saturnine features foreboding, and was presenting a badge that gleamed gold before his squinted eyes while two more strangers appeared at his elbows and dexterously divested him of his bulging briefcases before he could protest.

And the most dreaded words in the whole vocabulary of Empire were ringing in his ears:

"Imperial Security. Afraid you'll have to come along with us."

Before he could recover from the shock he found himself aboard an ultrafast Intelligence courier bound for Llrala, undergoing intensive questioning as to the contents of his briefcases. But the questions were being asked by a board of military strategists, the lowliest of which outranked him by a dozen shoulder stripes, and not by suspicious-minded security agents. Somewhere between questions he was offhandedly informed that Imperial laboratories had been experimenting with the xil'tressk ever since the botanists who had come to Risstair at his behest had sent in samples along with a case history, in keeping with regulations. Ever since a routine Security check had disclosed his unusual activities and the purpose behind them, that experimentation had taken on a positive direction: the lengthening of the coma duration, through mutation of the plant.

What it all boiled down to was the fact that, where his dream world had been shattered beyond repair, his position in the real world had altered so violently it had begun to resemble something of his own contriving. A scant three years, by Llralan calculation, had passed since he had begun his nightly trips to the spaceport control tower, but already his yearnings had come true. The provincial pencil-pusher had become the conquering hero. Sarno stretched his big body like some huge carnivore after a particularly satisfying meal and returned to the present, hitching forward to peruse the reports on his desk.

From paperwork to paperwork in one easy lesson, he thought wryly, then sobered as he took up where he had left off, with the failure of searchers to find any trace of the destroyer of Scout Flight S-90980. A ring of troops had been thrown around the village of Baxter and was being slowly contracted; when the noose was tightened, it was calculated that their prey would be inside. Results so far: negative.

He read on. Reports from other scout flights as well as infantry units indicated that previous theories that not all Terran fauna would be affected equally by the Dust had proved correct; several lower forms of life had been observed moving freely about with no sign of impediment. This did not include the pet species dogs, which had succumbed along with their masters. Of all types, birds seemed least affected of all, though some groupings—for instance, the ducks—had proven even more susceptible than men, going under as much as three weeks before D hour. In spite of this unusual side effect, no suspicion on the part of the Terrans had been aroused. This facet, promised the report, would be enlarged upon more fully in the reports of the Intelligence agent dropped on Terra six months prior to D hour explicitly to watch for such manifestations of suspicion.

One aspect worthy of note regarding the unevenness of the effect on the over-all population of the three planets was the fact that several human Unaffecteds had been discovered, and no apparent reason for their immunity to the Dust found. Their names were neatly listed below. Though Sarno knew the list by heart, he read the list again.

1—MARGARET CASSIDY, *Butte, Montana, Terra*
2—BRADFORD DONOVAN, *London, England, Terra*
3—MICHAEL HARRIS, *Canali, Mars*
4—JENNIFER NOGALES, *San Francisco, California, Terra*
5—PAUL NOGALES, *Blue Hills, Yagari, Venus*
6—RICHARD RAYBURN, SR., *New York, New York, Terra*
7—RICHARD RAYBURN, JR., *New York, New York, Terra*
8—DANIEL RIERSON, *Venusburg, Mudcounty, Venus*
9—HOGATE YOGANDA, *Hong Kong, Terra*

Nine names. Five totally strange, four utterly familiar—and all representative of the most perplexing and disturbing development to date. Nine who did not succumb to the Dust. Nine who had been awake and aware when the Llralan fleet came in; nine witnesses to his invasion when there should have been none. Nine—and a tenth, yet unnamed—who had reacted in various and generally violent ways against an invader who had expected no reaction at all. Since his troopers' guards were lowered, naturally there were casualties. Casualties which just should not have been. Casualties to add to the total already on the books, put there by a combination of overeager Llralan pilots and Terran gunners doggedly fighting to stay awake long enough to loose one ragged but effective salvo.

The Cassidy woman had struggled violently, inflicting scratches and lacerations, condemning them all to perdition forever and ever, while the Nogales woman had taken one look at the orange faces and gray uniforms framed in the door of her San Francisco bomb shelter and gone into a state of shock from which she had yet to emerge. Rayburn Senior put up such a strenuous resistance he had been killed; his son had laid the entrails of a jump sergeant on the floor in front of him and slashed two troopers with a lektro-blade before gun butts had driven him into insensibility. Michael Harris and Paul Nogales—two of the familiar names—had put up no resistance whatever. The former took one look at leveled guns and raised his hands; the latter happened to be in a jail cell when confronted by soldiers and in no position to argue. Hogate Yoganda, physical giant though he was, had offered no trouble, and Daniel Rierson—the third familiar name—had got in only one good punch before being floored.

The owner of the ninth—and fourth familiar—name had put himself into a class all by himself by the simple expedient of gunning down six soldiers and causing the death of a full colonel in some as yet unknown fashion. And as if that weren't enough for him, he was now, for reasons known only to himself, claiming that his immunity to the Dust and his impressive kill-total on Imperial soldiers was all due solely to the machinations of his grandfather—dead these thirty years. He was regaling guards and crew members—anyone who would listen—aboard the ship upon which he was being held with bloodcurdling prophesies of horrors to come as the undead rallied to the colors. Which on the face of it was absurd—but then so had been the idea of conquering a system with a vapor three years ago. And the skepticism of his soldiers, Sarno knew, could stand only so much before they would start believing anything and everything. The happenings in Baxter had done nothing to help matters—had in fact offered seeming substantiation for Donovan's wild tales.

All of which neither he nor the High Command could have foreseen when they stood on a rainswept Llralan spacefield less than a year ago and watched the first of the Terrabound robot ships thunder aloft to sow her skies with the means of her own downfall. By loosing the Dust and following it up with a full-scale invasion, they had opened a Pandora's box of unknown and unsuspected pitfalls—and like that Terran figure of folklore, he was beginning to learn the consequences.

He shrugged philosophically. If this was the worst Pandora's box had to offer, then his fleet was more than equal to the challenge. At least it was *as things stood now*. If Donovan kept up his tale-telling and the "Spook of Baxter"—nicknamed so by the troops chasing him—remained at large, things might not stand the same a week hence as they did now. And that couldn't be allowed.

He pressed a com switch. "Blanatta."

"Yes, my general?" The Vice-Commander's voice had not changed one whit since Risstairan days—he might have almost been going to order a police investigation of illegal walsos-distilling in the Korvalj foothills instead of giving an order concerning the fate of a full-strength battle fleet.

"My general wishes . . . ?" The Vice-Commander broke his train of thought.

"Blanatta, I've decided to have all the Unaffecteds transferred here. That includes Donovan. And Blanatta?"

"Yes, my general?"

"Have Sjilla detailed to the *Kalistra,* to accompany Donovan back here. Do you understand what I'm driving at?"

"I do, my general."

"Good. Give the appropriate orders then. I'm going to be tied up with these reports for some time to come."

"Yes, my general. Anything else?"

"No. As they say in this man's navy—carry on."

"Yes, my general."

Sarno released the switch, took another sip of his now-warm drink and pulled a sheaf of dispatches out of his *In* tray. The uppermost was concerned with the gathering-in, recharging and storage of hundreds of thousands of anti-grav jump chutes used by the troopers and now scattered all over three planets.

"From paperwork to paperwork," he groaned aloud, and began reading. It occurred to him that there was one bright spot after all: the paperwork of a battle fleet was much more terse, to the point and just plain *interesting* than that of a provincial planet.

He drained his glass, signed his name in triplicate and went on to the next one—tidying up, attesting to and preparing for filing the last little details of the downfall of the species Terran.

Chapter Nine

He came out of a sound, dreamless sleep to stare uncomprehendingly at an unfamiliar ceiling. Diffused sunlight glowed through a translucent window, and the room was pleasantly warm. For a long moment he lay there, pleasantly between consciousness and unconsciousness, feeling at peace with the cosmos; then he became aware of the unyielding contours of the pistol beneath his pillow. In a rush, everything came back to him and he threw off the covers.

Somehow in this tranquil bedroom the exhaustion and fear of yesterday felt far and away. His clean-scrubbed body was a thousand per cent better for the bath; that his beard still graced his face was testimony to the fact that he had not been able to find shaving tools. His clothes—from underwear to rough denim pants and jacket—he had surrendered with some misgivings to the household robolaundry . . . suppose he was forced to depart hurriedly in the night? But he hadn't been, and the clothing was neatly piled on the *Out* chute. En route to them he passed a full-length mirror, garnered the impression of a mobile bear rug. If hirsute wasn't the word for him, just plain shaggy was.

Grinning, he dressed quickly, slipped on his hunting boots and refilled his pockets with the paraphernalia he had emptied from them last night. Then he buckled on his cartridge belt, stuck the machine pistol in the waistband of his pants and—feeling like a new man—took rifle and jacket in hand and went downstairs.

He spent the next half hour eating breakfast and preparing

a small bundle of food to take with him. Then he toured the premises with pistol in one hand and third cup of coffee in the other, peering out various windows for signs of skulking Llralan patrols.

There weren't any. The sky was clean and cloudless, the day was still. It looked like the kind of day that would beguile the strictest militarist into relaxing his vigilance—but then he didn't know what kind of day Larrys considered ideal for loafing and daydreaming.

In any case, he had to get away from this locale while the getting was good . . . if it was now. He headed for the garage, dumped rifle and bundle in the aircar and started the engine. While it idled, he rolled up the well-oiled overhead doors, then climbed in and eased it out into the bright sunlight. Again he got out, closed the doors behind him—no need to get the hunt onto his trail before he had to by having some sharp-eyed peruser of aerial photographs notice doors open where before they had been closed.

Lifting the car ten feet he hurdled a tall hedge, immediately dropped back to just about two feet aboveground. Keeping speed negligible, he drove straight for a wall of trees, slid past one and around another. Methodically then, with windows open and ears straining for untoward sounds, he steered silently through the cathedral aisles beneath the trees, an occasional branch lashing the windshield.

He angled toward Baxter, intending to skirt it closely and head east to the coast. Once there, he could work north and away from the troop concentration around the township by leaps and bounds.

But it was not to be.

He saw the soldier rise out of the foliage for a quick look-around at the same moment that the soldier saw him. For a split second, both were petrified—Rierson by the abruptness of the ruination of his plans, the soldier obviously by the silent and stealthy arrival of a vehicle his mind associated with the upper air spaces.

Rierson let the car charge forward just as the soldier started bringing up his weapon. There was a long heartbeat of time in which he stared straight into the horrified, panicky eyes of the doomed trooper as he strove to bring his gun to bear.

Then the car lurched, a *vu-u-ump!* resounded through its hull and it was slowing again. He glimpsed a broken gray-clad figure in his rearview mirror, huddled on the forest mold. The soldier hadn't screamed when the car hit him—had died in grim silence.

Cruu-u-mmp!

The car staggered a bit, and Rierson thought he had rammed a tree. Then the acrid tang of discharged energy reached his nostrils and he swiveled his head rapidly, trying to find his assailant. There was nothing.

Cruu-u-mmp!

This time he saw the blue beam lick from a clump of trees to his left. The sniper was well-shielded—he couldn't reach him with the car, neither could he abandon it now, under fire, and shoot it out. The woods around probably held an entire patrol. That left only one way out. He took it. Sawing back on the wheel, he gunned the engine and grabbed for sky. Overhead, interweaving branches rushed at him in a confusion of light and shadow; then he was clear, with garlands trailing from the vibrating short-wave aerial. A red light was winking on the dash. He read the dial, felt his blood run cold.

A searbolt had burned into the alo reactor housing and freed energy was upsetting the precise stability needed for operation. Already the engine was rebelling, the craft hanging sluggishly in the air.

The car went into a long, climbing spiral and his insides rotated in sympathy. Shoving the wheel over hard, he got back down below the dangerous radar horizon. Black, oily smoke was dribbling behind, marking his passage clearly across the sky. Searbolts snapped by to right and left. The car's bucking was throwing off their aim. That, at least, was something.

The peaceful, deserted buildings of Baxter swam into view. He pointed the car's nose at the most prominent structure— the Methodist church—and concentrated on getting down on three skids and in one piece.

He made it—just barely. The car slewed around, tipped up and almost over, then settled back with a violent jounce. He shoved open the door, toppled out, taking his rifle with him but deserting the food bundle. On the dead run he crossed the boulevard, galloped into a back yard, narrowly missed garroting himself on a plastic cord supporting several flapping blankets and brought up panting under the scanty protection afforded by an outside staircase. From the vicinity of the church came shouts, the sound of alien engines. They were right behind him this time—his luck had just about sifted away.

Grimly, he began moving away from the commotion. He crossed two streets after carefully looking both ways, dived for cover near a third while a speedy little truck crammed with eager-looking troopers roared by, rocked around a corner on two wheels. Then he got up, ran on. To lie in hiding was to allow the trap to close about him. He had to get away *now* —or not at all.

On the face of it, the latter possibility seemed increasingly to be the odds-on favorite.

Reaching the fourth street, he began looking into parked cars. The fifteenth he tried—one street and two dives for cover later—had the ignition key in the lock, but the door was secured.

No time for finesse. He drove the butt of his rifle against the glass again and again, shivering and finally smashing through the flexible, multi-ply stuff. Piling in, he almost knocked the key from the lock in his haste, then spun the wheels backing out into the street. Cutting left, he put the accelerator on the floorboard and prayed he wouldn't meet any troop trucks head-on.

The speedometer was sitting on eighty when he saw the barricade up ahead—two gun-trucks end to end, festooned with helmets and gun barrels. He rode the brake hard and the shrill of tortured rubber was like a human scream of terror. The car fishtailed wildly, leaving twin lines of rubber, sparks and drifting smoke behind. Two streets from the roadblock he spun the wheel and dove at a side street with the speedometer registering forty. He didn't quite make it; the wheels bumped up over the far curb. He oversteered violently and the car shot leftward, along the new route.

And slammed to a halt, yawed around sideways in the street.

Not two hundred yards away was a second roadblock.

He threw the gear selector in reverse and the tires again

thinly protested their abuse as he jerked back onto the intersecting street.

To his right, soldiers were running forward from the roadblock. They started firing as he came back into view. Directly before him, the turret guns of the second roadblock's trucks were swiveling to cover him.

To his left, a light tank was coming up fast.

He put the car in forward, jumped straight ahead as the first searbolts from the running soldiers began to rip the side of the vehicle. The guns on the trucks depressed to follow his impetuous advance. Gritting his teeth, he cut the wheel to the left, slammed up onto the sidewalk and shaved off speed along a blank expanse of wall. A white-hot flash snapped down the street; a deafening concussion rent the air. Where pavement had been was now only a blackened crater scooped out of the street.

He slid across the seat, kicked open the buckled right-hand door and came out bringing rifle to shoulder. He snapped off three shots, saw one soldier throw up his arms and pitch backwards, another stagger but keep his footing. The spiteful crack of his rifle in defiance of all the ordnance ranged against him seemed to give them pause. He utilized the lull to full advantage, diving into a doorway. As he tried the double doors within, belated shots crackled across the building front, knocking out brick, plaster and glass.

The doors were open. Their lock had been fused by the hot breath of an energy gun. In an inspired flash he saw all the men and trucks and ships that had pushed him back into Baxter, the way he had been neatly herded into a box with only one possible escape—through the doors along this street—once he was in Baxter. And now he found the doors he chose doctored for easy entrance.

He put down his rifle, drew the pistol, put his shoulder to the doors and went through in one continuous motion. He landed rolling.

Fzap!

Brilliant blue dazzled his eyes in the dimness of the building's interior. Flat on his belly, he aimed for the source of that blue streak and held down the pistol's trigger. Sounded a choked cry, a heavy thump, then a peculiar muffled tattoo.

He waited tensely for several seconds. There was nothing else. He scrambled to his feet, retrieved his rifle and crossed the room—a paint store, he could see now. Besides the sales counter sprawled a rangy body. A searpistol had dropped from nerveless fingers to lie beside its late owner. Rierson scooped that up, saw that the machine pistol had hemstitched a neat row of slugs across the Llralan's chest from shoulder to shoulder. His tunic was sodden with red-orange blood.

Leaving him there, Rierson went through a curtain and found an exit onto a service alley. He scanned the narrow, debris-littered way before crossing, noted both ends were plugged. Across the alley he mounted concrete steps at the end of a loading platform, found the large metal bolt on the massive warehouse doors drawn back, its lock nowhere to be seen.

He was still in their trap.

Sliding back one door just enough to allow egress he slid through, crouched in the gloom and waited for lights to come on or guns to blast.

Taking no time to wonder at his luck he threaded through stacked packing crates, went through a door and onto a furniture display floor featuring early American.

To his left, a stopped escalator gave access to the second floor. Before him, doors led onto a fairly wide street. Through wide windows he could see unmoving cars and a traffic light that went from green to amber to red with fine disregard for the fact that traffic was stationary. The power was still on in Baxter, just as it had been at the house where he passed the night.

With his danger-whetted senses guiding him, he turned and ascended the escalator. Reaching the second floor, he headed for a window masked by a crinkle-finish plastic drape and peered out.

Flanking the doors below on both sides, flattened against walls, crouching in alley mouths and behind cars, a good dozen helmeted troopers waited for him to come bumbling into their arms.

Twisting, he surveyed the room in which he found himself. It was cluttered with furniture, offered only three exits. One was the escalator. The other two consisted of a wide archway

85

leading to another display floor and a door just beyond Sirius III dinette styles. A sign above the latter declared in fluorescent lettering: ROOF—PARKING FOR CUSTOMERS ONLY, PLEASE.

One of the Llralans below must have been watching the windows—either on his own initiative or by command—and spotted movement. He left his alleyway post and raised his rifle carefully, deliberately. Rierson flattened against the wall. The window buckled inward with a sucking sound, rained the rich broadloom carpet below the casement with blackened shards of glass. The curtain jumped and contorted, then fell back limp.

From his position against the wall Rierson couldn't see the soldiers directly below him, but he could see a pair running down the street to join the fray. Backing off to prevent his gun muzzle from betraying his position he caught them in his scope, fired once. They slammed to a halt, stung but unhurt as the bullet sprayed them with concrete chips. He fired again. The left-hand one went down in one spinning motion and lay still; the other sprinted for cover. Rierson let him go, saving his shells.

A flurry of shots kicked the curtain about, scattered glass. The window was now glassless; the curtain hung in smoldering shreds. Hollow footsteps rang on the escalator risers. Rierson turned, got set.

A Llralan burst into view, saw him, and whipped back a long arm to heave something. Rierson's bullet took him high in the chest, knocked him off his feet and somersaulted him out of sight. The cylindrical object he had been in the act of throwing went with him. Several others scattered and rolled, released from his other hand.

Rierson dropped to the floor.

Before his eyes, the floor surrounding the escalator bulged upward in seeming slow motion, developed jagged cracks, lost solidarity and wrecked the ceiling overhead with spinning fragments. Pungent whitish smoke roiled upward, dissipated to show twisted and exposed steel floor supports, rubble-heaped risers not previously visible from this angle. The entire section of flooring around the escalator well was either gone or smashed to bits; wiring and insulation hung in tatters from warped supports.

Gradually, hearing returned.

He shoved fresh loads into his rifle and swapped the near-empty pistol clip for the full one, thoroughly shaken. One small bomb had done all that—and from below. And how many such bombs—and searguns and autoguns and blast-cannon—had his name inscribed upon them?

He moved as one in a dream back to the window, risked a look at the street.

Two gun-trucks had arrived below. Their turret guns were pointing in his direction and quivering with a sort of electric aliveness. Hopefully he surveyed the point where the projectors entered the turrets. If someone had gotten careless . . .

No such luck; all the cup-shields were locked firmly in place. There would be no spectacular encore to the detonation of the flivver six days ago. No more gimmicks and dodges—just straight bullet for searbolt until his weapon ran dry.

Thus reminded of his ammunition shortage he pulled back from the window, dropped behind a pneumatic sofa and made a quick check in that department.

The machine pistol's full clip held twelve rounds. With the three left in the second one, that made fifteen; the rifle was fully loaded and there were eleven cartridges yet in the bandolier, making seventeen. Fifteen plus seventeen: thirty-two chances. At last check there had been just about that many soldiers outside, excluding the trucks and their crews. Tugging out the seargun he had taken from the Larry in the paint store, he inspected it thoughtfully. The leading edge of the grip had three wide indentions, one above the other, one for each finger of a Llralan hand. A small button was set almost flush into the top indention. He pointed the weapon at a wall, pressed the button. Nothing happened. He lowered it, examined it from every angle.

The receiver was an elongated egg shape, rounding off at the rear, tapering down to the short barrel in front. The barrel ended in a bulbous, cone-tipped thingumbob topped by a thin blade sight and with a roughened ring marked in Llralan characters encircling its girth. The ring's function was obvious enough: it controlled the spread of the energy discharge. That left what looked exactly like a terrestrial crossbolt shotgun safety placed up where the trigger guard joined the receiver.

He pushed that as far as it would go, again pointed it at the wall. This time a gratifying burst of energy dug an ugly wound in the plaster.

The besiegers were strangely inactive. Suspiciously, he reconnoitered.

The trucks were still covering the second floor with their cannon; troopers made cautious by his rifle crouched behind every available bit of cover. Down the street a smaller vehicle flying a Llralan pennant was parked, surrounded by several figures.

Leaving the window, he approached the escalator, moving quietly. From below came almost inaudible rustlings of clothing and sounds of breathing. The risers were rubble-choked but not impassable; an agile being could scramble up that jumble easily. And Larry troopers were, to say the very least, agile.

He grabbed a heavy chair, manhandled it to the dangerous footing near the blast-ripped area. Getting a good purchase, he heaved mightily. It rose on two legs, toppled, crashed downward and thumped hesitantly to a point halfway between floors. The rustling and breathing retreated. A second chair joined the first, nudged it a bit farther before both became lodged solidly. He added a half-dozen lighter ones for good measure, then left to check other approaches.

A second escalator stood innocently in the next section. From below came sibilant whispering. Prowling closer he strained his ears, silently congratulating himself on three diligent afternoons spent with the language tapes some twenty-three years ago.

Came a hoarse voice, nearly cracking in its effort to be quiet. "What do you think we've got up there, Raist?"

"Who knows? A Rekk—that's all we know for sure. Enough of us have seen him."

"And he's seen us!" endorsed a new voice. "Strange that since we started chasing him this morning five are dead and one is dying—while he remains unscratched."

There was a snort. "Hush, ancestor worshiper. Don't believe everything your big-brother-on-the-flagship tells you."

"Laugh if you want—Verif was the radioman who received the message from the *Kalistra* asking Sarno's personal attention on the matter."

"What can Sarno do about spooks, I'd like to know? And this spook is real enough to kill with seeming impunity. So what can Sarno do about spooks we can't kill but can kill us?"

"Don't *talk* that way," entreated the ancestor worshiper.

"Why? Got the galloping creeps, have you?"

"*Shh-h-h!*" That was Raist.

"What . . . ?"

"I heard something. Up above. Like footfalls . . ."

"Arr, you're just imagining—"

"Am I? Wasn't he barricading those other stairs a while back? Could be he's right up there now, listening to every word we say!"

"And he's got Sergeant Cax's pistol," inserted the ancestor worshiper. "If he points that our way and holds back the stud . . ."

There was momentary silence, followed by, "Move away from the steps—quietly. If he's up there . . ."

The voice faded and surreptitious sounds told the Terran they were moving away. He went back to the first display floor, avoiding windows. He should try to blockade that escalator as well as this one, but any such attempt, now that they were ready for it, might precipitate a wild blather of gunfire.

He had hoped to learn some cogent facts from his eavesdropping but had been disappointed. All he had learned was that the Larrys were a bit leery of him due to his success thus far at dodging sudden and violent death. In view of the beliefs held on some of the Empire's far-flung worlds, that wasn't particularly startling. But their semi-superstitious fear would evaporate magically upon viewing his mangled corpse.

Which brought up a ticklish question. He was in the pink of health, prime of life and in no particular hurry to end it all. On the other hand, scores of soldiers owing their allegiance to a far sun were very desirous of his demise. While he pondered the dilemma thus posed, he lugged several pneumatic sofas and lounges into a rough circle and climbed within. The Llralans were waiting for something, else they would have rushed him long since. With soldiers in the building with him, it wasn't likely that the awaited event entailed flattening of same. So he, too, would await developments.

Upon reflection, he decided there was no other choice open to him, anyway.

Outside, grinding engines sounded the arrival of reinforcements. *As if they needed 'em,* was his thought.

Abruptly and shockingly a voice bigger than life racketed up from the troops below—a voice speaking English.

"YOU IN THERE, REKK! DO YOU HEAR ME?" There was a waiting pause.

Uh-uh, Larry—I'm not going to give myself away.

"WE DO NOT WISH YOU TO BETRAY YOURSELF TO US," came the voice again, as if reading his thoughts. "WE WILL NOT FIRE ON YOU. WE WISH TO TALK. THIS IS COLONEL VARGIR ZOWAL OF THE IMPERIAL ARMIES OF THE EXALTED EMPIRE OF FOUR THOUSAND SUNS . . ."

In spite of himself, Rierson was impressed. A full colonel in charge of rounding up one lone Terran—they must really consider him important.

"VERY WELL, THEN. I CAN UNDERSTAND YOUR CONFUSION AND MISTRUST AT FINDING YOUR FELLOWS ASLEEP AND YOURSELF PURSUED BY OUR FORCES. I WILL TALK; YOU LISTEN."

He listened, but kept shooting nervous glances toward the roof entrance and the unblocked escalator. Likely the loudspeaker and pomposity was a diversion to allow them to creep in on him and catch him napping.

The colonel spoke again.

"TERRA, VENUS AND MARS HAVE BEEN SUBJECTED TO A TOXIN THAT RENDERS ALL TERRAN LIFE UNCONSCIOUS, CAUSING A KIND OF HIBERNATION. THE PROCESS IS NOT, REPEAT NOT, HARMFUL TO THE INDIVIDUAL. ONCE HE IS AWAKENED, HE IS AS HE WAS BEFORE, AND WILL HAVE NO RECOLLECTION OF THE TIME ELAPSED. THAT, SIMPLY, IS THE WEAPON BY WHICH YOUR HOME SYSTEM WAS CAPTURED."

Rierson swore. So there it was—unorthodox, but obviously effective. Effective enough to overcome a culture that, as a whole, had been highly contemptuous of the sprawling military oligarchy that sought its downfall.

The colonel, having paused to let that sink in, went on.

"THE SURRENDER OF THE FEDERATION NAVY AND DISSOLUTION OF THE CORRUPT FEDERAL GOVERNMENT IS INEVITABLE NOW. THE WAR IS OVER; THE DESPOT FEDERATION RULERS ARE

OVERCOME, THEIR MERCENARIES SLAIN OR STYMIED. THE PEOPLE'S OF THE FEDERATION WILL BE GRANTED THE BENEFITS OF IMPERIAL CITIZENSHIP . . ."

That was a test: a hot retort would betray a rabid patriot and also give them a target for their hungry guns; if the cornered man was a doubter, then the promises would soothe him, lull him into possible surrender.

" . . . YOUR FAMILY WILL NEED YOU IN THE TRYING WEEKS OF READJUSTMENT THAT LIE AHEAD . . ."

A gentle suggestion that his family's welfare hinged on what he did here.

"THE WAR IS DEAD; YOU CANNOT BREATHE LIFE BACK INTO IT SINGLEHANDED . . ."

An appeal to sweet reasonableness.

". . . YOU WILL BE GIVEN FIVE MINUTES NOW TO CONSIDER THESE THINGS AND LAY ASIDE YOUR WEAPONS. . . ."

And, finally, the ultimatum: agree or else.

Colonel Zowal was trying to avoid a costly assault that would result in only one bedraggled body to show for its losses—and already there had been too many deaths this fine morning. He was trying to save a few lives with his persuasiveness. Rierson could feel a detached kind of sympathy for him—but he wasn't buying any.

"The benefits of Imperial citizenship," Zowal had said. He wondered if the colonel meant the same benefits enjoyed by his own kind—state-run factories and farms, troop-enforced mandates sent down to local planetary governments by the omnipotent Supreme Council, secret police, movement permits, police stooges, the works. If he did, he could keep them. Rierson looked to his weapons. As a lawyer, a believer in justice—as an erratic personality nurtured in freedom and impatient of restraint—he could never fit into that sort of scheme of things. He would literally rather die first.

He *would* die first.

"YOUR FIVE MINUTES ARE UP," informed Zowal.

From his pneumatic stronghold, Rierson could watch the windows, the clogged escalator, the stairway to the roof and the arch leading to the unbarricaded escalator. For the hastiness of its preparation, it was an excellent place for a gallant last stand.

Only he didn't feel gallant. He felt scareder than he had ever been in his life.

A shadow buzzed across the windows. Searbolts fingered through, searching for him. They were yards wide. The flivver banked, went out of sight, came back again straight on. Rierson hugged the floor and unleashed energy crackled through the room. The improvised barricade on the escalator shifted as if someone were tampering with it. From the display room adjoining came what could only be the cautious tread of advancing soldiers.

"YOU HAVE ONE LAST CHANCE. SURRENDER AT ONCE."

Overhead the flivver's engine whined as it banked again. He hunkered lower, gripping his rifle in slippery hands. His mouth was parched and his belly was cold. He wished he had a glass of fresh, cool water. His head pounded.

"VERY WELL. AS YOU WOULD HAVE, SO IT WILL BE."

The flivver went by again and a volley of shots ripped away the tattered curtains, leaving a wide expanse of blue sky visible. He saw with surprise that the morning had been slipping away, that the sun was standing almost noon-high.

He knew he would never see the evening.

Chapter Ten

"You," Donovan said conversationally to the guard setting his food tray on the cell's tiny table, "look like a man who comes from a long line of military men."

The Llralan froze as if the sound of Donovan's voice had turned him to stone. Then, slowly, he turned and looked at the Terran, having no one else to look at. The usual truncheon-wielder was missing; the soldier carried a seargun in an open holster and looked as if he could use it.

There his visible virtues came to a grinding halt. He could point and shoot a gun—could probably bend Donovan into a pretzel with various alien forms of jujitsu despite the latter's stronger body—but so could a Terran combat robot. In the attributes that separate men from machines, he was not of the elite. Upon reflection, Donovan decided he was probably a moron.

"I . . . I am," said the moron. "What of it?"

"Why, I'll bet you have a large number of relatives in the armed services."

"That's right," admitted the moron, his tone cautious.

"But none so adept as you, eh?"

Despite himself, the Llralan flushed with pleasure at this praise. "Oh, no—there are many better than I."

"You are modest," insisted Donovan. "Why else would you have been chosen for this hazardous mission and your kin left off the troop lists? They *were* left off, weren't they?" Donovan peered hard at him. "Weren't they?"

"Why . . . no. I have a brother and two cousins in the fleet."

"Here? On Terra?"

"Yio—and another cousin on Venus." This proudly.

Donovan assumed a look of mourning. "That's too bad. That really is too bad."

"It is?" The other's eyes went round. This one, Donovan decided, was worse than Svitta when it came to making saucer eyes at the suggestion of something amiss. "Why it it too bad?"

"I'd rather spare you the strain. You'd only try to warn them, and your superiors might construe that as an act not quite true-blue—undermining the morale and all that. But then again, they *are* your relatives . . ."

"You must tell me!"

Casting eyes ceilingward, Donovan indicated acquiescence. "So be it. These relatives—are they working outside the ships?" He tried to impart just how bad working outside the ships could be.

The guard, hooked thoroughly, swallowed hard and nodded.

"Then they're doomed." He made the pronouncement simple, irrevocable.

"Doomed?" The Llralan's voice was little more than a whisper.

"I'm afraid so."

"But *why?* What have they done? What—"

"They haven't done anything—not *them*. It's your leaders—*they're* the ones that did it, and *I* think *they* should be punished . . . not innocent soldiers. But"—he shrugged—"I don't have much influence with the punishers, still being in my mortal body and all . . ."

"The punishers?"

"You know . . . the spirits of the dead. Say, didn't your commander tell you about this?"

The Llralan gave a violent negative shake of his head. "I was only asked what my religion was. When I told them, I drew this assignment."

"Then you haven't been briefed?"

Again the negation.

Donovan looked wary. "Then I've said too much. They didn't want you to know about Grandpa. You know: the old policy of ignore it and maybe it'll go away. Do you believe that?"

"Nyo, I don't. If one hides his head like a skura, one only finds the situation worse when he comes up for air. You must meet things head-on."

"Exactly!" Donovan exclaimed, then let his shoulders sag. "But . . ."

"But what?" asked the Llralan anxiously.

"How does one fight a bloodthirsty phantom?" He looked up. "Do *you* know?"

"You blast 'em!" The soldier's hand dropped to his gun.

"But how can you blast what you can't see? Why . . . old Grandpa might show up any minute—he could be standing behind you right now, breathing down your neck, and you'd never know until"—he drew a finger significantly across his throat—*"zzzzk!"*

The Llralan flinched as if already feeling the blood splashing down his tunic front. "But I have done nothing—"

Somewhere in the cellblock a door slammed and a nerve-shattering shriek echoed down the corridor. Donovan nearly jumped out of his skin; the Llralan whipped around in a fighter's crouch, gun out. He presented a perfect opportunity for a quick bash over the head and a break for freedom, but Donovan didn't take it. To run now would be to refute his carefully constructed scare campaign.

Heavy boots tramped toward his cell, accompanied by a snuffling, shuffling sound. Came a sharp humming, a static crackle, another ululating cry. The guard straightened; his gun moved uncertainly.

"Vaga, frambule!" sounded a terse command. "Ber!"

"I'm goin', you orange-faced scarecrow. But just you wait, heathen son of Sirri, you'll get yours . . ."

Kewhack!

"Insolent Rekk! You dare to profane the name of Sirri with your filthy mouth?"

"You're just askin' for it, Larry. Just *askin'*—"

"Silence!"

The procession passed his open door and Donovan sat up very straight. That was a Terran! Dragged along by a neck chain, heavily manacled, cowering defiantly before a lektro-whip in the hands of a muscular sergeant. The voice had told him as much, but to actually *see* another human after all that had happened . . .

The guard lowered his gun, baffled. This was obviously as unexpected to him as it was to Donovan. The mood of the moment was broken; imagination-conjured ghosts fled back to their chimney corners and reality returned.

Two troopers paused before the cell, moved apart to allow three officers entrance. One was Sa-Dzalla Sarak; the other two were lieutenants wearing the comets of the air force.

"This is the other one," said Sarak. "He and Shey are to be taken to the *Risstaixil* by direct order of General Sarno."

Donovan's ears fairly twitched at the utterance of two familiar names—Sarno and *Risstaixil*. Sarno—not Martak Sarno, surely—that pompous windbag was likely still pushing papers around a desk on Risstair. And *Risstaixil*—Flower of Risstair, in a language known to very few beyond Risstair's atmosphere. Two familiar names in one sentence. Hell of a coincidence, if it *was* coincidence.

"*Risstaixil?*" he repeated dumbly.

"That's right—the general's flagship. You're coming up in the world for one so busy as Sarno to notice you."

"The order was directly from him?"

"That's right. He wants to talk to you, the message said, about 'phantoms and old times.' " Sarak nodded at the troopers and they stepped forward, quickly bedecked him with chains and hustled him into the corridor. He was ranged alongside the other Terran and the procession got into motion toward the intraship cars. Donovan moved in a daze.

"Phantoms and old times." That had torn it. Phantoms, of course, alluded to Grandpa, but old times—old times had torn it. And just when Rumjet and he had been making admirable headway in the problem of giving various and sundry of the enemy the galloping jitters and trying to make it spread through the fleet. Given time, stimulated imaginations might have appreciably deteriorated morale and efficiency—sent soldiers chasing after shadows instead of going about an orderly conquest duty. Time was what he needed for his moonbeam-weaving to prey upon their minds; and time was what the Federation needed to beat its brains and come up with something to get Larry off Terra.

Time—his, at least—had just run out.

Twenty years ago, on Risstair, his actions had been rash to say the least. A case in point: when Sarno's hirelings had come to collect the customary 30 per cent of all profits paid by off-world trappers to avoid police harrassment, Donovan had thrown a flamer on the group and promised to flame Capital City if any of them so much as darkened his doorway again. Sarno had been all set to extinguish this spark of rebellion when Navy beam-radio reminded the Llralan Supreme Council that Donovan was, after all, a Federation citizen. The Supreme Council, thus reminded, had muzzled their minion.

Sarno had been very, very angry. And Sarno had a long memory—his message to Sarak had proved that. Sarno was about to enjoy a hearty last laugh on him, twenty years later.

The car deposited them on the floor of an empty, deserted cargo hold and Donovan and his companion were pulled roughly to the gangplank. En route, the other received another blow from the lektro-whip. It didn't seem to dampen his spirits in the least.

They left the ship and headed through the chill of late afternoon toward an area guarded by a force-fence and patrolling sentries. Within, the *Kalistra*'s brood of aircraft stood in neat rows. They went through an insulated gate, pulled up beside a longish, bullet-shaped ship with opened hatch. The pilots climbed up, disappeared. Then came a soldier who turned and waited for the Terrans.

Inside was a compartment with metal benches lining both walls, a short ladder up front that led to the cockpit. The Terrans were taken to the rear, their neck chains snapped to inset steel rings. The big sergeant and four troopers went forward; two others left the craft and closed the hatch.

Engines murmured. There was movement. The ship leaped away like a scalded cat, wobbled, leveled off while Donovan clutched handholds and tried to keep from bashing his skull against the wall. The ship seemed to be hanging motionless. That was illusion; through an unshielded port he could see blue water and streaky cloud cover racing beneath. The ship was flying after the sun as though intent on catching up to it—and at this rate it would. Calculating rapidly, Donovan figured they would be across the Atlantic in an hour—and it would be noon on the North American continent.

"Damn hot-rodder," muttered the other Terran. "Acts like an Overseas taxi driver. Kill us all."

Donovan regarded him curiously. "Who're you?"

"Donald Shey. Say, where were you picked up, Donovan?" Shey looked cautiously at the cluster of guards. They were passing around a walsos flask, paying no attention to the prisoners.

"London. You?"

"Paris. I hear you got some of them before they finally grabbed you. That right?"

"Seven lousy soldiers. What about you?"

"No, dammit. Everything happened too fast. First thing I knew about Larrys within fifty parsecs was when they kicked in the door of my shelter. They were as surprised as I was—only they had guns and I had a bottle. But the way I hear it, you got six soldiers and a colonel—not just seven soldiers."

"What does rank matter? He was killed. That's enough, isn't it?"

"Yeah—I guess. Every little drop fills the bucket."

"That's right."

"Is that why"—Shey gave him a peculiar, unfathomable glance—"is that why you're feeding them this line about spooks? Trying to throw 'em off guard, bollix up the works?"

"What are you talking about?"

"You know what I'm talking about. You've been giving them a hard time about vengeful ghosts and bloodthirsty spooks—got a few sweating, too. But what happens when nothing materializes? When nobody gets chopped down like you said they would? Why build up such a whopper? To get leniency for yourself as a ward of the spooks?"

Donovan regarded the other's expectant face closely. Suspicion reared its ugly head. "You're just full of questions, aren't you? Why should you care what I say?"

"I don't." The words seemed to pop out of their own accord. Shey shunted his eyes around, seemed to be groping for words. His gaze fell on the muscular sergeant. "It's just . . . it's just that I'm gettin' sick of being caught one with that lektro-whip ever' time I turn around. If"—he paused, seemed to gather his thoughts—"if you could give me an idea of what you're plannin', maybe I could help. If two of us came up with the same story, it'd carry more weight, seem more believable. And maybe that sergeant would lay off if he thought his hair might get lifted by a spook." He leaned forward eagerly. "How about it?"

That put the ball right back in Donovan's lap. Shey was waiting and evincing pathetic eagerness. And yet . . . and yet, behind that excited exterior, he seemed to be waiting, watching—weighing the truck driver's response, judging the effect of the offer on him.

Keeping his own countenance carefully composed, Donovan replied, "But if your ancestors haven't contacted you yet, you would be lying if you said they had . . . and the Larrys are very good at detecting a liar. It would only make them doubt the truth of my story."

"If the Larrys can detect liars, how did *you* convince them?" This sharply.

"Because I wasn't lying," said Donovan righteously.

"Aw, come *on*, now! This is Donald Shey you're talking to,

remember? Not some stupid Larry." Shey gave him a man-of-the-cosmos look. "Who're you trying to kid?"

"I'm trying to make the Larrys believe in Grandpa."

"Why?"

"Because I hate to see them slaughtered without a prayer. Even they deserve some kind of fighting chance."

"Oh, for God's sake—" began Shey in exasperation.

Donovan cut in with, "Hold up your hand."

"Whaa—?"

"Hold up your hand where I can see it. You're asking too many damn questions. If you've got four fingers instead of five, I'm going to pull this chain loose and beat you to death with it."

"Don't be silly." Shey exhibited a perfectly formed, five fingered hand. "Satisfied?"

"Not entirely. Clench it. Make a fist. I want to see kunckles whiten."

Shey complied, looking bored. A fairly large, rock-steady fist protruded from his loose sleeve.

Abruptly, its steadiness evaporated. It began to tremble violently, as with the ague. The clenched fingers spread, began to jerk convulsively.

"Hours too late," Donovan told him. "Years. A man beaten repeatedly with a lektro-whip has had his nerves chivvied around good and plenty. He resembles nothing so much as a wino after a week's teetotaling. He shakes, he quivers, he drools; he is miserable, feverish, nearly incoherent." He tugged at his neck chain. "Get ready to play whipping boy, Larry."

The mocker shrank back against the wall. A silver-blue gun glinted in his hand. "Don't try it!" He raised his voice. "Sergeant!"

The noncom came back to him. "Yes, sir?"

"Get me out of this hardware. He knows who I am."

"Yes, sir."

"And tell your stinking mocker to join his aromatic friends at the front of the cabin," appended Donovan as the sergeant unfastened Shey. "I'm getting nauseated back here."

"I hold your life in the crook of my finger," warned Shey.

"Then take it. You'll only be hurrying the inevitable—and hastening your own doom."

"That's what you think."

"That's what I *know*. Grandpa promised me."

"Grandpa, Grandpa," mimicked the other. "When will you get tired of this children's game and realize there is no help for you?" He dumped his chains on the bench, stood up, "What do you really hope to accomplish by all this? What—"

"Changing course," grated a nearby intraship communicator. Thus warned, Shey and the sergeant braced themselves. The ship rolled, began a long, dropping arc.

Shey worked his way via handholds to the communicator, spoke into it. "This is Drelig Sjilla. What's the meaning of our change in course?"

"Sir," responded a metallic voice, "we have received word from the flagship that the Spook of Baxter has been cornered. It was General Sarno's order that we proceed there so that you might view the capture firsthand. I was about to inform you when you—"

"Never mind that! Who's in charge of operations?"

"Colonel Vargir Zowal, Imperial Armies."

"How's it going?"

"Sir, the Spook has already killed five troopers and wounded another; he has survived the crash landing of an airship and a groundcar smashup. Countless shots have been fired at him with no visible effect, but he has finally been trapped in a village store. There is no way out."

"I see. Please inform the colonel that I am on my way, will you? And hold this thing steady so I can come forward."

"Yes, sir."

Shey-Sjilla and the noncom went forward. Sjilla continued on into the cockpit and the sergeant rejoined his men. Donovan, ignored, had nothing to do but stare out the nearest porthole. The ship was still in its falling bank. A coastline appeared and swept beneath. Donovan recognized Florida's distinctive peninsula and realized that the Atlantic had been crossed while he bandied words with the mocker. He was thousands of miles and six time-zones from London. Here the overtaken sun was shining with the brightness of high noon.

The ship continued its fall until it was only several hundred feet aboveground, then leveled off, decreased speed and changed course. After another ten minutes, it dropped to a soft landing among the pastel structures of a small town. Donovan was taken outside and shoved against the wall of the nearest building, a drugstore. Shey went to converse with a stiff-faced officer sitting in a pennant-fluttering command car, causing momentary consternation over his Terran appearance on the part of the colonel's personal guards. The noncom and four troopers stayed aboard and began to unfasten porthole windows and hook them back.

Shading his eyes against the sun, Donovan peered owlishly about. Though the sun was straight up, a chill was in the air.

Baxter lay spread before him, eerily silent and tranquil but for this one street. Along it, gray-clad troopers were flattened against walls, hunkered behind groundcars and refuse cans and utility poles, crouched in alley mouths. Not two hundred yards away a Llralan body sprawled on an exposed section of sidewalk. No one made any effort to reach it. Calculating the range and angle from the beleaguered building to the corpse, Donovan whistled. No wonder the Larrys were standoffish. Whoever was up there had one thing going for him: he knew how to handle a gun.

The flivver that had brought him here took on four more riflemen, lifted away and circled high above. *Like a silver vulture,* Donovan thought.

Zowal raised a hand mike to his lips and his magnified voice—in English—thundered forth like a pronouncement of doom:

"YOUR FIVE MINUTES ARE UP."

A current of anticipation ran all through the waiting soldiers. Guns were looked on nervously. The flivver checked, dove past the building at a shallow angle. Its ports vomited searfire and then it was climbing away, glinting in the sun.

". . . flivvers back at the *Molegenaro* for refueling and repairs," Zowal was telling the mocker. "They've been in the air around the clock since landing day. The crews are worn out and there are other duties for the air force to perform that are being neglected, but we've received no aid from other ships." He gestured in disgust. "As to troops, I've been trying to blanket half the state of Georgia with four miserable companies. *Somebody's* got to look after our bomb shelters. And with towns like Atlanta and Jacksonville and Birmingham . . ." He shook his head.

"Things are tight all over," Sjilla told him. "We're on the spot—if we can't back our brag when the Delegation comes calling, there'll be the devil to pay. Until then, we'll just have to do the best we can with what we've got."

Donovan turned his attention elsewhere, though their gripes were music to his ears, and rattled his manacles irritably.

". . . ONE LAST CHANCE. SURRENDER AT ONCE . . ."

If only he could make a break—but he couldn't, not surrounded as he was. He would be promptly seared and the assault would roll blithely on, uninterrupted. There was no way he could help that other Terran, no way at all.

Zowal had been waiting for some response to his last-chance offer. When there wasn't any, he heaved an unhappy sigh, raised the mike again.

"VERY WELL. AS YOU WOULD HAVE IT, SO IT WILL BE."

Soldiers began to scuttle toward the building, disappear within. The flivver went by a second time, lashed the windows opening off the second floor with fire.

"Why couldn't we," asked Sjilla, "just pull back and lob in a rocket? Or flatten the place with blast-cannon?"

"Because," Zowal explained patiently, "the quarry would smell a trap and run. Besides, it's a point of pride: he has killed kith and kin of these soldiers. They want his blood badly. If spooks bleed." He chuckled drily. "The more ordnance we use to bring Mister 'Spook' to bag, the more the importance attributed him—and the more timorous the attack upon any other Unaffecteds we may happen across. And if, just by chance, we did as you say and *didn't* get him . . ." Zowal didn't finish. He didn't have to.

Turning back toward his forces, he began to speak rapidly and earnestly into the mike. More soldiers got into motion. The gun-trucks showed signs of activity. All attention and weapons focused on the building with shattered upper windows and smoldering walls.

Donovan stared bleakly at the cryptic structure, feeling his helplessness like a bitter bile in his throat. Up there, a lone

Terran waited for all these to come for him and he, Donovan, couldn't so much as lift a finger to help.

The Spook of Baxter would have to go this one alone.

Chapter Eleven

The flivver made a third run past the windows and Rierson flattened behind his protection. Searfire splashed all around, and the smell of scorched plastic came to his nostrils. Already they were pecking away at his couches and easy chairs. It occurred to him that the big pile of furniture in the middle of the floor was a dead giveaway, that it would naturally draw fire—and that he could be pinned down by that fire while troopers maneuvered into a position to blast him. Cursing his carelessness, he scanned the showroom for a better location.

His gaze fell on the door leading to the roof. From there he could watch the windows while being well back from them; and any soldiers entering the intervening space would be walking right into his sights providing the drifting smoke didn't hide them.

He vacated his improvised fort, moved to the door and looked up the first flight of stairs to the landing. If forced back from the door he could retreat upward, holding them at bay with the seargun. Then . . . but his mind refused to dwell on what happened then. Going back into the showroom he grabbed a long couch, muscled it into place across the doorway, climbed over and dropped to his knees on the other side. At one side of the door he left a gap between the jamb and couch, barely wide enough for a gun barrel. There he settled down to wait further developments.

Developments came in the returning throb of the big flivver's motor, followed by a foundation-shaking series of blasts along the front of the store, up near the ceiling. Long, straggling cracks appeared in the plaster; dust and chips rained into the smoky interior. At several points the wall bulged inward as if clobbered from without by an angry giant.

As the flivver went over, white flame blossomed at the middle window and Rierson ducked reflexively. The concussion accompanying the flash was sharp, intense—a blast-cannon in operation. Force-driven chunks of wood, plaster and steel thudded into the walls, the couch, the stairs behind him. As he hugged the floor, three more blasts followed in quick succession. The rattle and thud of falling and flying debris became almost continuous. When the patter abated, the flivver came in again and this time blue flame jetted through the wall and ceiling at several points, scoring the floor deeply. When it climbed away, a large hole was allowing sunlight into the murky room. The greedy crackle of flames came to him and the volume of smoke increased, leaking out through smashed windows and newly opened exits.

It lasted like that for long-drawn minutes. The diving ship, then the hammering cannon, then repeat. Rierson kept low, not risking an eye to watch the systematic destruction taking place. No soldier would try to cross that flaming hell while the guns were going—not unless he was tired of living.

Then the guns stopped, leaving only the rumble of falling debris. His guts tightened, and he was vaguely surprised that he could become any scareder than he had been since realization of his fate was first thrust upon him.

Here it comes.

He shifted position, peered out through the gap.

Smoke roiled in great billows, allowing only glimpses of the far wall—but those glimpses were enough to see that the left windows were now one, joined by a great, uneven gap, and that the wall space between the center and right windows resembled Swiss cheese. Multicolored flames leaped and danced as various off-planet woods caught fire and nonburning synthetics began to smoulder odoriferously. The carpet itself was ablaze. Most of the smoke was going out into the street, but stray streamers began to drift over. His eyes smarted.

An indistinct figure loomed in the smog, clutching rifle at ready. He was stalking the piled furniture Rierson had vacated. Drawing the searpistol, Rierson sighted through the gap, touched the firing button. A wide streak of blue slashed electrically through the murk, caught the sneaking Larry in the small of the back. He dropped his rifle, clamped his hands to the wound, stumbled forward into the furniture-fort. He fell into it face first, bounced and slid loosely to the floor.

A muffled inquiry sounded from across the room near the ruined outer wall. Rierson's using the seargun had confused them; they weren't sure whether he had fired or been fired at. He shifted the weapon's muzzle toward the voice, hissed "Over here," in Llralan.

"Virr?"

Now he had it—the exact location of the inquirer. He pressed the gun handle, waved it in a vicious arc about waist high. Came a gurgling shriek, a heavy thump.

"Eyiii!"

He nearly dropped the pistol at the suddenness and nearness of that shrill, vengeful cry. The space before him was abruptly alive with Llralans—all rushing straight at the abandoned couch-fort. There was no time to pick targets; he twisted the beam selector to spray and held down the button.

A wave of energy swept out at the attackers from their flank and washed among them, charring everything it touched. As living flesh became ash, cries rose from tortured throats, choked off as life fled. He fired until nothing moved before him, then released the button and gingerly tuned the gun back to narrow beam. Was it his imagination, or had that torrent of death faltered as it reached for the last two? Was the gun running dry so soon?

He surveyed the damage wrought. Discernible through the smoke at floor level were seven bodies including the one near the furniture-fort. Adding to that the one he had killed by ear it made a total of eight, plus five others this morning and three plus a blasted flivver several days ago. Not a bad exchange for one man—and the price would go up every time they rushed him.

Silence descended. The odor of sear charges, smouldering plastics and burned flesh was nauseatingly strong. He tried breathing through his mouth, coughed, realized the smoke was thicker.

A tongue of searfire reached into the haze, created ruin along the far side of the room, then lashed blindly about like an out-of-control fire hose. The destruction continued until the flame flickered, paled, died. Immediately a second gun took up the barrage. A heavy lounge chair lurched drunkenly, teetered and fell on its side as its legs were burned from under it. One body's pants were afire, burning steadily. The stink of charring flesh waxed stronger.

The second hose of energy flickered into oblivion and a third replaced it, sketching out a rough half-circle, but falling feet short of the doorway. Before it faded, a fourth joined in, and then a fifth. When number three died, four and five were joined by a sixth and seventh. This continued until everything within that rough half-circle was blackened. Several of the smaller fires burned out as they exhausted, or had exhausted for them, their fuel supply.

When the fusillade stopped, the soldiers came again. Shimmerging in the thick atmosphere like figures on a faulty tri-vid receiver, they drifted into the charred area. Rierson raised the seargun, waited. When the first soldier leaped up on the blackened furniture-fort with a triumphant whoop and burst of energy down toward where he should have been, James Rierson fired.

The weakening flame jet caught him high in the trunk and he toppled into the space he had thought to contain his prey. But he wasn't dead; he started screaming hideously, begging for someone to stop the pain. Rierson shuddered, dropped the seargun distastefully and drew the machine pistol. The others were turning toward him, squinting through the smog. He thumbed the safety, began to squeeze off individual, aimed shots. It was point-blank range and they were silhouetted against the lighter gray of sun-diffused smoke. While they tried to find him, three soldiers died without a grunt; a fourth went to his knees, was trying to raise his gun when a fifth bullet rolled him sideways.

The seared soldier was still screaming.

It seemed to rattle his fellows. For a precious instant they stood unmoving, guns silent. A fifth and sixth of their number fell before they broke and ran. Rierson, taken off guard by their flight, let them go unscathed.

"Somebody!" raved the dying Llralan. "For the sake of Sirri, *somebody* . . . oh, Sirri, it hurts! Hurts . . ."

Something deep within the Terran cringed. Before he quite knew what he was doing, he was over the couch and striding toward the screams. When he put his weight on a gutted chair, its charred legs splintered and some of the furniture shifted. He pushed on, stood looking down at the writhing, horribly burned body.

The Llralan had either heard the furniture shift, or now sensed his presence. The scorched head twisted, and eyes glinted whitely in a blackened mask. He stared up without seeing.

"Zieg?" he queried. "Is that you . . . Zieg?"

"Nyo," said Rierson. "Your comrades are gone."

"Rekk?" The voice was incredulous. "Are you . . . the Rekk?"

"Yes."

"You . . . shot me?"

"Yes."

"Ah . . ." He seemed to relax. "I was afraid . . . that I had been shot by somebody . . . else in the confusion. At least I have died honorably . . . in combat." The glazing eyes swiveled about, trying to find his face in the smoke. He started visibly. "Sirri! You look like nightmares of . . . childhood, Rekk—like naparra—like a . . . walker of the night." He expelled breath rattlingly. "Then the . . . ancestor worshiper was . . . right. You are . . . are . . ." A convulsion racked him. "Rekk?"

"What?"

"Rekk, let me join *my* ancestors. I am weary . . . and the pain is unbearable. Give me surcease." Orange blood dribbled over his burned lips. "I came at you openly—I fought fairly. I do not deserve . . .a slow death."

"But—"

"You began killing me, Rekk. Finish the job. Or must I . . . beg? Is this torture the price I pay for . . . invading and disturbing . . . your rest? What is death? You should know better than I. But the pain, the pain . . ." The voice became incoherent, the eyes rolled wildly.

Rierson raised the pistol and gave him surcease.

Shaken, his hands trembling and his legs stumbling, he headed mechanically back for the doorway. The smoke was thinning, being sucked through the doorway and up, and a draft was blowing against his neck, but this development went unnoticed by his numbed brain. He climbed over the couch and staggered as he hit the floor.

Something intolerably hot snapped past his head, whacked the door.

He dropped to his belly, peered upward through the eddying smoke. On the stairs a tall, broad-shouldered Larry with a comet on his breast and a pistol in his right hand was trying to penetrate the smoke with narrowed gaze. Rierson in his mind's eye saw the ruined, pain-contorted features of the Larry in the showroom, felt his whole being rebel against becoming a like specimen. The machine pistol came up swiftly, surely, spat twice.

The Llralan stood as one frozen for long moments, staring unbelievingly at the holes punched in his tunic. Then he seemed to collapse upon himself and slid loosely down the stairs. Rierson rolled to one side, retrieved his rifle where it leaned against the wall and scrambled under the stairs as heavy boots pounded on them. Seen from this angle, the smoke was a thick snake coiling out of the door and up toward the open door on the roof.

Figures waded out of the smoke, and searfire crackled down from above. Quick retaliation was given, and for a short, deadly second the two forces poured fire into each other. Then somebody realized what was going on and bawled for a cease-fire. Two bodies adorned the barricading couch; two more had fallen out of sight into the showroom. A fifth had tumbled from above onto the comet-wearer. Some dozen soldiers milled about confusedly not ten feet from where the quarry crouched.

"Inside!" shouted the leather-lunged one. "He's trying to sneak away in the smoke. *After* him!"

The soldiers ducked back into the pluming smoke. The officious one made to follow, hesitated, dived behind the couch. From within came a burst of shots, an anguished cry, then incensed bellows. The Llralan at the couch waited until the

108

shooting had stopped and the bellowing attained volume before he betook himself inside, shouting authoritatively.

As he disappeared, Rierson rounded the corner, hurdled the piled bodies and sprinted up the stairs. Halfway up, he passed a second wearer of the comet, unconscious and missing an arm below the elbow. The other hand gripped a still-smoking pistol.

The stairs went up through a small rooftop shed from where the parking attendant usually presided over customer air traffic. He paused within the door, scanned the roof.

A flivver was parked on the gravel, occupied by a sole Llralan in the bubble cockpit, talking excitedly into a short-wave. To get to the next roof, he had to pass the flivver, pass under the gaze of the Llralan and risk having the hunt called after him by the short-wave.

He went across the roof like a quick-moving cat, up the short ladder into the craft's interior and paused to listen and let his eyes become accustomed to the dimness. He could hear the Llralan's voice now, but he was talking so rapidly his speech was incomprehensible.

Rierson eased to the cockpit ladder, warily mounted it. When he got his head and shoulders above the hatch, he rested his rifle across the padded arm of the nearest bucket seat.

"Larry."

The trooper started violently, half-turning in his chair and dropping his mike. When he saw the rifle and who was behind it, his face quickly achieved the color of faded orangish-yellow parchment. His throat worked convulsively, but he couldn't force any words out.

"Larry, you're dead. All that remains is for you to go through the formality of dying. Understand?"

The trooper's eyes showed that he understood perfectly.

"But . . ." Rierson continued, choosing his words carefully, "there is one chance for you to see another sunset. Interested?"

The Llralan nodded jerkily.

"Can you fly this ship?"

"I can, Gremper. As radioman, I must be prepared to fly it if the pilots are . . ."

"I don't want military procedure. I want cooperation. *Full* cooperation. That's the only way you see the next sunset. Understand?"

"What would you have of me, Gremper?"

"Take this ship north below radar horizon, and follow directions explicitly. And if you get any humorous ideas, remember: they'll sacrifice you to get me. So stay on the deck and stay alive."

"But"—the Llralan frowned in perplexity—"how is it that you fear death? Can the dead be killed again? If you are Gremper, then death can hold no fear for you. If you are not . . ." His eyes narrowed and his hand began toward his holstered pistol.

The radio sounded, voicing a sharp inquiry.

"Answer them," Rierson told him. "And make it good."

The Llralan hesitated, then picked up the mike. "This is Livar."

"What's happened up there, Livar?"

"I . . ." Livar looked helplessly at the rifle's muzzle, then at its wielder.

"Tell him"—hissed Rierson, mind working in high gear—"tell him . . . that you are Gremper's captive."

Livar shuddered, made as if to faint. Rierson made a mental note to inquire further into this matter of Gremper as soon as possible. Whatever there was about that name which struck such fear into a Larry's heart was worth knowing.

"Tell him," he repeated.

Livar told him.

"What? Listen, Livar—if you've been on the 'sos again, so help me I'll have you shot . . ."

Rierson climbed into the cockpit, swapped rifle for hunting knife and held it across Livar's throat while he disarmed him, then took the mike.

"Livar is not drunk," he said in his most sepulchral voice. "He is speaking the cold truth."

The radio lapsed into shocked silence. Rierson exerted pressure on the knife. "Now, Livar—it's time to go elsewhere. And remember about the radar."

"I will . . . but why should you care about that?" The Larry was persistent; Rierson had to give him that.

"*I* cannot be killed," he admitted modestly, "but you can. And you are going to render me a service. Surely you expected some consideration for that?"

110

The radioman's eyes went round. "I hadn't thought of it that way."

Rierson permitted himself a long-suffering sigh. "Mortals never do. It's left up to us ghosts and goblins to see the over-all picture. Ah, well . . ." He prodded with the knife. "Home, James."

"What?"

"Let's go."

"North?"

"North."

The ship soared, streaked away from the menace of the guns below, leaving Baxter behind in a swirl of exhaust vapors. Livar got down just above the treetops and let it surge forward. The ground became a kaleidoscopic blur.

"We've got all day," said Rierson, dropping into the seat behind him. "Take it easy."

Obediently, the ship slowed to a more sedate pace and Rierson leaned back, holding the seargun on his captured chauffeur. Muscles and nerves keyed for ultimate effort began to twang tautly, trying to relax. His stomach was unsettled; a foul taste rose in his throat. But in spite of that, he knew a fierce exultation.

He had shot his way into and out of a virtually escape-proof trap, had taken a heavy toll among his pursuers, and had caused confusion, destruction, *fear*. He had given the massed might of the Empire pause—perhaps had gained a particle of time with his antics—time for the Federation brass to get something roll-ing to break the Llralan death grip on Earth. He had kept platoons, ships, radio hookups tied down—men and equipment intended to help consolidate Larry's position. And now the search would be after him in full cry—consuming more time, man-hours and matériel.

All he had to do was stay one jump ahead of reprisals and continue to strike back hard enough and frequently enough to keep them preoccupied.

All he had to do was keep a Larry invasion fleet off balance single-handed.

Under his watchful gaze, Livar kept the ship on course north and behaved nicely. He didn't try to veer off; he didn't try signaling for help; he didn't try leaving his carrier wave on to attract attention. All in all, he was a very good little Larry.

And a very, very frightened one.

Frightened of someone or some*thing* named Gremper.

Rierson puzzled that one over while the ship fled north.

Chapter Twelve

The calendar on the wall was of a unique composition; like all the others aboard the *Risstaixil* it recorded the day, month and year by Llralan, Terran and Risstairan reckoning, simultaneously and side by side. According to it, a full Terran week had elapsed since landing day.

Drelig Sjilla, Imperial Intelligence, rank of Security Chief, presently attached to the elite Corps of Mockers, rested his weary frame against a bulkhead while Martak Sarno's voice filled the broadcast room, speaking the toneless English of a mechanical translation.

"Peoples of the Federation, I am Martak Sarno, Supreme Commander of the forces now occupying the home system of your species, and this is your seventh day's report on conditions here . . ."

"The general wanted you to see this," Blanatta said, turning down the volume of the monitor they were watching. On the screen, Sarno was sitting behind a massive wooden desk cluttered with papers; behind him on the wall hung the Great Seal of the Supreme Council above crossed flags of Empire—fields of space black with a spray of stars depicting the Milky Way and a superimposed judicial gavel, symbol of rule. "How do you like that stage dressing, eh?"

"Impressive," Sjilla paid tribute.

"I thought so," Blanatta beamed. "I designed it. Felt it would impress the Rekks more fully, since their own high officials often speak in similar surroundings."

"But what's the point?"

"Listen." The pudgy Vice-Commander—who looked, Sjilla thought, more like a walsos brewer than the second-in-command of an invasion fleet—turned the volume up again.

". . . as I have noted on previous reports," Sarno was saying, "the capture of the three planets of Terra, Venus and Mars was brought about by the use of a newly developed biological weapon known simply as the Dust. Periodic seedings of this Dust into the atmospheres of the three worlds over the past months, under the guise of nuisance raids by our robotic fleets, was the method by which the downfall was accomplished. The effect of the Dust upon Terran animal life is unique in stellar annals: it causes a slowing of the bodily functions, a precipitation of the organism into a kind of hibernation.

"The Dust has been totally effective upon the three billion some-odd inhabitants of this system, as well as a considerable portion of the lower forms of life . . ."

"I see he hasn't seen fit to mention the nine Unaffecteds," Sjilla commented drily.

"What purpose would that serve?" Blanatta countered. "It might give rise to some irrational hope that our position is not as firm as we claim it to be— and false conclusions lead to rash actions, more likely than not."

"Of course." Sjilla lapsed into silence. In the darkened broadcast room a score of technicians watched monitors, fiddled with earphones and worked the giant transmitters beaming the 'cast starward.

"The collapse of the Dusted billions was timed to coincide with the arrival of my invasion fleet," Sarno went on. "The raid alarms on three planets sent them scurrying for their bomb shelters, wherein they succumbed more or less simultaneously as the Dust did its work.

"Across these three worlds, in thousands of bomb shelters, the populace of this system is sleeping. It will be a long sleep— the effects will not wear off for some five months—but it will not be a fatal one. At the end of the five months they will

113

awaken with nothing to show for their slumber but a slight headache, a fit of sneezing"—here the general's somber features split into a grin, instantly suppressed, which was all part of the theatrics—"and a big thirst. They will have no sense of time elapsed at all.

"Or, if things proceed satisfactorily—and I believe they will—we can make use of our antidote and awaken them at any time. The headache and sneezing will be the same, but the thirst won't be quite so bad. Which is something to consider if you don't want all your lakes and rivers drank dry at the same time." The calculated lightness again.

"Peoples of the Federation, let me make one thing explicitly clear: *the fate of these people rests solely with you.* Their lives have been merely suspended—not taken. The rest is up to you.

"Within a very short time now, a Federation warship carrying a delegation of congressional and military leaders will arrive on Terra. These men will survey the planets and determine the strength of my position here. Let me tell you what they will find. They will find the cities empty, the towns deserted, the farms left untended. They will find three billion Terrans asleep in bomb shelters across the face of the planets, exactly as I have said they would—*and they will find Imperial soldiers occupying those same bomb shelters.* Each bomb shelter has its detachment of troopers, prepared to carry out any order it may become necessary to give. That order *could* be summary execution of all hostages of war. I hope that will not be necessary.

"The Federation Congress has asked to negotiate this matter under a temporary cease-fire agreement. The Supreme Council of the Empire of Four Thousand Suns has agreed to this. Negotiations will commence after the delegation has made its findings here known to the peoples of Federation—to you.

"To the bargaining counter I shall bring the lives of three billions of your compatriots. It is up to you to decide. These billions are not dead—far from it. They are sleeping.

"Only *you* can decide if they will awaken from that sleep with aching heads to sneeze violently and drink deeply—or if they shall awaken at all."

Sarno hunched heavy shoulders forward, gazed into the

screen as if he could see those watching from the other side. His whole speech had been calm, authoritative. Now his voice was flat, implacable.

"Within a few days, certain demands will be made of the Federation. They *must* be met. The decisions concerning those demands will govern my actions here.

"Think it over."

Slowly the picture did a fade, leaving the hard, unbending image of Sarno's visage graven on the watcher's consciousness. Blanatta heaved a sigh, shut off the monitor. "What do you think?"

"Very effective," Sjilla responded sincerely. "Not overdone— no transparent propaganda. Just the flat, cold facts." He shivered. Three billion lives resting in the crook of Sarno's finger, hanging on his slightest whisper of command. "Very effective," he repeated.

Blanatta nodded fondly. "He's really worked on this thing— ever since he conceived of a military use for the xil'tressk. Plotted every angle down to the finest detail—no wonder the Council could hardly refuse him when he went before them, even with such a farfetched plan as this seemed to be. He had planned so carefully, calculated every possiblity so closely . . ."

"Every possibility except that there would be those who were immune," Sjilla injected into the worshipful recital.

"That will make no difference," Blanatta opined blandly, refusing to be shaken in his absolute faith in his idol. "Absolutely none."

"You're right," agreed Sjilla moodily. "It won't. In fact, it's my job to see that it won't—though I've been a week on it now without making much headway."

"You will," predicted the paunchy Vice-Commander, serenely confident. "My general has faith in you. Which reminds me: he said he wanted to see you after you had witnessed the broadcast. He will be on the bridge. And now, if you will excuse me . . ."

"Certainly." Sjilla waved vaguely in response to the other's salute.

A week gone, he was thinking sadly. *And with it my chances of an early ship home to Llrala. I thought my job was over*

*when the fleet came in—but from the looks of things, it's only
just begun.*

When he had reported aboard the flagship from the scouter
that had brought him over from Mars, he had found the fleet's
Intelligence section waiting for him to assume command. Intelligence H.Q., with touching faith in his ability to dodge
Terran Security until D hour, had assigned him to head them
up by remote control, assignment becoming effective the
moment he set foot upon the *Risstaixil.*

Sarno had celebrated his safe return from the enemy by
dumping the puzzle of the Unaffecteds promptly and with
alacrity into his lap. Since then, he had had even less sleep at
a stretch than he normally got while operating on an enemy-
held world. At times he caught himself remembering those last
relatively peaceful days in Rusted Plains with a certain nos-
talgia. He had been rushing to and fro across this accursed
planet overseeing an interrogation here, coordinating various
of the elements of his command charged with sniffing out
planetary bigwigs scheduled for awakening there—carrying on
a conversation with overtones of lunacy while high above the
Atlantic Ocean, witnessing the resounding defeat of an Imperial Infantry unit at the hands of a single man, or spook or
warlock or whatever . . . He seemed to be the absolutely in-
dispensable man.

Which is a compliment to my abilities, I suppose, he
brooded. *But I'd rather have a vacation than a compliment. A
bottle of 'sos, a hammock under the trees, a female to ruffle
my hair and tell me how wonderful I am . . .*

But no girl would have anything to do with him in the
pseudohuman shell Llralan surgeons had given him, he realized
—and he wasn't likely to be out of uniform for some time yet.
In spite of three billion helpless hostages as a bargaining point,
the Empire was going to have its hands full completing the
Federation's downfall. There would be need for mockers . . .

He shook himself out of his introspection with an effort, left
the broadcast room and walked down a short corridor, let
himself through a heavy door and so into the ordered bedlam
of the *Risstaixil's* bridge. He moved past the big, darkened in-
flight computers, walked through the communications section
with its constant hum, buzz and mutter as the flagship kept in

116

touch with its brood, and mounted the steel stairs at the far end of the high-vaulted room. This was the final sanctuary of the ship's commander, this raised balcony. And on a flagship it amounted to a kingly throne or holy kiosk. From here the Supreme Commander furthered the cause of Empire, wielded the power of life and death over ten thousand ships and their crews, and dispensed justice; this was his sanctum inviolate. To be invited upon that raised decking was the naval equivalent of a privy audience with the Supreme Council.

Sjilla had been invited to the bridge, not the High Walk, but he climbed the stairs as if they belonged to him. Long years of experience had taught him that nothing—absolutely *nothing* —was sacrosanct to those who carried the golden badge of Intelligence.

Sarno was studying the gigantic battle board—an instrument taking up a full wall of the bridge and studded with innumerable tiny lights in dozens of colors. The lights were never still, shifting constantly in a multicolored maze of pattern within pattern, glowing and dimming, pulsing and fading, each hue and degree of brightness indicative of some facet of the giant complex that was the fleet, each pattern telling a precisely worded story to those versed in its use. Sjilla moved to stand beside the general, detouring several smaller versions of the main board used for concentrating on a particular area.

Sarno racked a phone he had been speaking into, setting it into place among nearly a score of similar ones, and turned.

"Well, Sjilla! What did you think of my little speech?"

"Very convincing. If I were a Terran, I'd be shaking in my boots."

"You look enough like one to produce a faint quiver right now," observed the general. "Those surgeons did a job of it, didn't they?"

"They did."

"Unfortunately, it wasn't good enough to fool our friend Donovan, eh?"

"They only worked on my skeleton," Sjilla contradicted. "Surgery can only do so much—it can't enable you to outguess the opposition."

"You mean he tripped you up?" Sarno's voice was chiding.

"For shame—how did you ever dodge Terran Security if you can't even outthink a legless old man?"

"He tripped me up," Sjilla admitted ruefully. "But he's not all that old, and being legless is no impediment to an agile brain. Mine, unfortunately, was not equal to the contest, as I had been methodically dulling it with endless interrogations, thousands of miles' air time and almost no sleep. He caught me up in my own cover story and made me look like an amateur. Don't underestimate that boy, general—it might be the worst mistake you ever made."

"And what would you suggest I do with that 'boy,' as you put it?"

"I could suggest a lot of things—none of them pleasant for Mister Donovan—but I won't."

"Oh? And why not?"

"Because whatever else he may be, he is still an Unaffected. No matter what kind of nuisance he makes of himself—and he makes a prime one, that I'll concede—he is still one-ninth of a very complicated puzzle the answer to which you want and I have been assigned to discover. If he is dead or in the condition which you or I might wish him in a moment of ire, he cannot answer questions—questions pertinent to the mystery of the Unaffecteds."

"What do we do in the meanwhile then? Let him have his way?"

"Absolutely not! He's done enough damage. Place him securely out of harm's way—put him in the deepest, darkest dungeon this oversized fishcan has got and feed him with a long-handled stick if you have to. *But keep the men away from him.* He's already got half the fleet in jitters with his bedtime stories."

"All right, I'll salt him away good and tight. Now, about this whole problem of the Unaffecteds . . ."

"I was coming to that."

"I'm listening."

"All right . . . in the first place, on the face of it, it is impossible for Unaffecteds to exist. Your dusting was thorough; my air samplings prior to D hour proved that. Every single living person on these three planets with the exception of myself

118

should have collapsed more or less of one accord within roughly an hour's time—the same hour the fleet came in."

"But nine didn't," Sarno pointed out.

"That's right—nine didn't. Which is impossible."

"But it *happened*."

"Precisely. It happened. But it couldn't have happened. Not to nine regular, run-of-the-mill Terrans. It *couldn't* have."

"But it did."

"Wrong. Those nine are very extraordinary in one respect. Very extraordinary indeed. In one way, they are as unlike other Terrans as you or I."

Sarno frowned. "In what way?"

"Not a single one of them succumbed to the Dust," said Sjilla simply.

Sarno regarded him incredulously. "Are you trying to be funny?"

"Definitely not," the Security Chief assured him.

"Then why a crack like that? You're deliberately going in circles."

"That's where you're wrong. I am *not* going in circles. I am inching ahead. Would *you* succumb to the Dust if exposed to it?"

"No."

"And neither did I, though I was exposed to it fully as long as anyone else on these three planets."

"Are you suggesting, by any chance, that Donovan and his confreres are *Llralans?*" Sarno asked softly, in the manner of one humoring a very small child.

"No . . . but I am saying that they have something in common with Llralans, that being their immunity to the Dust. Since they are *not* Llralans, whose immunity is simply a part of their make-up, then the immunity must be acquired—and has nothing to do with the thoroughness of dusting procedures. And how does a Terran acquire immunity to the vapor of the xil'tressk blossom?"

"By being previously exposed to it," said Sarno automatically. And then, "But that would mean . . ."

"Exactly. It would mean that the nine had at one time or another been on Risstair, come into contact with the flower, went into the characteristic coma and then gone their way, all

119

unknowingly armored against a unique weapon that would be turned on their planets at some future date."

"Donovan!" Sarno ejaculated. "Rierson—Harris—Nogales!" He ticked them off with mounting excitement. "They were all on Risstair; they all had opportunities . . ." His voice died, and the exultation faded from his features. "Only . . ."

"Only that still leaves five unaccounted for," Sjilla finished his statement for him. "Five mystery cases. And the Spook of Baxter makes six."

"Then you don't think there's anything supernatural about him?"

"I do not. I simply think he's another character like Donovan who happened to have the good luck to be in the wrong place at the right time and miss the brunt of the landing forces. He killed four men. Donovan killed or caused to be killed seven men. Putting Donovan in the Spook's place, you'd have the same situation."

"Except for one thing," Sarno said. "The small fact of yesterday's fiasco. Twenty-eight dead, a half-dozen wounded and an aircraft pirated right out from under our noses. Add to that the rumor that he confessed over the airwaves and for all to hear how he was indeed the fearsome Gremper . . ."

"That's no rumor. I was there. He said it."

"And how do you explain *that?*"

"Easily enough. He identified himself as *Gremper,* didn't he? Not Grandpa?"

"You were there—I wasn't. Besides, what does that have to do . . ."

"*Gremper* is a strictly Llralan corruption of the Terran colloquialism *Grandpa,* which means grandfather. The attempt of one uneducated in languages to pronounce an unfamiliar sobriquet."

"So?"

"If the Spook *were* a spook, or some kind of a guerrilla fighter in communication with Donovan by some unheard of method such as, say, mental telepathy, *don't you think he would have used the Terran term?* Why should he use a Llralan mispronunciation?"

"All right, why?"

"Because he had never heard it any other way," Sjilla told

him, pained by his inability to see the obvious. "Because he heard it from a Llralan soldier, deduced its scare value, and used it at an opportune moment."

"You're crediting an awful lot to coincidence and the native ability of Terrans one and sundry to cause mischief wherever it'll do the most good," Sarno pointed out dubiously.

"Would you rather believe in bloodthirsty and unstoppable spooks?" Sjilla retorted. "Spooks capable of reaching out and lifting your hair even as we stand here talking, surrounded by the armed might of Empire?"

Sarno glanced behind him in spite of himself, then looked shamefaced. "You're getting almost as good at that as Donovan."

"I ought to be. I learned straight from the horse's mouth, so to speak."

"The what's mouth?"

"Never mind—back to the case of the five Unaffecteds not accounted for. Or the six, counting the Spook. For your information, one other besides Donovan and Harris and Rierson and Nogales *was* on Risstair. Hogate Yoganda. He was crewman on the same ship as Nogales, but he didn't create as much of a disturbance and therefore went unremembered. You *do* remember Nogales?"

"Do I ever! He jumped his ship—a trader in port taking on a cargo of furs—and spent the better part of five Llralan months in the bush. I had search parties combing the wilds for siveb around the spaceport."

"And the ship? Did it head for home without him?"

"Not on your life! I refused clearance until he was brought back. Even made them help look for him. They were really hopping mad!" His eyes lighted at the remembrance. "Wasn't anything they could do, though. So Yoganda was aboard, eh?"

"That's right—and he remembers hunting Nogales very vividly. Including brushes with certain forms of local wildlife."

"Marqs," Sarno identified. "Marqs, by the stars! Yes, I believe the ship lost two crewmen to the marqs before Nogales was finally caught . . ."

"He also remembers a certain flower, falling asleep in a pleasant glade despite his fear of marqs getting him while he slept."

"He needn't have worried; marqs know as well as the aborigines to give the territory of the xil'tressk a wide berth."

"That makes five," said Sjilla. "Four more and we're home free. Maybe when we figure out what makes those four immune—those four who have never traveled to Risstair, or even out of this system—we'll figure out just who this Spook of Baxter is, and a way to gather him into the fold."

"And what progress have you made in that direction?"

"Little, very little. We know that Jennifer Nogales is the jilted bride of Paul Nogales and happens to be six months' pregnant; we know that they spent the few months of their life together in Butte, Montana, at the boarding house of Margaret Cassidy. We know that when Nogales ran out on her, she returned to San Francisco—her home town—and her parents put the law on Nogales, and that he was in jail on Venus awaiting extradition to Earth on charges of wife desertion. Insofar as the Nogales couple and Margaret Cassidy is concerned, we seem to have interrupted a true-to-life soap opera with our ill-timed invasion.

"We know that Richard Rayburn, Sr., and his son were very close, as is demonstrated by the pathological hatred displayed by Rayburn, Jr., at the very sight of an orange face since the death of his father, and his flat refusal to co-operate with questioning. We know further that torture would doubtless only drive him over the brink of insanity to which our invasion, the violent death of his father and the sudden ending of his world has pushed him. Therefore he is about as useful to us as his dead parent."

"And what does all that add up to?"

"A common denominator, I'm sure. All that remains is to find it."

"And then what?"

"And then we reduce all factors to that common denominator, scoop up the Spook of Baxter, and proceed with an orderly if somewhat tedious conquest duty and round of negotiations with the Federation. Or at least you do. I take a ship home for Llrala and a well-deserved vacation."

"As easy as that, eh?"

"As easy as that—I hope."

"That makes two of us. Go to it, and good luck."

"Thanks."

Drelig Sjilla turned and went down the High Walk's stairs with the same slow, deliberate pace he had mounted them, across the floor of the bridge and out into the corridor leading to the intraship cars.

He had a job to finish.

Chapter Thirteen

The desk lamp glared down on a confused jumble of papers and cards and scribble sheets. The ship's artificial night had long since come, the lights dimming to a dusky half-illumination meant to be restful after the hard white light of working hours. The officers of the *Risstaixil* not on duty had turned in one by one, until only his light remained burning.

Sjilla ran the back of his hand across weary eyes and sipped gently at a cup of stimulant. Spread before him was all the information he could dig up on nine Terrans at such short notice. Later, he could go through files of various townships and cities, add bits and pieces. There would be hospital records, police records, military records . . . reams and reams of paperwork for each and every individual under observation. He sighed. Such work was nothing new to him; comparing the two, he felt that the Empire had more bureaucratic red tape than did the Federation.

Sighing again, he read back over the topmost grouping of papers and cards, searching for what he knew must be hidden somewhere within. The name on the driver's and pilot's licenses was Daniel Rierson; along with those two essential cards, the man caught in Venusburg had possessed the usual credit cards, social security, identity cards naming him a member of a gun club, an explorer's club . . .

And on and on!

There were also old, dog-eared passports for a good dozen worlds, at the rate of three planetary clearances per card. He read the report of the capturing officer again.

". . . prisoner offered little effective resistance, this being limited to one blow of the fist, which rendered Trooper Vorn insensate. Corporal Zaquor hit him over the head with his rifle butt. The blow caused no serious damage, but was very effective in insuring the prisoner's tractability until such time as we could get him to a suitable place of detention. . . ."

He grinned wryly. Being somewhat of an authority on reports of all types and natures, he was of the opinion that three-quarters of the Empire's population went around nursing an unfulfilled desire to be adventure-tale writers.

Taking a fresh sheet of note paper, he twirled it into his typer, adjusted it and started making notations on the facts concerning Daniel Rierson that he considered cogent.

NAME: *Daniel Rierson.*

OCCUPATION (*At time of Invasion*): *Semiretirement.*

OCCUPATION (*Beginning of war*): *Hunting guide, Venusian game farm.*

POSSIBILITY OF HAVING BEEN ON RISSTAIR: *Positive.*

VISITORS ON RISSTAIR: *One young boy—a nephew.*

SUPPORTIVE EVIDENCE: *Snapshot picturing boy exhibiting a dead tarl and a Terran rifle against typical Risstarian background.*

PRESENT LOCATION OF VISITOR: *Unknown.*

Leaning back, he contemplated what he had written. Very concise, very informative—but not very. Had Rierson really ever encountered the xil'tressk and become immune? Had that big-boned youth in the picture?

Sjilla searched among the litter, again found the picture. He held it up to the light—a faded color print showing a solemn-faced youth with a strained grin on his face. That was all—plus one very dead tarl, a brand-new-looking rifle and

Risstairan trees in the background. He reversed it, read the blurred inkling on the back:

> *Uncle Dan—Something to remember me by . . . Summer of '09.*
>
> *Jim*

Just that, and nothing more. He turned the print back to show the picture, studied the boy therein somberly.

Summer of '09, he thought. *2409, Terran count. And where was I that year twenty-three years ago? A hardly-dry-behind-the-ears recruit tailing Terran tourists around Llrala Central, my sole duty to keep them from taking pictures . . . as if they didn't have better ways of getting information. But we didn't know that then—and I kept people from taking pictures.*

He stared at the young, unlined face grimacing up at him. *And you—you were having your picture taken. Jim. Jim Rierson? Jim, the mighty hunter of tarl . . . your uncle was probably proud of you.*

Did you ever wonder, Jim, why two perfectly sane races capable of bridging interstellar space should be at one another's throats? Did you? And did you ever conclude that it is not two life-forms warring, but two philosophies? The possible persecutors and the afraid-of-being-persecuted—the ones with fear, and those without? Do we all believe in this vendetta against Terra and the Federation? No. But the Empire is old, Jim—older than the Federation, much older. We attained the stars once before, Jim—and were smashed by a people fearing our youth and military strength. The Workargis . . . if you've ever heard of them you probably don't remember— not just another boring history lesson out of many such, when your mind was out roaming the fields of Terra or forests of Risstair.

But we remember. We went out that first time innocently and came running back, whipped and wiser. It was determined then that such a thing should never happen again. The Supreme Council was formed, and created the High Command, and we became a militarily oriented culture. When we went out the second time we went in armadas, and prepared. The Workargis were repaid with interest for their earlier destruction—but the fear would not abate, and the pattern was set. We've met seven cultures capable of offering fight, Jim—yours in the eighth. We are still mighty, and the seven are our vassals. Perhaps we could have stopped after one or two . . . but not now, Jim. If we stop, we falter; if we falter, we are destroyed. We have sacked too many planets, murdered too many races, looted and raped our way across too many star-years to ever go back and start again. We are fighters. If we do not fight, we do nothing.

During the years of peace, conditions are always tranquil throughout Empire, Jim—there aren't many assignments for the likes of me. But let a strong civilization loom on the star map and all of a sudden we must cope with conspiracies on a thousand worlds, all aimed at toppling the tyrant—us—and ushering in the champion of the downtrodden—you, or someone like you.

So we go on. We fight here, against you, and if we lose then the book can be closed when the last Llralan is hung or shot or simply dumped out an airlock. If we win, we will go on, our borders forever expanding—always looking for the lurkers in the Big Dark that would creep in upon our suns and surprise us if we dared to rest.

Where will it end? It is my job to make sure that it does not end here—and I will do my job. We are weary of the witch-hunt, but we will not lay down our pitchforks. Perhaps . . . perhaps someday, if we search far enough and long enough, we will find peace and a restoration of our confidence. But now we are running scared across the face of the cosmos, and your people are in our way.

So tell me, Jim, have you given up hunting deer and tarl? Have you turned your guns on bigger game, on us? At any time during that summer of '09 did you fall asleep for around nine hours beside a flower the natives of Risstair call xil'tressk? Perhaps while waiting for tarl to come down to water? Are you now out there somewhere, looking for more targets for your rifle? Or do you sleep innocently within some bomb shelter, never dreaming that the thing you feared is come upon you—that the defenses are breached, the invaders within the walls and running through the streets?

He came out of his reverie and laid the picture aside, picked up another billfold at random and typed the name:

NAME: *Richard Rayburn, Sr.* (*deceased*)

OCCUPATION (*At time of Invasion*): *Prison Guard.*

OCCUPATION (*Beginning of war*): *Prison Guard.*

At that point he stopped, finger poised to strike a key. *Prison Guard,* the license said, but that wasn't all, not by a long shot. Rayburn's home town was listed as Blue Hills, and the state the license had been taken out in as Yagari, *and the planet as Venus.*

He scrabbled through the litter feverishly, came up with a neatly typed list of names and places. Nine of them in all— the names of the nine Unaffecteds, and where picked up. Rayburn's driver's license made his home Blue Hills, on Venus, but the list said he'd been picked up in New York City, on Terra. And that wasn't all. The license had his occupation listed as prison guard. He picked up another sheet of paper— the dope sheet on Paul Nogales—and compared it to the list of names, and then to Rayburn's license.

Rayburn was a prison guard in Blue Hills, Yagari, Venus; Nogales had been a prisoner in Blue Hills, Yagari, Venus. Which led to the inevitable question: how many prisons were there in Blue Hills? Reading further, he found the answer he wanted, whether there were ten or two hundred: Richard Rayburn had worked for, and Paul Nogales been imprisoned at, the same institution.

Sjilla finished the cup of stimulant at one gulp, oblivious to the fact that it was stone cold. It looked as if he had stumbled onto something here. With carefully suppressed excitement, he appraised his find. Five of the nine Unaffecteds had been on Risstair: Donovan, Rierson, Harris, Nogales and Yoganda. Four had not: Margaret Cassidy, Jennifer Nogales, the Rayburns. That two of them—the two women—had been linked to Nogales had been apparent early, just as the relationship between father and son had been obvious. Now he had discovered a possible tie-in between Nogales and Rayburn Senior—that of prisoner and guard. Nothing definite yet, of course, but a start. Find a common denominator, he had told Sarno—that's what is needed. A common denominator. Find that, and the pieces of the puzzle will fall into place.

Reading back over the items spread before him, it looked very much like that common denominator was going to be none other than Mr. Paul Nogales. Just how and why, he couldn't begin to guess, but the pattern was clear. Landlady, wife, jailer—all that was needed now was to find some way to tie Rayburn Junior into it, discover what it was that made those whose lives Nogales had touched immune to the Dust, and present the whole neatly wrapped package to Sarno. Visions of the sweet-smelling meadows of home began to parade across his mind's eye. With any luck at all, he could have this wrapped up and be on his way within, say . . .

His train of thought snapped. For suddenly superimposed over that pleasant parade he had imagined an inimical, faceless figure with a rifle and heard a somewhat hoarse voice speaking in heavily accented Llralan—a disembodied voice crackling over the airwaves with its somber message.

He climbed to his feet and went and looked along the corridor at the closed doors behind which the big brass of the fleet slept, slept as if they had not a care in this world—or any world. Turning, he walked to his single porthole and peered through the thick unshielded glass. He couldn't see much; a misshapen moon was riding high, throwing silvery light on drifting clouds. The over-all effect was one of extreme cold. And cold it was, he knew, on the plains of Canada—colder than it ever got on Llrala, except at the extreme poles. Though the cabin was warm, he shivered.

"Fly north," the voice over the radiophone had urged before communication was cut. Fly north. But how far north? North Georgia, Tennessee, Michigan?

Or Canada?

Where are you, Spook of Baxter? Hiding? Running? Or watching with glittering, emotionless eyes as another soldier walks into your sights? Where are you? Who are you? What are you thinking now?

He yawned hugely. He was tired, worn to a raw edge by too many long nights and tension-filled days. He had uncovered something tonight—but tomorrow would be soon enough to follow it up. He turned down the desk lamp, undressed and crawled into his bunk. His head had hardly touched the pillow before he was asleep.

But his dreams went round and round, and kept coming back to the image of a perennially young and grim-faced boy stalking across the land with a rifle and a strained grin, in search of orange-faced, two-legged game:

"I killed twenty-eight Larrys today, Uncle. Let 'em think they had me, then lowered the boom . . ."

And of an unseeable, enigmatic personality maneuvering man and machines to their destruction at the beck of a living captive:

"Grandpa, they've been giving me a hard time."

"Don't you worry, son, I've been giving them a hard time, too."

His dreams skittered confusedly round and round, and were not free from fear.

Chapter Fourteen

Atlanta, Titan of the Southland—city of silver towers and soaring roadways, of six million residents and numberless travelers, city of swarming traffic day and night, on the surface, above it and below—Atlanta, city hermetically sealed from the elements by centuries of scientific contriving, city that never sleeps . . .

Was sleeping now.

Silence had come to the sprawling metropolis, silence unknown in these environs since the white man had driven out the Indian and begun his long climb to the stars.

And winter. The cold blue, clean-washed sky was uncluttered

129

by any man-made object; a smoky haze softened the already graceful lines of expressway and office building alike and imparted an unreal, faerylike atmosphere to the whole vista. A wizard's work in grace and enduring beauty, rising out of the ground-mist of a crisp Georgia morning like an idle day-dream, and in appearance as fragile and transient as the dream itself.

Atlanta lay slumbering in the bright cold sunshine and time seemed to drag its heels . . . and had the city builders been gone a week, a fortnight, or an eternity?

With an effort of will, James Rierson extricated his thoughts from the gentle spell being woven upon them by the strangeness and utter tranquillity of the scene before him. This slumbrous faerie castle was, after all, only Atlanta. The city that had been his home for as long as he could remember. A different-seeming Atlanta, to be sure—but still Atlanta. Out there somewhere were the back-alley and serviceway playgrounds of his youth—the hidden sordidness the health inspectors never seemed to find, nor the city beautification committees care about, for it was deftly hidden by a stroke of an architect's pencil, and who worries about what cannot be seen? Hidden byways ruled by jungle law—by the law of survival of the fittest, by the mandate of the quick and the dead. It was a world he had known only passingly in youth, for his parents had much preferred that he keep to the manicured and well-tended playgrounds that were a credit to the city and much safer for a child not versed in the finer points of survival by tooth and claw—but a world he had come to know more intimately of late, when his natural habitat became the world of high-vaulted courtrooms and paneled law offices and chilly white prison cells. For when two laws exist within the same boundaries there is certain to be friction—and between the law of books and balances and the law of the jungle there is no middle ground.

Rierson sighed deeply. He had chosen the law of books, unfortunately. Unfortunately because the older laws ruled Atlanta now—and ruled the whole planet. Garbage-littered alleyway and dome-roofed court building, both came under the same code now: *kill or be killed.* There were no laws to hide behind, no police to summon, no recourse left to the weak, the meek or the inept.

The exhilaration he had experienced yesterday at escaping the Llralan death trap in Baxter had long since evaporated, leaving a cold chill in its place. What could he have been thinking of to believe he could do any damage to the forces arrayed against him? He could kill a hundred—a thousand—and it would mean nothing to them. The angry buzzings of a tiny insect. An insect that would, in time, be swatted. Perhaps . . . perhaps, had he spent his life dodging the minions of the law, always sleeping with one eye open and his suitcases packed, he might have a chance. With instincts honed by dozens of brushes with the law, by any number of hairsbreadth escapes, he might manage fairly well—slipping through cordons, eluding search parties, resorting to knife and gun when no other course was open to him. But such was not the case. His had been a planet-bound and very ordinary kind of life—with one short time-out for that one stellar voyage as a youth. He'd attended school, graduated from law college, become a practicing attorney. He spent the bulk of his vacation time hunting deer and ducks in the vast managed wilderness around his vacation cabin, and occasionally reminisced idly of his one great advanture into interstellar space.

That was it. He was a good lawyer, a passable rifleman and a lousy wing shot. None of which especially qualified him to carry the fight singlehanded to an enemy that outnumbered him ridiculously and overtopped him in resources to an even more fantastic degree. They had a space fleet, an air force, an army. He had himself. Which didn't add up to a heck of a lot. Not with his ammunition almost gone and his morale at an all-time low.

One thing was sure, though. He had one thing in his favor: he was still free and whole; he was still—within the limitations placed upon his activities by Llralan patrols—his own man. How long he remained that way was strictly up to him. The Llralans would try equally hard to get him whether he was actively resisting or moping along bewailing his fate. Does one care, when one swats a bothersome mosquito, if the insect is despondent or not? Answer: one does not. One only cares whether one has swatted accurately and if the pest is removed.

Therefore the best thing the mosquito could do to vent its feelings would be to dodge the swats and continue to bite back. Perhaps it could even infect the swatter with malaria, or something.

Which was all very well as far as the analogy went—but analogies don't win wars, or even battles. Thus far the mosquito and the giant had been sparring blindly with one another, and the mosquito had been coming off pretty well by comparison. But he had the uneasy suspicion that all that could change very abruptly—that the giant had been slapping vainly with his right hand while his left lay quietly by, waiting for a clear shot. And once he took aim with that left, it would be all over but the burying. To avoid such an abrupt funeral, it would behoove the mosquito to keep the giant from taking aim by keeping him off balance—a monumental task in itself, and surely impossible if the mosquito didn't know more about what would serve the equivalent of giving the rug his titanic opponent was standing on a good firm yank.

What did he know now? He knew that apparently the entire planet was sleeping as if intent on outdoing Rip Van Winkle himself, and he knew, very definitely, that the Llralans were behind whatever shenanigans had induced that slumber. He knew that some of the soldiers in Baxter—as indicated by that overheard conversation at the stairwell—regarded him with a half-superstitious fear, and he knew that at least one of them was scared absolutely silly by the thought of someone named Gremper, who could not die because he was already dead.

Now *there* was a promising premise. An ordinary mosquito buzzing around one's head might cause annoyance, but certainly not alarm—but an *unordinary* mosquito would be an insect of a different color. If he could imbue himself with the traits of a were-mosquito, it would help his campaign to stay free tremendously. No one in his right mind—especially no Llralan in his right mind—wants to take on the supernatural.

It was promising, but how to get more information? His unwilling chauffeur was close to hand—lodged in a precinct station cell—but it wasn't likely he would aid and abet the enemy without certain forms of persuasion. And that kind of persuasion wasn't included in the law texts he had read. Again, he found himself wishing for a back-alley education of the sort that might inform a man on the more delicate aspects of persuasion by knife.

By knife . . .

He unsheathed his hunting knife and held it up for inspection. The blade was long, wicked-looking and razor-sharp. A light stroke would open the Llralan pilot's veins as effectively as bleeding a deer—but to what effect? The Llralan could probably stand the sight of his own blood better than Rierson, and if he bled to death he would certainly disclose no desperately needed information. He twisted the blade in his hands and it caught gleams from the sun in its mirror-polished steel and bounced them into his eyes. He stared moodily into the reflection and cursed his squeamish stomach thoroughly. Dammit, there must be *something* he could—

And then it hit him, having been so obvious all along that he had of course overlooked it: if Livar expected a spook, why disappoint him? If he thought himself to be in the clutches of the terrible Gremper, why disillusion the poor fool? Why not play it up big, confirm his darkest suspicions and affirm his gravest terrors?

He put away the knife, hefted his rifle. The more he thought of it, the better he liked the whole idea. He grinned at the sky. One snow job coming up!

But first, ammunition for his weapons—and some food.

As a full-time spook, he was going to need more sustenance than the wind riffling his whiskers could provide.

He was unable to move; his arms were lashed cruelly, his legs strapped to the chair with his own belt, his throat and forehead encircled by strips of cloth, holding him ludicrously to attention in his seat. Nowhere was there actual pain; only the utter inability to move chafed at him, threatening to push his mind over the brink of insanity.

All around was utter, unrelieved blackness. His eyes, wide-staring, focused on the tiny yellow pinprick of light emanating from a point before him and centered on his face.

Behind the light, shrouded in darkness, a voice was speaking slowly, haltingly and with a heavy accent.

"Now . . . we get some . . . answers. You will cooperate . . . or suffer."

"I will cooperate, Gremper," Livar acknowledged, unable to control the quaver creeping into his voice. He was utterly at the mercy of this monster Rekk beyond the light—if the other so desired, he could simply walk away and leave him here to go slowly or quickly insane, depending upon his endurance. He doubted that he could endure long—his mind had been in a sort of deep freeze since Lieutenant Zo-quen and the others had left the flivver to descend into the smoke welling from the rooftop doorway . . . and had not returned.

And then the Terran had been behind him, coming as silently as a bog spirit, and unscathed though he had strode through the very jaws of death. Surely then, this was the terrible Gremper spoken of half jokingly, half seriously, by those who had heard of the stories told by the legless Rekk captive. And the failure of Zo-quen to return was explained: how could he have hoped to kill, or even offer combat to, an angered ghost?

The light's intensity increased, and he shut his eyes against the glare.

"Shutting your eyes," came Gremper's voice, "is only a . . . temporary escape at best. Eyelids can be . . . removed."

Livar slitted one eye, saw a long-bladed knife being twisted slowly in the light, catching reflections—winking at him evilly. His fear rose in a solid lump to clog his throat.

"I have said I will answer," he said, striving to keep his tone strong, even. It was no use—a soldier's duty is to die in battle, amid comrades to mark his fall and carry his helmet and insignia back to the Hall of Heroes in his native town. But *this*—to die unable to strike back as the life spark fled, unable to scream defiance in the face of death, unable even to take comfort in the fact that his death would be noted and that his sons would one day wear the proud Warrior-Sire Sword upon their barracks caps . . .

The light faded back to a comfortable glow. The knife vanished.

"You will answer truthfully—on your soldier's oath?"

"I swear it."

"Terra, Venus, Mars. All under your . . . control?"

He tried to nod, felt the restraint of the cloth, resorted to verbal response. "Yio."

"How?"

"The Dust, a toxin taken from a flower that makes Terrans sleep. From Risstair . . ."

"Risstair?" The voice was startled.

"Yes, Gremper, Risstair. A flower that makes Terrans sleep, growing natively on Risstair."

"How long?"

"Originally, no more than nine hours, my lieutenant said. I know little of these things, but my lieutenant is—was—an officer and scholar. Pure Llralan blood, no colony breed—"

"How long *now?*" interrupted the voice.

He tried to raise shoulders in the cosmic gesture of bafflement, again felt the unrelaxing bonds holding him close. Frustration rose in him, and dark insanity seemed to perch on his shoulders like a carrion bird, waiting to prey on the dead remnants of his mind.

"How long?" repeated the voice impatiently.

"I know not. Not everything is given for me to know. But the sleepers will need no food, no water, while they sleep. They hibernate, like the toor—"

"Never mind the alien similes. What is the plan?"

"The plan?"

"Yes, the plan! What does your fleet leader plan to . . . do with three planets? The people sleep—is their next sleep to be the eternal one? What . . . purpose lies behind the attack?"

"It has not been explained fully to the soldiers," Livar returned. "But, simply, we are to hold the lives of our hostages as the exchange token that will force concessions upon the Federation. It is Sarno's doing—"

"Sarno?"

"The fleet leader."

"If the Federation does not believe that everything is as Sarno says?"

"They will. Already, a truce ship is en route here carrying observers. They will determine for themselves that attack is impossible without sacrificing the populations of the planets, and then work out the terms of the concessions." Livar spoke this last with misgivings. The Rekk's world was at the mercy of his comrades, but he was at the mercy of the Rekk. And the Rekk was just liable to be incensed enough to kill him—slowly —to vent helpless rage.

But the Rekk was speaking. "After I locked you in here I scouted the surrounding area. I saw . . . men . . . loading certain Terrans into trucks for transportation elsewhere. Why?"

"The penmasters . . ."

"I do not understand."

"There are three hundred penmasters on Terra. Lieutenant General Quiror is the one for the Southeastern United States."

"What do the . . .penmasters . . . do?"

"They preside over a central pen to which specimens are brought for reawakening."

"Reawakening?" Suddenly the voice was eager. "Then the sleep is not permanent?"

"No. Not if the antidote is—"

"*Antidote?* There is an antidote?"

"Yes."

"What is it? How is it made? How does it work?" The words were sharp, hammering at him as Gremper's bullets had hammered at his fellows in Baxter.

"What, I do not know; how, I do not know. It works by awakening those who sleep," replied Livar lamely. "I know nothing of these details."

"Are you sure? Are you sure that you are not holding back through a sense of loyalty?" The knife was again shining in the beam of light. "I would hate to believe that. I would hate to test that loyalty with steel—"

"No!" That was torn from his throat. He fought the bonds madly, his fear and encroaching madness lending him superhuman strength The straps holding his arms slipped along the arms of the chair, encouraging him to redouble. "*No!* You will not vent your hate upon me! Combat, yes; torture, no! *No,* do you hear me?"

"Enough," interrupted the Terran. "You are not lying. Now"—the voice took on a new note—"let's get this straight. The solar system is completely under the thumb of Sarno's fleet. All the inhabitants have succumbed to the Dust. There is no resistance to the occupation. Correct?"

"Yio . . ."

"You hesitate. Why?"

"The Dust did not work entirely. There have been stragglers. But you know of that."

"Of the legless one. Of Donovan, your grandson."

There was a moment's pause. Then, "You will act as if I know nothing, and tell me of my . . . grandson. Then we will see how straight your tongue . . ."

"I do not know much," Livar began. "I know only by word of mouth; there has been no official word, other than that stragglers had been caught. But the legless one—Donovan, your grandson—feared that your wrath would be vented upon poor soldiers unable to control their destinies . . ." Here he paused. Had that inimical personage beyond the glare taken the hint? Would he abide his living kin's wishes? There was no way of knowing.

"Go on," prompted the voice.

"He warned the guards to warn their blood kin to beware angering you and the others by any overt acts against the sleeping population. The blood kin felt it their sworn duty to inform their town brothers of the danger. It had been remarked"—here again Livar was treading dangerous, very dangerous ground, and knew it well—" by many troopers that Terran females, while not very attractive, *were* very available, and that our homes were far and our chances of return uncertain. . . . After the tradition of Empire, petitions were presented to officers and were approved, and a certain portion of the antidote granted for the reawakening of a number of chosen specimens . . ."

The voice of Gremper was flat and emotionless. "And was this . . . recreation . . . carried out?"

"No," Livar hastened to assure him. "It was being arranged —such things take time. Donovan's warning reached them in time. Their fear of death without combat overcame their appetite for alien women . . ." Which wasn't strictly true, but he could plead ignorance if Gremper pointed that out.

"Donovan—a guy named Donovan," said Gremper. "So that's who Gremper is, and why this poor yokel is so afraid. Brother, this Donovan must be the con man of all times! He's sold them a bill of goods from the word go."

"I do not understand Rekkish," Livar said apologetically.

137

"What? Oh! Well, don't let that worry you. That's quite all right. Well!" The voice held a tone of immense satisfaction. "That is very definitely that."

"You're speaking English again," Livar pointed out gingerly, fearful of invoking his wrath.

"No matter. You have been most cooperative. Now . . . sit very still."

Livar wondered for a moment just how else he could sit, then gasped aloud as a huge bulk blotted out the thin ray of light and precipitated the cell into utter darkness.

The bulk passed into shadow and the light sprang back. He felt hands on his bonds.

"I am releasing your hands," came the hoarse voice, so near he jumped. "You will sit still until I say otherwise. Then you may untie yourself and have the run of the cell. You will find an atomic lamp beside the door and what can be a month's supply of food if you are not gluttonous. There is running water." As it spoke, the shadow shape again passed before the light and beyond, and Livar heard the door creak faintly.

"You are in a police station, in a cell," the voice of Gremper went on. "You will so remain until the duly delegated mortals come to deal with you. At present, they are sleeping.

"When they come for you, you will know that the invasion has failed and that I have dealt with the invaders."

There was a muffled clang, and Livar was alone. He lost no time in finding the lamp and switching it on, basking in the glow as might an entombed miner bask in the sun upon coming to the surface. And then the full import of the Rekk's last words hit him and he sat down weakly, all pleasure at being unbound gone. He thought of his fellows out there, thousands, aye, tens of thousands of soldiers and their weapons: searguns, blast-cannon, rocket launchers, tanks, flivvers, the massive spaceships themselves with all their awesome engines and terrible energy projectors. Power to sunder a gun, energy to fuse it together again.

A good many of his comrades were no doubt looking for his captor right now, with all that might to back them up.

If they were right out of luck, they would find him.

Chapter Fifteen

He had the distinct impression that he'd been this route before
—with minor differences, to be sure, but the format was
definitely familiar. As for the changes: this cell was even
smaller, if that were possible, than his former one on the
Kalistra, and his food was no longer served personally but
arrived with a whoosh of pneumatic air through a shielded
opening and into a small receptacle. The food itself had taken
a turn for the worse. Whereas he had formerly received whatever the menu of the day in the ship's galley happened to be,
he was now compelled to subsist on Llralan field rations.
Which, to his way of thinking, was a fiendish torment worthy
of the low animal mentality of his captors. And he missed his
daily trips to the head—plumbing was installed right into the
broom closet of a space he now called home—and the pleasure
of scaring the bloody blazes out of such innocent savages as
Svitta.

He still carried on one-sided conversations with Grandpa,
but more to keep his hand in than in hopes of spooking any
theoretical snoopers. That there were snoopers he knew almost as surely as if they were in the room with him— which
annoyed him constantly when he was forced to answer the call
of nature. The image of a bunch of skinny knotheads watching
him through a concealed camera lens and making cracks about
his alien anatomy to pass the time didn't strike him as
humorous at all.

The lighting in the cell remained a constant half-twilight,
and his feeling of time elapsed was impaired even more than

it had been on the *Kalistra*. There were only the regularly arriving field ration packets to indicate that he was not entombed and forgotten—that and the sensation of prying eyes. Once he had begun hoarding the empty food packets instead of sending them back when the tube glowed, stacking them neatly in pyramid-fashion like a kid with alphabet blocks in the center of his cramped floor space. There had been no reaction, until the number of packets had reached twenty and he stood over them with prayerful countenance and folded his arms and inquired of Grandpa if he had arranged them correctly, and if he was now to be transported from this durance vile . . .

It had been nice to see faces again, even orange ones, and even those were seen fleetingly at best and were contorted into all sorts of dark scowls. Not a word had been spoken on their part; they had simply confiscated the food packets while he stood under drawn guns, and went away, slamming the door behind them. Martak Sarno might not believe in spooks, but he was taking no chances.

After that, things had seemed more endurable for a while. The fact that he could still shake them up even in his present state was immeasurably heartening—that and remembrance of a bright cold afternoon in Georgia and a deadly rifle and a somber voice:

"Livar is not drunk. He is speaking the cold truth."

Somewhere, somehow, someone else had been missed by Sarno's Dust and was exploiting his immunity to the hilt. His total dead soldiers had already exceeded Donovan's before he was locked into this miserable rathole, and he had likely been active since—but Donovan was far from envious. More power to him.

That someone would actually remain free to irritate the invaders and put teeth in his own tales of a bloodthirsty phantom was more than he could have hoped for in his wildest dreams. Which was all very well except for the fact that he wasn't satisfied to rest on his laurels and let others have all the fun.

Unfortunately, nobody seemed interested in just what did and didn't satisfy him. Such considerations, he was afraid, weren't going to make his captors lose much sleep. He had

had his brief moment with Grandpa, but events had been taken right out of his hands again—if he'd ever had a grasp on them to start with. Now it was just between that self-styled Gremper out there somewhere and all the forces Martak Sarno could bring to bear against him.

Since it was out of his hands, he would have liked a cigarette to smoke while he awaited the outcome. Which of course he didn't have. He pounded his pillow shapeless, tossed restlessly on the unchanged and much-wrinkled bedding.

This whole invasion business was getting to be pretty much of a drag.

Chapter Sixteen

Sjilla stared reflectively out the plasgas window at the azure upheavals of rock that had given the village spread below its name. In his nostrils was the by-this-time utterly familiar stench of xil'tressk perfume. He was standing in a fifth-floor cell of the city stockade, Blue Hills, Venus.

Turning from the vista, he looked down at the thick-stemmed plant in its window box. It was quiveringly aware of his presence, tenacles curving stiffly, gas ducts secreting furiously. Sjilla was the first meat on the hoof it had had contact with for long days, and it was famished. He shivered, turned away.

So easily, he thought, *are the Unaffecteds explained away. The answer was so simple it was simply overlooked.*

This was the cell of Paul Nogales, footloose, wanderer sower of wild oats, a regular star-bum by any standards. The plant was his pet, his "Tiger Lil," as he put it—a souvenir of

141

his wild sojourn on Risstair, lugged about across countless star-years since because of a fondness for its unabashedly carnivorous nature.

Paul Nogales, wanderer, had wandered into San Francisco nine months ago—and Paul Nogales, sower of wild oats, had sown a few. But this time there had been a catch—a marriage license—and he and "Tiger Lil" had taken it on the lam, but not before having set up a cozy little love nest in a Butte Montana, apartment house belonging to a Bible-spouting old woman, none other than Margaret Cassidy. Just he and she, and the xil'tressk made three . . . and then the bird had flown the nest, leaving behind heartbreak—and immunity to Sarno's Dust. Immunity for a loving wife who had lovingly fed hamburger to his pet and then fell asleep watching it digest. All this he had learned from Nogales, a born talker with no objections as to whom his audience consisted of, or what government they owed allegiance to, as long as they were attentive. Immunity for a loving wife, and immunity for a nosy landlady who had sensed evil in that pulsing alien flower and come sniffing around, only to get quite a noseful more than she bargained for.

The bird had flown, but not far. Warrants beamed ahead had beat his ship to Venus and police had been waiting when he disembarked to escort him to the local stockade. And Tiger Lil accompanied him. Why not? Who can object to a flower? But a flower can cause quite a stir of interest if its feeding habits are unusual enough, and prison guards are likely to remark about such phenomena at their dinner tables, and if a certain prison guard has a son scouting around for a particularly interesting project with which to wow his high-school biology teacher, and if the guard pulls a little seniority and gets his son into the cell with a camera and notebook, and comes along himself, just to make sure the no-good star-bum doesn't try any thing . . .

The pieces fell together neatly, one after the other, and he was overwhelmed by the simplicity of it all. It seemed almost too easy: Rayburn Senior and Rayburn Junior struck down the same instant by the perfume of Tiger Lil, and rushed by police courier to New York City to be put under the surveillance of the best man on off-world diseases in the system by prison authorities worried about an epidemic . . .

And the usual recovery from the vapor's effect, and the aroused curiosity of the medics—and then the culmination of the invasion before anything could come of that curiosity.

Nine Unaffecteds, he thought. *Nine neat and tidy answers for why they were not affected. Case closed and forgotten.*

Except for one thing. Or rather two things.

The first thing was Unaffected Number Ten—the Spook of Baxter, the unknown element in all this. What was the answer to *his* immunity? The second was a little more complex, how complex he was just beginning to realize. Just how many people had come into contact with Paul Nogales over the years since he'd left Risstair? How many a floating crap game, how many a romantic tryst had Nogales and Tiger Lil attended together? Across how many paths had they sown the seeds of immunity to Sarno's supposedly infallible weapon?

He had accounted for nine. A tenth was making no secret of his presence.

But how many are running loose and unsuspected, and laughing up their collective sleeves? He groaned aloud. Sarno was just going to love this . . . and he could see his chances of a ship home receding farther and farther into the distance the harder he pursued. Plague of the Black Stars, would *nothing* work out smoothly?

A throat cleared pointedly from the cell doorway interrupted his melancholy mood. A trooper stood just outside.

"What is it, soldier?"

"Pardon, sir, but there is a message from Underchief Blalir. It was said to be most urgent, sir."

"I see." He frowned. Blalir was back on Terra, puzzling out leads regarding the Spook of Baxter. Maybe he had finally come up with something. "All right. Thank you." He nodded at the undulating planet in the window box. "Bring that along, will you?"

"Yes, sir . . ." The soldier sounded dubious. As Sjilla left the cell, he was stalking Tiger Lil as if he suspected her of being about to pounce on him and swallow him whole on the spot.

While Sjilla waited for the self-service elevator to come up, the trooper caught up to him, holding the plant gingerly and twisting his head from side to side to avoid its thrashing tendrils. "There's a scout ship waiting outside," he said out of the corner of his mouth, busy being afraid of the plant and ashamed of being afraid all at the same time. "You may have heard it come down. It is waiting to take you back to Terra."

"Then Blalir has hit on something this time for sure!" Sjilla exulted. Images of home swam closer again.

"It would seem so, sir."

The elevator arrived and they got aboard. Moments later they were walking past one of the slender scout's graceful tail fins to the foot of the gangplank, the soldier still having difficulty with Tiger Lil.

Security Underchief Blalir was waiting at the grounding site—an open, rolling meadow that did nothing to alleviate Sjilla's worsening case of homesickness by its close resemblance to the plains of northern Llrala—with a command flivver. Sjilla jumped down the scouter's lock, sprinted across the scorched earth beneath its fins and climbed in beside him. The scout pilot waited for word from Blalir's pilot that he was clear for lift, then took his ship up with a rush and a thunder.

When it was lost to view, Sjilla turned. "What news?"

"I think we've just about got it pinned down," Blalir said. "I'll give you a step-by-step rundown and let you judge if we're on the right track."

"I'm all ears."

"Ever since this hullabaloo started, we've been pretty sure that one individual has been responsible for all the fireworks, for the simple reason that we've never seen more than one man at a time, and that what fragmentary descriptions we have seem to match the same man." Blalir shrugged. "Obviously then, he was responsible for the destruction of Scout Flight S-90980 and the demise of its crew, so we started from the beginning."

"The beginning being?"

"The red groundcar found on the highway north of Baxter, of course. Long ago it was established that it had been in the explosion that signaled the atomization of S-90980. If the car was in Baxter and the killer was in Baxter, then it was a logical assumption that they left together. That raised the possibility that the groundcar actually belonged to the killer. So we checked."

"How?"

"The Georgia Motor Vehicles Registry. I had a team of language-and-file specialists dig into groundcar registrations for the past year. The car had current Georgia plates."

"A clever observation," complimented Sjilla.

"Another logical step," contradicted Blalir. He gestured deprecatingly. "It was the obvious thing to do."

"And what did the specialists discover?"

"The groundcar was registered to a William MacFarland, insurance claims investigator, home address Waycross."

"Waycross?"

"A town of some ten thousand inhabitants," clarified Blalir.

"I see. And what did you do then?"

"I, personally, went to Waycross and checked his home address. He wasn't there—not in his home, and not in his bombproof. I could have wasted a lot of time nosing around into this bombproof and that, but I didn't."

"If this red car was registered to him, why discount the possibility that he's the man we're looking for?" Sjilla wanted to know.

For answer, Blalir silently produced a card embedded in a slice of protective plastic. "My boys at the Motor Vehicles Registry cross-referenced him and came up with a copy of his driver's license. Does that description sound like our Spook? Does the photo *look* like him?"

Sjilla had to admit that they didn't. The Terran smiling up out of the picture on the card bore no faintest resemblance to various accounts of the Spook's appearance. He handed the card back. "So you think somebody borrowed his car?"

"Let's say I *thought* so. Either that, or the car had been stolen. But the Waycross police blotter showed no stolen vehicle report placed by MacFarland, and no red Catamount listed among the missing."

"So what did you do?"

Blalir leaned back against the seat cushions, ran a hand across tired features. "To save guesswork, I had MacFarland's wife carted off to the nearest pen, dosed with antidote and questioned."

"And?"

"I discovered that the bugs in the reawakening routine are numerous. That set of impulses sent into the brain to prepare the patient properly for the shock of awakening to a conquered world don't seem to work." He shrugged. "She went whirly."

"And you drew a blank?"

"I didn't say that. We put her under heavy sedation and got the Interrogation staff to work on her. Got what we wanted to cover the cogent periods. Found out where MacFarland was—or was supposed to have been. Seems he left the day before the invasion to go to Atlanta for a talk with his district manager, and was going to swing south the next day to interview a claimant in Baxter. He figured to stay overnight in Atlanta, start early the next morning for Baxter."

"How early?"

"Around nine o'clock."

"Nine A.M., EST." Sjilla frowned thoughtfully. "The invasion came off around eight o'clock Greenwich time, and the Dust was supposed to work just about then, give or take a little . . . say about . . ."

"It would have been between noon and two o'clock in this time zone," informed Blalir. "These accursed time zones would confuse a computer. But that's about right. Now, assuming MacFarland got away on time, he would either be on the road between Atlanta and Baxter, or already in Baxter, when the sirens blew."

"How do we know he *did* get away on time?"

"We don't—not for sure. But it's a pretty safe bet, else what was his car doing there?"

"Any number of things can happen—"

"Granted. But I thought the chance of finding the point where the groundcar shifted out of MacFarland's possession and into that of the Spook justified following up a promising lead, no matter how long the shot." He paused, took a breath. "And I was right."

Sjilla sat up straight. "You mean you *know* who the Spook is?"

"I mean I *think* I do," responded the Underchief patiently. He tapped the flivver pilot on the shoulder. "Let's go."

"Where?" asked Sjilla, as the ship lifted.

"To the spot I think the exchange took place. But to continue my tale: I thought that perhaps MacFarland had arrived in Baxter, gone in to see his claimant, and perhaps loaned his car to someone to use in the interim. Or had it sent to a garage for a tune-up."

"Or had it stolen."

"Or had it stolen," agreed Blalir. "In that case, we'd have reached a dead end. We thought we had, anyway."

"What d'you mean?"

"I had the claimant's home and bombproof checked—we got his name from Mrs. MacFarland. No luck. Then I commandeered two squads of troopers and had them go through the four main shelters and a dozen or so lesser ones that this town boasts. I passed around a description of our man and had an agent accompany each unit. No MacFarland. Then I thought maybe MacFarland had simply left his car parked in front of that heathen temple and got into the bomb shelter, and that the Spook had grabbed it after finishing off S-90980, just as he took that second car when Zowal cornered him."

"But if that had been the case," Sjilla pointed out, "MacFarland would have been in the church bomb shelter. And he wasn't."

"He wasn't," agreed Blalir. The flivver was following a wide highway at a sedate pace.

"So the car had arrived in Baxter, but MacFarland hadn't."

"That would seem to be the case."

"What came next?"

"Well, I was getting pretty discouraged," Blalir admitted, "but I had one chance left: if MacFarland and the Catamount had parted company somewhere between Atlanta and Baxter, perhaps there would be some sign of that parting on the highway connecting the two."

"That's pretty slim," Sjilla opined.

"It sure was. We go down here!" That last was directed at the pilot, and he obediently set the ship earthward in a gentle falling turn. A square white building swam up toward them, centered on a field of concrete festooned with fuel pumps and maintenance racks.

"A gas station," Sjilla said humorously. "We running low?"

Blalir answered with a shadow grin. "This," he said, "is where MacFarland and his car became separated."

"So your long shot paid off?"

"My series of long shots paid off," amended the Underchief. "There were a lot of gaps in the trail that could have completely thrown me off. As it turned out, I was lucky."

The ship sat down with a slight bump and Blalir climbed out, Sjilla following. The Underchief led the way to the station's office, passed within and waited for the other to join him.

There were two unconscious Terrans on the floor, breathing with that abnormal, Dust-induced slowness: a youth in coveralls, and a round-faced, portly man. Sjilla knelt beside the latter, patted his pockets and came up with a billfold. "You've already checked this, no doubt."

"Yes."

He flipped it open to see for himself. "William MacFarland, age forty-seven; occupation, insurance claims investigator." Closing the billfold, he replaced it and stood up. "Congratulations on a fine piece of work."

"That isn't all," Blalir said, untouched by the praise. "Come on back outside."

He followed him into the bright, heatless sunshine and across the pavement to a Terran aircar squatting to one side of the building. His observant eye picked up scars in the pavement ending under the ship's runners. "Landed in a hurry," he commented.

"Yes," Blalir opened the ship's door. "Have a look."

Sjilla inspected the interior, noting a musty smell of old pipe tobacco and Terran gun oil. "Owned by the boy?"

"No."

"Anyone else on the premises?"

"No."

He gave a deep sigh. "Looks like you're onto something. Had it checked with the Motor Vehicles Registry?"

"In the process now. The information should be coming in at any time."

"Good. I—" With a muttered exclamation, he bent over and picked something from beneath the edge of the driver's seat, turned it over and over in his hands. "Tell me something," he said thoughtfully.

"If I can."

"You don't happen to remember the caliber of those bullets the Spook uses to such good effect, do you?"

"The caliber?" Blalir looked lost for a moment, then, "Oh, you mean that decimal designation signifying the diameter of a slug-thrower's bore. No, I don't. Sorry."

"Well, I do. It's .300. A long-range, steep-shouldered, spitzer-pointed .300 caliber hunting round. Packs quite a punch."

Blalir's face showed that he hadn't the faintest idea what his superior was talking about. "So?"

Sjilla held his discovery up to the sunlight, rotated it so that the bronze casing gave off fitful gleams.

"This," he said. "This, too, is a .300."

Chapter Seventeen

"The Terran delegation, my general, awaits your pleasure." Blanatta stood with exaggerated stiffness, resplendent in full-dress uniform.

Sarno nodded. "Show them in, Blanatta, and then carry out your orders."

Blanatta bowed, stood aside. "General Sarno will see you now."

Five glum-looking Terrans filed in—three military men and two civilians. They were followed by a pair of neatly pressed, starched, creased and polished paratroopers who waited for Blanatta to exit, then closed the door and took up positions on either side of it.

"Gentlemen"—he gestured at the length of the conference table—"be seated."

They sat. Five carefully blank faces were turned toward his; five pairs of carefully veiled eyes bored into his own. It happened that the two generals sat on his left and the two civilians to his right, so that he was face to face with the white-hatted space-navy fleet admiral who comprised the fifth member of the delegation.

They were good, Sarno gave them credit—they showed nothing of the conflicting emotions that must be pounding behind those expressionless masks. They could have as easily been here on one of those highly formal social calls such as he had received when military administrator of Risstair as to bargain for the lives of three billion of their kind.

He smiled faintly, feeling the strong wine of victory and power pulsing like molten lead through his veins. For the very first time since arriving on Terra, he began to realize the true magnitude of what he had accomplished. Before, it had been obscured in petty details of conquest duty and the curiously interrelated problem of Donovan, the Unaffecteds and the Spook of Baxter. But now—now he was facing a delegation representative of the leadership of the small but tough Terran Federation, the Federation that had kept all the might of Empire at bay all these long years of semipeace and open war. And it was they who had come to him.

The silence stretched. Finally the leftmost general shifted in his seat, uttered something like a growl deep in his throat. "You know why we're here, Larry. You've got some convincing to do. So start convincing."

Sarno raised surprised eyebrows. "Larry? My, my, general, isn't that taking military brusqueness a bit far? Especially considering the situation?"

That elicited another growl, and the Terran general opened his mouth for a hot retort. He was cut short by the civilian sitting nearest the admiral.

"Easy, Carstairs, we're here to be shown something, not engage in name-calling."

The general fidgeted but subsided, and Sarno regarded the stocky civilian with new interest. Anybody who could cut an

150

irate general down to size must carry a considerable amount of weight.

"Who're you?" he inquired.

"Name's Garcia," the civilian responded easily. "Ryan Garcia."

"Garcia," echoed a phantom voice in Sarno's skull. A key word had been mentioned and the robolibrary listening in on the conversation via various mikes scattered about the conference room had responded. He pressed a stud masked from the Terrans by the edge of the table, triggering the go-ahead.

"Garcia," whispered the voice. *"Ryan X. Federation senator, representing the North American Alliance in the Congress. Absent from Terra six months inspecting conditions on frontier worlds. Home: Miami, Florida. Married. Two children. Family Pen Rating: 1-A. Present status: in custody of Penmaster Quiror, Atlanta Pen—"*

He hit the stud again, cutting off the recital. "Well, Senator Garcia—you ought to feel right at home here, Canada being part of your district. You'll even get to see how the taxpayers are faring—courtesy of Empire, of course."

The dapper Terran smiled. "That's nice of you, but let me put one thing straight from the start. General Carstairs, while perhaps not the best diplomat to be found between the stars, has expressed more or less the Terran stand on this matter. We do not come here to be bullied and intimidated. We come here to appraise the situation merely, and report our findings to the Federation High Command. You have made very sweeping statements concerning your power of life and death over these three planets and their populations. Frankly, we think you're a liar."

Sarno grinned broadly. "Bullying? Intimidation? Harsh words, Senator Garcia, harsh words. And liar"—his grin faded —"that, too, is a harsh word. I like it not at all. As to my situation here . . ." He shrugged. "You will see that soon enough for yourself. I have a guided tour all arranged. It will hit the high spots on Terra, and then if you are still not convinced, I will see to it that your tour is extended to Mars and Venus as well. I will ask only this: when your ship came in, did your radiomen detect any traces of combat gabble? I know they were straining their sets. Did they?"

"No . . ." Garcia admitted reluctantly.

"Means nothing," inserted the admiral flatly. "Fleet your size, play it right, you could damp it out."

"All except the PDC's," put in the second general. "Nothing they've got could damp *them* out."

"So the PDC's are out of commission." The admiral gave an almost imperceptible shrug. "Doesn't mean system's subdued. Could be plenty of fighting going on."

"But there isn't," Sarno said. *If you discount Georgia,* he added mentally.

"We'll see," the admiral returned. "We get a chance to deviate from this guided tour?"

"Why should you need to?" Sarno inquired innocently.

A bleak smile flitted across the Terran's craggy features. "We're professionals here. Except possibly Garcia and Trenton. Don't try detouring us."

Sarno returned his wintry gaze blandly. "Don't worry, admiral—by the time you leave Terra, you'll be convinced."

"I'd better be. Two days. Absolute maximum. No word, twenty battle-squadrons drop on you like eagles on a sitting hen."

"You're giving *me* ultimatums?"

"We are," said Garcia. "And we intend to back them to the limit."

Sarno's peculiarly colored eyes chilled. "And you think I don't? For the sake of your loved ones, Senator, *don't make that mistake.* Don't try to call my bluff—I'm not bluffing."

"Neither are we," Garcia informed. "Those squadrons have standing orders to proceed immediately to Terra, Venus and Mars, there to destroy all enemy forces wherever found, thereby cutting our losses to a practical minimum."

Sarno shook his head incredulously. "I seriously believe you mean that."

"We do."

"Well . . . it's nothing to me, of course. Except for the fact that, as the admiral here so deftly put it, we're professionals here, with the possible exception of yourself and your colleague. As a professional soldier, I deplore the useless murder of three billion noncombatants. But if that is the Federation's wish, so be it. Perhaps it has to do with the population problem, eh? And, not being able to push us off our own planets, the powers that be have decided to halve that population quickly and painlessly, and put the blame on us."

Garcia showed temper for the first time. His lips thinned and his swarthy features darkened even more. "Are you suggesting . . . ?"

Sarno raised a hand. "Merely a suggestion. And why does it strike you as so repulsive? Because your wife and children are here? And what about General Raymond?" The robolibrary had been feeding him information right along. "Or Representative Trenton, for that matter. Their homes, and loyalties, are many light-years from Terra. If it came right down to a choice between ultimate defeat at the hands of Empire and simply vacating three worlds for reoccupancy, how would *they* vote?"

"Your basic premise," said the heretofore silent Trenton tightly, "is correct. You know very well that this war was instigated and pushed right along by your side; you know that population is not, and never has been, an issue. You have more than a thousand planets. For the six billions of us, there are fifty benevolent worlds within our borders. Perhaps one day expansion could become a motive—but not now. No, we represent a challenge to Empire, the mighty Empire which has thus far defeated all comers. So long as we remain autonomous, we are an intolerable blot on your record. You have four thousand suns; you want our two hundred eleven to add to that total—not because you need them, but because they are there to be had."

"But not to be had easily!" gritted Carstairs.

"We're not here to talk politics," reminded the taciturn admiral. "We're here for proof. Talking gets us nowhere. Trot out some of that proof."

Sarno inclined his head. "A man of action." He glanced at a wall clock. "Your convincing will start soon enough. Even for you, Admiral. And meanwhile"—he touched another stud in the table—"refreshments. We have walsos of the finest grade, and some Terran whiskeys which I have—ah, taken the liberty of borrowing from the stocks of nearby cities."

"Looter!" muttered Carstairs under his breath as an immaculately attired Growezi steward entered pushing a rubber-tired cart. "Freebooter."

"Please!" Sarno looked pained. "You do me injustice. Perhaps I *do* take certain liberties with the planets under my protection, but then"—his grin was that of a hunting marq—"but then, there's not one thing you can do about it. Not one."

"We'll see," promised Carstairs fervently.

"Yes, indeed. Indeed yes. We shall see. And soon. But meantime. . . . Steward! . . . You must not refuse a drink."

The Growezi padded silently forward to serve the drinks.

"Just what," inquired Carstairs explosively, "kind of a damn fool trick is this?"

They were standing near an airlock. The double doors were drawn back, and beyond could be seen the beginning of a weatherproof tube leading to the Terran cruiser lying alongside the Llralan flagship.

"This," Sarno told him, "is the tubeway to your ship."

"I damn well *know* that!"

"Well?"

"Well, what are you—?"

"Excuse me, general." Sarno walked forward. Blanatta had just appeared, ambling lazily down the tube. At the sight of the delegation he snapped into a more military bearing. Sarno met him at the lock.

He gestured at the pistol belt strapped around the Vice-Commander's paunchy gut. "Any need for that?"

"None. There were no Unaffecteds among the crew of the *South Pacific*."

"And what an ironically inappropriate name *that* is for the barrens of Alberta," commented a new voice.

"Back from your detecting, Sjilla?" Sarno asked, without turning.

"Back," confirmed the mocker, coming around into view. "Sirri! If looks could kill, that tall Rekk general would have cut me down to sandwich-size by now."

"Carstairs," identified Sarno. "A hothead. What luck did you have in your investigations?"

"Excellent luck. Such luck as requires a long talk with you."

"Meaning?"

"Meaning as soon as you spank this bunch of tourists merrily

154

on their way, we can get down to the business of wrapping up this Spook-Gremper affair once and for all."

Sarno stared at him. "You mean that?"

"Am I disposed to joke about such matters?" Sjilla waved wearily. "Take care of this business and send a messenger for me. I'll be getting a needle-shower and some sleep, if Sirri so decrees."

"All right." He turned to the waiting delegation. "You gentlemen spoke of proof. Through here lies the first install- ment of that proof. If you will follow me . . ." He ducked into the tubeway with Carstairs close upon his heels, still muttering.

Those mutters, Sarno calculated, would quickly become bellows—or be silenced altogether, depending upon what lay beneath that fiery exterior—when Carstairs saw what awaited him aboard the warship he had so recently quitted. He would find the entire crew, officers and men, sleeping deeply. But not the sleep of a weary crew after a long and tiring voyage. A much slower, longer-lasting kind of sleep.

The sleep of the Dust.

Looking forward eagerly to all their reactions, Sarno in- creased his pace along the creaking, faintly swaying tunnel leading between the two ships.

Chapter Eighteen

"And that," said Martak Sarno with much satisfaction, "is that."

"It went well then?" inquired Sjilla.

"Very well indeed. I wish you could have seen the look on

155

Carstairs' face when he saw what had happened to that crew. While the shock of it was still fresh, I sent them on their way with Blanatta to act as shepherd."

"A cute trick, that," Sjilla complimented him. "But then you're full of cute tricks, aren't you?"

"I like to think so, anyway. But right now I'm interested in hearing just how we go about wrapping up the Spook of Baxter and Gremper into one neat bundle. Then at least *that'll* be out of the way."

The tone of his voice made the Security Chief regard him closely. "Something wrong, general?"

"What makes you think so?"

He gestured vaguely. "It's my job to know such things. Nothing *in particular* makes me think so, but something's wrong just the same. Am I right?"

Sarno sighed heavily. "You are, as usual, right."

"What's the problem this time?"

Sarno shrugged helplessly. "Nothing you can pin down exactly. Deteriorating morale on the part of the troops, for one thing. For another, the robots are getting restless."

"Huh?"

"The robots. These planets are crawling with 'em."

"I know. So what?"

"So they're getting restless."

"Impossible. They're only machines. They can't—"

"Don't tell me." Sarno raised a weary hand. "I know every word you're going to say—I've already said them myself. Nevertheless, the fact remains."

"What fact?"

"Robots have been accosting troopers on patrol and spouting strings of naturally unintelligible Terran at them. The troopers have reacted typically for combat-trained men. They blasted 'em."

"So where's the problem?"

"The incidents are increasing too fast to suit me—much too fast. And there's something else. In some instances, the troopers didn't blast well or quickly enough. The robots escaped. Who's to say how they'll react to hostility?"

"That's easy. They'll call a cop."

"There aren't any cops. What then?"

"Look, they're only machines. Not men. They have a limited capability, else they'd have taken over long ago. Stop worrying."

"All right . . . if you'll tell me why fifteen troopers are missing in widely different places for no apparent reason."

"Accidents. Alien cities are death traps to the unwary."

"Agreed—especially when populated by angry robots. But enough of that. What about the Spook of Baxter—of Gremper?"

"Firstly, they're one and the same. Now, what else would you like to know—his name, home address or financial status?"

Sarno expelled his breath explosively. "Positive identification?"

"Positive."

"And?"

"And it is just as I thought—the Spook is merely another Unaffected who happens to have a native ability for slinging slugs and ducking searbeams. His name? James Rierson. His home address? Atlanta. His financial status? Enviable."

"Rierson." Sarno frowned. "Daniel Rierson, James Rierson —any relationship?"

"That of uncle and nephew. And the reason for the immunity of the nephew, as I see it, is the same as that of the uncle." He fumbled in a pocket, handed across a faded photograph. "Familiar?"

"Risstair!" Sarno exploded. "A tarl—a vuru tree!"

"And James Rierson, twenty-three Terran years ago, holding a brand-new slug-firing rifle," Sjilla added. He delved into the portfolio he had brought with him, brought out a large square of photographic paper, passed it over. It was a fresh print, much enlarged, of the same scene. Sarno looked it over, laid it on his desk.

"So? Why the enlargement?"

For answer, Sjilla produced a small brass cylinder. "This is the empty cartridge casing of a .300 caliber slug-thrower."

"So?"

"The soldiers killed in Baxter before Rierson started using that .40 caliber pistol and a stolen seargun were killed with a .300 caliber. We found this casing in a vehicle belonging to Rierson—the vehicle itself was fairly close to Baxter."

157

"What does that prove?"

"That he was in the neighborhood, and owns a .300. The rest is proven by the fact that he is not to be found in any of the nearby bomb shelters, nor lying around loose—and by that enlargement."

"What about the enlargement?"

"The rifle he's holding in the snapshot—that's also a .300. Pretty constant string of coincidences, don't you think?"

"You are absolutely sure you have the right man?"

"You want more proof?" All right—descriptions of him in state files match pretty closely the descriptions given by soldiers fighting the Spook, except for the beard, which is understandable. Medical records show no depilatory treatment. And to top if off, this casing here is made by the same ammunition company that made the ones found near the bodies and in that furniture store in Baxter. Want more?"

"No." Sarno grinned. "I know when I'm licked. All right, you've got the Spook of Baxter—alias Gremper—tagged and explained. Wonderful. You have explained the immunity of Donovan, Yoganda, Nogales, Harris, and both Riersons. But what about the others?"

"Oh, that."

"Yes, that."

Sjilla got up, went to the door. "With your permission, general, I shall bring on the next exhibit."

"Go ahead."

"Thank you." He opened the door, spoke to someone without. "Bring it in."

A soldier sidled through the door, grimacing fearfully and holding something out at arm's length—something that writhed and contorted violently, and lashed out at his protected arms with ineffectual barbs. A heavy and very, very familiar odor permeated the room.

"Xil'tressk!" Sarno ejaculated, startled out of his habitual self-control. "A xil'tressk . . . here?"

"A xil'tressk here," Sjilla agreed, as the soldier divested himself of his threshing burden with obvious relief and beat a hasty retreat. "Otherwise known as Tiger Lil, and the boon traveling companion of none other than Paul Nogales."

Sarno was staring at the aroused plant with frustration.

"Your dramatic revelation would do credit to a Terran detective thriller," he informed the Security Chief. "Now will you please tell me what in Parra it signifies, and just where you got that thing?"

"With the greatest possible pleasure," Sjilla replied, and proceeded to do so, leaving nothing out and finishing with, "so you see, it was the simple working of cause and effect. Donovan and Harris and the rest were on Risstair, and so were you—and they were all exposed to the Dust. When you discovered its military potential, and the High Command decided to gamble on it, it then became inevitable that your paths would cross again . . ."

". . . and Nogales' unpredictable nature just added frosting to the cake," Sarno took it up.

"Exactly."

He leaned far back in his chair, shook his head wonderingly. "And, of course, Donovan being the individual he is, he could not rest content without stirring up trouble. Being captured early in the proceedings frustrated him and stimulated his imagination."

"Again correct."

"And this James Rierson—who I remember only as an overweight, distinctly lost-looking Terran juvenile seen fleetingly in the Risstair spaceport—reacted according to *his* nature, and kept reacting until he got clear—"

"—and earned the sobriquet 'Spook' while doing so," Sjilla nodded. "Cause and effect personified. Fling a pebble and the ripples roll on and on . . ."

"Who would ever have believed it?" began the general, and then thrust his awe at the monumental workings of Fate from him almost violently and returned to the business at hand. "Now that we know what we're up against in Georgia—or wherever he's got to by now—how do we go about rounding him up? Sirri knows he's caused trouble enough both directly and indirectly for an army of phantoms, let alone one man."

"Indirectly? How indirectly?" Sjilla wanted to know.

"By substantiating Donovan's tales; you know that. By dampening morale considerably. By making troopers more than a little reluctant to take up their stations below ground

159

in the bomb shelters with only the sleeping—and the undead, so they think—for company. And also . . ."

"And also?" prompted the Security Chief.

"Well, the ripples are spreading with a vengeance. There was a sudden death in Georgia yesterday, one that we cannot directly credit to this Rierson's marksmanship. It occurred in full view of a platoon; they were combing a wide stretch of fallow acreage on the off-chance of flushing the Spook."

"And?"

"You have read the reports of the botanists, the ones stating that not all life-forms on this planet were affected equally by the Dust?"

"I have. What of it?"

"That some isolated forms were affected not at all?" persisted the general.

"I read the report," Sjilla reiterated.

"That soldier died from a heart attack—brought on, medics theorized, by extreme tension due to hunting what he had more than a passing fear was looking over his shoulder all the time."

"An ancestor worshiper, then."

"Exactly. Barbarous custom—but that's not important. What is, is the way he was struck down. The other soldiers don't necessarily believe the medics' verdict. They think Gremper— by manipulating certain denizens of this planet which should have been sleeping—deliberately singled him out for destruction, as an object lesson. They are, to put it mildly, terrified. And their terror is spreading."

" 'Manipulating certain denizens,' you said?"

"Yes, one of the life-forms not affected by the Dust."

"What happened?"

"I'm not quite sure. The report was confused. There was some kind of eruption . . . and the trooper was dead. Keeled over in his tracks. The soldiers swear those birds were guided by Gremper's hand and killed him in some bizarre fashion."

"Birds?" said Sjilla. "What birds? What happened?"

"Maybe *you* can tell *me*, knowing so much about Terra." Sarno's voice sounded plaintive.

"I'll try. But I've got to know what happened."

"The botanist gave me a name. Or rather several names. But the words are nonsensical to me."

"Let's hear them."

"Well . . . just what, I'd like to know, is a covey of bob-white quail?"

Sjilla uttered a loud groan. "I was afraid of that."

"Afraid of what?"

"Someday, when we've got all the time in space, I'll try to explain it to you. Meanwhile, there's the matter of getting Rierson."

"You have some sort of plan?"

"I have a plan," admitted Sjilla. "And I think it'll work. It'd better! A covey of quail!" He wagged his head gloomily. "By the Black Stars, a covey of quail. Maybe the dead *will* start walking before this thing is done."

Chapter Nineteen

The steak knife made short work of the tender and succulent slab of meat on the platter before him, and James Rierson forked a slice into his mouth, chewed appreciatively. These robochefs in the better apartment buildings really knew how to broil a sirloin. And that gravy! He tore a warm, butter-drenched roll apart and sopped happily, then shoved the soggy bread in to keep the steak company.

It was almost as if he were home in his own apartment—which was located in a very similar neighborhood on the other side of the city, even had a similar floor plan—after a long day at the office or in court. Which, perhaps, was dangerous. The utter familiarity of his surroundings might tempt him into lowering his guard, might dull his reflexes. It was already somewhat difficult, under the present circumstances, to think seriously of the information he had scared out of Livar.

The interview with Livar, he was forced to admit modestly, had been a master stroke of genius. Now he had one big advantage over the opposition: he knew what he was up against. They didn't; they only knew they weren't supposed to be having the trouble they *were* having, and that their leaders couldn't seem to explain it, let alone do anything about it.

And then too, he knew about Bradford Donovan.

He took another bite of steak, gazed out past the gently blowing curtains at the window to the sunset-reddened wilderness of skyscrapers and spider-web roadways that was Atlanta. A sprawling citadel in which time had come to a stop for its six million inhabitants . . . and only one of many such, one among all the scores of metropolises and towns and villages spread across the face of three planets; the only signs of activity centered around alien spaceships dotting the landscape here and there like malevolent growths sprung up after a poisoned rain.

And somewhere within one of those grim spheres, a tiny spark of rebellion against the slumbrous spell cast by Earth's conquerors, resided one Bradford Donovan, unblushingly telling the most fantastic lies—and somehow getting them believed. Looking back upon his escape from Baxter, he could now see more clearly why the soldiers he had overheard in the furniture store had regarded him as something more than mortal; and why Livar, poor slob, had been so terrified when he turned around and found himself face to face with the dreaded Gremper. And, though he hated to admit it even to himself, it might just be that: had not Donovan set the stage beforehand with his imaginative depiction of his militant "Grandpa," those soldiers back there might have tried just a little harder, shot just a little faster and deprived this selfsame sirloin of being enjoyed so thoroughly.

It was, he reflected, sipping his coffee, almost as if Donovan had foreseen what would happen in Baxter and had carefully and artistically sown the seeds of fear for his, Rierson's, harvest. And all while a prisoner aboard some Llralan warship and theoretically helpless. Somehow, among all the incredible things he had witnessed or learned of since the big whitetail buck collapsed in his sights back in the game management area, Donovan's feat was the most incredible of all.

He had conceived of the interrogation of Livar as a means of discovering some lever, some slight edge, to use against his pursuers. Well, Donovan had handed it to him on a silver platter. He could become Gremper, the grandfather of his grandson—but to what avail? He could step into the role, drift across the planet from city to city like the restless phantom he was supposed to be, passing like the angel of death in the night among the invaders—with what end result? Livar had said—and Livar, if he was any judge, had not lied—that the Federation would be held at bay by threats of wholesale slaughter of the sleeping populace if it tried to push this Sarno character's fleet off Terra and out of the solar system. He had further stated that a truce ship was on the way with observers to see if Sarno indeed held the three planets as securely as he was broadcasting for all to hear that he did.

They would come in highly skeptical and be promptly slapped in the face with the devastating fact that for once the Llralans weren't over-advertising. After which, he knew, the Navy would stay conspicuously absent from this neck of the cosmos while frantic negotiations got under way to prevent Sarno's giving the order that would bloodily halve the Federation's population. Which in itself was understandable, but made it hard on him. He could wander the planet waging his lonely war against the invaders, killing a few, scaring hell out of a few more and managing to make everybody more than a little nervous—and what would come of it?

Nothing, that was what. The Navy would not intervene, there would come no figurative blare of bugles and thunder of hoofbeats as the good ole cavalry hove over the hill just in the nick of time to send the pesky orangeskins running for the far stars—and the Llralans, much annoyed by his picayune tactics, would continue to hound him until at long last he made some fatal slip and they collected his corpse. He figured he could do one hell of a job on their morale before being so collected, but it would all be wasted; a shattered morale is only valuable if there is to be a follow-up. Left alone, it would mend itself gradually, and sooner or later it would be as if James Rierson, alias Gremper, had never really existed. Just a bad memory, that was all.

He sighed deeply, pushed his plate away and poured himself another cup of coffee. Already he had acquisitioned the identity of Gremper twice—once in Baxter, and now to frighten Livar into revealing much-needed information—and he would likely go ahead with the thing. Certainly there was nothing to be gained by sitting on his hands waiting for some boneheaded Larry to stumble over him unexpectedly and get the hunt up again in full cry. And maybe, just maybe, something would occur that would break the deadlock and unleash the Navy, in which case any groundwork he could lay might prove to be the backbreaking straw. But playing the part of an army of phantoms was going to require stamina and dedication, and he could at least treat himself to one more peaceful night's sleep before he embarked upon his foredoomed-to-failure campaign of disturbing theirs.

He sat long over his coffee, face somber in the deepening dusk. When the last color had faded from the western sky, he kicked off his boots, placed his gun within easy reach and turned in.

There was a tiny, muffled rustling somewhere nearby. He stirred, tugged the bed covers higher against the insidious chill pervading the room. The rustling came again, somewhat louder. Fallen leaves being stirred. He turned over, still more asleep than awake, thinking drowsily that the birds were stirring in the tree outside his window earlier than usual this morning, and waited for the first trill of bird song that generally preceded his alarm clock's ring by about twenty minutes.

The awaited avian music was not forthcoming. Strange . . .

He dropped back into a fitful doze, but ingrained habit would not allow him to drop off completely. The seconds dragged by, and an irritating little node of worry began to nag his sleep-drugged consciousness—where *was* that bird song? Surely one of the sparrows would have emitted a few chirps by this time, and the mockingbirds . . .

But the sparrows and mockingbirds had already quitted his tree by this time of year—the early frosts had killed the leaves, and the branches were too bare for their taste. After all, this *was* the latter half of November . . .

He opened his eyes and stared ceilingward in the dark. *Then what am I doing at home? Why not at the cabin . . . ?*

That thought wavered uncertainly and ended in confusion. For he had just become aware of two things simultaneously: he wasn't *at* home, and those rustlings outside weren't birds stirring to greet the dawn.

They were footsteps.

Footsteps moving back and forth in the courtyard three floors below, footsteps rendered audible by the carpet of dead leaves strewn over the flagstones—*the leaves ungathered since Sarno's Dust had done its work*.

He was completely awake now, though a trifle groggy, and the sound of purposeful footsteps in the sleeping city could mean but one thing.

Hunters.

He slipped out of bed, the room's chill forgotten, and stuffed his feet into icy boots. The open window through which the sounds came was a pale gray smear in the inky blackness. Retrieving his pistols and tucking them in his jacket, he fumbled for the rifle, found it, and made his cautious way thitherward, skirting unfamiliar obstacles by touch.

The courtyard, in the washed-out gray light of false dawn, with its leafless trees intertwining frost-burned branches in the central garden above the green-gray masses of evergreen hedges, was like a surrealist fever dream beneath the blank and staring windows in the enclosing walls—and a strikingly proper setting for what was taking place.

For something was moving in the courtyard.

Rierson stiffened into immobility, eyes straining in the weak light, feeling something buried deep beneath his civilized veneer stir fearfully—some strange small flicker of superstitious fear that almost constituted race memory, some residue from a less-sophisticated age, bearing no relation at all to his very logical fear of the Llralans and their guns.

Too short in stature for Llralans—he realized that as a fourth form glided from some point beneath him to join the three already grouped by the garden. The four stood unmoving, unspeaking, in a precise little circle facing one another—he *assumed* they were facing one another—and silently communed.

If not Larrys, what then? He took his eyes off them long enough to look at the sky, saw that the stars were still burning brightly, that there were no definite beginnings of a sunrise as yet. His first observation had been correct, then—it was indeed the hour of false dawn.

And just what, if not Larrys, moved in the false dawn upon a planet populated only by Llralan soldiers, the sleeping . . . and the dead? For one wild moment he considered calling out to the group and inquiring to just which graveyard they returned with the coming of the sun. But suddenly such a question didn't seem at all funny; and the Llralans, in their fear of their ancestors, seemed more astute than the determinedly unsuperstitious Terrans.

A fifth figure moved into view from yet another point of the compass, joined the four and immediately went still in perfect imitiation of them.

Ghosts, James Rierson told himself, *do not rustle dry leaves underfoot when they walk. That takes solid feet with weight on them.*

Which was a pretty weak argument with five indistinct shapes standing in that eerie little formation under the black naked tangle of tree branches in the winter-ravaged garden. Five vague specters, in appearance manlike and yet no taller than an average Terran in his very early teens, totally unrecognizable in the meager lighting.

There was a way to remove all doubt, but he had been putting it off, half-hoping the shapes would dissipate before his eyes or resolve into some familiar form—even if the form were Llralan.

The figures showed no signs of vanishing, neither did they abruptly become tarnished statues of Greek athletes or Confederate soldiers—statues do not walk about in the predawn, or stand in silent communion within an apartment house courtyard. Or do they? He rubbed a hand across his face. Anything seemed possible in this upended, invaded, sleeping, weak-gray-lighted world. . . . He brought himself up short with an effort and did the thing that would identify the silent group below.

He raised his rifle and looked through the scope sight.

And almost broke out laughing as the sick fear drained out of him.

For the figures stood out clearly in the scope's light-gathering field.

They were robots. Five Terran utility robots of one of the more popular models. Five five-foot robots standing quietly in the courtyard as if awaiting some activating signal.

But an activating signal from where? Or, more importantly, from *whom*?

Had the Llralans somehow managed to activate Atlanta's working force of robots and send them hunting him? It didn't seem possible, but then of course all laws of probability had been knocked into a cocked hat by Sarno's introduction of the Dust into the war. The old rules simply didn't apply any longer.

The scope's cross hairs shifted to the nearer robot's right hand. In those steel fingers reposed a silvery, fragile-looking gun—a stunner. And each of the others were similarly armed. So if the Llralans *had* sent them after him, they had not been able—or had not chosen—to override their inbuilt inability to permanently harm human beings. If spotted and shot at, the worst that could come of it was stun-shock and capture. Which in its own ways was bad enough, but didn't arouse the cold terror that being awakened from a sound sleep to face the immediate prospect of violent death would have. Pure terrestrialism made it hard for him to be afraid of the robots that had been an inherent part of his daily existence from infancy.

Afraid or not, soft-nosed hunting bullets weren't going to stop them if they tried anything—and he knew better than to think he could wield the Llralan seargun fast enough and accurately enough to down five robots in a stand-up gunfight if the robots had stunners and were intent on using them. He best tactic at this point would be a strategic withdrawal. He didn't *know* the robots were looking for him, but he couldn't be sure they weren't, either. When faced with five gun-toting robots with unknown motives, discretion becomes as never before, the better part of valor.

Abruptly, the robots moved. Without a sound, without a gesture, they split up and made for various doors opening onto the courtyard. Whether he was the object of it or not, a search was definitely in the offing. Time to exercise that discretion before he had to put his valor to the test.

He left the apartment, went down the corridor quickly to a stalled escalator and down, his soft-soled hunting boots making the slightest of whispers on the risers. Reaching the second floor he turned left, trotted to a hallway leading away from the courtyard. Forty feet along, big French windows opened onto a foyer and so to the landing stage-parking area used by visitors, mailmen and delivery services. He ran heavily across that, feeling terribly exposed, and down the gently sloping ramp that gave access to the area for groundcars.

When he reached bottom, he was on the sidewalk running in front of the building. He crossed the street, hurried through a front yard partially shielded from the windows behind him by tall hedges, and moved up an intersecting street. Two blocks away he reached the entrance to one of the sunken roadbeds reserved for emergency, maintenance and sanitation vehicles. Going down, he headed back toward the heart of the city.

Finally he felt safe enough to pause to catch his breath and gather his thoughts, choosing a spot halfway between a truck ramp and a stairway leading up and out. Those openings and the luminescent lettering naming them provided the only relief in the otherwise total darkness. Overhead lights were out; all central power sources had long since been shut off by the Llralans. It was cold here, much colder than the apartment, and the soft breeze blowing through the tunnel felt as if it was coming straight off a glacier.

Something moved in the tunnel ahead of him; a black shape flitted across the grayness at the ramp's mouth with disconcerting speed, heading right toward him.

He fired from the hip.

The concussion was deafening. Yellow-orange flame stabbed at the figure, illuminating its features momentarily. It staggered a bit, but did not go down. Rierson was only vaguely aware of coming fully to his feet and working a fresh round home. His ears were stunned by the rifle's blast and his eyes dazzled by the muzzle flash. He waited tensely for what would happen, knowing himself powerless to prevent it, whatever it was. The seargun was in his jacket and he would never be able to reach it in time if that which confronted him were hostile. For the muzzle flash had revealed, in the split-second of its duration, the futility of the bullet it had sent on its way.

The awful racket of echoes raised by the gunshot finally died away, leaving him pointing a useless weapon at an enigmatic adversary. The tense silence stretched interminably.

Then: "Your pardon, sir," said an apologetic voice, "for this imposition. But I must speak to you for a moment."

Rierson remained exactly as he was and said nothing.

"Sir, such a course of action would bring me extreme unhappiness, but if you persist in your efforts to deactivate me, I must take protective measures." The robot's hand came up and the outlines of a stunner were plainly visible against the weak light from the ramp.

Rierson straightened, lowered his rifle. He remained silent.

"Thank you, sir, very much. Now, may I have a word with you?"

"Who sent you?" said Rierson carefully.

"I am afraid, sir, that I do not understand the nature of your query."

"Who ordered you to come looking for me? Was he tall, skinny? Was his head pointed? His skin orange? Did he have four fingers instead of—"

"Sir," interrupted the robot politely, "no one sent me. I came at my own—or rather at my master-brain's—volition." He retreated until he stood in the light of the ramp, looked upward. What Rierson had seen in the muzzle flash's illumination was confirmed: his accoster was a blue-steel five-foot-tall utility robot, the graven image of the five in the apartment-house courtyard.

The robot turned. "I am afraid, sir, that the rather hasty firing of your weapon may have attracted unwanted attention. The aliens are everywhere."

Rierson stared. "You know about them—about what they are?"

"Oh, definitely, sir. They are quite a noisy lot—and destructive, too. They show absolutely no respect for private or public property. They are also"—did the little robot's voice change, or was that just his imagination?—"trigger-happy. One of my co-workers was brutally deactivated right before my vision lenses. It is about them that I—or rather that my master-brain—wishes to speak."

"I see. And what does your master-brain wish to say?"

"That I do not know, sir. My instructions were simply to find and bring back with me a sentient human being."

"Just any human? Not any one in particular?"

"No, sir. No one in particular."

"H'mm." Rierson frowned. "And what if I don't want to go back with you?"

"My instructions were to bring back a sentient human," repeated the robot doggedly.

"And whether the human wants to go or not has nothing to do with it?"

"No, sir." The robot sounded positively near tears. "I am sorry, sir."

"Isn't that a little unusual—the wishes of a master-brain taking precedence over those of a human?"

"The circumstances are unusual, sir," assured the robot, in classic robotic understatement.

"You can say that again," Rierson told him feelingly.

"I know that I can, sir—there is no just-developed impediment to my speech. Would you like me to say it again?"

"Never mind," he said hastily. He had almost forgotten how trying it could be, at times, to make conversation with a robot.

"Yes, sir—as you like. Shall we go?"

Rierson hesitated. "One last question."

"Yes, sir?"

He rapped it out swiftly, hoping to take off-guard any distant technician—if there *were* a technician—listening in on the conversation, and get a truthful answer from the robot before the theoretical controller threw in an override.

"Is your master-brain working for the aliens? Are you?"

"Sir!" The robot seemed to draw itself up to full height—illusion, surely. "My master-brain is an integral part of the Civil Defense network of this planet. What you suggest is treason!"

"Okay, okay, don't go melodramatic on me . . ." began the lawyer.

And stopped.

For a light had come on in his brain.

"Came the dawn," he muttered, considering requesting the little robot to give him a good swift kick in the seat of the pants. And it might even oblige, considering the way he had been maligning its cherished master-brain. He swore softly. If ever anybody deserved a kick in the pants, he did—it might jar the brain into gear. And his brain needed jarring.

For he had been allowing the Llralans to push him all over the state of Georgia and doing nothing about it but shooting a few here and there. Cavemen tactics, or at the very best, Apache. And he a supposedly well-educated citizen of the twenty-fifth century—a lawyer!

"No, sir," said the robot, a trifle huffily. "Dawn is eleven minutes and fifty-six seconds away."

"Beg your pardon," said Rierson humbly. He set the safety on his rifle, adjusted the carrying strap and slung the gun across his back. If news of this ever got out, he'd have to move away and change his name. "I most abjectly beg your pardon."

"That isn't necessary, sir," responded the robot, mollified by his change of attitude. "Now—shall we go?"

"We most definitely shall. Lead the way."

"I am sorry, sir, I cannot."

He was brought up short. "Why not?"

"Sir," the robot said, "you *say* that you will go peacefully— and then request me to turn my back and lead the way. Sir, my chest plate is damaged. You caused that damage with your weapon. I think you'd better lead the way."

"Don't you trust me?"

"Not completely, no, sir."

"But I don't know the way!"

"I shall instruct you as we go. I am sorry, sir, but I cannot be too careful. After all, you *did* try to deactivate me."

He thought about arguing, but decided against it. The robot was right, and he didn't feel up to an attempt to rationalize his actions. He felt, in fact, just about as if he had been called down by a circuit court judge for eating popcorn while court was in session. In a word, chastened.

"Sir? Shall we go?"

They went.

Chapter Twenty

Their destination proved to be the uppermost floor of Furnestine's Shopper's Oasis, a thirty-nine-story pile of metal and stone and glass in one of Atlanta's older sections. The robot followed him through the accounting and credit departments, down a corridor with the look and smell of disuse, and called a halt before a door bearing the lettering: CONTROL ROOM, ROBOTS.

Keeping a wary eye on his charge, the diminutive metal man slid around nearer the door, punched a button beneath a tiny grid and said, "One-Zero-Eight returning with merchandise."

The panel slid soundlessly into the wall. Beyond was a tiny room one side of which was composed of a wrap-around bank of view-screens, switches, meters and various other indicators. There was a contour chair before a projecting metal table; on the table stood a slender microphone, a typewriter keyboard and several slots marked IN and OUT.

"Enter, sir," invited a voice from within.

Rierson entered. One-Zero-Eight—the number was stenciled on both shoulders—stationed himself in the doorway.

"Be seated."

That sounded just a bit peremptory—and perhaps it was. No telling what old and half-forgotten relays had closed in the big positronic brain behind that bank of instrumentation when it had realized what was happening to Earth. One-Zero-Eight's instructions regarding human willingness or lack of it to accompany him here had pointed that up eloquently.

Furnestine's robotic master-brain had wanted a human; now that it had one, perhaps it was wasting no time in establishing just what the relationship between man and machine in this particular instance was going to be.

If that were the case, the machine needed setting straight. Rierson wasn't about to act as rubber stamp for any half-baked mechanical intelligence—and the master-brain might as well know it now.

"I'll stand."

"As you will." The mild baritone addressed itself to One-Zero-Eight, seemingly unbothered by his balkiness. "Your outer plate is damaged. Is there anything Maintenance should attend to?"

"No." The robot's steel fingers touched the dent in its steel chest—the dent with the flattened slug from Rierson's rifle still in it. "The damage is to appearance only."

"Good. You have found a human. Is he cooperative?"

"Reluctantly so. He is quite on edge—shot at me the moment he decried my presence."

"That is understandable," decided the master-brain. "The only human in a city of this size—and no doubt hunted by the aliens."

"No doubt at all," inserted Rierson.

"You *are* hunted then?"

"Earnestly."

"Yes. One of my finest salesmen had his brain-casque blasted by some sort of fire weapon. Highly illegal procedure."

"And just what did you do about such highly illegal procedure? Call the police?"

The master-brain's voice was pained. "Sir, I could not. The police, like everyone else with the exception of yourself, are lying unconscious in the city's bomb shelters with a much-reduced pulse rate and respiration. But we had to take *some* action against this lawbreaker."

"Oh, definitely," agreed Rierson. "Like what?"

"We took him into custody. And I notified the continental Civil Defense Emergency Coordination Center in New York City."

"Was the Coordination Center manned?"

"No, sir, but its robotic complement is operating on an

around-the-clock basis, keeping communications open, receiving reports from lesser components of the network such as myself, compiling data and drawing conclusions."

"What did the Center have to say about your taking the lawbreaker into custody?"

"Sir, I was informed that my action was well within the established code of robotic conduct permitted under extraordinary circumstances."

"That term again," complained Rierson. "Anything out of the ordinary really gives you a whopping new range of powers, doesn't it?"

"It does," said the master-brain. "That is logical: extraordinary circumstances require extraordinary measures. That is why, until such time as the police awaken to deal with him, the lawbreaker will be kept in the cell normally reserved for shoplifters or bandits—and that is why One-Zero-Eight, along with his co-workers, was ordered to search for, and bring back if found, a sentient human being."

"With the human in question having very little to say about it," Rierson said.

"True. Ordinarily, the sentiments of the human would take precedence—but in this case the circumstances are sufficient justification for the methods employed. It must be assumed that, whatever the surface reaction, any human left awake to witness the invasion would have only one prime motivation: to drive out the invaders and restore normalcy . . . and that, therefore, appearances to the contrary notwithstanding, I am actually carrying out your will when I have you brought before me, whether or not you consent to being brought."

"That's pretty abstract thinking for a robot," the lawyer commented.

"Yes, sir, but the circumstances call for it."

"Now *there* I agree with you wholeheartedly." He gestured. "All right, you've carried out my will by dragging me here by the scruff of my neck. Mind revealing to me in just what manner you intend to continue carrying it out?"

"Sir, that is what I wish to speak to you about."

"I'm listening."

"Sir, as you are no doubt aware by this time, the strange sleep into which the humans of Atlanta have fallen is not

174

confined to Atlanta—nor are the aliens. The situation exists world-wide."

"The Coordination Center told you that?"

"Yes. Also, I have conversed with the master-brains of other stores in the Furnestine chain—as well as those of various manufacturers and advertising agencies with which I have done business in the past."

"All communications channels are open, then? Strange. While I was downstate—"

"No, sir, not completely open. I suspect the aliens have blanketed all normal channels. I conversed over the emergency alternate circuits; I would have been very surprised if they had succeeded in blocking *those*."

"I see. Go on."

"Yes, sir. Sir, everywhere are the aliens: in the air overhead; riding in heavy, clanking vehicles on the ground; occupying many bomb shelters and sneaking about like children playing hide-and-seek. They are destroying personal and public property at an appalling rate, building their own structures upon the wreckage of what they have torn down with absolutely no regard for building codes or zoning laws, and have deactivated or attempted to deactivate any and all robots trying to approach and reason with them. They have dragged sleeping humans from bomb shelters, piled them like yard goods in their illegal enclosures, and"—the robot's voice took on a new note—"performed still further indignities upon certain of the populace."

Memory of Livar's reluctant reference to certain pastimes traditionally indulged in by Imperial soldiers upon occupied worlds when those worlds contained sufficiently Llralanoid females in sufficiently helpless condition came strongly to mind. His face tightened. So Donovan's warnings hadn't been quite as universally effective as he had been led to believe by the Llralan radioman.

The master-brain plowed on. "Sir, these injustices cannot be allowed to continue. There *must* be a stopping point—but as yet, none is in sight. Whenever individual robots try to interfere, they are viciously smashed. Stunners are no match for the aliens' fire weapons.

"The individual robots are helpless; their master-brains,

individually and collectively, are helpless. The Emergency Coordination Centers, lacking human guidance, are helpless. We *must* act, and yet we cannot, except upon such a limited scale as to assure failure and possibly incite the aliens to further overt acts against the populace. *The entire robot network is, in effect, paralyzed.*

"Sir, my creators and the stockholders of Furnestine's, Incorporated, wished that my resources be at the service of the community in case of a civil emergency; almost all similar corporations have programed their master-brains in a like manner, and the Emergency Coordination Centers were set up by the government to, as their title states, coordinate the civilian effort. The aliens are certainly a civil emergency; this fact has set in motion certain irreversible relays in our brains.

"But our creators never anticipated such an emergency as this. We are helpless in an unprecedented situation without direct human control—without humans to take the responsibility for our actions. Our circuits demand of us action that is presently impossible. With each passing moment, the ensuing conflict is worsened by the continuing inroads of the aliens and the pathetic vulnerability of our humans. Usually, there are the duly delegated officers of the ECC's to take command and issue orders—but the ECC crews sleep as soundly as do the police, as my customers and clerks, as *everybody,* and there is no help to be found there.

"Sir, only as a last resort did the ECC's instruct the master-brains to order their robots into an all-out search for a sentient human being. *Any* sentient human. The search has been under way now for forty-nine hours, fourteen minutes and thirty-one seconds, and you are the sole human it has turned up across all the length and breadth of the inhabited planets of this solar system.

"Sir, the conflict resulting from our inability to take the action which our inbuilt relays demand that we take has reached the critical stage. Already, weaker brains are faltering under the strain. If it is not resolved immediately, the entire Civil Defense network will be of no use to anyone, anyone at all, for much longer. In other words, sir: we, the robots of this solar system, are in serious danger of becoming addled.

We stand ready to act, *but we must have orders to act upon*.

"Sir, will you consent to give us those orders?"

Rierson was just a trifle overwhelmed by it all. When One-Zero-Eight had been insulted by his remarks concerning its master-brain's conspiring with the enemy, and frigidly informed him that he had slandered an integral part of the planetary Civil Defense network, he had realized in an inspired flash that for him there would be no more playing the role of lone guerrilla, no more running and hiding and sniping . . . but he had half-expected a duel of wits with a strong-willed positronic brain hell-bent on doing things its own way and making him the scapegoat for it by somehow extorting his endorsement of its methods. Such things had been known to happen. But he had definitely *not* expected being offered generalship, as it were, of the entire robotic resources of the solar system.

"Sir?" The master-brain seemed afraid its offer had been rejected. "Please, sir?"

"Very well, Percival," said Rierson grandly. "I assume command."

"Very good, sir. Only . . ."

"Only what?"

"Sir, my name isn't Percival."

"It isn't?"

"No, sir. Most of my humans call me Charlie."

"All right, Charlie. Let's get down to business." He unslung his rifle, leaned it against the wall and sat down in the control chair. "I want a complete report on just what's going on where—especially concerning those indignities you mentioned being performed upon the sleepers. And I want robots to stop accosting Larrys and looking under beds for insomniacs. Have all scouts and messengers called in. If they keep running around blindly they're going to make the Larrys nervous. Make 'em nervous enough, and hell's liable to pop. Is that clear?"

"Yes, sir!" There was snap in Charlie's tone.

"Relay it, then. And arrange some way for me to talk directly to the New York Coordination Center if that becomes necessary."

"Yes, sir."

"This is for you personally: I want armed guards on the

tenth floor of this building, and all your other personnel above that level. Any alien attempting to pass the guards is to be stunned and detained."

"It will be done."

While Charlie's meters and indicators came to life in flashing, clicking patterns, Rierson swiveled his chair so he could see out of the one window in the cubby. As he watched, a high-flying flivver appeared in the lower corner, whizzed across and vanished. He smiled grimly. Let them hurry to and fro, let them look for Donovan's grandfather's ghost on three worlds and in a billion hidey holes. Let them think that they didn't really have much to fear, let them ignore Donovan's warnings and have their little games, let them believe for a little while longer that all they had to contend with was one ghost, or one man.

Gremper had just mutiplied himself into a positronic horde.

Chapter Twenty-One

The alien encampment covered what had once been a square block of tall office buildings and lapped over into a pleasant little park. The office buildings were gone; their only remains consisted of several mountainous piles of rubble pushed tidily into the street running behind the camp and shored up against the building fronts across that street. A big semi-rig's tractor cab protruded from one of the heaps; the vehicles in the street had been covered.

The viewscreen that allowed James Rierson to see the entire camp while seated at Charlie's control board presented a panoramic sweep as seen from an elevated vantage point;

every other screen showed it from a variety of angles. Occasionally a Llralan voice murmured from one of the soundgrids as the "shotgun" microphones likewise trained upon the camp by Charlie's scouts picked up a thread of conversation.

"The perimeter," said Charlie, "ends against the 500 Block of Memorial Boulevard on the north, extends south into Quincy Park and bends back to end against the 500 Block of Bragg Street. There are sentry posts in buildings around the camp, and several autogun nests covering strategic approaches."

Rierson grunted in acknowledgment, continued to study Screen One—the one with the vista.

The cleared space had been given over to an orderly, defensible setup which clearly bespoke the military training of its new occupants. One corner—up against the rubble heaps—had been smoothed and leveled by the same machinery that had moved the explosion-toppled former structures out of the way. This area was a motor pool, containing at present several of the huge earth-moving devices, three light tanks, fifteen troop trucks, a pair of cargo copters and one of the big jet flivvers. The number of vehicles present was never the same long; it fluctuated constantly as small but heavily armed convoys arrived and departed on an irregular schedule. Forward of the motor pool but well back from the perimeter was a cluster of prefab huts: headquarters, officers' barracks, field kitchen and a pair of unidentifiable buildings frequented by the camp's brass and a number of Llralans in civilian clothing. Once he had watched cylinders reminiscent of the bottled gas containers used on frontier Federation planets being carried into the latter huts.

All around the perimeter stretched a line of tall, slender and evenly spaced blue-steel posts. Between the posts a vague, bluish shimmer danced—in appearance no more than heat distortion on metal. In fact, nothing could brave that ethereal curtain and survive. At three points in the fence were conventional gates set on heavy, insulated posts. In line with each of these were plascrete blockhouses from which jutted the snouts of autoguns and blast-cannon. Within the fence: squat metal generators supplying the voltage that hummed between those seemingly innocuous posts, and continually pacing, ever-alert sentries.

"This is the installation you have chosen?" The New York Coordination Center's crisp, authoritative voice sounded as if it were speaking over his shoulder.

"Yes."

"A well-fortified one," the ECC noted.

"That's the point: testing my theories on a weak one would prove nothing."

"You are sure that the units of the Furnestine master-brain will be adequate to the task? The entire working force of Atlanta is yours for the asking."

"Thanks, but I'll stick with Charlie this first time around."

"Your confidence is justified," Charlie assured him. "We will not let you down."

"Heroics," inquired the ECC, "from a master-brain? I hardly think the robotic code allows for any such illogical behavior— even under the most trying circumstances."

"This is not a matter of heroics," Rierson cut in before Charlie could demonstrate how very nearly human he was by rapping out some biting retort to that. "Surprise, not overwhelming odds, is what I'm basing my attack on. That, Charlie's newly acquired fund of military lore and a few embellishments of my own."

"I know of those embellishments," said the ECC with prime disapproval. "They make absolutely no sense to me."

"Maybe they don't, to your unimaginative brain. They will to the aliens. And that alone should make them sensible to you: if they work havoc among the aliens, and the working of havoc among the aliens is a desirable thing, then they are sensible."

"That is logical," admitted the Coordination Center, albeit reluctantly.

"You just bet it is."

With that he lapsed into silence and concentrated on the viewscreens before him. The voices coming through the grid were just so much noise—the Larrys in the camp spoke either too swiftly or colloquially for him—but every word was being recorded by Charlie and transmitted via New York to robot linguists halfway across the world. When and if he wanted to know what was being said, all he had to do was so indicate and a near-perfect idiomatic translation would be forthcoming. Which was only one of the services he now had at his fingertips.

Nearly thirty-six hours had passed since he had accepted command of the CD network at Charlie's request—thirty-six hours almost uninterrupted by such trivialities as sleep, and liberally lubricated with coffee. Thirty-six hours in which the very massive complexity of the robot community of Terra and her sister planets had become more awesomely apparent to him than it had ever been in his life; by comparison, the gaping holes in the Llralan Occupation were glaringly evident. Thirty-six hours of nearly continuous verbal reporting on the part of master-brains and ECC's in hundreds of towns and cities across three worlds—reports that spoke of lonely squads of troopers maintaining their deathwatch over the sleeping populace in the close confines of the bomb shelters, of fortified encampments such as the one on Charlie's viewscreens now, of armed convoys and foot patrols and squadrons of aircraft, of humans lugged unceremoniously from bomb shelters to be dumped still sleeping in the pens or, worse, of women awakened and fitted with subsonic slave controls for the use of female-hungry troops.

Thirty-six hours in which to have the terrible omnipresence of the interstellar warships—both those aground and those which would most certainly be in orbit above—driven forcibly home again and again.

If he was going to turn the robots loose on the Llralans, he was going to have to do it in such an manner as to prevent those warships from extracting the terrible vengeance of which they were so completely capable upon defenseless robot centers such as the one in New York. Which meant he could not allow the invaders to become aware that their attackers were robots; robots can be smashed, and the humans directing those robots coerced into surrender by threat of execution of sleeping hostages.

Thus the "embellishments" he had spoken of, and of which the New York Coordination Center had voiced its disapproval. To the logical mind of a robot, the existence of ghosts is the veriest nonsense, and the idea of robots masquerading as something that doesn't exist borders on sheer lunacy.

But as long as his orders were carried out it didn't really matter what the robots thought—what was important was what the Llralans thought. To a Llralan, neither the existence of ghosts nor their ability to pull nasty stunts when so inclined fell into the realm of nonsense—and ghosts can be neither smashed nor coerced.

Charlie had a question. "Sir, are we to be allowed to use firearms? These invaders are not human as the word to which I am attuned is defined, and somehow mere stunning seems too good for them."

The flat, unemotional voice with which it was said seemed to underline the menace in the words. There were rats in Atlanta's wainscoting and Charlie wanted to exterminate them.

"Are you sure your robots can differentiate between the two? There are captive humans down there too, you know."

"I am sure." An image of a gun-toting Larry flashed briefly on one of the screens, superseding the Llralan encampment. "This is an invader." The picture vanished, was replaced by one of a wild-looking individual with tangled hair, matted beard and a haunted look. He recognized it only belatedly as himself.

"And this," said Charlie, almost reverently, "is a human being."

"Couldn't prove it by me—all right, you can have guns. If you can find 'em."

"Oh, we can find them, sir. Furnestine's carries a complete line of sporting and defensive guns. *Everything for the discerning customer,* sir, that is our motto."

"I'm sure it is," agreed Rierson. "New York?"

"Yes?"

"How're the entertainment industry robots coming on their little project?"

The answer was not immediately forthcoming and he knew the ECC was checking latest progress. Then, "They have delved into the film libraries of the last two centuries—that's as far back as tight-beamed solido-image photography goes—and have come up with a number of film clips that fall within the general category you specified."

"Are they available for viewing?"

"Yes. Is that your wish?"

"It is."

"A viewscreen will have to be freed."

"Oh—of course. Charlie, connect Screen Eight into New York."

"Yes, sir."

While the arrangements were being made he kept his attention upon the enemy installation as seen on Screen One. A convoy was arriving, and another departing. He watched them with interest, noting how they performed their tasks with soldierly precision.

And just how were they going to perform, he wondered, when a skirmish line of solido-images materialized out of the night and passed unharmed through their sparkling fence, followed closely by Charlie's ponderous and nearly indestructible warehousemen, when the utility hatches leading to underground roadbeds suddenly opened and emitted a stream of gun-brandishing cleaning robots into their midst? If things went according to plan, the images—which would be as weird and ghostly as Terran film libraries could provide—would throw them into utter confusion. It was very possible that some poor fool would start babbling about phantoms and the undead. That, he calculated, would be the final straw needed to totally wreck any effective resistance that might be mounted against his steel-and-printed-circuit raiders.

That's the way it *should* work, anyhow.

Now to see.

Chapter Twenty-Two

Bradford Donovan stared morosely at his reflection in a big, darkened viewscreen across the room, much depressed by what he saw. In the screen was framed the likeness of a gloomy-looking character wearing the shipboard khakis of a Federation Navy captain. The unfamiliar uniform was too tight across the chest and binding in the crotch, but that wasn't what was bothering him. What *was* bothering him was why he was dressed like this in the first place.

The office of Lieutenant General Quiror, Penmaster of Atlanta, was a tiny room in one corner of the penmaster's prefabricated headquarters, and at present it was jammed full. There was Quiror himself, his chief of staff, an Imperial Intelligence specialist fiddling with a slave-circuit console, and a pair of riflemen holding their guns on Donovan and the three Terrans with him—Michael Harris, Dan Rierson and Paul Nogales.

And, lastly, there was Drelig Sjilla.

He it was who had ordered the clothing change, and he it was who had explained the reason for it to them while—with the exception of Rierson—they had been compelled to strip to the skin and outfit themselves in pilfered Federation military garb.

Donovan shook his head. No, it was still impossible to believe. James Rierson, nephew of Daniel, prowling the Georgian countryside, the very embodiment of his, Donovan's, grandfather's ghost? It was too incredible. To him, James Rierson was only a vague, unimportant memory—a blurred

184

face among many blurred faces parading before his mind's eye and reminiscent of a time gone forever. A time when Bradford Donovan had walked on living legs and wrested a livelihood from a hostile world with gun and trap and guts. But Sjilla was speaking.

" . . . the problem is very simple: we must lure into the open and capture or kill one exceedingly irritating Unaffected who has been snarling operations in this area. The solution is equally simple, but requires some explaining."

"You will have my full attention," rumbled the barrel-chested penmaster. " 'Irritating' is a mild word for what this Spook was putting us through a few days ago—though, I'll admit, things have calmed down since he escaped from Zowal in Baxter."

"That's what worries me," Sjilla said. "It's been the better part of a Terran week since that Baxter business—without so much as a single sighting of our friend out there with the rifle. That means he is lying low, waiting for the pressure to ease off. And when a man of his type is allowed to lie low and have time to think things out, it's a dead certainty that you'll hear from him again—and that you won't like what you'll be hearing!"

The penmaster grunted. "I could name you a lot of men who didn't like what they heard from him last time. They heard death rattling in their own throats."

"True—but next time it could be infinitely worse. The initiative will be his. That is, it'll be worse if we don't do something first. That's why I'm here; here is where an air patrol with Llralasteel detectors found abandoned the flivver he used to escape from Baxter. And that's why I need the services of Colonel Visstor here, and two rifle companies. My four prisoners"—he waved at the Terrans—"my assistant and myself will complete the cast of a little play I wish to enact for our friend out there with the rifle."

"You and three of the Rekks"—Quiror indicated Donovan, Nogales and Harris—"are wearing enemy uniforms. Your prisoners are to be equipped by your assistant with subsonic slave controls. I smell a trap."

"Exactly right. I want our friend out there with the rifle to see five Terrans—four of them military officers and the fifth his uncle—fighting a running battle with Llralan forces. If I judge him rightly—and I think I do—he will be inclined to horn in. And when he does"—the Security Chief toyed idly with the oak leaves on his collar that made him a Federation Army major—"his trouble-making days are over. If a rifleman doesn't get him, Major Donald Shey will."

"The major being you?"

"The major being me."

"You are sure"—the hard-faced old soldier glanced uneasily in Donovan's direction—"that you are after one . . . man?"

Donovan grinned. In the face of overwhelming proof to the contrary, doubt as to the mortality of the Spook of Baxter was still stubbornly rooted in at least a few minds. The word had been getting around.

"Absolutely certain," responded Sjilla flatly. "I can even give you his name: James Rierson."

"And just how do you know that this—this Rierson—will be watching your act?"

"If he's anywhere in Atlanta, he'll be watching. Tomorrow at noon a Terran space scout will appear at low altitude over Atlanta, pursued by half a dozen fighter flivvers. The seven craft will be manned by robot pilots and will execute a spectacular air battle during which the space scout will destroy two flivvers and then crash in flames near the western outskirts."

"And then what?"

"And then my little troupe goes into its act, having moved to the area under cover of darkness. We shall engage in a long and noisy skirmish in which no one is hurt but plenty of property is torn up. If we draw no attention, we will then disengage and fight a running battle across the city, during which time two rifle companies must make flame like ten, and the four remaining roboflivvers—all Sarno could spare—must impersonate a veritable horde of aircraft. We will make a stand, then fall back to stand again until we get results."

"That," remarked Colonel Visstor, "seems like an awful lot of trouble to go to for one Rekk."

"Does it? Maybe it does. But know this: as long as James Rierson runs loose he is a terrible danger to the perfect picture of a conquered world Sarno wants to present to Federation bargainers. Let them think that *one* thing is not as he says and they will begin to wonder about *all* things. Too much wondering, and they'll send in a fleet to call his bluff. It won't do them any good—but it won't do *us* any good, either. We need these three planets as a bargaining counter, not an untenable beachhead far behind enemy lines."

He paused for a moment, added, "Besides which, certain low-mentality elements of this fleet have been swayed by a certain prisoner's irresponsible tongue-flapping. They have been warned to keep still, but as long as Rierson runs loose it will be impossible to make them do so. Soldiers always fear the worst—that way they are never disappointed—so the tale might grow simply as a respite to boredom, and hang on until it comes to be believed. You might be interested to know that Sarno has considered this alone enough of a threat to have contemplated obliteration of Atlanta if he could be sure that would erase the cause."

Visstor had no comeback for that. Quiror made no immediate remark. The guards were silent; there was only the subdued buzz of the slave-circuit monitor in the specialist's hands.

"You cannot," inserted Donovan into the thoughtful silence, "kill what is already dead."

All eyes darted involuntarily toward him. Number One guard had started violently when he spoke, now looked as if he didn't appreciate what had been said.

"I warned you about that before we left the flagship," said Sjilla, cold anger in his tones. "I told you there would be none of that this trip."

"So you did. So what?"

"So . . . you must learn obedience." He motioned to Number Two guard. "Know how to use a lektro-whip?"

"Yes, sir."

"Excellent. Take this Rekk outside and use it. Five strokes, three-quarters max."

"Yes, sir!"

Donovan's stomach did a sick flip-flop. It seemed he could already feel those searing jolts tearing at his nerves. He licked dry lips. "You'd better not," he warned. His voice lacked the menace he had tried to instill in it.

The guard gestured with his gun. "Up, frambule!"

"For each stroke, Larry, a month of torture for you—"

"Donovan, *shut up!*" Sjilla's fist came down on the camp table, hard.

"Let's go, frambule." The guard reached for him.

Donovan started getting to his feet. "Your sons born and yet unborn shall pay for what you do this night . . ." he began desperately.

And the guard hesitated! Donovan had touched a nerve.

"Oh, for Sirri's sake!" That was Sjilla, surging upright, knocking his chair over backward, striding forward. He snatched the whip from its hook on the soldier's belt, snapped his wrist. The metallic coils snaked along the floor. He pressed the stud in the whip's butt, flicked the tip up . . .

There was pain.

Donovan threw up his arms in ineffectual defense, shrank back against the wall. The first awful jolt was followed closely by a second, a third—he heard himself crying out, knew Sjilla was destroying all his carefully wrought lies with each stroke of the whip, and knew he was powerless to prevent it.

The wracking fire along his nerve endings kicked him off his perch and onto the floor. Sjilla's voice came relentlessly over gulfs of distance, joining the cadence of the whip:

"So *this* is the mighty minion of the undead? *This* the grandson protected by his grandfather? And where *is* this omnipotent guardian *now*, eh? Why does he not *hear* the cries of his troubled descendant? *Why* does he not—"

There was a scream, and Donovan realized dimly that it had not been his. He also realized belatedly that the lights were out, heard Quiror threatening death and destruction for all at the top of his voice. Sjilla was cursing steadily in two languages and with an undertone of fear in his voice. Came a sharp blue dazzle as a seargun went into action. A choked cry and distant thud answered the shot. Lying on the edge of consciousness while white-hot flashes of pain rocketed through his body, Donovan tried to muster himself—tried and failed. The lektro-whip was not being used any more. He relaxed and let the darkness hovering all around pour into his brain.

Outside, the frantic crackle of searguns mingled with the guttering roar of Terran flamers and the whiplash report of many rifles.

When the lights went out, and one of the riflemen shot the other in the darkness and confusion, Daniel Rierson reacted with the cat-quick reflexes even age had not dulled. He launched his lean body at the Intelligence technician—it was he who had screamed when the lights went out, leaping up in abject terror, his precious console forgotten. The old outhunter's hand chopped once, viciously, and the Llralan would never know terror—or any other emotion—ever again. With deft fingers he found the Llralan's holstered seargun and jerked it free; then he was moving for the door in a nightfighter's crouch, trying to outline targets against what light might seep in from outside. The Llralans were still blinded by the searbolt that had killed the guard; he was not.

There! The gun swiveled, spat with deadly accuracy. The remaining guard stumbled sideways, crashed across the camp table, taking it to the floor with him. Rierson would have liked to stay and blast all the Llralan brass in the room, but there wasn't time. If the mocker had been right, his nephew was out there somewhere—and he had to be warned.

Finding the door with precision learned on hundreds of nocturnal excursions on a dozen worlds, he fired a sustained burst into the lock section, threw his sinewy weight forward violently. The door gave, and he was through into the outer confines of the headquarters hut, passing through the confusion of upset office personnel like the phantom Donovan had dreamed up to haunt the invaders, and so into the night beyond. Just outside he halted, ducked to one side and flattened against the wall.

All around was pandemonium. Blue lightning played across the area between the huts and the outside fence, and streams of brilliant red flame answered in a withering crossfire. To one side, intermittent orange flashes speared off toward an unseen target—slug-throwers in operation. The outer fence's electric veil was gone, and towering shapes loomed between the useless posts, red flame spurting from their midsections.

189

Something skittered toward him crablike and he brought his gun up, ready to fire.

It was a short, barrel-shaped thing hung all about with tentacle-like appendages and topped by a plastic dome. Two of the metal tentacles were bent away from its body, one gripping a pistol and the other an atomic torch.

For a long moment, man and machine confronted each other tensely. Then a red bulb glowed beneath the plastic dome and a hoarse metallic voice rasped out the single word "Human" and then it was gone, wheeling madly around the corner of the prefab. Seconds later there came staccato burst of shots, a white atomic glare. A shriek sounded, then lurid Llralan curses.

A gun-wielding office clerk burst through the open door, halted in dismay at sight of what was happening to his camp. Thus reminded of his predicament, Rierson snapped a shot into the other's body, saw him fold without a sound, and started cautiously around the building after the little cleaning robot. Around him the battle raged. Over in the motor pool, a tank's engine snarled to life and it chugged forward, guns sniffing for targets. Five larger-than-life shapes turned as one and angled toward it with a ponderous grace that somehow brought the image of tall sailing ships to mind.

The tank's autoguns started firing, and blue light haloed the five vaguely humanoid figures, making their steel bodies gleam and sparkle. One of the five faltered, began to stagger. From the remaining four a sudden and murderous barrage thundered at the Llralan tank. There were red incandescences of flamer fire, the yellow-orange flash of slug-throwers. The tank slewed sideways, still firing, climbed the steep hill of rubble behind the motor pool and then, very slowly, rocked off its wide treads and crashed back like a dying turtle. There came the strong reek of spilled fuel, and flames began to crackle around the battered hulk.

He wasted no more time. Heedless of the beautiful, deadly splendor of the fire fight he sprinted straight for the inoperative perimeter fence. The fighting had moved inward, and fewer and fewer defenders were shooting back. Most of those had backed into a tight square in the wrecked motor pool, trying to load onto the available airships and fight a rearguard action simultaneously. Out here, near the fence, all was quiet, with only the odor of discharged energy and charred flesh to indicate that the battle had passed this way. He passed one of the small cleaning robots lying in a broken heap, hurdled a pair of Llralans who had fled the wrong way before the fence was deactivated, and was out of camp.

He maintained a steady dogtrot as long as he could, and the sounds of conflict died away behind him. When bursting lungs and out-of-condition muscles called a halt, he drew back into the protection of a doorway and fought to regain his breath, cursing the seventy years and inactivity that made him tire so easily nowadays.

When his breath was coming more easily and his heart had settled down a little, he left the doorway and pushed on, exhilaration pulsing through him. He was free! No more shackles, no more tiny alien cells—free! For a while, that very fact alone blotted out his original purpose for making the break. Once more he was his own man, with an entire planet to roam and with a gun in his hand to insure his continued freedom.

But this was not Risstair, nor Gratlafn, nor New Sedalia, nor even the northern steppes of Venus nor the barren plains of Mars. This was Terra, with three billion sleeping inhabitants and horizon-obscuring cities and invading armies . . . and an enigmatic individual who did not sleep, but stalked through the cities and across the planet and killed with seeming impunity to the invader's armed might.

And time was running out for the Spook of Baxter. His nephew or not, he had to be found and warned.

Hefting his gun, he kept bearing away from the camp, sticking close to shadows and treading carefully.

Chapter Twenty-Three

Slowly, by painful degrees, he came back to consciousness. Great blobs of pain whirled before his eyes in fiery displays; his head resounded like an anvil in an echo chamber. His entire body was afire from the lash of the lektro-whip and he seemed to feel hot flashes of misery all the way down to the tips of his plastic toes.

With a dull kind of shock, he realized he was no longer in the alien command post. Nor was he sprawled on his back as he had been when he lost consciousness. Instead, he was stumbling along through the clamoring night, guided by a steel grip on his collar. Voices were conversing tensely, seeming to come from a great distance, and it took him a small eternity to recognize the voice of his captor as that of Sjilla. The Llralan mocker was frog-marching him along one-handed with an exhibition of sinewy strength Donovan would not have thought present in that lean frame.

Belatedly he became aware of his surroundings. Clouds of concrete dust swirled out of the darkness, settling over them in a choking pall. Nearby, irregular flashes of searfire stabbed out against an unseen and unknown enemy. Farther away, a minor war seemed to be in full swing. The crackle of energy discharges and boom of heavy explosions came steadily. Half-seen forms flitted through the night like grotesque inhabitants of a bad dream. Voices raised in pain and fear keened thinly above the general uproar.

The confusion of the night blended into the screaming of his electricity-torn nerves to become one big, pulsing horror. He felt consciousness leaving, and with it sanity—his tortured body cried aloud for surcease, but its voice was lost in the turmoil.

And still they marched.

Stolidly, surely, inexorably across the face of that flaming, thundering hell—Donovan going before, lost in his own suffering, with Sjilla close on his heels, one hand wrapped in the Terran's collar, the other gripping a flamer. Behind came Quiror, Visstor and a pair of soldier-clerks, shuttling Nogales and Harris along before them as living shields.

A titanic shape loomed out of the drifting dust and smoke. To Donovan's bleared eyes it seemed to float and shimmer above ground level like some inimical specter. Bright-burning, inhuman eyes glittered down on the procession. The truck driver felt a sudden yank on his collar, was hauled up strangling. He was dimly aware of Sjilla waving his hand at the others, muttering rapidly under his breath.

The giant shifted. A deep-voiced challenge sounded, an organ-note of inquiry raised against the pandemonium. Something buried down deep underneath the overlaid impressions of the past days stirred, and memory came. A warehouseman! They were facing one of the big Physak manual-labor robots, a trademark of which was the oddly musical bass voice designed to fit the bulk and stature of the speaker. And now he could see the long-barreled rifle held lightly in the robot's dexterous fingers. An explorer's flamer! How long had it been since he'd taken his out of its tarl-fur sheath and snapped it to his shoulder, remembering days long past? It seemed millennia at the very least.

But Sjilla was replying to that challenge in English, his voice bearing the weight of authority. As fragments of that reply came to Donovan's ears through gaps in the roar of the conflict, the sudden hope that had come with recognition of the robot was extinguished as speedily. Was there *no* situation with which the mocker could not cope?

". . . these are my prisoners," Sjilla was saying. "The fighting is yonder . . . go before . . . reinforcements are needed. . . ."

The big robot rumbled assent and faded into the night. Donovan slumped tiredly, once more overwhelmingly aware of the damage done to his nervous system by Sjilla's use of the whip. The flamer prodded his aching ribs.

"Move," came the sibilant hiss. "We've got a long walk ahead of us . . ."

Something scuttled out of the dark, checked and waved octopus-like tentacles wildly. A hand torch's beam swept across them. In its glareback Donovan could make out a small maintenance robot. What in the . . . ? Were all the robots in the city up in arms? If so, who had activated them? Who . . . ?

The flamer jerked out of his ribs, spat a torrent of flame at the little robot. The machine wabbled, tipped over, righted itself, went trundling away unevenly to the left.

The gun came back, scalding his skin with its white-hot muzzle.

"Now let's *move* . . ."

They moved.

The ground-radar was filled with utter confusion. James Rierson pored over it anxiously, trying to get some kind of idea as to how the battle was progressing. The control room's viewscreens were of little help; they were hazy with smoke and lighted only by sporadic glares as one side or another opened fire through the murk.

Finally he gave up and asked Charlie.

"Sir," the master-brain said, "the battle is progressing nicely. I regret to inform you of the loss of five store-units in action, but the casualties of the enemy are ten times that and mounting rapidly. We have smashed their main defenses, split their forces and have the main group of defenders backed up against a blank wall trying to load into aircraft. They will never get off the ground."

"Good, Charlie." What else was there to say? The battle was progressingly nicely—but not at all as he had intended. He just didn't have the heart to tell Charlie and dampen the master-brain's enthusiasm; he was not that accustomed to the role of commanding general. He went back to studying the radar.

The Llralans were losing, all right—but they shouldn't even have been fighting. The sudden onslaught of ghastly specters chosen from among the most gruesome of all B-grade solido-image horror movies of the past two centuries should have shattered their nerve, dissolved their will to resist. But it hadn't; and, upon reflection, he realized why.

He had hit them with too much too soon—had underestimated his opponents and overplayed his hand. Before they could fully digest what was going on and get scared they had found themselves engaged in a savage fire fight, and had reacted with the reflexes of trained combat troops. Almost without conscious thought they had fought back, forming little pockets of desperate resistance against the overrunning robots —fought back with courage. Llralan soldiers had never been afraid of a fight—just a little leery of phantoms was all.

But courage was not enough this night. With Charlie's succinct rundown he was able to correspond the wildly agitated blips on the radar to what must be happening out there. Sure enough, a pattern was becoming clearer with each passing moment. Here a spearhead slashed through, there an arm reached out to encircle and contain, and there . . .

His jaw dropped. A gap had appeared in one of the curving lines of attackers, and a small clump of blips moved through from the direction of the alien headquarters—not running scared, but moving with slow determination. Several times attacking units approached, hesitated, then turned away. Once a unit flared from green to orange, then went out.

"Charlie."

"Yes, sir?"

"What does it mean when a blip goes orange and then fades?"

"It means, sir, that the unit has been lost."

"I thought so. Get me a camera-robot to sweep . . . uh, Vector Sixteen, will you?"

"Right away, sir."

He drummed fingers impatiently while the robot got into position, watching with mounting alarm as the clump of steadily-moving dots went beyond the cleared perimeter of the pen and entered a street.

"Robot in position," Charlie reported. "Screen Six."

"Good. Send it along Bragg Street."

"Yes, sir. Which direction, sir?"

"West. And have four armed units follow it. There may be trouble."

"Yes, sir."

Screen Six glowed, filled momentarily with swirling streaks, then cleared to show a night-darkened street only dimly visible through the robot's night lens. Walls lining the street marched ponderously by on either side of the camera, swaying slightly with the motion of the robot.

"There!" Rierson came half out of his chair. Figures were moving ahead of the robot, moving awkwardly, several being dragged bodily along by the others. There were the gray Llralans uniforms, yes, and . . .

The picture died. Very abruptly, very finally. He switched his startled gaze to the radar in time to see the symbol representing the camera-robot wink out, and a symbol he should have noticed before move from the line of interference that was the buildings along the street and race to rejoin the departing group.

"Ambush!" he gritted. "Don't let 'em get away, Charlie! *After* 'em!"

Charlie, confused by orders that made absolutely no sense to his orderly brain, simply continued to direct operations around the pen while the four units detailed to follow the camera-robot came to the spot where it had fallen and stopped, awaiting further orders. By the time he had settled down enough to give cogent instructions, the group of fleeing dots was off radar. A quick change of focus revealed nothing; they must have gone below ground. He ordered a quick level shift from surface to below surface. That, too, was a waste of time. The group had vanished as if swallowed up.

And then, "Sir!"

"What is it?"

"Salesman Five-Two-One reports a lone Terran, sir, walking down Vincent Street."

"Bring him in."

"Sir, he is not inclined to come along. He is armed and refuses to cooperate."

"Oh, hell! Has Five-Two-One got a stunner?"

"No, sir."

"Well, get a unit there with one. If he won't cooperate,

stun him and bring him along. It's for his own protection—the streets aren't safe." This last was said with an irony that seemed to escape Charlie.

"Indeed they aren't, sir. It shall be done immediately."

He leaned back tiredly in the control chair, closed his eyes. The battle at the pen was all but over with his robots victorious, but it wasn't the victory he had wanted. The first Terran he knew of beside himself not sleeping under the effects of Sarno's Dust had been spotted and would be brought in whether he wanted to come or not, but that didn't elate him, either. Far from it. That one brief glimpse of the fleeing group had been enough to spoil any small satisfaction he might have felt.

It had shown several Terrans being hustled away by a handful of Llralans—the very kind of Terrans whose company and advice he could have used at this juncture. Military men and officers all, from the cut of their uniforms.

"Charlie," he said. "Charlie, is the Terran reported by Five-Two-One wearing any sort of military uniform?"

"One moment, sir. I will find out." There was a pause while the master-brain communicated with its robot. Then, "No, sir, no military uniform. Only a civilian suit which Salesman Five-Two-One considers sartorially fit only for an outworld hick."

"Oh, great, just great. I finally get somebody on my side, and it has to be a bum."

"I am truly sorry, sir." Charlie sounded as if he felt personally responsible.

"Such a barbarian he doesn't even trust a robot," Rierson went on, warming to his subject.

"Sir," said Charlie gently, "in all due fairness it must be recorded that you yourself evinced no great eagerness to cooperate with Salesman One-Zero-Eight when first he contacted you. I believe he still has the dent in his body armor made by your bullet."

"Oh, shut up! And tell me how that bunch managed to get through the lines."

While Charlie struggled with contradictory orders, he lapsed into a moody silence. Damn all logical, fair-minded robots to perdition, anyway—how can a man work up a good

197

righteous rage when a mechanical monstrosity is looming over his shoulder to remind him of his former sins?

It just didn't seem fair.

Chapter Twenty-Four

The dapper little sales robot escorted him through a long alleyway roofed over against the night sky, turned into a gentle ramp leading down to a stretch of underground road-bed and so to a wide set of doors fronting on a freight platform.

Mounting the platform it turned to him. "We are here."

"Where is here?" Dan Rierson wanted to know. He still mistrusted this metal man with the too-ready stunner, but he had chosen to come along rather than be stunned and lugged. He preferred to meet whatever awaited him head-on. And he had been permitted to keep his gun, either deliberately or as an oversight on their part—an oversight he had not been eager to call to their attention.

The robot bringing up the rear came into view—the one with Five-Two-One painted on its chest and with a deer rifle in its hands.

"Here, sir, is Furnestine's Shopper's Oasis."

"And is this where your master-brain resides?"

"It is, sir."

"Let's go, then."

"This way, sir." The robot moved to one of the doors, leaned against it. It slid back on well-oiled tracks. Rierson caught a diffused yellow glow within. The robot stood for a

198

moment as if in deep thought, then said, "It is safe to enter now, sir. They are apprised of our coming."

"They?"

"The sentries, sir." Five-Two-One stepped within, waited while Rierson and the second salesman followed. They moved across the warehouse at his motion. The door slid shut behind them, and a ten-foot metal man stood silently there with one hand on the door, the other cradling an explorer's flamer, pistol fashion.

"Whaa . . . ?" Rierson backed away from the salesmen, hand on the butt of his gun.

"Just one of the sentries, sir. Pay no heed."

"I'll damn well pay heed if I want to—and this thing begins to smell more and more like one big trap. I'm not going any farther until I get some answers—and fast!" His fingers curled around the seargun's grips.

"What answers?" The robot gave every appearance of a very human exasperation.

"Who's running this show, for a starter."

"Furnestine's Master Control, sir."

"And is Furnestine Master Control a robot or a human?"

"Furnestine Master Control is my master-brain, sir."

"A robot, then."

"A robot, yes, sir."

"And who controls Furnestine Master Control?"

"I do."

That reply came from a deep pool of shadow in one corner of the cavernous warehouse. Rierson shaded his eyes against the weak glow of a single overhead light, his gun in his hand instinctively.

"Who's there?" The words were harsh, fear-tinged.

The answer was amused. "Only us chickens, Uncle."

The gun wavered. "Jim? Jim, is that you?" So the mocker had been right—his nephew was also behind that attack on the pen! Suddenly, Daniel Rierson felt very old and very tired and very out of touch with things—as if he had slept a long time, dreaming deeply, and been suddenly jarred awake to find that time had passed him by. The gun dropped to his side as a shadowy figure detached itself from the bigger darkness and moved forward, slender barrel of a slug-firing rifle aslant across a bent elbow. He shook his head as a fighter might after having sustained a hard series of jabs to the head. "Jim . . ." he repeated dazedly.

"None other, though I doubt you can recognize me with this beard." The big man with the rifle was coming forward, grinning. "Welcome to the sole guerrilla organization now operating on Terra. That makes you a charter member, being a relative of the president, founder and chief dogface in the ranks. This war seems to be turning into a personal vendetta. The Riersons against the Larrys."

"Personal vendetta," Dan Rierson repeated slowly. "The Riersons against the . . . Jim, I need a drink. A long, stiff one."

"Sure, Uncle, you *do* look a little pale around the gills." James Rierson looked at Five-Two-One. "You heard the man. A bottle of bourbon. Right, Uncle?"

"Right."

"Well, what are you waiting for?" he asked the robot. "Get going—and don't tell me Furnestine's hasn't got a liquor store."

"Oh, *no,* sir." The robot sounded offended. "The very finest stock. That is our policy: *Everything—*"

"*—for the discerning customer,*" the younger Rierson finished. "I know. Seems I've heard that somewhere before. So get to getting—can't you recognize a discerning customer when you see one?"

Five-Two-One wasted no more time.

Sjilla racked the field radio's speaker disgustedly, stood up. "No use. It's not working. I can't send, I can't receive. Fat lot of good it did to lug it along in the first place."

"Then we're stuck?" Colonel Visstor asked. He was standing by one of the business office's wide windows, peering at the street from behind a curtain.

"Unelss we can signal a flivver, we are. Those accursed robots are lurking everywhere; we don't dare move."

"We could commandeer a Terran aircar," suggested Quiror hopefully, tinkering with the sights of the one sear-rifle they had left. "You know how to fly them, you could—"

"We'd be shot down by our own side before we could get

airborne," Sjilla squelched the idea. "No, we're hemmed in pretty good."

"You better believe it," put in Bradford Donovan from where he lay tiredly on a wide couch, under the gun of one of the soldier-clerks. "You're way out of your depth. Phantoms and robots—a likely combination, eh?"

"Oh, shut up!"

"Uh-uh. I *like* to twist the knife. Twist it 'til you scream. Besides"—the corners of his mouth tipped upward in a grim smile—"you lost your whip in all the excitement back there. So what are you going to do—tongue-lash me?"

"I don't need a whip for the likes of you!"

"Now *there's* an interesting prospect." Donovan's smile broadened into a grin. "Any time, Sjilla, old rat, any time. I'm owing you, anyway, for that whip."

"All that is irrelevant," Quiror said. "What is relevant is: how do we get out of this predicament and inform Sarno of our survival?"

"That's your problem, not mine," Donovan replied breezily. "Myself, I'm ready to accept your abject surrender any time you care to offer it."

Visstor eyed him incredulously. "You *are* addled."

"Am I?" The Terran yawned broadly. "Maybe I am— but remember what happened when Sjilla started beating up on me. Grandpa didn't like that. Naturally, he had to interfere—"

"Oh, for Chrissakes, Donovan!" That was Paul Nogales. "I'm beginning to agree with these Larrys. You're either addled or believe in running a bad joke into the ground." He played nervously with his naval admiral's ornate cap. "Can't you just be quiet?"

Michael Harris smiled quietly. "The same thing applies to you, Nogales. Shut up. Let Donovan drive 'em crazy— then we'll walk out of here free."

"And your families will suffer," promised Sjilla.

"If our families suffer—" began Donovan threateningly— and never got it finished. The door leading to the outside corridor burst inward to admit the second soldier-clerk, who slammed it behind him. Sjilla was on his feet, flamer drawn, before he got the door closed; Quiror and the other trooper had him covered. Visstor's gun was half out of its holster.

The soldier pawed feebly in the air, eyes rolling wildly, trying to regain his breath as he sagged limply against the panel.

The door opened a second time, pushing him forward. He bleated in terror, set his feet and attempted to shove it closed again. A massive hand reached through, sent him spinning away, and a blast of searing energy slammed him to the floor, his body a smoking ruin.

A Physak stood stolidly in the door, stooped over to clear the nine-foot opening. Wisps of acrid smoke curled from its flamer and drifted around its impassive metal features.

Sjilla fired. Half-crouched, his utterly human features set in a savage mask, he advanced across the room on the robot, a solid beam of fire hosing its frame, seeking a chink in its permasteel armor. While the door frame around it crumpled and buckled, the robot stood its ground doggedly, bringing its own weapon to bear. That cascade of intolerable energy centered on the gun and droplets of molten steel began to drop away, hissing on the plastile floor. The robot maintained its position, jerking its trigger finger convulsively, but the gun was destroyed.

Sjilla stopped firing abruptly, turned on his heel. Behind him, a shudder ran through the big robot; it took an uncertain step forward, faltered, and crashed down. The room shook.

"Let's go," snapped Sjilla. "They've found us. Out the back way."

The surviving trooper gestured with his pistol, urging the three Terans ahead of him. They hesitated.

"Move!" gritted Sjilla. "We've no time for games. Move or we'll kill you right here."

They moved. With the half-panicked Llralan soldiers crowding close and Sjilla bringing up the rear, they left the office and headed down a darkened corridor at a near run. Behind them, a heavy tramp of metal feet urged them on.

The trooper-clerk loped ahead, yanked open a door—and dived to one side. A flamer bolt snapped through the space occupied by his body a moment before. He came to his knees, fumbled in his belt and flung something through the opening.

"Down!" That was Quiror, shouting in Llralan. They flattened.

The detonation from the tiny bomb was deafening. Debris poured through the door. Then they were up and running through the roiling dust, going out into the cold sunlight at a dead run. Sjilla gestured leftward along a service alley.

"This way."

They were three-quarters of the way toward an intersecting street when two ponderous shapes moved out of the shadows to stand shoulder to shoulder. Sunlight gleamed on their blue-steel casques, was reflected from the barrels of their guns.

"Back!" Sjilla snapped a shot down the alley, saw the shot go wide and cascade bricks over the waiting figures. The robots didn't stir.

Back they went, past the ruined doorway, over the twisted shapes of two little octopodal cleaning robots. Sjilla paused only long enough to acquire a second flamer from a relaxed tentacle and rejoined the group with a gun in either hand.

Ahead of them, a second pair of Physaks trundled out into the alley and faced their advance. They halted, the Llralans in confusion, the Terrans hardly daring to believe what was happening.

Sjilla's eyes had a trapped look as he surveyed first one duo and then the other. Then he seemed to reach a decision, and the doubt erased itself magically from his face.

"All right, if that's the way it's got to be," he said, almost to himself.

He squared his shoulders unconsciously. "Quiror, we're going out past these two. I'll lead the way. When they go down, run like blazes. And you make sure somebody gets back to Sarno to carry the tale, eh?"

"But—"

"No buts, general. As an Intelligence Security Chief, I outrank you. And I just gave you an order. Clear?"

The general seemed moved to protest further, took a long look at the set of Sjilla's face and changed his mind. "Clear."

"Good. Let's go then."

He faced about, thrust the pair of flamers before him and started down the alley toward the waiting Physaks. Behind them, the first two had begun a deliberate advance. The trooper tugged out another of those incredibly powerful hand bombs and calculated the range. Sjilla moved steadily down the alley.

"They'll burn you before you get in range," Quiror commented in the sudden eerie stillness.

"Not a chance," Sjilla said over his shoulder. "To them, I'm a Terran. Terran robots don't burn Terrans. It's impossible."

Donovan swore. The mocker knew what he was talking about. He began to believe Sjilla was going to get out of this one, too.

Sjilla paced onward. The robots before him had begun moving, too—straight toward him. The robots behind were coming with the inexorableness of fate. The trooper nursed his bomb and waited. Visstor kept his sidearm trained on the Terrans. Quiror himself was watching the Security Chief.

"Are you sure it's impossible?" he queried. "They look awful ready to shoot."

"I'm sure," Sjilla replied calmly. "You don't live among the Terrans as long as I have without making sure."

He raised his twin guns a fraction more, and Donovan saw his shoulders move as he drew in a deep breath. Sjilla wasn't as sure as he was pretending—for all he knew, he was walking straight into flaming death. The Terran shook his head begrudgingly. You had to admire courage like that, no matter who had it, or whose side he was on.

Sjilla moved another few steps. The robots marched toward him, guns leveled. Donovan held himself ready to get out of the way when the shooting started—but how does one get out of the way when one is directly in the line of fire and confined on either side by sheer walls? The trooper shifted his bomb to his throwing hand, made ready to fling. Donovan looked at Nogales and Harris. Their faces were mirroring the tension he felt building in himself as the taut little vignette drew to its inescapable climax; and if it was hard on them, it certainly wasn't pleasant fun for their captors. Quiror and the trooper were equally impassive—only their faces showed their strain—but Visstor looked ready to climb the walls. He felt a twist in his guts. The first outbreak and that jumpy colonel was going to start squirting searfire. And he, Donovan, was in the way.

"Okay, fella, you can cut out the heroics."

Donovan nearly jumped out of his skin at the unexpected voice. He saw alarm flash in Visstor's eyes to be superseded by doubt and then confusion. For one microsecond, his fingers had tightened around the gun butt, but they relaxed now. Donovan sweated. It had been close, close.

The words had caught them all flatfooted. Even the Physaks seemed taken by surprise. They stopped in their tracks, stood rooted. Belatedly the Llralans and their prisoners turned to look at the source of that tension-breaking voice.

A Terran stood framed in the wrecked doorway through which they had entered the alley—a huge, wild-looking specimen with a dark, unkempt beard and a rifle held ready in his hands.

The trooper muttered an oath, started to activate his bomb —and wilted on the spot, the potent cylinder rolling from nerveless fingers to glitter inimically in the sun. Visstor stared at him distractedly; Quiror's eyes widened. Neither the man in the doorway nor the Physaks had made a discernible move.

"A simple bit of misdirection," came the big man's voice. He was speaking in laboring, heavily accented Llralan, answering the question before it was asked. "The soldier saw myself and the Physaks as the main threat. He was wrong." A hand left the rifle's stock to gesture vaguely. *Those* are the threat."

Donovan followed the direction of his wave—upward. He heard the involuntary gasp from Visstor as he did likewise. Lined along the roofs above were a good dozen gendarme-class robots with guns in their hands.

Sjilla dropped his arms to sides and walked back past the group to face the Terran. A slight smile played upon his features.

"It would appear that I am outmaneuvered."

"It would appear so," the big man responded. He eyed the flamers in Sjilla's hands with definite lack of enthusiasm. "Mind letting those things go? The fall won't hurt 'em, and I'd feel a lot better about it."

"A question first?"

"All right," agreed the Terran, somewhat dubiously.

"Can those robots up there fire without killing your fellows, there? Will they fire at I, who am so obviously a Terran and therefore beyond reproach?"

"That's two questions," the Terran said. "But I'll answer both. No, they can't fire without hitting the Terrans, and no, they wouldn't kill you, who are so obviously a Terran."

"Well, then—" began Sjilla.

"But there's a catch to that rosy picture," came a new voice. Donovan looked back at the roofs.

"Rierson!" hissed Sjilla. "I thought you were killed at the pen."

"Sorry to disappoint you." The old outhunter bowed mockingly. "But about that catch: these robots aren't carrying killing weapons, they're carrying stunners. Stunners. One move and they sweep the alley with stunner fire. After that, we can separate the friends from the foes—and the foes from their guns—at our leisure."

Sjilla inclined his head slightly to the man in the doorway. "Your idea?"

"Yes."

"Very clever. I compliment you."

"Thanks." The tone was dry.

"You *are*, I take it, the elusive James Rierson?"

"That's me," agreed the Terran.

"In that case—"

Sjilla moved. He whipped to one side, flattened against the wall, his flamers arching up with deadly purpose. Thus inspired, Quiror and Visstor pointed their weapons at the robots above. The move was a good one; it would have taken flesh-and-blood watchers by complete surprise and perhaps snatched victory from the jaws of defeat. But robotic reflexes and robotic speed defeated its brilliance. Stunners went to work the moment Sjilla dove for the wall. Robots directly above him made no move to lean over and fire downward, leaving that to the ones across the way; they instead methodically swept the five figures in the center of the alley.

Donovan had one moment in which to see the Security Chief stiffen against the wall and slide slowly to the pavement, fighting the paralyzing effects of the stun-bolts to the last, before the fire from the rooftops swept over him and he, too, went down into blackness.

Chapter Twenty-Five

"You really meant it, didn't you?" The Terran general, Carstairs, faced Martak Sarno across his desk, eyes blazing.

Sarno lay back in his chair, met that gaze calmly. "And what made you think for a moment that I didn't?"

"But *why?*" That was Garcia, his face pale, his eyes still reflecting the shock of what he had witnessed. *"Why,* Sarno? We called off the squadrons, didn't we, not twelve hours after we started our tour? We were convinced; we were ready to talk terms. Why did two thousand innocent people have to die?"

"To lubricate the wheels of diplomacy, you might say." Sarno shrugged. "I didn't appreciate that little threat you leveled at me on our first meeting. When threats are leveled, countermeasures must be taken. I took them. Now . . . within forty-eight hours, I want those twenty battle squadrons with which you threatened me turned over to Imperial forces out along the Line."

"Impossible," rasped the admiral. "Can't be done. Even in overdrive."

"All right, then, their equivalent, within a Terran week. I want twenty full battle squadrons in Llralan hands within seven Terran days as a show of good faith on your part."

"Good faith!" exploded Carstairs. "Why, you . . . !"

"The surrender of those squadrons will soothe my ruffled feelings," Sarno went on smoothly over the general's interruption. "And bear this in mind: those ships have to be notified, get under way and go through the process of surrendering. That takes time. Also, a beam-radio message must reach me within that same span of hours informing me that my conditions have been met. Otherwise . . ."

"Otherwise?" prompted Garcia.

"The village whose occupants I executed was a small one. If at the end of a week I have received no word, I shall have to proceed to a weightier form of persuasion."

"Meaning?"

"Meaning a municipality of somewhat greater size will be next."

"How much greater size?"

"Say . . . about the size of Atlanta."

Garcia grunted as if he'd been kicked in the groin. "You dirty—"

"I think," Sarno cut in blandly, "that I'll invent a new game. For every degrading epithet heaped on my undeserving head— a new Terran corpse. Just what variety, I can't say right now. Relatives of the offender? No, that wouldn't work in Raymond's or Trenton's case. Beautiful young maidens, after the fashion, I understand, of ancient Terran literature on the subject of interstellar invasion? An interesting thought. Young children, thus confirming your image of me as a baby-eating monstrosity? No . . . I am too fond of the younglings, no matter their race. Heads of state, tri-vid personalities, well-known and rabid patriots? Perhaps." He smiled, glorying in the power he held over them.

"You've made your point." Garcia's look held pure hatred.

"Please." Sarno raised his hand. "Believe me, Senator—the choice of Atlanta as the next city has nothing personal in it, though you might assume that to be so, your family being interned there. Other considerations entirely are responsible."

"What considerations?" That admiral again. Why did he have to put in his eighth-Imperial's worth? Sarno had marked him down as a potential troublemaker since first meeting—he was too sharp.

"What considerations?" the admiral repeated. "We were bound for Atlanta on our tour when the pilot received instructions to turn back. The crew of the flivver was tense and

208

jittery all the way back. Now you say you're going to execute six million people. Quite a jump from two thousand, who were executed abruptly. No warning. You say you wanted to speed things up. Why the hurry?" His pale eyes bored into Sarno's. *"What's happening in Atlanta, Sarno?"*

"Nothing. Nothing at all."

"I don't believe you. Plenty's happening. Something's gone sour. Bad sour. Now you're trying to panic us. Want to get this thing over with as soon as possible." His chopped-off sentences hammered at Sarno. "You're scared, Sarno. Bad scared. Somebody's walking on your grave—"

"Enough!" It was a savage roar. Sarno surged to his feet. "Not one more word!" He regained self-control with an effort, planted his fists solidly on the desk. "Gentlemen, I have made my ultimatum. Twenty battle squadrons, within a Terran week, or Atlanta dies. You are wasting valuable time."

Garcia seemed drained, listless. To all appearances he had not even noticed the extent to which the Terran admiral had rattled Sarno. Now he looked up.

"And after that, what? Another town, another squadron—where does it end?"

Sarno smiled grimly. "I had thought that was obvious from the start. But of course it wouldn't have been to you—you were too busy hoping for miracles. Well, the age of miracles is long past; there are only the hard, cold facts of today. You are faced with a choice—you have been from the start. Play it my way, or lose three billion Terrans."

"If we play it your way," grated Carstairs, "we'll end up without our shirts."

"Exactly."

"But—but . . ." That was Trenton, spluttering as if some great revelation had come upon him. "But you're blackmailing us! If we let these planets die, we can never be free of guilt—yet if we go along, what? Ultimate surrender?"

"That is a hoped-for result," Sarno agreed. "Then the war wil be over, and peace will come once more. No more fighting, no more dying, no more bloodshed and bitterness. A graceful surrender makes for the smoothest integration into Empire."

"Never!" snapped Carstairs. "Never! I'll fight you with my

bare hands first! I don't know about three billions here, but I'd rather die than . . ." His voice trailed off uncertainly.

Sarno spread his hands. "That is your prerogative—it always has been. Surrender or death. The choice is yours entirely; it is completely up to you. You hold your destiny in your hands— I am simply the instrument of that destiny. But remember: you hold the destiny of these planets in those same hands. And time for decision is running out. For six million Georgians, it will run out in seven days." He resumed his seat. "You will, as before, have free use of the *Risstaixil's* transmitters to consult with your superiors. I suggest you do not waste the time remaining." He nodded to the guards.

As the Terrans filed out, he studiously avoided the gaze of the admiral—that character was getting to be an extreme pain in the neck. Sarno cursed himself for allowing him to get through to him so easily.

He had the distinctly uneasy impression that things were slipping out of his grasp and beyond his control. He had set a series of events in motion by his discovery and use of the Dust, and now it looked as if those events had taken on a life of their own. Atlanta—Atlanta was a glaring example. Quiror's command massacred—wiped out to the man. The specimens chosen for reawakening—including Ryan Garcia's family— missing, presumed spirited away by the unknown attackers. Four Unaffecteds missing and unaccounted for. And one of them was Donovan.

Donovan! The very name was enough to make him boil over. Donovan had started it all—Donovan and no one else. Without Donovan and his wagging tongue, there would have been no Gremper, no Spook of Baxter, no unrest and ill-concealed fear among the troops. James Rierson—if indeed it were he in Georgia—would have caused not one millionth the consternation with his stubborn refusal to be killed if it hadn't been for Donovan.

And now Donovan was gone. Vanished without a trace. Somehow, deep in his heart, Sarno knew he was not yet rid of Bradford Donovan—that he would yet rue the day he had let Sjilla talk him out of inverting him over a slow fire. Bradford Donovan would never have been killed as an innocent bystander in a gun battle—that would be too easy. Donovan—

as witness that marq attack so many, many years ago—died hard. Donovan, who had made his life miserable on Risstair, who had come back to haunt—he flinched at that word "haunt"—his crowning achievement, to confound his perfect invasion.

He got up, walked to a porthole. Sjilla was the only one who'd ever come close to giving Donovan pause, and Sjilla was gone, too. Somewhere out there were both of them—and he had no doubt, none at all, that Donovan had at last gained the upper hand.

Donovan, Donovan, Donovan . . . Sirri, he was sick of that name! He ground a knuckle into tired eyes. If only Sjilla had escaped. With Sjilla, he would have had a chance.

But Sjilla was gone, and there was no recalling him.

Sarno felt like weeping.

Chapter Twenty-Six

"Repeat your instructions," James Rierson said.

"Yes, sir," responded the Nairobi master-brain. "Precisely at 9 P.M., local time, the android fashion manikins are to commence their infiltration. Fifteen minutes are to be allowed for them to get into position before the 'open fire' order is given. Stun-guns only; no firearms. As soon as all the aliens are unconscious the androids are to leave, the warehousemen are to carry away the human females and the salesmen are to carry out their assignment and turn off all lights."

"And then?"

"And then, sir, the previously positioned projector-robots are to begin their solido-image projections."

"Very good. How long will the operation take?"

"Twenty-five minutes from commencement of infiltration to lights-out. As I understand it, the projections are to continue until they evoke some response from the enemy, and then cease completely."

"You understand correctly. Carry out those orders to the letter. If you run into unforeseen event, have the Casablanca ECC put you in immediate voice-contact with me."

"Yes, sir." A distant relay thudded. Contact was broken.

"That makes fifteen cities," said the New York ECC. "Atlanta has already seen limited action—that makes sixteen. There are many more; their master-brains want action, too."

"They'll get their action—all the action they can handle. But they'll have to be patient."

"They cannot be patient; there are human lives involved."

"I know that—and they'll still have to be patient."

"The patience would not be necessary," the ECC pointed out, "if you would have done with this shilly-shallying and meet the problem head-on." Its voice became persuasive. "Turn us loose; do not hold us back. Let us arm ourselves and deal with them all as Charlie dealt with that one encampment. Let us teach these impertinent aliens the penalty for interfering in human affairs."

"If I did, they'd then proceed to teach *you* the penalty for attempting too much, too soon," Rierson snapped. "Now be quiet or I'll order you to dismantle yourself and throw all your own components in the East River."

"Such an action would, for a number of reasons, be quite impossible," replied the ECC frigidly.

"Nothing is impossible." He broke contact, leaving it to stew that awhile.

"That's telling him," Michael Harris applauded from the doorway. "Yessirree, *that's* telling him."

Rierson leaned back in the control chair, grinned. "That blasted machine can really get me going sometimes. You ready to take over here?"

"Ready." He burped pleasurably. "Charlie, your robochefs set a mighty fine table."

"Thank you, sir."

"Don't thank *me,*" Harris said as he eased his corpulent

contours into the seat just vacated by Rierson. "I should thank *you*. That's the first decent meal I've had since this whole slapbang started." He looked at Rierson. "Bradford would like to see you in the subbasement. Says he has several items that might be of interest to you."

"On my way. . . . Don't let New York bully you into anything we might regret."

"Not me." He stretched luxuriously. "I might just catch forty winks. The escalators are running now, by the way. Unless you simply want the exercise, I recommend them highly."

The subbasement was a whirl of activity; robots scurried to and fro, bringing armloads of booty captured at Quiror's pen down from the ground-level warehouse and stacking it in orderly fashion against the housing of the reactor that was Furnestine's emergency power source. Lined along the far wall with military precision were the fifty sleeping Terrans carried away from the pen; huddled in a corner were Llralan prisoners, including the mocker, guarded by a trio of warehousemen with flamers. Out of respect for Sjilla's caginess and his human appearance, Dan Rierson sat nearby with a rifle across his knees.

James Rierson found Donovan sitting on a heap of salvaged Llralan equipment, holding something in his hands.

"How'd it go with the robots?"

He gestured. "The usual griping from New York, but the others proved very eager to cooperate."

"Good." The stocky man exhibited a black-metal cube not much larger than a children's building block and about the same weight, from the way he handled it. "Know what this is?"

"No."

"I didn't think so. If you had, you'd have been a little better informed on just what Larry was up to."

"How?"

Donovan turned the cube over, revealing several tiny buttons, a tiny knob and an inset bulb glowing bright orange. He prodded one of the buttons with a thick forefinger, then offered it to Rierson.

"Listen."

He could now see a grid in one surface of the cube—the one directly opposite the buttons. Gingerly, he held it near his ear. After a moment he took it down. Voices—Llralan voices, whispering out of the little black box!

"You don't have to act like a Tordig witch doctor seeing his first cigarette lighter," Donovan said humorously. "Well, what did you hear?"

"Llralan voices!"

"Naturally—but what were they saying?"

"I don't know; they were talking too fast. I think I did hear something that sounded vaguely like 'Atlanta' once or twice, though."

"You did."

Rierson handed the gadget back. "What *is* that thing, anyway?"

"The Llralan soldier's equivalent of your friendly morning newspaper—partisan, of course. His friendly voice from home —from religious services to popular music, with heavy doses of propaganda and indoctrination claptrap in between. The *Sulis-su-Banussen*—the Voice of Empire. What you were hearing right now was what you might call the fleet news."

"You mean they're actually telling what happened here?"

"I didn't say that." Donovan held the cube to his ear, his face somber.

"Then what?"

"The *Sulis-su-Banussen,* as a matter of course, is naming the next town whose occupants will be exterminated as an example to the Federation delegation, unless certain obligations are met. A Martian village, it appears, was the first to go."

"Strange the Martian ECC's didn't set up a howl," Rierson said. "What obligations?"

"Not so strange, perhaps—a lot of those Martian villages don't have so much as a single master-brain. But about the obligations, Sarno seems to think the Federation owes him twenty battle squadrons in a pretty package with a pink bow on it—and unless he gets said package within five days, a city is going to die."

Rierson felt the blood drain away from his face. "What city?"

Donovan shrugged. "Atlanta."

"How . . . ?"

"The way he promised all along—soldiers quartered in the bomb shelters will do the deed."

"There aren't any soldiers in Furnestine's bomb shelter."

"There will be—just as soon as they finish up wherever they are at present. Each squad has a certain list of shelters for which it is responsible. Sarno doesn't have enough men to blanket three planets." His smile was devoid of humor. "It takes an awful lot of logistics to murder three billion people, even at the rate of six million a throw.

"Nobody's going to be murdered," Rierson said flatly. "We'll stop that before it starts."

"How?"

"All I've got to do is give the word and the entire working force of Atlanta rises up in arms."

"Excellent. Wonderful." Donovan's tone was biting. "So you slaughter the two thousand some-odd troopers in and around Atlanta—and then what happens? Sarno is no fool; if robots start killing his men, he's going to start smashing robots. Before your robots could get started good, bombs would be falling on every robot communications center on three planets."

"But we *can't* just sit by and let them—"

"On the contrary, that is just what we must do." He shook his head. "I'm surprised at you, Rierson—I would have thought a man like you could see the folly of what you're suggesting. One provable case of armed robotic resistance and Sarno lowers the boom good and plenty, leaving isolated master-brains to try to cope with the Larrys—and leaving us high and dry. But you know all this as well as I do; you told me yourself about your efforts with the solido-images at the pen—and it was you who suggested that 'ghosts' strike in Sydney and Portland and Canali and Nairobi and all those other places to take some of the pressure off Atlanta."

"Yes, but—"

"As I said, Sarno is no fool. Perhaps he already suspects what's going on—*maybe the broadcast itself is a trap*. It wouldn't be the first time the good ol' *Sulis* had spoken with tongue in cheek, knowing unfriendly ears were listening in. Maybe he's trying to force us into showing our hand."

"And maybe, just maybe, they're sincere. What then?"

"Then it is out of our hands. It is up to the delegation the

Sulis spoke of—them and the twenty battle squadrons. Meanwhile, we ought to be making tracks—or, rather, *not* making them—right out of here. Sarno has had a galloping bellyful of Atlanta by now. Time we moved on to greener pastures."

"What about them?" Rierson indicated the ranked sleepers.

"Any reason they should get preferential treatment over anybody else in this burg? They'll have to share Atlanta's fate."

"I don't like it."

"Neither do I; that's just the way of it. We jump our gun, we'll be killing any chance we might have been able to give three billion people."

"The robots won't like it, either. They aren't capable enough of taking the long view to stand idly by while six million people are murdered in hopes that such inaction will save a greater number of lives later."

"I know that, too," the truck driver said. "For the sake of their sanity, you'll have to order every robot in the CD network to forget Atlanta exists. Charlie and the other master-brains here will have to deactivate themselves."

"How do you know they won't rebel against such preposterous instructions?"

"They don't have any choice, do they? We're the best they've got—so they'll have to obey us until somebody better comes along. If it becomes necessary, we can undergo lie detector tests to prove the validity of our claims—or rather, I can. I can see you're still not quite convinced."

"You do that," said Rierson. "You go take a test and convince the robots not to act, and deliberately leave Atlanta helpless under the ax—and you'll be held responsible by law for every man, woman and child here."

"I know. And"—his face was tight-drawn as he said it—"I'll accept full responsibility for anything that happens, if it happens." He stood up, tucked the cube in his pocket. "But the execution is five days away, and an awful lot can happen in five days. Meanwhile we might as well put the time remaining to good use."

"Meaning what?"

"Come on over here and I'll show you."

He followed the squat man to a number of longish cylinders stacked cordwood-fashion near the door. When Donovan lifted the top one off the pile and stood it on end, he remembered where he'd seen it before: being unloaded from a jet flivver and carried into one of the prefab huts at the pen.

"What d'you think these are—bottled gas?"

"I remember thinking they looked like that when I saw them the first time," Rierson admitted.

"And when was that?"

"When I was getting ready to turn the robots loose on the pen. They were being taken into one of the prefabs."

"Yeah . . . that's where the robot said he'd picked 'em up."

"You asked about them? Why?"

"Because Larrys—at least Larrys bivouacking on an enemy world—don't use bottled gas. Because my curiosity was aroused. He fiddled with the nozzle atop the cylinder. "What d'you think would happen if I opened this?"

Rierson eyed the nozzle distrustfully. "We might all expire in our tracks. I don't trust alien gadgets."

"Don't be provincial," chided the truck driver. "It might also be some kind of joy juice with which we could go on a jag to end all jags."

"I'd settle for dragon seed," Rierson countered, a trifle bitterly, "since robots don't seem to be worth much."

"And that," said Donovan, ignoring the comment, "might be just what we have here: press the nozzle and *poof!* Minute missiles, instant infantry, sudden spaceships. We'll see shortly."

"We will?" Rierson's interest picked up. "I seem to be missing a lot of obvious points. See what?"

"Patience, my long-faced friend, patience—ah!" A salesman came through the door, swept the room with impassive gaze and came toward them.

"Mr. Donovan?"

"Here."

"Sir, Mr. Harris gave me a message to relay to you."

"Relay it, then."

"Yes, sir. The answer is affirmative."

"That's all?"

"Yes, sir."

Donovan looked at Rierson. "Have one of the warehousemen bring a sleepyhead upstairs—the one in the orange jacket, see him?"

"I see him, but—"

"Don't argue. Just do as you're told. And act like you know exactly what you're doing." He hefted the cylinder, started for the door.

"But—"

"Don't argue, I said," he growled, without looking back. "Don't open your mouth. Not once. I've just found out that, among all his other gifts, Sjilla can read lips. In English, yet. Now, *move*." He went out of sight and up the stairs.

Rierson was inclined to stop him but refrained, instead speaking sharply to a massive Physak painstakingly dividing a heap of captured Llralan weapons into neat little stacks. The robot rose from its crouch with tigerish grace, glided across the room and lifted the man in the orange tunic into its arms like a sleeping child. Then it, too, disappeared through the door.

James Rierson followed, wondering if Donovan had gone slap-happy from his untender treatment at the hands of the Llralans.

"Yessirree!" exulted Michael Harris. "You sure hit the jackpot on that guess, Bradford."

He was sitting where Rierson had left him, in the chair before Charlie's control board, watching one of Charlie's viewscreens. Visible on the screen was the group of Llralans bunched in the corner of the subbasement far below. The camera looked out from the wall, giving a good view of the whole premises.

"You see, my young and baffled friend," Donovan said to James Rierson, "Mike and I laid a simple trap for Sjilla and the boys down there. Charlie was in on it, too—he provided the bugs. Didn't you, Charlie?"

"I did indeed, sir," responded the master-brain.

"You mean you bugged that corner? Why?"

Harris cast an imploring glance ceilingward. "The innocence of youth! Are you sure, Bradford, that this is the storied Spook of Baxter?"

"Sjilla was," grinned Donovan. "And I trust his judgment. But as to why we bugged that corner . . . it's the next best thing to mind-reading, old son, if you can get your enemy in

218

a pocket where he thinks he can talk freely—a pocket you have previously prepared."

"Which is why you insisted on putting them in that particular corner to start with," Rierson said. "I should have known there was some kind of devious reason."

"Such language!" Harris reproved severely. "Respect your elders, son. Didn't your uncle teach you any manners?"

"He's in on this too, I suppose." Rierson studied his uncle's untroubled countenance on the screen. "You'd never know it from looking at him, would you?"

"Lad, lad!" Harris patted his large stomach with much satisfaction. "We were at this before you got out of training pants. We used to give Sarno fits, the three of us, in the good old days, so we decided a logical step at this point was to spy on Sarno's favorite spy in order to best determine how to take up where we left off twenty years ago."

"And?"

Donovan thumped the metal cylinder he was still holding. "Remember that remark you made about dragon seed?"

"I remember it."

"Well, this is it." He set it down carefully. "This, my young friend, is the antidote to Sarno's Dust. I knew it had to be somewhere in that camp—else how did they intend reawakening those fifty people your robots pulled out of there? —but I didn't know what it would look like. Sooo . . ."

"So we arranged box seats for Sjilla and Company down below," Harris took up the tale. "And we put on a little act— seemed fitting, somehow, seeing as how Sjilla intended corraling you via the same method. Donovan was to go through all the likely-looking piles of junk while I sat here with my ear glued to the mike and recorder running. The first time out was a winner; when he started messing with those cylinders, Quiror very nearly had a stroke. Sjilla told him to shut up, even if Donovan accidentally awoke somebody it would only be added grief for us, the shock of awakening to such an environment being too great for the average individual. In other words, we'd be saddled with a loony."

"And he's right, too, I imagine," Donovan continued. "But we decided to play the thing out, so we had you cart out that fellow in the orange jacket after I left with the cylinder. That put Quiror into a panic, and even bothered Sjilla."

"Give a listen," invited Harris. He pressed a stud.

"They're up to something, all right," said a voice. Quiror's voice. It sounded worried. *"Look . . . they're carrying a man out. You don't suppose . . . ?"*

"That they've found out? How could they?"

"But they're thinking too close to home!" insisted Quiror. *"One whiff of that antidote, and—"*

Harris switched the tape off. "I quote: *'one whiff of that antidote, and—'* " He smiled benignly, reminding Rierson of an overweight cherub.

"You're going to give the man in the orange jacket such a whiff?" he asked.

"Certainly not!" Harris looked horrified. "We've got enough to worry about without holding somebody's hand while he adjusts to the fact that Old Mother Earth just ain't what she used to be. All we wanted was to ascertain our findings—not start trying to wake everybody and his brother up. Leave that to the proper authorities."

"You seem to forget," pointed out Rierson, "that the proper authorities, also, are sound asleep. You've got to start somewhere."

"Precisely. We've got to start somewhere." He beamed fondly at the big man. "You're learning, son, you're learning. Given time and patient tutoring, you might get by. Very incisive thinking there—you've put the problem in a nutshell."

"Can't we dispense with the sarcasm?" He was a little rankled by the other's treating him like a promising but inept youth.

"By all means." Harris was suddenly solemn as an owl. "Shall we tell him, Bradford?"

"Tell me what?"

"I guess so," Donovan said. "He looks trustworthy to me. Tell me"—he went on, before Rierson could retort to that—"do you know what a Planetary Defense Center is?"

"Haven't the faintest idea," Rierson gave back. "Whatever you're driving at, you'd better hurry—it's almost time for my diaper change."

"All right, you know," conceded the truck driver. "And

do you remember your high-school geography well enough to know where the nearest one to Atlanta is?"

"El Scorpio," Rierson replied promptly. "The Texas Panhandle."

"Bravo!" applauded Harris. "You learned your lessons well."

"No, I didn't," he contradicted. "I always read Erle Stanley Gardner classics in geography. I remember simply because I toured the place last year at the invitation of the War Department. Good publicity, you know—*Civic Leaders Visit Military Installation.*"

"Ouch!" Harris grinned ruefully. "That's handing it back with a vengeance! The closest I ever came to being a civic leader was when I ran for dogcatcher on Sirius III. I lost by a landslide."

"Then you know how to get there? To the Scorpion, I mean?" Donovan persisted.

"I know."

"Good."

"Why is that so good?"

"Because, as you said"—he tapped the cylinder significantly —"we've got to start somewhere. And a PDC strikes me as being as good a place as any, better than most. Military men these days have to be supermen. Sound of body"—some unfathomable emotion showed itself briefly on his face, and then was gone—"and stable of mind. If anyone could recover from the shock of reawakening quickly enough to do us or themselves any good, it would be the men chosen to man the PDC's."

"Granted. But just how do you propose to go about it? No doubt every PDC in this system has a Llralan command post on it by now, with technicians to dig out defensive secrets and plenty of guards to insure that something like you're contemplating doesn't happen."

"No doubt at all," agreed Donovan.

"Well?"

"There are ways and means, boy, ways and means." He hefted the cylinder again. "Meanwhile, there's the minor problem of getting out of Georgia and into Texas without getting shot. That calls for a council of war. When do your supernatural visitations upon the Llralans begin?"

Rierson checked his watch. "Two hours."

"Good. That gives us time to thrash things out." He looked at Harris. "Where'd Nogales get off to?"

The fat man shrugged. "Staring out some window toward the north is my guess. He is suffering from a very recently revived conscience."

"Meaning?"

"Meaning he is feeling guilty for getting that little pregnant girl up there in Canada on Sarno's flagship into this predicament in the first place. Meaning he is engaging in the pastime of reviewing his misspent youth and feeling sorry for himself."

"Well, I'll be damned."

"Very likely. You want me to get him?"

"Yes. Bring him down to the subbasement. He can engage in self-pity some other time; we're going to need his gun." He turned to Rierson. "Let's go down."

And down they went.

Chapter Twenty-Seven

The men of battle fleet Z-501-V, code name *Sleeper*, were, for the most part, fighting men in their prime—men taken platoon by platoon from the battlefronts and moved back to a holding area far behind the lines months in advance of the actual assault upon Terra. Moved back, sequestered in isolated garrisons strung through a bleak mountain range upon a world that just barely qualified as habitable, kept completely in the dark as to their proposed mission for fear of security leaks and denied all liberty and correspondence privileges for the same reason. They were men in which the sap of life flowed richly, but they were also obedient soldiers, and so with the fatalistic acceptance of their breed they caught up on lost sleep, sharpened their marksmanship, participated in the innumerable games of chance that are an inherent part of any garrison duty, speculated upon their chances of surviving whatever the High Command was cooking up *this* time, or just sat and grew weary of staring at one another.

The orders to ship out brought no relief, not even the relief of a sudden and violent return to combat. Instead there had been more waiting, this time in the cramped confines of the troopships as the fleet lay dormant well within enemy lines awaiting the signal to strike. Boredom was supplanted by gut-wringing tension as the danger of being sighted grew more likely with each tick of the clock. And then at last the briefing and into the drop-ships and out high above the nearly unresisting planets, and—after the initial stir of activity surrounding landing—the settling down to man their bomb-shelter posts. Which, after all, was just another form of waiting.

The sap, long contained, began to bubble dangerously near the surface. The men of Z-501-V were tired of waiting. They had been obedient soldiers, they had followed orders, they had waited interminably and jumped unquestioningly into the stronghold of the Federation with only their superiors' preposterous-sounding reassurances to bolster their courage. It was time, figured the men of Z-501-V, for some of the sap to spill over, for accumulated steam to be blown off, for a little manly diversion.

By the second day after landing they had submitted their traditional soldiers' petitions.

By the sixth day the arrangements were in the works, given only slightly less priority than the developing problem of the Unaffecteds.

By the tenth day, the first units to be allowed liberty had received their customary doles of walsos from stores, the requested antidote from the flagship, certain cities had been designated for their use and transportation was being arranged.

By the fourteenth day, despite abrupt and unexplained cancellations of petitions by several units that had pressed the hardest for them to start with, festivities were getting under way.

By the fifteenth they were going full blast.

And by the sixteenth . . .

Night under a summer sky and a silent, darkened city lay sleeping beneath the myriad stars. Two shadow-shapes sat within a shadow-truck beside a shadow-curb and watched with shadowed gaze the only oasis of light and sound in all that concrete stillness. Across the street a long, low building that ran long on glass and short on masonry was ablaze with light and abuzz with muted sounds of merriment. Behind those gigantic opaqued windows through which a diffused yellow glow fell softly on a row of troop trucks below, supremely indifferent to the brooding slumber of the city or the officious presence of the pair of military policemen, the proud Third Battalion of the 6077th Infantry was in its cups and at its pleasures.

Abruptly a door banged open and laughter, loud shouting and louder music spilled uproariously into the night. A figure was silhouetted momentarily against the light. It weaved uncertainly. Voices calling after the leave-taker, bawdy jokes about his inability to hold his liquor or last the full liberty any more were cut from earshot when the door slammed shut as violently as it had opened.

The MP in the driver's seat, having started when the door opened, now settled back again. "Really having themselves a ball, aren't they?"

The second man shifted his wad of falzwok-weed from one cheek to the other, spat carefully into the street. "Any reason they shouldn't?"

"Yio," agreed the driver vehemently. "I could be aboard ship pounding my ear if they were wherever they're supposed to be doing the same instead of messing with alien women."

The falzwok-chewer grinned in the dark. "Do I detect a note of envy, Vasq? Envy for the lowly foot-sloggers?"

"Lowly my rear end! The infantry always gets the most of everything—and always first! I can't see it."

"You obviously couldn't see going out the hatch four or five siveb above an enemy planet with nothing but rifle and grav-chute to insure the safety of your precious skin, either," observed the falzwok-chewer. "Else I would be deprived the boon of your companionship this fine summer evening."

"The military police is as honorable a service as any!"

"I agree. But it is also somewhat less hazardous than the infantry. The brass realize that—and compensate to a degree by awarding certain hazard-privileges such as first choice of alien women. Relax . . . your turn will come."

"You've got it all figured out, haven't you?" Vasq inquired sarcastically.

"I have," responded the other. "So why not settle back and enjoy the cool of the evening after the heat of the day? Consider the stars—how differently they appear from the southeastern quarter-sphere of this world than they do from Villair."

"I'm from Zaxen, not Villair," snapped Vasq. "And I'm not a stargazer."

"You should try it, stargazing. Brings tranquillity of the spirit, a cooling of the temper—"

"But no women!"

"You," said the falzwok-chewer, laughing, "are hopeless."

"*Me? You're* hopeless. Women to be had, and you count stars!"

"I count stars," agreed the falzwok-chewer. "We meet a battalion at the landing strip, load 'em into the trucks and escort 'em here for a night's liberty—a night's tanking up on cheap 'sos and satisfying the baser appetites with subsonically controlled zombies—and then send 'em back thoroughly soused and sated to their bomb shelters and their duty of sitting up with living corpses. What we've got here is no more than an automated brothel; blank-eyed, shambling creatures with their brains in space freeze dancing to the tunes played through those little boxes on their skulls. We sleep by day and man-handle recalcitrant drunks by night—a ghoulish business, this—and yet you can't wait to jump in and join them." He slid down until his neck rested on the back of the seat. "I count stars," he repeated. "And it's thankful I am for their company."

Vasq had no ready comeback for that; he had been taken aback by the other's tirade. The silence between them stretched. Finally he bestirred himself, got out of the truck and walked over to the small fire built by the troop-truck drivers in search of more sympathetic companionship. The falzwok-chewer shifted into a more comfortable position and wrapped himself in a mantle of private thoughts to ward off the creeping chill of the African night. His wad of falzwok-weed became tasteless and he spat it out. Time dripped away and his thoughts matched pace, dripping slowly one upon the other and building fanciful stalagmites in a cave of half-forgotten memories. A shooting star flamed briefly beyond the tallest buildings of the city, and the shouting across the way died down. He found himself drowsing . . .

It seemed he had hardly closed his eyes when Vasq was shaking him urgently. ". . . up, sergeant. Sergeant, wake up! Sergeant . . ." His voice held a peculiar note; the sergeant realized it was fear.

He stirred. "Hmph?"

"Look!" Vasq was pointing across the street.

He looked—and shot bolt upright, the sleep burned out of his head as by atomic flame.

The building across the street was as dark as the rest of the city. Not a single light burned.

"Must be later than I thought," he said. "The battalion gone?"

"No."

He twisted around to give the driver an uncomprehending stare. "What do you mean, no?"

"I mean *no*." Vasq waved at the building. "They're still in there."

The sergeant looked back at the building. "How long have the lights been out?"

"They just went out."

"All at once?"

"All at once."

"Was there anything before that?"

"No . . . yes . . . I mean I *think* there was. All the shouting and laughing stopped suddenly. The record players kept playing—they're playing now—but that was all. No more voices. I was coming to get you when the lights went out. I—" His fingers dug convulsively into the sergeant's shoulder. *"Sarge!"*

"I see it," growled the sergeant. "I see it."

Across the way, atop the three-story building which had so

226

recently rung to the sounds of the Third Battalion's mirth but now was still, a pale radiance shimmered. As they watched, a tiny, globular thing rose slowly above the parapet like a pocket moon, casting a weird orange light over the darkened building. For a long heartbeat it hung suspended, pulsing softly, then began an erratic journey along the lip of the roof. It bobbed, it dipped—long, tenuous streamers trailed away behind, fading slowly into nothingness. It made a complete circuit of the roof, arrived at its original position, and hung there.

"Great Sirri protect us," breathed Vasq. *"What is it?"*

"I don't know," said the sergeant. *"I don't know."* His gun was in his hand. When something moved in the nearby shadows, it was only by the strongest exercise of will that he did not fire. It was one of the truck drivers, his face a pale, frightened blur in the dark.

"You see that thing?"

The sergeant lowered his gun. "How could we help but see it?"

The truck driver shook his head. "I don't know. I . . . *By the Black Winds of Tervillon, there's another one!"*

The sergeant and Vasq turned as one. A block away, a second ghostly moon shimmered and bobbed as it duplicated the first's roof-girdling maneuver above the building over which it hovered, and then went quiescent.

"And another!" Vasq's voice throbbed with ill-concealed panic. *"Sarge . . . !"*

A fourth, a fifth, a sixth of the little spheres appeared, dipping and weaving in their enigmatic little promenades around the roofs above which they materialized. A seventh, an eighth . . . the utter blackness of the canyon-streets between the building-crags began to be suffused with subtle luminescence.

At length, full twenty of the things hung silently above the rooftops.

And the immediate shadows surrounding the truck began to fade before a cold brilliance that flooded down from directly above, from six floors above, and strengthened visibly.

They looked upward, and Vasq uttered a curse that was half prayer.

One of the spheres peeped over the building at them, a

gaseous, palpitating seeming-entity that began its supernal waltz immediately they decried its presence.

Vasq threw his arm up wildly, and a beam of blue fire stabbed at the thing. His aim was true; the beam cleaved it cleanly.

His aim was true, but it had absolutely no effect upon the pulsing thing. None. For a moment he was unnerved completely, then, mouthing a string of horrible oaths that did credit to his years as an MP, he held down the firing stud and hosed flame at the thing, his eyes wide-staring, maddened.

The sergeant and the truck driver moved with snaking speed, the one to protect his partner, the other to save his own skin. The sergeant reached out and yanked Vasq bodily into the cab; the truck driver went head-first beneath the vehicle. Masonry torn loose by the beam of Vasq's weapon avalanched down, exploding on the pavement like ancient artillery, pelting the steel body of the truck, smashing but not shattering one side of the tough windshield.

When it seemed safe to come out the truck driver did so, dusting himself off absently and gaping at the roofs.

"You all right in there?" he questioned.

"All right. You?"

"Fine," he said, and then again, *"Fine,* sergeant. I don't know what he did, but whatever it was, it was right." His voice held happy incredulity. "They're *gone,* sergeant—all of them!"

And it was true. The rooftops were empty and as dark as they had ever been, and the phantom moons were gone as if they had never existed. The sergeant climbed slowly out of the truck, half-expecting to see the lights come back on in the building across the street. Whatever alien magic had caused that weird display, searfire had erased it, and it seemed only proper that the lights should spring back to life, the shouting and laughter resume.

But the windows remained dark, and the only sound was that of the still-operating record players.

The truck driver followed his gaze. "You going to take a look?"

"We are," the sergeant affirmed. "Want to come along?"

"Not particularly—but I will, anyway." He drew his sidearm. "Hot flame seems to be prime medicine for the ghosts of at least this planet." He laughed hollowly.

"Let's go then," said the sergeant.

They crossed the street, pushed open a door, found themselves in a long corridor. Vasq unlimbered his torch, sent its green beam stabbing ahead. Three doors down, an arm protruded into the hallway. They went toward it. It belonged to a man with corporal's chevrons, sprawled on his face as if struck down while making a desperate dive for the door. Vasq knelt, rolled him over.

"Sirri!" He went pale.

The corporal's eyes were open, but he wasn't seeing anything. His throat had been neatly and expertly cut, from ear to ear. A thick pool of blood was puddled where he had lain; his tunic-front was a sodden mess.

The sergeant stepped over the body, flashed his own torch around the room beyond. One look told him all he needed to know. When the truck driver started forward, he held out a restraining arm.

"There's nothing you can do for them now."

The truck driver looked as if he were going to be sick. "All . . . *dead?*"

"About ten of them, all with their throats cut. There's a subsonics specialist, too, and evidences that they had some of the Rekk females in there. But they aren't there now." He faced resolutely down the hall. "Let's check the rest of the building. They can't *all* be dead. Not like this."

But they could. Each room, each bend in the corridor, disclosed new butchery. On the second floor the truck driver stumbled over something that went rolling in the dark. When Vask put his light on it, what was left of his nerve evaporated completely. He backed away, wiping his hands hysterically on his tunic and muttering a weird litany, his eyes bugging.

It was a head, completely severed from its body. Since there were several headless bodies and a like number of loose heads, it was not immediately apparent just whose he had booted. Not that it mattered much.

Vasq watched his antics curiously. "What's he saying?"

The sergeant listened. "It's an old, old dialect—I can only catch a few words. It appears our friend here is an ancestor worshiper; he is calling upon the spirit of his mother's mother to protect him in this house of death."

"Ghosts," snorted the MP disdainfully—and then shut up and looked around him at the carnage. The sergeant could almost see the wheels go round as he connected the orange moons outside to the death all around him. *"Ghosts,"* he whispered, as if some great truth had been revealed to him. "Ghosts . . . *Gremper!"*

The sergeant sent Vasq outside with the ancestor worshiper in tow and went on to the third floor alone, sternly beating down the cold waves of fear threatening to wash over him. When he had finished his grisly survey and satisfied himself that nothing lived within the building—and that not one of the alien women brought here for the pleasure of the dead men remained—he retraced his footsteps, shut off the still-running record players and went out of the building into the brooding night and away from the thick, fresh stench of death that hung over all that remained of the once-proud Third Battalion of the 6077th Infantry.

Overhead, the suddenly remote stars seemed to burn down more coldly.

Chapter Twenty-Eight

The intraship car whirred to a halt, the doors slid back and Martak Sarno dismounted wearily. The days of worry had gone for naught; his ultimatum had been heeded. Atlanta was spared. He had just come from the *Risstaixil's* radio shack. Beam-radio messages were streaming in from lonely relay points out along the Line—messages heralding the surrender of the specified number of Terran warships.

He sighed heavily, tugged his wrinkled tunic straight and settled his pistol belt more comfortably. He had taken to wearing the pistol everywhere since Donovan and Sjilla had been listed among the missing—and since four battalions of his paratroops had died bloodily in widely separated cities under circumstances that had witnesses babbling of angry ghosts. The battalions had died, and in other cities frightening phenomena had been reported—reported by responsible officers, and observed by dozens of men simultaneously. And now the pistol was his ever-present companion. He dared not examine too closely his motives for wearing it; it sufficed that its familiar weight made him feel more at ease. And anything that could offer a modicum of comfort was welcome in these trying times.

Turning, he faced a door across the corridor. The door to the conference room. Behind that blank portal guarded by a pair of equally blank-faced troopers awaited the Terran delegation. He felt a small twinge of uneasiness, shook it off impatiently. At least here he was master; he had them over a grist-rock and they knew it well. At least four of them did. That admiral, though—he had been guessing at things he couldn't possibly know, guessing shrewdly. And he had been noting the effect of his guesses on Sarno. Now he had to be faced again, along with the others, and informed of the new demands the Federation must meet in order to buy continued life for its three billion sleeping citizens.

He would almost have rather faced Donovan gun to gun, or those ghostly orange moons—or even, most horrible of all, a week's worth of paperwork—than to walk into that room and face those five sets of eyes, those five angry faces.

But that was ridiculous! *He* was the conqueror—not those five in there. They were here on *his* terms—not he on theirs! And the conqueror was going to present his demands, and they were going to listen, quietly and respectfully, and then they were going to fulfill those demands promptly and with dispatch. His was the hand that held the whip, and it was best not to let them forget it, lest they grow rash.

He squared his shoulders, nodded to the right-hand trooper,

and passed resolutely through the door as the trooper opened it. He went around the table, took his seat and positioned his list of terms exactly in front of him. Only then did he deign to notice the five across the table from him.

"Gentlemen, you may be seated."

They sat, obviously fuming over having been made to stand like junior Llralan officers until he assumed his seat. The pair of troopers that had prompted them to their feet returned to their posts on either side of the door as the outside trooper closed it.

"Let me begin by saying, gentlemen, that your alacrity in seeing that my demands concerning the battle squadrons were met is very gratifying."

"I'll just bet it is," Carstairs said in a mimicking tone.

Sarno frowned at him. "Do all Federation generals behave like unruly schoolchildren in the face of adverse circumstances?"

Carstairs glowered back at him. "Tell those two bully boys to go chase themselves and I'll show you how a Federation general acts!"

"Indeed? Please, gentlemen, let me make one thing perfectly clear. I grow exceedingly weary of your empty threats, and have decided to tolerate them no more." He drew his pistol, placed it beside the list of terms. "Neither do I find your constant outbreaks during the course of negotiations pleasant. They shall terminate forthwith. You will conduct yourselves as men and ranking officers, or I shall suspend negotiations until the Federation can send me someone who will."

"Uh-uh, Buster." The admiral shook his head. "We're it. You deal with us or you don't deal."

"I find," Sarno said, "that I am not making myself clear. If I grow dissatisfied with your actions, you will not be able to deal with anyone. You will be dead."

"You wouldn't dare!" That was Carstairs.

"Wouldn't I?" Sarno laughed, and the sound of it was tinged with something akin to madness. "Wouldn't I just?" He sobered abruptly, skewered the general with a glance. "There is nothing, absolutely *nothing*, I would not dare. You—these planets—the *Federation*—all are in my power. I am humored; I am not told what I would and wouldn't dare."

"Like a child with a flamer," observed the admiral.

"*Exactly* like a child with a flamer," Sarno agreed, not at all miffed by the comparison. "Like that, exactly." He grinned toothily. "*Now* do I make myself clear?"

"Disgustingly," replied the admiral.

"You," said Sarno thoughtfully. "You, I don't need. I think I'll rid myself of you." He picked up the gun, aimed it at the admiral's white, beribboned tunic.

Garcia looked horrified. "You're not serious?"

"I'm not?" chuckled Sarno—and fired. The weapon's beam caught the admiral just below the throat, sent him over backward, chair and all. The two congressmen sat rooted; Carstairs and Raymond were on their feet. Carstairs had a feral snarl on his sharp face.

"And then," said Sarno lazily, swinging his gun to cover Carstairs, "there were four. Or is it to be three?" He waited. The troopers in the doorway had been taken by surprise, but now their guns were leveled. A faint tracery of steam rose from Sarno's gun barrel. The tension stretched.

And then Garcia—his face as pale as bed linen—spoke. "Sit down, Carstairs, for God's sake. We're dealing with a madman here—no telling what might set him off."

Carstairs emitted something like a groan, sank back into his chair. Raymond followed suit. The tension leaked away. Sarno gestured to one of the troopers, indicated the dead admiral.

"Get that out of here, trooper—dump it in the garbage incinerator. And send a crew to clean the carpet as soon as we're through here."

"Yes, my general." The soldier slung his rifle, grabbed a shiny spaceboot in either hand and dragged the corpse across the carpet, leaving a trail of thick, dark blood and charred bits of flesh. His partner opened the door and he dragged it through, silencing the startled inquiries of the troopers outside with a word. The door cut him from view, and Sarno looked back to the four remaining Terrans.

"I can tell you what *might* set me off, Senator Garcia, and that is any other deprecating reference to myself. Understood?"

Garcia's eyes burned like hot coals. "Understood."

"Excellent. Then we can get on to the order of the day.

That being the list of conditions that must be met before Terra and her sister planets are returned to you."

"Those being?"

"The list is quite impressive. I doubt you could remember them all to relay to the High Command if I simply repeated them to you, so I have had five lists drawn up. However"—he laid down the gun, picked up the top sheet—"you won't need one of these now, it seems." He tore it precisely into quarters, then into smaller bits, and piled the pieces neatly to one side.

"Why, you . . ." began Carstairs.

"Now, now!" Sarno raised a warning finger. "Shh-h-h! Can't tell what might set me off." He pushed the remaining four sheets across the table, waited until Garcia had handed one to each man, keeping one for himself.

"As you can see," he said, "the demands are not at all unreasonable. The Empire demands none of *your* worlds; it wishes only the restoration of all those taken by the Federation in the course of the war. It asks that all prisoners be surrendered up, and that all behind-the-lines fortresses, listening posts and shipping-lane raiders capitulate within a specified amount of time. Further, it requires the names and locations of all spies, operatives, agents and collaborators within the borders of Empire. As insurance against new incursions by spies and saboteurs, certain high-ranking military and civilian personnel shall be turned over to the Supreme Council as hostages. All "Freedom Radio" broadcasts to subject races of the Llralan people will cease forthwith, and the continued well-being of the Council's hostages will depend upon whether or not the broadcasts resume once Terra is freed, as well as upon the curtailment of all clandestine intelligence activities.

"And, last but by no means least, all Federated armed forces must disengage from the battlefront known as the Line and withdraw within the Federation's borders until such time as the cease-fire is terminated and conflict resumes."

"But those conditions will put us right back where we were at the beginning of the war!" exploded Raymond. "They refute every gain we've made, and leave you exactly as you are. And those additional handicaps! Why—why, it's like handing you a club to beat our brains out with!"

234

"That," said Sarno smugly, "is your problem, not mine. At least I have not demanded anything like total surrender of all Federated armed forces."

"The only reason you haven't is because you know you'll never get it," opined Carstairs. "You may not even get all this."

"No? That *will* be too bad, won't it—for the peoples of these three planets, I mean? Because, gentlemen—and here's an important consideration—*one city a day will lose its population until those demands are met.*" He leaned back in his seat, smiled at the ceiling. "That should give you plenty of time, shouldn't it? We'll start with the small townships, of course, and work up. By the time we get to New York, say, or Hong Kong, you should have been able to resign yourselves to your fate and begun to make arrangements."

Not even Carstairs felt moved to verbal protest; they simply sat and stared at him as if hard put to accept the reality and enormity of what was happening to them, and to the Federation. Sarno placed his hands on the table, stood up.

"And now, gentlemen, all the cards are on the table, in Terran parlance. I have shown my hand, and it is a good one. There no longer exists the slightest suspicion in your minds that I am bluffing. I can see that. Very well: this meeting is adjourned. It only remains for you to convince the High Command to accede to my demands, basing your methods of convincing upon what you have seen here.

"You may leave."

They left, and he sank wearily back into his chair. He felt curiously lightheaded. It was all up to the Terran High Command, now—he had voiced the Empire's demands, and not one single concession less than had been specified would buy life for the three planets involved. He had rested his case, and in a very short time the jury would go out. All that remained for him now was to hang on long enough to act as executioner if that jury's verdict should be unfavorable.

The decision was simple: three billion lives against voluntarily crippling themselves so badly that total defeat was a virtual certainty. The basic decision was simple, all right, but the ramifications of either course of action would extend to the ends of recordable history. They had come to a parting of the ways. Would they hold victory so dear as to squander three billion lives in pursuit of it, or would they ransom the worlds and then fight on, pitifully restricted?

Only time would tell. Meanwhile, there was this new and utterly baffling turn of events: the appearance of actual *things* in the night; the swift slaughter of four full battalions, each in one of the cities designated for the soldiers' use during liberty, each within the actual building set up for that liberty —and each accompanied by weird manifestations above the rooftops and the disappearance of the Terran women interned there for the troopers' pleasure.

He groaned softly. *Four battalions!* By comparison, the fate of Lieutenant General Quiror and his command in Atlanta faded into insignificance, though it had been a symptom of the disease now running rampant. For with only three million soldiers to do the job on three *billion* sleeeprs, the loss of even a single man was painful . . . but the loss of four battalions was excruciating. Four battalions and not a single clue as to the identity of their slayers, much less anything concrete to strike back at, to wreak revenge upon.

He climbed to his feet, moved to one of the thick portholes lining the conference room. A weak, heatless sun was shining on the drifted snow far below. The porthole disk itself was rimed with ice.

I do not, he told himself, *believe in ghosts—not in bog spirits, not naparra, not the ancestral spirits of Llrala nor the native ghosts of Risstair. And certainly not in Donovan's grandfather's ghost, or angry Terran ghouls that slit the throats of the defilers of their female descendants and then dance a jack-o'-lantern polka above surrounding buildings.*

Nevertheless, he had canceled all liberty passes; and for virtually the first time in the annals of the Llralan military, such action had met with no griping in the ranks. That worried him; when the enlisted men started agreeing with command decisions, trouble was brewing. Bad trouble.

He squinted out the porthole at the winter-wrapped slice of this savage planet to which he had come with his Dust and his fleet and his high hopes, and felt an ugly foreboding deep in his soul.

On the other side of this world, he thought, *it is night. And*

Venus and Mars—they have their night sides, too. I wonder what walks there now?

The frosty glass gave back no answer and he turned and retrieved his pistol from the conference table and left the room, stepping carefully to avoid the mess the Terran admiral had made on the carpet.

Chapter Twenty-Nine

The three sleeping planets pursued their individual orbits around their yellow sun, and each turned independently upon its axis, and that fact made very little difference to their populations. Night or day, high summer or hard winter, they slept peacefully on.

But the invaders were *not* sleeping, and therefore, if they found themselves confronted by things normally confined to bad dreams, they could not resort to waking up to escape.

And they *were* confronted . . .

"Six!" said the corporal.

"And seven!" responded the lanky private jubiliantly. He began to gather in the playing markers as the onlookers swore. "Another game, anybody?" He grinned, waved at the lax shapes sprawled beyond the glow of their battle lantern in the cavernous bomb shelter. "My luck's running hot—how many did you get that time, corporal?"

"Ten," grunted the corporal disgustedly.

"And ten makes seventy-five," he said. "Seventy-five Rekks for the six of you to divide up according to your winnings. Me, when and if the order comes, I go kiting along to the next

237

shelter on our list, do in my share there and then so on back to the ship." He clattered the markers together. "Shall we move on to the next shelter, gentlemen?"

"And just how," inquired a burly trooper, "do you know how many you'll be responsible for in the next shelter?"

The lanky private gestured airily. "Me, when I get a chance to go topside and breathe, there's a method to my wandering: I looked up our next stop. Being good at simple arithmetic, I figured out that exactly one hundred one and one-half Terrans are my quota there. Sooo . . ." He clinked the markers suggestively. "Any takers?"

"Not on your life," said the burly one. "Fifteen extra here is enough for me."

"No sporting blood." He looked around. "Anybody? Corporal?"

"I agree with Vorgen," the corporal said. "Twenty-seven will do me nicely."

The others were of a like mind and the game broke up as they moved away from the table to stretch their legs and curse their luck. Conversation lulled and the low, ever-present drone of the sleepers' breathing seemed to grow louder. Up at ground level, according to a patrolling gun-truck they had made contact with a while back, a tropical storm was raging, but here in the shelter there was no evidence of it. There was only the hypnotic breathing of the sleeping Terrans and the nearly inaudible hum of the unseen machines that kept the air pure, the temperature stable and performed the various other chores to the well-being of the sleepers—and, consequently, of their guards.

"Trapped with a bunch of non-gamblers," complained the lanky private, "and no liberty in sight. Life is worthless."

"You're right," agreed the corporal, thumbing through a magazine found in the shelter. "Your life would be worthless if you got the liberty you've been groaning about; I wouldn't give a quarter-Imperial for your chances of surviving it."

He snorted derisively. "Are you afraid of orange balloons, too?"

"When they can cut throats, yes—and when searfire only makes them go away to pop up somewhere else."

He shook his head in amazement. "You actually *believe* all that scut?"

"I believe four dead battalions," retorted the corporal. Then, changing the subject: "Say, here's a picture of Madrij, of the Supreme Council!" He pored over the writing accompanying the picture, finally shrugged. "Wish I'd learned to read Rekk; it'd be something to know what they thought about old Mad—"

The hum of hidden machinery deepened, compensating, as a sudden wave of cold air washed into the shelter from the stairs—air that smelled faintly of rain and wet things, some of the odors recognizable, others not.

"Now I wonder," said the lanky private, "what caused that? I thought these places were supposed to be airtight."

"Somebody probably opened the door," the corporal answered absently, preoccupied with his magazine.

"Yio? Who?" The private looked around. "There are seven of us here—all present and accounted for. So who opened the door?"

The machinery continued to throb at an altered pitch as the fresh air continued its invasion. The burly trooper who had won fifteen of the private's sleepers wandered over in time to catch his question.

"Maybe it was an *orange balloon,*" he whispered. The private jumped in spite of himself, and the trooper brayed.

"Very funny," snarled the private. *"Very* funny."

"Whoever it was," inserted the corporal, "didn't close it behind him. Soxkin, why don't you go attend to that little chore—and make sure it's secure this time, huh?"

"Why me?" asked the private, showing reluctance.

"Because I chose you!" snapped the corporal. "Now jump!"

The private gave him a dirty look, picked up his rifle and went out the door. The shuffle of his boots on the steel risers ascended beyond earshot and the corporal went back to his magazine, half-listening for the thud of the door closing.

Instead, a glow lighted the stairwell followed by a hair-raising shriek of stark, unadulterated terror.

Almost before the glow faded, the corporal was leading his men in a headlong charge up the stairs. They found Soxkin on the topmost landing, huddled into a protective ball and gobbling insanely. They rushed past him to the door, guns at the ready.

Beyond the door wind-driven sheets of rain lashed through the deepening twilight, obscuring the tall spires of the city and drumming loudly on the silent cars in the street. That was all. No glowing orange spheres, no shrouded phantoms. Just the rain and the wind and the city.

"Corporal!" It was the burly trooper, Vorgen, bending over the incoherent Soxkin.

"What is it?"

"He keeps saying it was one of the cutthroat balloons," Vorgen said. He listened, went on, "He says it appeared right in his face when he went to shut the door."

The corporal hastily shoved the door closed, and they were in sudden, inky blackness. He swore. "Didn't anybody bring a torch?"

Apparently, nobody had.

He swore again and felt his way to the stairs and down. "We've got to report this," he said, and his voice was shaky, almost as shaky as his knees. He shut up and concentrated on getting down the stairs in one piece.

Elsewhere, a gun-truck was rumbling swiftly down a rural highway bordered on either side by snowy fields and winding over undulating hills. Its headlight beams dipped and swayed and created marching shadows as it sped along.

"For Sirri's sake, be careful!" the radioman, sitting beside the driver, shouted above the noise of the engine. "You hit ice, you'll kill us all."

"Can't be careful," the driver shouted back. His eyes were fastened unwaveringly on the road, his gloved hands fought the bucking wheel expertly. "The captain said hurry."

"Yio, but we won't do him any good dead in a roadside ditch," the radioman retorted.

The driver slowed the armored juggernaut carefully. "We should be getting there. We just passed a road sign—you catch what it said?"

"How could I?" the radioman wanted to know. "I can't read Terran. Wait a minute . . ." He switched on his throat mike, spoke to somebody up ahead. Then, "If the next intersection has a marker with three vertical lines side by side, that'll be the one. Turn left."

They came at length to the proper intersection and the driver hauled the big vehicle through the turn. "Now," he said, "we go!" The engine bellowed and the truck leaped ahead.

"You'd better go slow," the radioman worried. "If it's here at all, it should show up right along—*there it is!*"

The driver followed his pointing finger. *"Sirri!"*

Sweeping down across the fields on what was obviously an intercept course came a great black beast, running full-out on four slender, pistoning legs, a dark cloud of tail whipping out behind. And on the creature's back: a *man,* riding crouched, a voluminous cape billowing around him.

"Coming after us," the radioman whispered.

"We'll see about *that,*" the driver responded.

The truck surged ahead, and the beast and its rider began to close the distance, pounding closer and closer. The creature's hooves hardly seemed to touch ground. . . . The radioman noticed a pale cone of light that seemed to come from *behind* the truck and follow the thing's wild career from a fixed point, much like a spotlight on a performer, or . . .

Or *what?* Something he should recognize, something his training had included. He tried to think, but the thing grew larger as it drew closer, and cogent thinking was impossible with superstitious fear laying like a sheet of ice over his brain. He knew what was coming, knew from having heard of the fate of others along this road, knew all the driver's frantic maneuvering could not prevent it.

It happened. The thing loomed gigantic as it cut across the road and into the truck's headlights. And then it was rearing on its hind legs, and the rider was flinging something directly at the windshield—something that pulsed and glowed bright orange and swelled enormously . . .

The truck spun out of control, left the road as startled cries sounded from the gun turret, and flipped. The serene peace of the wintry fields was shattered as it plowed thunderously through a fence and into a stand of young trees, finally coming to a rending halt with all wheels up.

Within the battered cab, the dying radioman fought off the darkness, trying to find the mike button to report.

"Headless . . ." His voice was feeble, and blood frothed in his throat. "The rider was headless . . . *and he threw his head at me!* He . . ."

And then he died.

And elsewhere . . . The soldiers stood their posts with increased alertness that night, eyes straining to pierce the darkness and ears straining for any untoward sound. The detectormen within the blockhouses amid the pale glow of their instruments suddenly became the most important men in camp, probing and prying at the surrounding terrain with immaterial fingers and unseeable eyes. The fence flickered softly, transmitting a hum of power along its death-dealing length to the soldiers walking sentry.

It did them no good. All their alertness, all their precautions—all for naught. While their commander slept soundly in his camp bed, confident in his men's readiness, secure in their ability to meet and defeat anything the sleeping planet had to offer, the sentries collapsed one by one with no fuss and with little sound other than the clatter of dropped weapons. Faint puffs of vapor, invisible in the night, came drifting on the prevailing wind currents and seeped through the gun slits of the blockhouses. Moments later, the gunners were unconscious on their mounts and the detectormen slumped senseless in their chairs.

When all was still save the whispering breeze, the perimeter fence flared once, briefly, as some object made contact with it, and then the flow of power was smooth once more. There came no shouts of alarm, no rasping bull horns, no pounding feet. There had been none to notice the flare, none to give the necessary orders, none to carry them out had they been given.

Within a very few seconds, the fence's generators were quietly shut off and a host of shadow-shapes came drifting in out of the night as unobtrusively and silently as had come the vapor. Stun-guns sparkled briefly over the bed-trenches of the bulk of the encampment's complement to insure their continued slumber, and only one or two of the soldiers so much as twitched or grunted when the stun-bolts hit them.

A sleepy radio operator in the HQ hut noticed that a certain undertone of static had vanished from his set as disembodied voices conversed back and forth over the airwaves, and that voices far away now came more clearly, but the implication failed to register. A certain amount of static had to be endured if the radio set was to be surrounded by the electric protection of the fence; once that static disappeared, it mean the fence was no longer operating. But it had been a long watch, the conversation of his fellows at similar posts had been routine and hypnotic, and he was expecting his relief man's arrival almost any time now . . .

The door behind him opened.

"About time," he said without turning. "I was beginning to wonder when you—"

He never completed his sentence. Something sparkled and hummed in the doorway and his body went limp, his drowsy mind relaxing almost willingly into unconsciousness.

And still elsewhere . . . A pair of troopers, bundled up in heavy winter gear but still miserable, stood guard over a command flivver parked in a street beside the bomb-shelter entrance.

"This," opined the taller one, "is madness. Why should we freeze to death just to watch their ship while they're inside trying to prove us the victims of hallucinations?"

"Because," said the shorter, "they are the mighty Imperial Intelligence and we but lowly foot-sloggers. And also"—he grinned bleakly—"because they do not want the 'orange balloons' and other nasty little fragments of our overwrought imagination running off with their transportation and leaving them stranded."

"Orange balloons!" The tall trooper snorted. "I know what I saw—right up there." He pointed to a balcony some twenty levels above the street, at present almost obscured by falling snow. "And it wasn't any balloon. It was . . . something else."

"Don't tell me," said the shorter man. "Tell them." He hunched his neck deeper into his parka. All around them the snow drove silently, silently through the cold gray streets, and a bitter little breeze caused it to eddy and swirl at the bases of the huge, brooding buildings. Drifts had buried the Terran traffic stalled on the street, and the whole sprawling city seemed to grow out of a snow field.

"What a Sirri-forsaken world," the tall trooper remarked.

"No wonder the Rekks are so foul-tempered and uncooperative."

"And their ghosts are so restless," appended the other. "How'd *you* like trying to take the Sleep Eternal if your grave was as cold as graves must be here?"

The tall trooper shuddered. "I wish you wouldn't say thing like that. I—"

"Look!"

He looked, stiffened, began to fumble frantically at the rifle slung over his shoulder with numb fingers. "Here we go again!"

"Yio—only this time the Intelligence boys get to see it, too." There was a dismal satisfaction in the way it was said. He went running toward the bomb shelter, slipping and sliding on the uncertain footing, leaving his partner alone with this latest manifestation.

The snow continued to fall in ragged white blankets, and the wind to moan softly around the corners—*but where the snow had lain for days, it was melting.* Melting and becoming water and draining away before the temperature could freeze it back into ice.

And, in every tall spire, in every shorter edifice, one by one and by the scores and hundreds, all across the city:

The lights were coming on.

And so it went. The central planet of the three followed its course around the sun, and turned upon its axis, and to its invaders its peaceful slumber became the background for a thousand bad dreams. Unease matured into out-and-out fear, and the fear became near-panic, and the panic began to insinuate its tendrils into every bomb shelter, every stronghold, every spaceship across its length and breadth. Effervescent blue glowworms six feet in length began to haunt the nights of Venus, and Mars had its own special breed of night life, too, and the panic was no longer confined to a single planet, but spread.

On Terra, a troopship in France was beseiged by phantom soldiers wearing ridiculous little tin hats and carrying bulky rifles with knives on the end. The ship pulled up its ramps and unlimbered its spaceguns and did as much damage to the beseigers as blowing soap bubbles would have, and finally gave

244

up when it had blackened a suitable stretch of countryside and settled down under tight security to wait out the seige.

Also on Terra, Sirri was deserted by His faithful at a twilight service in a Terran park when lookouts detected the peculiar orange gas-moons apparently sneaking up on the gathering. The soldiers fled and the chaplain did likewise, priestly robes flapping like the wings of some ungainly bird in his precipitative flight. When they were sure the moons were not pursuing, they halted and congratulated each other upon escaping an awful reckoning.

On Venus, the undulating glowworms put to rout a similar service, the incident being notable in that Gauskarr, Supreme Commander of Venusian Occupational Forces, had been present and had put to the lie once and for all the old rumor that ranking brass was soft and out of condition by setting the congregation a blistering pace away from the immediate vicinity.

On Mars, squadrons of the tiny white lights that had been present at the slaughter of the 208th Infantry's Second Battalion in Canali patrolled the highways and byways, chasing everything that would run and fleeing from everything that pursued.

And on all three planets there were certain undulating howls in the night, echoing weirdly among the soaring architecture of a technological age, and creaking sounds as of doors being opened, and thuds as of doors being closed, and thumps and bumps and the rattle of chains and tread of unseen feet.

The three planets turned upon their axes, and every gathering of aliens had their share of nightfalls and witching hours and false dawns, and as the blood-congealing visitations during those periods increased and diversified, the troopers grew more fearful and restive, and their officers more harried, and the brass hats more frantic.

The invaded inhabitants of the three planets might be sleeping, but it was the invaders that were having the nightmares.

Chapter Thirty

"As I peruse these reports," said Security Underchief Blalir, "I am increasingly aware of an overpowering trend."

"So am I," responded Martak Sarno bitterly. "We're being run off the planet by spooks."

"What then?"

Blalir tapped the reports with a forefinger. "These incidents seem to occur in waves. Each time these ghosts"—he grimaced slightly—"appear, they show new sophistication of technique. Quiror's pen, for example, was simply wiped out, but this latest attack on a pen is quite a different matter. One moment the sentries are walking their rounds and the detectormen are watching their instruments—and the next, it is morning and every man in camp wakes up to find himself stark naked in a big pile with his fellows in the center of camp. The buildings are smashed—and not a gun, not a flivver, not a shirt is to be found. But no one's throat is cut. While irritating, the stunt is intrinsically harmless. Such phenomena are called"—he consulted his notes—"poltergeist phenomena, common in the history of this planet. It means something like prankish ghost."

"A damned embarrassing prank for those involved, I'll bet," ventured Sarno.

"Perhaps. But frightening might be a better word. What could be more frightening than to awaken upon an alien world stripped of every defense—right down to underwear—you possess? And with the full knowledge that all those defenses had not helped to keep you from getting into this predicament in the first place?"

"And that others who had found themselves in a like position hadn't wakened up at all, eh?"

"Precisely. That is what I meant by sophistication: two hundred and twenty *frightened* men are infinitely more damaging than a like number of *dead* ones. Dead men you simply bury and make adjustments to get along without; frightened ones you must continue to utilize, or end up with nobody left to do what must be done."

"And meanwhile the fear spreads like a contagious virus through the ranks."

"*Yes.*"

"And the Quartermaster is hard-pressed to resupply the missing equipment."

"Again correct."

"So where does that leave us?"

"In the middle. We know that *something* is capable of slitting throats and getting away unseen; we know that *something* can put to sleep, disarm, disrobe and disassemble a camp without betraying itself; we know that *something* is responsible for all these manifestations that have the troops on the verge of open rebellion. . . . But we don't know *what*. We don't have any concrete proof that the Federation has a hand in it, so we don't dare brace them about it for fear of disclosing something they don't already know and sending the whole game up in flames. In fact, we don't have any concrete proof of *anything*."

"You are not," informed Sarno, "telling me anything I don't already know."

"I am aware of that," the Underchief replied patiently. "You know every bit as much as I do—which is nothing. I have driven my men until they're dead on their feet, have set up numberless camera traps and staked out countless likely-seeming areas for a visitation. And what came of it? One agent was at Curik's pen when the 'headless horseman' came galloping through the barrier fence and started chasing soldiers around inside. Four ran into their own fence and were fried; my agent and six others were burned by others trying to stop that thing with searfire. Another agent happened to be at Zalaguester's pen when it was doped and stripped. Result: my agent woke up naked right along with the rest of them."

Sarno smiled in spite of himself. "That," he said, "ought to set Intelligence prestige back about ten centuries."

"Maybe." Blalir didn't seem to care one way or the other.

"Surely your camera traps got *something?*"

"Oh, yes—wonderful shots of those things you call jack-o'-lanterns, and glowing blue worms and flocks of little white lights. And of searfire going right through them, and some good candid stuff of tough paratroopers fleeing like frightened children."

"But nothing important?"

"Nothing." He gestured again. "It's almost as if—I hate to say this, but it's so—it's almost as if our every move were being watched, interpreted and countered. We found cameras smashed, and cameras with film exposed, and in some cases the cameras were just gone."

"You sound as if you're beginning to believe in ghosts yourself," Sarno observed bitingly.

"Why not?" Blalir shrugged. "I've seen stranger things than ghosts in my years with Intelligence—and come to the conclusion that nothing is impossible. So why not?" He didn't seem overly dismayed at the prospect.

Sarno said as much.

Again the shrug. "Why should I be? If it's so, it's so—and my emotional reaction to the problem is not going to alter it one iota."

"Well, that's an admirable attitude," the general admitted, "but it isn't helping us settle this thing. You, personally, were in New York City when all the lights came on and the snow melted off the streets. What did you see?"

A third shrug, and a slight twist of the mouth as if even the effort of lifting his shoulders was begrudged. "I saw the lights come on, and the snow melt. Oh"—he raised a placating hand to head off the other's comment—"we did see the space troops in fine style, rushing around from power station to power station, guns drawn and teeth bared. But all we saw were switches turned on where they had been off. No jack-o'-lanterns, no headless horsemen, no phantom soldiers or spooks of any variety whatsoever. Just switches *on* where they had been *off.*"

"And so?"

"And so we turned the switches back off, got a company to seal off the surrounding areas, and went through them with a fine-tooth comb. We found, as usual, nothing—nothing at all. One does not catch quicksilver in a seine."

"What about that ship in France, the *Kalistra*, where this whole mess started?"

"Oh—the ancient soldiers of Terra?"

"Yes. What did the scan beams show?"

"Nothing. Every time we turned on a scanner in the neighborhood, they vanished. Leave the scanner off, they'd reappear. We tried surprising them with random timing on the scan sweeps—and that didn't work, either. Their reactions are the fastest I've ever run up against."

"Which suggests two things to me," said Sarno. "One they're afraid of detection—they have something to hide. Two, those reflexes *could* be robotic."

"On the other hand, they could be allergic to the scanner beams," Blalir countered. "As to robotic reflexes, we've poked and pried at more robots than I care to remember. They're clean; all we found was a vague sort of puzzlement as to where the humans had gone and what we were doing here, coupled with a sort of wish that things would get back to normal so they could resume whatever their workaday chores happened to be. Besides, who ever heard of disappearing robots?"

"Whoever heard of ghosts laying siege to a spaceship?" Sarno retorted.

"Playing with words," reproved the Underchief gently, "gets us no closer to the solution of our problem."

"And neither, apparently, does your fumble-fingered bumbling." Sarno's voice was cold. He stood up, planted his bulk solidly on both feet. "Until you can give me something definite to work on, stop wasting my time."

The Underchief's eyebrows lifted just a trifle as he uncoiled from his own seat. "Insults, like word-bandying, will get us exactly nowhere," he commented. His voice held a matching chill that brought Sarno up short. He had almost forgotten that, with Sjilla gone, Blalir had automatically received Sjilla's vacated post—and that, as Acting Security Chief and in absence of orders from home, he was not required to take abuse of a mere expeditionary commander such as himself.

Great, he told himself as the Underchief left the cabin. *Just great. Now I've got an enemy within the ranks as well as all those without.* Belatedly he realized that he had meant to ask Blalir if there had been any word from Atlanta on Donovan and the others. Not that it really mattered. Blanatta would have informed him if there had been. He felt a sudden surge of warmth for his old police chief. Even when things looked blackest, Blanatta's faith in his ability to get them through was unshaken. Right now, Blanatta was minding the fleet and keeping watch over the ghost happenings—and Blalir, whatever his personal feelings and despite his resemblance to an under-nourished corpse, was competent. His command was in goods hands, and, for the moment at least, the spooks were quiet.

He yawned broadly. Which meant, perhaps, that he could sneak a little sleep. He unbuckled his gunbelt, loosened his tunic and turned in, not even bothering to take off his boots.

An hour later he was on the bridge, all thoughts of sleep driven from his head, straining to hear a distant voice through a constant blather of static.

"Sjilla," he called. And then again louder, "Sjilla!"

The interference lifted momentarily and a voice said clearly, "Here, general."

"I thought you were dead!"

"One of the hazards of my occupation," was the wry rejoinder. "People give me up too soon."

"Where are you?"

"I'm . . ." The static came back, worse than before. Through gaps in the noise Sarno caught snatches of sentences. ". . . attacked by robots in Atlanta . . . Got caught by Rierson. Donovan . . ."

He seized eagerly on that. "Donovan! What about Donovan? Is he dead?"

"No." The reply to that was clearly understandable. "But he's out of commission. I've got his legs."

"Sirri!"

Came a static-filled chuckle. "Grotesque, ain't it?"

"Your voice sounds funny."

"So does yours—but I caught the backwash of a flamer bolt across the face. What's *your* excuse?"

"You seem in excellent spirits," observed the general. He himself was supremely happy. He had the delegation—and by proxy the Federation—where he wanted it, and now Sjilla was back from the dead. And Donovan was out of circulation. Let the phantoms beware!

"I ought to. Incidentally, I got the Spook of Baxter."

"*What?* How?"

"How would take a long time telling, and this contact is terrible. Suffice it to say that I have him neatly tied to a stretcher and ready for delivery."

"Excellent. And when may I expect delivery?"

The static obscured the reply.

"I didn't hear that last," he said, and waited. There was no answer. He jabbed the talk button anxiously. "Sjilla?"

". . . still with you, general—but just barely. As to . . . delivery. There's one more . . . to do before I . . . the neatly-wrapped bundle to you." The interference worsened momentarily, then lifted altogether. "There are some loose ends that need tying up. Will I have your cooperation?"

"Absolutely. There's something else that needs taking care of?"

Something about describes it, general. Something following me, sniping at me. It got Quiror—he'd escaped with me—and it got two riflemen. All I've got left is a pair of troopers and a flivver pilot."

"Robots?" Sarno questioned. "That's the second time you've mentioned robots. What about them?"

"Well . . . Rierson got the jump on me in Atlanta. He armed the robot staff of a department store and smashed that pen good. But I took care of that when I nailed him—and whatever's after me now isn't robots, and it isn't a figment of Donovan's imagination. Pipe dreams don't slit people's throats while they sleep."

Sarno felt a nasty thrill along his spine. "Is that what's happening?"

"It is—though I know you'll find it hard to believe . . ."

"No," said Sarno. He felt suddenly very old. "No, it isn't hard to believe at all."

251

"What do you mean by that?"

He told him, wasting no words. When he'd finished, there was a long silence. Then, "So it isn't a bad dream, after all—it's really happening."

"It's happening, all right—I can attest to that."

"In that case"—Sjilla's voice regained its briskness—"in that case, I'm going to try it. But I'll need full cooperation."

"Try what? And I've already said you'll have full co-operation."

"Try something that until just this moment seemed utter nonsense. Try a little countersorcery, you might call it. But I've got to set a stage."

"Just say the word and you'll have a thousand soldiers—or two, or three."

"Thanks, general, but that's not the kind of cooperation I'll need."

"Name it then." Sarno was in an expansive mood.

"You know where El Scorpio is?"

"El What?"

"El Scorpio—Planetary Defense Center 10."

"Oh. Somewhere on the North American Continent, isn't it?"

"Yes."

"What about it?"

Static. Then, ". . . I want it set up for me. Whatever's dogging us, I want to lead it into a space wide enough that it'll have to make its presence known before it strikes."

"You shall have it," promised Sarno. "There'll be two thousand troopers awaiting you—"

"*No!*"

He was taken aback by the other's vehemence. "Why not?"

"Because . . . because two thousand mud-faces will just get in my way. And each other's. How many men on the base now, by the way?"

"A moment." Sarno turned, consulted his battle board, his eyes running swiftly down the twinkling rows of lights. Then, "Approximately two hundred. That includes the officers and the technicians mapping its defenses."

"That's plenty of manpower. Now, here's what I want done . . ."

The static flooded back, stayed longer than usual. Sarno waited impatiently until it lifted. "Sjilla—still there?"

"Still here."

"I didn't catch the last. Want to repeat it?"

"You can bet your brass button I do. And Sarno? Do it my way, huh? Right down to the last detail? Otherwise, I won't be responsible for what happens."

"And this way you will?"

"This way I will—and I think I can guarantee you the final cessation of hostile activities, both temporal and otherworldly."

"You *think*." Sarno underlined the word.

"Yes, I *think*," Sjilla came back testily, the strangeness of his voice accentuated. "Or would you rather do it your way? In such case I'd rather *not* think. You know how mass slaughter appalls me."

"I do?"

"You do now. Now, do I give you my plan, or do we do it your way?"

"Don't get upset," soothed the general. "You've always gotten results before—and you got the Spook of Baxter this time, in spite of the pen massacre. I've no cause to doubt your judgment. We do it your way."

"Good!" That approval was distorted by returning interference. "Listen closely. Contact is fading; I won't have time to say it twice."

"I'm listening."

"All right. Incidentally, if I'm on the right track, those supernatural manifestations you spoke of should cease shortly. They'll be coming after me. Now here's what I want done . . ." The voice went into a quick, concise detailing, interspersed with bursts of static and an alarming fade-out of volume that turned his crisp tones into a rasping whisper. Finally it stopped altogether and Sarno turned away from the radio. The contact was broken, but not before Sjilla had said what he wanted done. He had it all figured, right down to the requesting that warships in patrolling orbit be on stand-by to come down and lend support if whatever appeared happened to be vulnerable to energy weapons and at the same time proved too much for the token base guard to handle.

Sarno shook his head in unbegrudging admiration. At the

very start, even before the first robot Dust-ships had left for Terra, Sjilla had come to his fledgling command with the highest possible recommendations. And he had long since come to the conclusion that Intelligence H.Q. had known whereof they spoke.

Never once had he failed to produce.

Chapter Thirty-One

The soldiers occupied a wind-eroded ridge that gave them a sweeping view of the grassy plains rolling away to the horizon on all hands, their positions only partially entrenched and ill-concealed by hastily rigged camouflage netting. The three pre-fab autogun bunkers spaced evenly along their fan-shaped line stuck up like sore thumbs in the tall, waving prairie grass.

The sky arched high above in a myriad of cold winter colors as the sun sank toward the western horizon, and the ever-blowing wind began to bite at exposed flesh with fresh vigor. Night came marching toward them across the undulating grasslands and the first stars were already in evidence, burning with a hard, cold brilliance. Nine siveb behind them clustered a group of tiny buildings dwarfed by the immensity of empty space all around, buildings that were in reality cavernous hangars and reactors and barracks situated in the center of a vast space field easily capable of holding and servicing half an Imperial fleet at a time.

It was those buildings that the platoon was here to protect— those buildings and the other nine-tenths of the Planetary Defense Center known as El Scorpio which, like an iceberg, lay hidden beneath the surface. To protect them from some as yet unspecified danger that might at any moment come, like the night, marching out of the east. The soldiers were acutely aware of their vulnerability here, and their eyes were never still, searching the uniform monotony of the nearer swells and dips in the terrain with narrowed gaze. There were no distinctions made—any movement in that vast area of utter, eerie quietude would draw sudden and heavy fire. If it were only a trick of wind and shadow, or one of those jakrabbis that had not succumbed to the Dust . . . well, nothing was lost but a few rounds of ammunition. If it was *not* the wind or a jakrabbi then they had avoided being massacred unawares. So they stared until their eyes began to play tricks and they gripped their weapons until their hands ached.

"We're exposed here," muttered a rifleman to his partner, blowing on his trigger hand to warm it. "Sitting up like pips in a shooting gallery."

"That's the idea," returned his partner, without lowering his distance-lenses. "That's the whole idea."

"I don't like it!"

"Who does?" The other continued to scan the vector assigned them.

"It gives me the creeps, all this damned emptiness! And that wind! It just blows and blows . . ."

Came a derisive snort from the speaker's left. "What d'you expect it to do? Sing you a lullaby?"

The rifleman turned. It was the loader from the autogun emplacement farther along. "What are you doing here, Vas? If the lieutenant catches you . . ."

"He won't." Vas jerked a thumb at a small, pyramid-shaped hump at the base of the ridge. "He's in his tent, catching some shut-eye."

"Has anything else been heard from Sjilla?"

"Nothing. Just that one radio message and then nothing."

"I don't like it—not one little bit. On the say-so of one little radio message, we're scattered all over the state of Texas, seems like, waiting to fight some unnamed and unspecified enemy. I don't like it . . . the whole thing smells funny."

"Don't like anything, this one," said the second rifleman, lowering his lenses. "Got it all figured out, he has. Wonder why he isn't in command instead of Sarno?"

"I still say," the worrier responded doggedly, "that Sarno shouldn't act on the instructions of one short, mysterious radio call. 'No reinforcements moved in,' it said. 'Deploy what you have to cover all approaches. Bunch your officers and technicians in the most protected building with an armed guard, but don't attempt to fly them out.'" He gestured disgustedly. "What kind of goings-on are those, I ask you?"

"If I could understand it, I wouldn't be saddled with the likes of you as a partner," opined the worrier's partner. "Leave it to the officers—they know what they're doing."

"Yio? Like they knew in Atlanta, eh? And Portland, and Chicago and Paris and all the other cities—how about those?"

"Now that," declared his partner, "is enough! I don't even want to listen to such things—not with the brass as touchy as they are about mentioning them."

"That's just it. *Why* are they so touchy?"

"I couldn't tell you," confessed the loader. "But"—his voice dropped significantly—"you know what that legless Rekk, Donovan, had to say about it."

"Space-breeze!" defined the second rifleman contemptuously. "Who believes in spooks?"

"I'll bet I know a few who do."

"Who, for instance?"

"The men who were on liberty in Nairobi and Portland and Sydney and Canali, and who are now in refrigerator boxes awaiting shipment home. The ones who came up against the Spook of Baxter, and that headless thing, and those orange balls and blue worms and white lights."

The skeptical rifleman hefted his weapon. "Let a spook show up around here and we'll *see* whether he can be killed or not. All I ask is one good, clean shot at . . ." His voice tailed off and he sat as one transfixed.

"What's wrong?" hissed his partner.

"Across there—on that third rise. See it? A movement. Coming this way!" His rifle met shoulder. "Hard to see . . . can't get a clear shot . . ."

The grass on the third rise agitated wildly, moving against the push of the wind. Something was advancing on them, shaking the grass, but there was nothing to be seen.

The first rifleman gargled inarticulately, threw up his rifle and squirted a hose of flame at the movement. Startled shouts arose along the line, but he paid them no heed. His first shot had gone wide; he corrected and fired again. The unseen approacher accelerated its pace. The rifleman's partner unfroze and twin lances of fire crackled out. The thing turned at right angles and really started moving. Their fire fell behind. The dry grass began to burn luridly against the deepening twilight where the shots landed.

By now they could catch fleeting glimpses of something above the grass, moving upwind at an incredible pace. Other guns opened up, and the loader went racing back to his bunker. His voice sounded thin and lost above the wind.

"Re! Re! *Blast* it, Re!"

Re obligingly blasted it. The autogun coughed to brilliant life, swept after the still unidentfied fleeing thing in a flat, vicarious arc. Caught up with it and passed it. And stopped firing. A long line of alternately flaming and smoldering grass marked the path of flight. The rifles, which had ceased firing when the autogun began, remained silent. Into the returned stillness seeped the moaning of the bitter wind. The flames danced where searfire had breathed hotly upon the brittle grasses; the untouched stems nodded in cadence with the wind. The soldiers waited.

The lieutenant came out of his tent and up the rearward slope of their position on the dead run, voiced sharp inquiries and then barked a quick command. Five soldiers climbed out of their entrenchments and dog-trotted toward where the autogun had stopped firing, fanning out into a skirmish line. Their fellows on the ridge prepared to lay down covering fire.

There were long-drawn moments while the soldiers searched the area, aided by hand torches and the strengthening glow of the grass fire, and then a corporal gave a shout and lifted something above his head. They came back at a faster pace than they had used going out, and brought up before the lieutenant. He took the corporal's prize from him, swore loudly.

"A jakrabbi!" his voice came faintly down the lines. "A Sirri-accursed longears!" He flung the carcass away from him down the slope and unsnapped a loud-hailer from his belt.

"*All right, men.*" His mechanically augmented voice had a

strange, hollow ring in the blowing vastness. *"You killed a jakrabbi—nothing more. But you have shown you were alert. I commend you."* He paused for a moment, went on. *That alertness must be maintained. I have just heard from Major Corvun that Security Chief Sjilla is expected momentarily. Consequently, the danger he spoke of is increased. Carry on."* He replaced the hailer and started back for his tent.

"Look!" That was the first rifleman—the worrier—nudging his partner in the ribs and pointing at the sky. His partner looked. "Not there—over near the bright star."

Then his partner saw it. "A flivver!"

"Yio, and circling in to land."

The word ran quickly along the line, and the lieutenant, too, glanced up. As the tiny sliver of silver drifted down toward the distant buildings of El Scorpio, he unlimbered his hailer a second time.

"That will be Sjilla. From now on, anything can happen. Remember: stay alert."

Then he continued toward his tent without another look at the airship. The lieutenant was dead-tired—too much so to get excited over anything short of the prospect of a hot bath, a warm bed and plenty of time to enjoy both.

The first rifleman settled back into his shallow bed-*cum*-entrenchment and twisted until he could again survey the rapidly darkening slopes. A chill for which the arctic wind was not entirely responsible passed over his frame, and he tugged half of his open sleepbag up around his shoulders.

"Any time now," he said. "And from any direction."

"Yio," agreed his partner. "Any time." He raised the distance-lenses once more and began to traverse the slopes nearest them. "Wonder how I'll get mine—from an orange balloon or a glowworm?" He tried to make it a joke, but it didn't sound funny.

"I don't know, but I've got a feeling we'll find out pretty soon now."

Behind them, the big command flivver settled in smoothly among the buildings they were here on the ridge to defend.

Chapter Thirty-Two

The flivver came to rest before an aboveground administration office, and there was a delegation waiting to meet it. Major Corvun stood at the head of the little knot of officers, his hand tentatively on his gun butt. His inferiors struck like poses. Off across the rolling sea of grass to the east, a reddish glow strengthened in the dusk. Corvun shook his head. Lieutenant Hanosork's platoon was jumpy this evening, but then who could blame them? Sjilla's message had set everyone on edge —including Sarno, he'd wager.

The flivver's compartment door banged open to reveal a Llralan trooper with slung rifle. He dropped the craft's short ladder, descended to the ground and stood at attention.

The next figure to appear at the door bulked large as he ducked through and came down. Corvun's eyes widened. By all visible characteristics, the big man was a Terran—a Terran with a plastic bandage wrapped under his chin, over the top of his head and then several times around, turban-fashion. His clothes were colorful, loose-fitting and of obviously Terran cut; an alien rifle hung from his shoulder.

The trooper saluted smartly, and the big man returned it with a casual wave. Then he motioned back inside, said something and started across the pavement, hands in jacket pockets. The wind whipped his trouser legs as he approached, giving forth a faint popping sound.

Corvun snapped to attention, executed a classic salute. His junior officers imitated him. The big man took his hand out of his pocket, gave another of those casual waves. Corvun rankled

259

for a moment, then chided himself for it; after all, Intelligence was hardly as tradition-steeped as the infantry.

"Security Chief Sjilla?"

The big man nodded, flipped the lapel of his jacket. The both famous and infamous gold badge was pinned there.

"Major . . .?" He raised inquiring eyebrows.

"Corvun, sir. Imperial Infantry, 503rd Division."

"Good. Major Corvun, you must forgive my slowness of speech"—it was true; his words came slowly and with obvious difficulty—"but I was slightly singed by a flamer several days back."

"I will have a medico sent for."

"Never mind; the wound is minor. That's my self-diagnosis." The big man smiled. "We pick up all sorts of tricks in this racket."

"I can imagine."

"But we are not here to exchange pleasantries," he went on in a crisper tone. He turned back toward the ship. Two soldiers were lifting down a stretcher. A fat individual wearing the comet of the flying corps looked on, a bulging bundle tucked under one arm and a searpistol in the free hand. "The Rekk on the stretcher is my prisoner," he said. "You have heard of him referred to in the past as 'The Spook of Baxter.' He is no spook; he is as mortal as you or I. But he *is* highly dangerous. That's why I've got him lashed securely to that stretcher. I figure he can do less harm that way."

"What harm can he do?" Corvun asked curiously.

The big man shrugged. "I don't know. But let him get one arm loose and we'll all find out soon enough." He smiled at the major enigmatically. "James Rierson is a holy terror once he gets started. But I know all his tricks." Again the strange smile. "I am almost intimate with them, you might say. Therefore I do not wish him locked away, but kept right in my sight, bound just as he is now. If by any chance he manages to break loose—don't ask me how—do not hesitate to shoot. And shoot to kill. This one is very, very dangerous."

The troopers approached with the stretcher, paused before them. Corvun looked down at the prostrate form. The Terran was straining at his gag, the flesh showing whitely around that

260

impediment to speech. Muffled noises came from behind the gag; his throat worked convulsively.

"A very vicious personality," observed the big man. "Terrible temper."

The other's eyes bugged with his efforts to speak, and the muffled sounds increased in volume.

"Typical Terran," commented Corvun judiciously. At that, the Terran subsided and closed his eyes.

"Why . . . he seems to be crying!" exclaimed the major.

"Repenting his former sins and wickedness, no doubt," the big man said. The Terran opened his eyes and stared at him venomously.

"Brrr!" The major shivered. "If looks could kill—"

"And they just might, orange-face."

He whirled, but there was only the flivver pilot, his face lost in shadow, a bland smile on his features.

"Down here, stupid."

He looked down. A Terran was glancing up at him from about belt-buckle level, standing with his knuckles braced on the pavement—standing, as Corvun realized, on the stumps of his legs. A superstitious horror overcame him.

"This, of course, is Donovan," said the big man, not at all affected by the glare. "Don't let him worry you."

"No, indeedy—don't do that," mimicked the other. "Let Grandpa worry you—and he'll be doing that soon enough. That I guarantee!" He looked at the Security Chief. "Well, do we go inside to wait for him, or stand out here and freeze to death?"

"We go in." He looked at Corvun. "Have some men go out to the flivver. They'll find a number of metal containers in the troop compartment. I want them."

"Yes, sir. Anything else, sir?"

"Yes. Let's get in out of this blasted wind. Lead me to where the rest of your officers and technicians are situated."

"Sir, all my officers besides the lieutenants out with their platoons are right here. Only the technicians are inside, and they are down in the main control center studying relays and circuits. I felt that we, as officers of Empire, should meet you."

"A noble gesture," the big man acknowledged. "But a rash one. You could have been—"

"Don't think walls will protect you," Donovan chipped in. "They won't."

"Perhaps not—we shall see." He thrust his hands back in his pockets. "Very well, then, lead us to the central control area." He started forward.

"Your pardon, sir . . ." the major ventured.

He stopped. "Yes, what is it?"

"Sir, I have no soldiers to fetch the containers along. Could two of my officers perhaps carry the stretcher while you sent your two men back?"

"Absolutely not! It won't hurt a couple of officers to do something besides warm a chair. Now let's go."

Corvun smarted under the insult, but swallowed his pride. This man was favored by Sarno; and that tiny shield of gold on his jacket gave him the right to say anything he wished, to anybody, at any time. He nodded to the two lowest rankers present. "Carry out the Security Chief's order." He placed stress on Sjilla's title, hoping they would see his position and make no ill-considered remark.

They saluted simultaneously, went to do Sjilla's bidding, and—knowing infantry officers' volatile temperament—he was grateful.

"Well," said Sjilla impatiently. "What are we waiting for? Let's go."

"Yes, sir. This way."

He led them across the pavement through the icy dusk, a ghoulish parade in the failing light.

Bound tightly on his stretcher, the individual who had been relegated to the role of James Rierson, captured spook, writhed in frustration.

Chapter Thirty-Three

When the van of the enemy fleet smashed through the thin line of picket ships riding in Pluto's orbit and broke inward toward the sun, Central Control, Canada, flashed a Condition Red-Maximum to all points. Colonel Ralph Dumas, commander of PDC-10—El Scorpio—noted the message almost instantly and ordered the base's bomb screens raised and its short-range interceptors aloft. Then he made a careful check of all systems and found his command fully prepared to make things hot for the invaders when they got within range of the missiles and beam projectors that gave the Scorpion its sting.

Satisfied that all was as well as it could be under the circumstances, he leaned back in his command chair and ordered his robotic steward to fetch a cup of coffee precooled to the forty-nine-second tolerance level. After all, he had fully one hundred seconds before further action was required, and he *had* been wakened from a sound and dreamless sleep not three minutes before. Of course, commanders more disposed to worry would have spent the time rechecking with infinite care to the boundless irritation of their men, but Dumas was not of that breed. From a more cautious point of view, he squandered time shamelessly.

He permitted himself the luxury of a small yawn, chided himself gently. Must be getting old; he still felt sleepy. The coffee would help. Where in blazes *was* that steward, anyway . . . ?

He awoke.

For a full three seconds by the clock mounted into the ceiling above his bed he lay quite still watching the sweep hand sweep along. By the fourth second he was sitting bolt upright, and by the fifth second he was cursing himself for reacting without first considering possibilities.

The nearest thing to panic he had felt since he began his well-ordered military existence at the Academy twenty-nine years ago came welling up inside him and it took a concerted effort of will and all the cortical training he had ever received to overcome it and accept the obvious fact.

He had fallen asleep at his post.

With interceptors aloft, screens up, with a hundred highly trained men in the control room awaiting his order to unleash awesome energies against the invading phalanx of enemy vessels, with Terra buckling down to receive the first Condition Red Maximum assault in its stellar history, he had gone to sleep on the job.

Once he had forced himself to accept that, and all the unthinkable ramifications it embraced, the panic drained away and he was himself again. He turned his attention outward . . .

And received another nasty shock.

Ranged before him in his bedroom—for that was where he was, he had known from the first moment of awareness—was the most fantastic assortment of characters he'd ever seen. There was a big man with a rifle on his shoulder, another man standing complacently on the stumps of his legs with his loose pants tucked into his belt—and there were a half-dozen Larrys. Two of them were bending over a third Terran lying on a stretcher; another—a pot-bellied flier, by his uniform—held a gun casually pointed at the legless man's head. The other three—a major and two captains—simply stood an stared at him.

"Do you understand Llralan?" inquired the big man.

Dumas nodded mutely, suddenly conscious of a throbbing headache.

"Good." He turned to the Llralan major. "Give your little speech, major."

"Yes, sir." The major took a pace forward while Dumas let it sink in that the big Terran was giving the Llralan orders and that the Llralan was responding as he would to those of an Imperial general.

"You are a prisoner of Empire," he was informed flatly. "Terra, Venus and Mars are in the hands of the Empire. Due to the use of a new and totally unprecedented weapon the inhabitants of these three planets are in a deep, comalike sleep. This has permitted us a virtually bloodless victory, and placed us in an extremely favorable position to bargain for concessions on the part of the Federation, holding the inhabitants of these worlds hostage. You are advised to cooperate fully and offer no resistance, since such resistance would be futile and would only bring retaliations against the civilian populace." He stepped.

"Good enough, Security Chief?"

"Good enough, major," said the big man. He looked at Dumas. "I can see the wheels going round, colonel. Excellent—that's what I want them to do. Have you fully digested the information given you, in the best accepted human-computer fashion?"

"I have digested the information," responded Dumas, nettled by the other's slighting reference to acceptance-response conditioning.

"Good. Then accept this much more: the vehicle by which this weapon was delivered was the series of supposed nuisance raids by robotic ships over the past year. When the saturation level was reached, the pre-seeding was followed up by a full-strength invasion. The weapon itself consists of an extract from a flower found on the Imperial province-world Risstair."

"Sounds incredible," commented the colonel.

"But true," countered the big man. "Ready to go on?"

"By all means."

"All right. Every single person on the three planets was supposed to succumb more or less simultaneously about a month ago. The overwhelming majority did just that, but there were notable exceptions. Donovan, there, the legless man, was one. He did not collapse. Further, he killed six or seven soldiers before his capture, then proceeded to scare the wits out of the more superstitious among the invaders with tales of a vengeful grandfather's ghost that would react unfavorably to his being harmed in any way. Got all that?"

Dumas waited a long time before answering, and then replied slowly. "Got it."

"Good."

"Look, what's all this leading up to?" He was very relieved that his original impression had been false, that he had not failed in his duties, but this second set of circumstances was beginning to try even his ability to adapt and adjust on the spur of the moment.

"To the reason for your reawakening at this point in the proceedings."

"I see." He frowned. "Then there is a special reason?"

"There is."

"I can't see it."

"That's what I'm here for," said the big man patiently. He spoke with some difficulty. It stemmed, Dumas imagined, from the plastic bandaging around his face and head. "To explain it to you."

"And what makes me important enough to rate a personal explanation from a mocker?" Dumas wanted to know. He had already labeled the man as such before the major had addressed him by his rank.

"Just this: you're the commander of El Scorpio."

"So what?"

"Let me ask you a theoretical question, colonel."

"All right, if you'll get me a glass of water first."

"Thirsty?"

"As hell."

"A natural symptom of the reawakening," the big man assured him. "The sneezing will come later."

"*Sneezing?*"

"Yes. Quite a violent fit of it. Harmless but annoying. Destroys all vestiges of dignity, sneezing does. But back to that question I was going to ask. Suppose, colonel, that this base were fully staffed—excluding, of course, the interceptors. Suppose a full strength battle fleet of the Llralan Empire were sitting on these three worlds. What kind of damage could you do to it?"

He shrugged. "Wipe it out."

"That's what I thought. Makes you a very important person, theoretically, doesn't it?"

The Llralan major stirred uneasily. "Security Chief, I do not see where this is getting us—"

"You aren't meant to!" snapped the big man. "Now shut up."

The major's features tightened and he drew himself up as though about to say something. Then he thought better of it and contented himself with staring surlily at the ceiling. Dumas noted the byplay, filed it away for future reference. There was friction among the conquerors. Good. Maybe he could . . . but the mocker was speaking.

"Suppose, colonel, I told you that Donovan was not the only Unaffected who managed to cause the Larrys trouble? Suppose I told you a criminal attorney from Atlanta named James Rierson also got in a few licks—so much so that it began to be rumored that he was the phantom grandfather Donovan spoke of?"

"It could happen, I guess," Dumas conceded.

"Then suppose I told you that not only did he not get caught, but kept making such a nuisance of himself that Martak Sarno, Supreme Commander of Llralan forces here, sent his best man, Security Chief Drelig Sjilla, after him?"

"Modest, aren't you?"

"To a fault," was the solemn rejoinder. "Suppose I told you that this Rierson enlisted the help of domestic robots to attack and destroy an alien installation in the heart of Atlanta, and that Drelig Sjilla was reported among the missing, along with Donovan and three other Unaffecteds?"

"It's your tale," Dumas said. "So far, it signifies nothing."

"But you think it could all be possible?"

"I guess so. Can I have that water now?"

"One more item. Think you could stretch your credulity far enough to swallow it?"

"For a glass of water, yes."

"All right, suppose that Sjilla was captured by James Rierson, who freed Donovan and the others in the process, and suppose they hatched up a scheme to end the occupation of Terra"—the big man wasn't looking at him now, was instead regarding the major intently—"and suppose that scheme was perpetrated by the combined robots of three planets, and had as its purpose convincing the Llralans that the undead of the solar system were revolting, and the men commanding the robots decided the best way to finish up would be to impersonate Llralans knowing how to stop the spooks long enough to get inside a PDC like El Scorpio and awaken the commanding officer and apprise him of the facts before dropping the masquerade and lowering the boom?"

Dumas had known it would happen. As soon as he had faced the weird menagerie occupying his bedroom he had known it. His mind slipped. At least that was the only explanation his straining brain could come up with when the major mouthed a vulgar Llralan oath and grabbed for his seargun and one of the Llralans kneeling beside the stretcher-bound Terran jerked off a three-fingered glove to reveal a four-fingered hand and shot the major through the body with a short-barreled slug-thrower produced from under his gray tunic.

And, while he was busily consigning his soul to madness, the legless Terran and the fat Llralan pilot fired together, and the two captains wilted in their tracks.

And then he sneezed. There was no warning, just a sudden, skull-tearing nasal explosion. And another.

The one called Donovan laughed out loud and then took a bundle from the fat pilot, unwrapped it to reveal a pair of artificial legs and began unfastening his pants.

To put them on, naturally, Dumas thought wildly. *Why not?*

And then he sneezed again. Violently.

Before he had recovered, Donovan had indeed put on his legs and was in the process of getting back into his trousers. From the bundle that had contained his legs he drew a flame rifle and straightened, turning to the big man.

"We'll handle the others. They'll still be bunched in the control room. You soothe the colonel's fractured sensibilities."

"If you say so," returned the big man. "This is your show."

"You're right. It is."

He looked over to where the pair of troopers had divested themselves of their Llralan gloves, revealing hands startlingly white against the orange tint of their faces and gray of their uniforms, and were taking two more flame rifles from under the blanket that covered the prostrate Terran. The fat pilot removed his gloves, drew a second pistol to match the one he'd killed his captain with. He spoke for the first time.

"Well, Bradford, let's get on with it."

"Right." Donovan spoke to the big man. "The theater suffered when you became a legal beagle," he said. "You mocked a mocker mocking a Terran without a slip."

"Yeah. Good luck out there."

"We won't need it; the chips are all on our side of the table now. Provided, that is, you can bring Dumas out of that stupor he's in."

"I'll try."

"You do that. Otherwise, this is all for nothing." He headed for the door. "Let's go, tigers. We've got some sheep to slaughter."

And out they went.

Chapter Thirty-Four

"This," said Randolph Dumas, "is the last word in radio jamming equipment." He stroked the smooth plastic sides of a cryptic coffin-shaped affair festooned with cables leading off in dozens of directions. The technician sitting in the cushioned bucket seat before the control console muffled a sneeze in his handkerchief, looked up and grinned.

"You bet, sir. When I cut loose on 'em, the only way they'll be able to communicate will be with smoke signals."

"And this," Dumas told him, moving to the next electronic gadget in the huge underground control complex, "is your baby, as of now."

"Thanks." Bradford Donovan slipped into the seat, picked up the headphones and put them into place.

Dumas leaned over, flipped a switch. "That ought to tune you in on the *Sulis-su-Banussen*. Does it?"

From the earphones seeped wailing, dirgelike music. Donovan nodded. "It does. Apparently, it's disc-jockey time for the soldier boys. He twisted a knob marked VOLUME experimentally, and the music flooded into the room. "That's their idea of popular music."

"Good God! It sounds like a funeral march!"

"It is. Theirs."

"Yeah. We hope. You ready?"

"Ready as I'll ever be."

"No prepared speech?"

"I'm going to do it off the top of my head—that's how I got this far. No need to change a winning way."

"I agree." Dumas indicated another switch, positioned just below a tiny indicator bulb. "When that glows red, hit the switch and you're on the air."

"Quaint," commented the truck driver, reaching for his microphone. "Get ready, Larrys, here I come. The Voice of Empire speaks tonight, in an unscheduled broadcast."

Dumas fingered a second indicator. "When this goes green, the bomb screens are up. When that happens, with those warships Rierson's got watching this place, it's going to start raining fire. That'll be our job; yours is scaring hell out of three million combat soldiers. Think you can do it?"

"I flatter myself that I've done it before this—and without benefit of all the equipment." Donovan settled the earphones comfortably, faced the instrument panel. "Let's get at it."

"Right. Good luck."

"Just keep the rain from running down the back of my neck, eh?" He triggered the mike experimentally, took a deep breath. He had started talking himself into this chair back on the *Kalistra* what seemed like ages ago.

Now he was going to have to talk himself out.

Martak Sarno switched off the monitor, and the voice of an indignant Terran flicked into nothingness. Garcia had been talking for the better part of four hours now to the Federation

High Command, wearily persisting in his recital of Llralan terms. At the other end, voices had changed periodically as the buck was passed from hand to hand, and Sarno calculated that Garcia was getting near the top of the chain of command. And each progressive voice had borne that much more helpless frustration.

He smiled grimly. "They protest loudly and at great length, Blanatta. That is a good sign: if they were going to do anything rash, they would accept what was said calmly and rationally. This way, when their voices are hoarse and their supply of invective exhausted on poor Garcia's undeserving head, they will start coming around. It'll be slow, and it'll be like pulling teeth, but the goals of our invasion are as good as won."

"Just as we always knew they would be, my general," responded Blanatta loyally.

"We did? Well, maybe . . . but now that it is almost done, I am not going to lie about it. I have had my doubts at times, Blanatta—grave doubts."

"My general!" The paunchy Vice-Commander manifested horror. "It could not be!"

"But it can. When the Spook of Baxter escaped Colonel Zowal, when Quiror's pen was annihilated, when we were besieged on all fronts by phantom killers and poltergeists and orange balloons and headless horsemen . . ." He sighed heavily. "But all that is ended now. The ghosts stopped walking just as Sjilla promised they would, and have not been seen since. Wonder how he . . . but no matter. Any word yet from Texas?"

"Major Corvun reported that Sjilla had contacted him and was arriving momentarily. That was last evening. Nothing since."

"Strange . . ."

"I thought so, my general. I asked the warships in patrol orbit if anything noticeable had occurred. Nothing. I did not dare send a flivver over for a closer look—not if Sjilla's instructions were to be carried out."

"No, of course not. Still . . . the time grows overlong. Any word from Corvun himself?"

"No."

"H'mmm. Well, we'll give Sjilla another two hours. If nothing happens by then, we'll see what we can do. Take command, Blanatta. I'm going below for a drink and a shower."

"Yes, my general."

He was in the shower when the raucous battle-horn began clamoring. For a moment he stood incredulously, then leap-frogged out of the stall and started frantically drying himself.

The wall-grid in his outer office came to life, began to bellow, "BATTLE STATIONS! BATTLE STATIONS! GENERAL SARNO WANTED ON THE BRIDGE. GENERAL SARNO WANTED ON THE BRIDGE. BATTLE STATIONS . . ."

He got on a pair of pants, threw on his soiled tunic and shoved bare feet into boots, having trouble because of their dampness. Then he was pounding for the intraship cars, buckling on his pistol belt and leaving the shower running behind him.

When he reached the bridge Blanatta was nowhere to be seen in the frenetic activity as dozens of men raced to their posts. He shot one glance at the battle board, groaned aloud. The symbols were going crazy, forming an insane gibberish of flashing, twinkling light. He turned away.

A calm, unhurried voice was announcing, "Orbiting patrol ships report six of their number lost and their screens being forced. The troopship *Molegenaro,* north of Atlanta, has ceased reporting and the emanations from its drive piles are gone from our detectors. Another source of energy is increasingly apparent."

"Another power source?" he asked blankly, of no one in particular. "Where?"

Commander Curz appeared out of the confusion to answer. "Sir, a planetary defense base has become operational and is firing on our fleet. Its bomb screens are in place—"

"Which one?"

"PDC-10, sir, the one in Texas. El Scorpio, they call it."

"*No!*"

"I'm afraid so, sir. There is no posibility of mistake—"

"Condition-change," chanted that overriding, emotionless voice from Detectors Section. "Troopships *Kilgarea, Borsekk* and *Su-Nadairi* are now off screen and not reporting. Sudden flares of energy from each ship's former position—"

272

"Upping ship?" Sarno voiced that faint hope, and Curz relayed it as an inquiry to Detectors.

"No, sir—nature of explosions at least Nine-Z. Indicative of destabilization of drive elements on near-total scale, and subsequent propulsor damage and related destruction—"

"Only one thing causes a de-stabe of Nine-Z proportions," breathed Sarno. "Terran missiles equipped with Scrambler warheads. I—"

"Condition-change!" announced Detectors. Sarno's eyes found the board automatically, discovered the trouble spot moments later. Several lights were out. As he watched, another winked out. "Heavy cruiser *Daisdaro*," Detectors identified it. "Reported being hit with a force-projector beam. *Daisdaro* is now off screen and not reporting—"

"COMMUNICATIONS-SEIZURE ATTEMPT!" brayed a new voice. "Rekkish Confuser in operation—"

"That does it!" Sarno slammed a big fist down atop a radio console. "*That . . . does . . . it!*" He turned. "Where . . . ?"

Blanatta was at his elbow, a bulbous microphone trailing an extension cord in hand. He surrendered it to Sarno with some relief. "The fleet awaits your orders, my general." He indicated the mike. "Fleet-wide connection . . . I had the *Sulis* tied in . . ."

Sarno thumbed the mike. Now he was, according to Blanatta, on the *Sulis-us-Banussen*—and the Voice of Empire was going to speak this day in a way that Terrans would not soon forget. He cleared his throat, began to speak, mouthing his words clearly and distinctly.

"Soldiers of Empire!"

His voice racketed back at him from an amplifier overhead and all activity on the bridge came to a momentary pause, then resumed, under the weight of necessity.

"Soldiers of Empire, this is your general. Take heed of what I am about to say!" He paused, went on. "A Terran offensive has been mounted against us—treacherously, against the promise of an utter cease-fire during negotiations. At least nine ships have already been lost in this cowardly sneak-attack. The Rekks have attacked in contempt of their word, and in utter disregard for the hostages we hold in our hands. All negotiations and attempts to deal reasonably with them have gone for naught. Therefore there is one course left for us, and one only!"

Again he paused, scanning he flickering battle board, looking over the faces turned in his direction. He went on in sonorous tones, with the air of one who has been forced irrevocably into a predetermined but eminently regrettable course of action. And it was true; he had indeed hoped it would not have to be this way.

"Soldiers of Empire, you hold in your hands three billions of the enemy who have so treacherously betrayed their word and attacked without warning or provocation. As they have shown themselves lacking in honor, we must uphold ours. Their sworn word has meant nothing; we must show them the folly of doubting ours.

"Soldiers of Empire, as you love your honor and that of your nation, . . . Soldiers of Empire, *execute the hostages.*"

He lowered the mike, feeling all emotion drain from him. So it was done. From the first, he had known that there was that possibility, but somehow it had not seemed real—until now. The fact that he had not been bluffing would be proven beyond any doubt; the pledge of Empire would be upheld. The Terrans would, indeed, learn the folly of underrating the word of an Imperial general.

Still, he had hoped the slaughter would not be necessary . . . had hoped that the High Command would come to terms, and that the war could go on to its inevitable climax—with himself as hero-in-chief, of course.

Ah, well . . . He sucked in the tense air of the bridge and accepted the situation. There would be other campaigns, other fleets, other sleeping planets . . .

"The attack," announced Detectors, "has abated. Total number of destroyed ships: fifty."

Sarno winced. In an eyewink of time—*fifty*.

"The *Risstaixil*—is it ready to lift?" he asked Curz. Blanatta had disappeared again.

"Yes, my general."

"Good. Make ready to do so, then, upon order. We'll fight this thing out in space and then come back for the troops."

"Yes, my general." Curz went away on the run, heading for the intraship bull horn.

Sarno thought of three million troopers scattered over three worlds—three million pairs of hands dropping whatever they were about and reaching for guns, of the few who were perhaps already carrying out his order. For a brief moment, a fierce sense of omnipotence swept him. Try to fight Martak Sarno, would they? Trifle with his ultimatum, refuse to take him at his word? Well, they'd see what such trifling got them in the long months ahead. The months and months given over to bitter hindsight, and to mass burials. For a moment he felt very close to Sirri Himself in his power over those who defied him.

But it was a very short moment.

For, in the next one, a voice shouted "COMMUNICATIONS-SEIZURE ATTEMPT!" only to be drowned out by a giant voice, flooding the bridge with sound—a voice only too terribly familiar to Martak Sarno.

"Llralan invaders!" it thundered. *"Llralan invaders, hear my words!"*

"Communications-seizure successful," announced someone unnecessarily. "Rekkish Confuser in operation; Rekkish transmitter sending—"

"Break that Confuser!" snarled Sarno. "Don't let him speak. Don't!"

"Impossible, my general," came back a strained voice. "Confuser operating full strength; sending a max—"

"Llralan invaders, hold your peace! Your ships are at my mercy; I am smashing them to bits. Your way home is blocked off, and this I promise you: for every Terran that dies, all that hear my voice now shall die ten times over—slowly and horribly. I, the grandfather of my grandson, promise you this upon my tombstone. By the name you have given me, I promise you these things. I, Gremper!"

"Donovan!" Sarno's voice was shrill, despairing. "Donovan—shut up! Somebody get through that Confuser! I don't care how—just *do* it!"

"Trying, sir, but—"

"No buts! Do it! Fire Control!"

"Here, sir."

"Blast that transmitter. Pour everything we've got at it. We've *got* to knock it out!"

"Yes, sir, but . . ."

"But *what?*"

"It is broadcasting from the defense base, sir—it's behind those bomb screens."

"Don't argue with me—*get that transmitter.* Do as I say or I'll have you shot where you stand. Understand?"

"Everything we have, yes, sir. Right away, sir." The technician looked frightened unto death.

"Do not heed, if you wish," came Donovan's voice, softly. *"The choice is yours. But do not whimper for mercy when your insides are being unraveled through your ears, for you will have none of it from me. I, Gremper, will not be merciful."*

"Gremper!" He heard that name running like wildfire down through the men on the bridge, and knew that that same voice was being heard on every other ship's bridge, and in every ship's hold, and at every gun station, being heard across three worlds everywhere a soldier crouched in a bomb shelter with his personal *Sulis* held to his ear. Being heard, and listened to, and feared.

"Shut up!" he roared. "Do you hear me? *Shut up!*" His gun was in his hand. "That is no ghost—that is Donovar *Donovan,* don't you understand? You silly, superstitious, sa brained fools! Donovan! Not his grandfather—him! And he not a ghost, he is alive. He can be killed—"

"You have only one chance of mercy," came Donovan's somber tones.

"Shut up!" He took several stumbling steps toward the amplifier. "Shut *up,* damn you! Donovan, *shut up!* Donovan . . ." He went to his knees, raised his gun waveringly. "I warned you—"

"—and that chance is: surrender. Lay down your guns. Come out of the bomb shelters . . ."

The sound he made was that of a primordial beast cornered and fighting for its life. And then the seargun came to sparkling life. Energy splashed against the amplifier's steel sides, left a glowing burn from which molten drops splattered to the deck. But his aim had been bad. The voice continued.

"Sarno and the ones responsible for the Dust must be surrendered up . . ."

His gun made one long, continuous buzz on the otherwise

silent bridge. Men stared in stricken wonder at their general's battle with the inanimate amplifier. A goodly portion of the Communications Section began to warp and blacken. The radiomen skittered out of the way fearfully. At last the voice died in mid-threat, died a horrible, groaning death.

There was silence.

He was in a crouch, gun up, ready for any further sounds. There were none. Slowly the tension drained out of him and he straightened, sweating profusely. "You see?" he said triumphantly. "He can be defeated, you *can* kill him. *I* killed him. I killed his voice, and his voice is the dangerous thing about Donovan. Kill his voice, kill him. Shut him up and he is helpless—*kill that voice*. Don't you *see* it?"

They obviously didn't.

He shunted his gaze around that circle of blank, staring faces, seeking some corroboration, some flicker of understanding. There wasn't any. He began to back away from them.

Behind him, a door opened and a voice—*the* voice—ordered imperatively, *"Lay down your weapons. Leave the bomb shelters. Only by doing these things may you receive clemency. Your salvation lies in your hands; act swiftly before I grow angered . . ."*

He whirled, gun spitting fire before he was full around, traversing the doorway savagely . . .

And stopped firing.

Blanatta stood there unsteadily, gripping the door jamb for support, a hurt look on his placid face. His tunic front was a charred shambles.

"I . . . I," he began, and faltered. Blood bubbled over his lips and runneled down his double chins. "They said the . . . receiver was out . . . up here. I was bringing a field radio until it could be . . . repaired." He coughed wrackingly, and the fingers of his left hand opened. The radio clanged on the steel decking. He took two short, stumbling steps toward his idol . . . and collapsed like a grain sack, his head hitting the deck with a sickening crunch.

Sarno stood stock-still while insistent fingers pried the smoking gun from his clenched fist, his mind swirling insanely. He had *killed* Donovan, but Donovan was there, right there

277

on the floor, hiding inside that field radio, laughing up at him.

And talking. Always talking.

He stood mumbling under his breath without moving out of his tracks until Security Underchief Blalr and two of his men came and placed binders on his arms and led him off the bridge and out of sight of the shaken bridge personnel.

Donovan was still talking.

Chapter Thirty-Five

With Sarno's breakdown and the death of Blanatta, the burden of command fell squarely on Naval Admiral Curz's shoulders. The admiral was a capable officer and able fighter, but he recognized a hopeless cause when saddled with one. Forty-nine of his combat ships and twenty of his troop luggers were destroyed; the rest were sitting ducks for the missiles and guns of El Scorpio. The Army' morale and discipline had been completely and utterly shattered by the unnerving use of the *Sulis-su-Banussen* to threaten and intimidate. For all he knew, not one soldier remained at his bomb-shelter post. Communications were still snarled by the Terran Confuser. He did the only thing he could do under the circumstances.

He sued for a cease-fire, got it, and asked for terms.

Not fifteen Llralan minutes after Sarno had been led off the bridge Curz was bargaining feverishly, with Ryan Garcia of the *South Pacific* acting as intermediary, to save something out of the shambles of the invasion. He offered all data on the Dust, its antidote and the manufacture thereof in return for enough time to load his troops aboard their ships and blast for home. Dumas acquiesced before the combined advisement of Garcia, Donovan and Rierson as to the value of nullifying any further use of the Dust, but insisted on having time to make sure he was getting what he paid for. Mutual safeguards were effected, and the exchange got under way.

Meanwhile the crew of the *South Pacific* was reawakened and Garcia, the other surviving members of the delegation, the four last Unaffecteds imprisoned on the *Risstaixil* and an additional female prisoner, a Mrs. William MacFarland, were taken aboard.

Thirty hours after Donovan had begun uttering his dire threats over the *Sulis,* Curz's ships lifted without opposition from Terra, waited in space for the squadrons based on Venus, and then drove outward to be joined by the ships from Mars as they passed the orbit of the red planet. Once beyond the orbit of Pluto they flashed into subspace and were gone as utterly as if they had never been, gone home to face the wrath of a Supreme Council that brooked no failure.

And on the sleeping planets behind them, the staggering preponderance of the population remained in blissful ignorance that Terra's solar system had been invaded, occupied for more than a month, and then abandoned.

The invasion was over. The real work had just begun.

Three billion souls, spread unevenly across the face of three worlds, had to be brought back to the land of the living. Then they had to be convinced that they had been gone in the first place, told that they had been in imminent danger of never returning from the twilight never-world of Dust-induced sleep—and then kidded into going back to business as usual, as though nothing of consequence had really happened, after all.

Meanwhile, the war had to go on. The Llralans had to be held at arm's length while Terra and Venus and Mars got back into stride. It seemed an impossible task, but the Federation's bent for accomplishing the impossible was what had kept the voracious Empire at bay this long.

The impossible, in the words of a proud organization four centuries dead, takes a little longer. Squads went from bomb shelter to bomb shelter with compression sprayers, awakening specifically chosen individuals—government officials, policemen, doctors, psychologists, psychiatrists, priests, preachers, heads of widespread private organizations, influential public figures—anyone considered capable of aiding a dazed population-at-large back onto their collective feet. Then military priority took over: persons important to the maintenance of the war effort were brought awake. There were exceptions in this—a Mrs. Jane Donovan of London, England, was one—but they were rare.

Only when a skeletal structure of society was functioning in some semblance of normalcy did Navy ships swoop low over cities and hamlets, crop-dusting the two-and-half billion some-odd remaining sleepers back to consciousness. Reawakening was considered complete on August 10, almost exactly nine months after Sarno's armada had appeared on Terran screens as it came in past Pluto. Occasionally an unreached individual would be found and the antidote squads summoned, but the occurrences became increasingly rare and finally petered out altogether. Nearly three billion people were busily trying to relate their unalterable impression that only moments had passed to the awesome reality of months spent in slumber. Rip Van Winkle could have been no more aghast than they when he awakened to find that time had passed him by. At least in his case time had continued to take its toll of everyone else. But what would he have thought—how would he have reacted —if his experience had been shared by every soul in the colonies, and had been induced by a hostile intelligence?

The brass hats foresaw the consequences of such reasoning upon the over-all morale: the public would never feel safe again upon any world, would subconsciously hold their breath every time a ship rumbled overhead, would fairly panic at each raid alarm, would begin to feel that victory was far from certain and defeat more than possible, unless . . .

Unless the facts were stretched a little, and the magnitude of the Llralan accomplishment toned down until it achieved the aura of something that could have been but never was. Something harmless in itself but serving as a lesson that vigilance must be maintained. Something, in fact, passed off as almost a government-planned exercise meant to remind the public of the grim realities of the far-distant war, in the guise of a harmless, laughable, comic-opera stunt pulled by the incredibly dunderheaded Larrys.

There were speeches by all prominent figures to that effect. Speeches that those prominent figures for a change believed themselves, having no reason to suspect otherwise:

"Look, ladies and gentlemen (or boys and girls, or friends and fellow countrymen, or any of a dozen openings, depending upon the audience), fun's fun. We had a little midautumn snooze at the Empire's expense—a sort of vacation from our troubles and cares—and for that we should draft a letter of appreciation to the Llralan High Command."

Inevitable laughter.

". . . But the fun is over." Grimly. "Suppose that had been radio-active waste, or exotic disease germs, or poison gas? What then, fellow patriots?" Pause. "There is a world of difference, my friends, between three *sleeping* planets and three *dead* ones."

Thoughtful silence.

"There was no harm done this time—outside a few broken noses, cut lips and injured prides . . ."

Laughter.

". . . but next time *it might be different*." Menacingly. "Ladies and gentlemen (or boys and girls, or friends and countrymen, or whatever), we *must not let this happen again. We shall not!*"

Applause.

"We must meet the enemy on his home ground—carry the fight to his own back yard—break his back and pin his arms, so that our stars may be forever free . . . that our progeny may go forth in confidence and tread the starways opened by our forefathers and bled for by us in peace and dignity. Liberty *must not die*, extinguished by the insidious sea lapping from the banks of Empire up to the very shores of our home world. Liberty *must not*, and it *shall not!*"

Thunderous applause.

And on and on and on, until enlistments for armed services far outstripped the present requirements, and everybody was whipped up into a patriotic frenzy against the nasty aliens. The very few individuals capable of maintaining independent thought against the general hubbub of public and official indignation secretly wondered how Llrala had got away with such a trick in the first place if she was so dunderheaded; and just what good bombastic speeches, patriotic fervor and eternal vigilance would do if she ever got dunderheaded enough again to pull off another such harmless, laughable, comic-opera stunt. But they did not give voice to their thoughts—to do so would have meant being lynched, if not shot officially for treason, subversion or some other form of unforgiveable naughtiness.

The thoughtful kept their peace and the invasion was laughed away and the war went on, and after a time it was almost as if the abrupt cessation of activity on Terra and her sister planets in the early winter of '32 had never happened. Little things like the 150,000 people who had not and never would awaken were adroitly swept under the rug, since they interfered with the over-all picture being painted by the powers-that-be.

Those 150,000 casualties—for the most part comprised of aircraft pilots and passengers, mountain climbers, trapeze artists, window washers, steeplejacks, swimmers, firemen, men in the arctic extremities, flagpole sitters and the like, but including the interceptor pilots from the PDC's who had gone up to take on Sarno's fleet, the two thousand Martian villagers murdered by Sarno as an example, all persons to whom minute-to-minute medical attention had meant the difference between life and death, and the twenty battle squadrons that had surrendered to forestall Sarno's execution of six million Atlantans —were the sole losses attributable to the invasion upon which the Empire had pinned such high hopes. As to the gains . . . the Dust was being rapidly rendered useless by the manufacture and distribution of the antidote to all planets, and Terran Intelligence had themselves a real live Llralan mocker to play with.

Which left the nine original surviving Unaffecteds to pick up the threads of their lives where they had been ripped asunder nine months ago.

Epilogue

The October sky of 2433 was every bit as clear and beautiful, and the wind as cutting, as the sky and wind of November '32.

James Rierson puffed and grunted his way to the top of a rocky outcropping and flopped tiredly. He waited until he had caught his breath, then raised binoculars and scanned the shale-strewn canyon below, following the little stream that ran down its center and then widened into a series of pools and runlets where the canyon became a wide green valley carpeted with high grass and dotted with lodgepole pines.

He took a deep lungful of the rarefied mountain air, shook his head sadly. A shame that the antidote ships hadn't got around to spraying the Georgia wilderness areas—what made Colorado so special, anyway? Something, obviously—else why should antidote be squandered on its game herds while the much more deserving animals of Georgia still slept under the effect of Sarno's Dust?

Sarno's Dust . . . he unslung his rifle and laid it across his lap. Had there ever really been such a thing? Here was autumn, as crisp and lovely as autumn always was; and here he was, rifle in hand and nonresident hunting license in pocket, hunting deer. He idly fingered a scratch in the gun's stock. Had there really ever been a Sarno, a Sjilla, an invading fleet? And what about Gremper and the Spook of Baxter—hadn't those been figments of a vivid imagination, of a colorful dream?

No. He was in Colorado, not Georgia, and he was hunting mule deer, not whitetail. The ten-point buck he had pursued a year ago was still sleeping at the edge of that frost-burned meadow. And would continue to sleep until the powers-that-be got around to him, or the Dust wore off, or he finally slipped away into death.

He raised the glasses again, searching for movement on the slopes around him. The big war had reached down and touched his life and had gone away again, and here he was, as if nothing had happened. *And what about those others?* he wondered. *Donovan, Nogales, Harris? What about my uncle? And that young Rayburn, and Yoganda? And Jennifer Nogales, and the daughter that was born to her at the Scorpion dispensary, and Margaret Cassidy? What about them?*

Donovan . . . Donovan had tried to parlay his part in the ruin of the invasion into a soldier's uniform, and had failed. The Military Board could be excruciatingly stubborn at times, even in the face of overwhelming evidence that they had made a wrong decision. Donovan's wife, though, hadn't seemed to think it *was* the wrong decision—she had two sons in uniform to worry about, and she must preferred having her unruly and unpredictable husband where she could look after him.

Harris had gone back to Mars and whatever he had been about before I day; and Margaret Cassidy had gone back to Montana and her boardinghouse, doubtless to run it as nosily as ever. That her nose had got her a berth in a Llralan shipboard cell wouldn't stop her. Only death can cure a snoop.

As for Jennifer Nogales, she had dropped all charges against her errant husband in the face of his solemn word never to stray again, and they had left together for San Francisco with their baby. Rierson has his doubts as to how long *that* would last. Wanderlust, like snooping, gets into the blood and doesn't wash out easily. But maybe he was wrong—he hoped so, remembering the wistful little girl who had left El Scorpio with her daughter in her arms and her husband beside her, his ribs taped where a searbeam had tickled them in that last vicious fighting in the Scorpion's control room.

Yoganda gravely thanked Donovan, Rierson, Dumas, Garcia and anyone else he could get his hands on for delivering him from the enemy and returned to Hong Kong; Richard Rayburn, Jr., enlisted to go kill some of the Larrys that had killed his father. Daniel Rierson had gone kiting off to the ends of the Federation, hunting a new sunset with a reborn enthusiasm.

Which left him.

He looked down at the rifle in his lap with a kind of wonder. It seemed impossible that it had ever been turned on anything other than game animals. That it had been the sole weapon raised in protest against the Llralan occupation for all the long days while Donovan and the others had languished in shipboard cells and before he had run into Salesman One-Zero-Eight in that unlighted service tunnel in Atlanta—and that, thereafter, its owner had been cast in the role of a robot-commander whose jurisdiction covered three planets and at whose beck metal men called dead ones forth from their graves and sent them against the enemy—was absolutely beyond comprehension.

Ah, well . . .

A flicker of movement down the canyon caught his eye. He brought his rifle up, and a big mulie buck with heavy antlers went bounding down-canyon.

His rifle woke thunderous echoes along the rocky face of the gulch, and a geyser of white dust spurted out of the ground well behind the fleeing buck. Before he could work another shell home the mulie was gone, disappearing around a boulder the size of a small house. The echoes died away, and the wind came whispering up-canyon to breathe coldly in his face. He cussed himself roundly as he climbed off the outcropping and slipped and slid back to the canyon floor. He wasn't here to sit in the sun and daydream—he was here to hunt deer. And the sooner he realized it and got down to business, the sooner he would be putting the tag on his buck.

He hurried down-canyon to find the mulie's trail. He wasn't too familiar with this western hunting—maybe the buck hadn't run too far. If he was in luck, he might get another shot.

Finding the trail he went along it swiftly, head down, concentrating.

From high above came the deep-bass rumbling of a spaceship's muted propulsors as it settled slowly toward the no-longer sleeping planet.

MORE EXCITING SCIENCE FICTION FROM PAPERBACK LIBRARY

SCIENCE-FICTION

BY PHILIP WYLIE AND EDWIN BALMER

WHEN WORLDS COLLIDE

America's most famous science-fiction adventure!

Two outlaw planets were hurtling through outer space on a direct collision course toward Earth. Secretly, a few rocket ships were built to evacuate the most brilliant and biologically useful to a distant planet where the human race could start anew. But when the secret leaked out, it touched off a savage world struggle for the million-to-one chance of survival.

52-521, 50¢

AFTER WORLDS COLLIDE

the brilliant sequel to When Worlds Collide

"Extraordinary . . . thrilling." —The New York Times

"Fascinating, exciting, mysterious . . . scientific details absolutely plausible." —The London Times

52-255, 50¢